1973

THREE PRIESTS

BOOKS BY JOSEPH DEVER

No Lasting Home
A Certain Widow
Three Priests

Three Priests

by

JOSEPH DEVER

Doubleday & Company, Inc.

Garden City, New York

1958

Library of Congress Catalog Card Number 58-6637

At long last,
to Margarita Pretiosa,
wife and mother

CONTENTS

BOOK FOUR: CLOSER TO THE THRONE

BOOK FIVE: THE MAKING OF A LIBERAL

BOOK SIX: THE GUERRILLA BISHOP

BOOK ONE

Rome Delayed

CHAPTER I

The Big League

UNTIL he smiled, Turtle Whelton was as homely as the slow-moving reptile after which his classmates at St. Brendan's College had named him. His head was somewhat oval-shaped and his strong neck seemed startlingly close to his thick, slanting shoulders. Long, sinewy arms dangling from a keglike torso threatened to rival the length of his short legs and made him seem the grotesque production of some assembly line that had run out of symmetrical parts.

Yet when he smiled, as he did now in the locker room of St. Brendan's barnlike fieldhouse, his features became a sunburst of warmth and the face of the turtle could not be seen on the land. Nor could the turtle's voice be detected in the vigorous baritone tones with which he answered his teammate's quip.

"If you could run like you throw, you'd be Frank Merriwell," second baseman Willie Klein had taunted in reference to Whelton's failure to score from second base on Klein's single to center. The play had taken place in the intra-squad practice game that same afternoon.

"If I could score from second on one of your blooper singles," Whelton said, chuckling, "I'd be on the track team."

"All right, Klein!" Coach Davis called abruptly over the thin partition of his private office and dressing room. "You do the running against the Illini tomorrow. Whelton will do the throwing. Okay?"

"Okay, Coach!" Klein punctuated his answer with the hollow slam of his locker door. "See you at practice tomorrow, Turtle," he added on his brisk way out of the locker room.

"See you, Willie," Whelton said, squinting into the fragment of mirror taped to his locker door and meticulously combing his sparse patch of dark hair. Too many showers, he thought with resignation as he faced the shiny-domed specter of early baldness, much too many!

"Vin," the coach called across the partition. "I want to see you for a minute before you go."

It would be about the big-league scout.

Willie Klein had told him about the scout's presence on the campus while they were dressing for practice. Klein had spotted the scout and recognized him while making a routine visit to the athletic director's office just before lunch. Later, in the cafeteria, he had asked young Father Larkin, an assistant dean, if the stranger really was Clipper Phillips, former ace pitcher and presently midwestern scout for the New York Giants.

"He is," Father Larkin had said with a tantalizing smile.

"Well—is he—is he here to look someone over?"

"He is," the priest had repeated, still smiling tauntingly.

"A pitcher maybe?" the second baseman had asked, suppressing momentarily his own searing ambition to play big-league ball.

"Maybe," Father Larkin had answered with the same noncommittal smile.

"Turtle! He's come to scout the Turtle! Excuse me, Father, excuse me!" Then the dash up the cafeteria stairs, two at a time, and the headlong flight across the campus to the fieldhouse.

Now, turning the handle on his locker door, Turtle Whelton thought with winy excitement of the big leagues. He imagined for a moment throwing his spitter at, say, Honus Wagner of the Pittsburgh Pirates. In his imagination he could anticipate the electric personal tension of such a pitch. The squat, goblinlike Wagner, batting terror of the National League, set for the pitch. Turtle vizualized his own slow, deep-dipping windup after tonguing the ball liberally. The pitch, the projectile speed of the rising, breaking spitter. The squat, eagle-eyed batter braced for him. The swing, the clock of bat against ball. The blurred, white flight to center—higher, higher, until the ball roosted high in the stands . . .

Whelton smiled at his own imaginative chagrin, slipped on his black and white varsity sweater, and rounded the corner into the office of Coach Davis.

"Sit down, Vin," the coach said, squeaking around toward Whelton in a splintery swivel chair. Davis was a long, lean man whose knobby red nose seemed alien to all that physical length. "Stretch," they had called him in his ballplaying days at St. Brendan's and later in the minor leagues. He had been almost impenetrable at third base, it was said, and at the bat had hit dependably to all fields. There had been an unsuccessful tryout with the Athletics, but his subsequent career with the Indianapolis club had been long and sporadically brilliant.

Open on the desk before him was a small black notebook in which he kept a record of the strength and weakness of his own squad and, whenever possible, similar data on St. Brendan's opponents.

"I've collected a few notes on this boy Stokes who plays center for the Illini. He's not All-State for nothing—hits a real long ball consistently."

"I've read about him, Coach. He murders a high fast pitch, they say."

"Glad you've already heard that. I was going to warn you against feeding Stokes your high, hard one."

"I'll be careful, Coach. What's he weak on?"

"The newspapers say he can hit anything," Davis said. "But I'm not sure about that. I saw him against Milwaukee Teachers the weekend you were down with the grippe. I'm pretty sure he's a sucker for a slow one, low and inside."

Davis paused and rubbed his nose.

"It just occurs to me. You low-balled that Wheaton club a lot in our second game."

"That's right, Coach. You'll remember, most of them were rangy guys. I tried a slow curve, inside and knee-high. It seemed to work real well."

"That's the pitch," Davis said. "I think I've got it here."

He flipped back the pages of his notebook.

"Here," he said, his face lighting up with fulfillment. " 'Whelton's slow inside curve against Wheaton tall boys very effective. Should come in handy again.' "

"Should," Whelton said, smiling.

"There's something else I want to speak to you about, Vin, something equally important. And it gives me a good feeling to be able to say it to you." Davis's small, intense blue eyes were shining and his lean, somewhat ravaged face screwed toward a precision of truth. "At the same time I—I wish your dad were here to do the telling."

Whelton warmed, thinking of his father's long friendship with this man for whom baseball was almost a religion. Davis and Vin's father had been boyhood chums on the west side of Lakeport. Both had played ball on the neighborhood sand-lot teams and had been offered athletic scholarships to St. Brendan's.

Stretch Davis had accepted his scholarship, but the lingering illness of Grandfather Whelton had made it necessary for Vin's dad to take over the affairs of the Whelton Lumberyard, thus sacrificing any chance he might have had to go on to college.

Vin's father, now ward alderman and a moderately successful lumber merchant, had followed Davis's baseball career with avid, friendly interest.

When finally given his unconditional release from Indianapolis, Stretch, still a bachelor, had moved back into the old west-side neighborhood. He was well on his way to becoming a reminiscing barfly in the neighborhood tavern when Mr. Whelton used his influence to help secure him a coaching job at St. Brendan's.

Now young Whelton sat before him, facing the prospect of a big-league career, and just for a moment a bitter wind of memory lashed against Davis's heart. For he remembered the big chance in Philly, his cockiness, flippancy of tongue, and refusal to abide by training regulations—he remembered the uncontrolled cocksureness of youth which may have cost him a long big-league career. Had there been a connection between staggering into his hotel room at 2 A.M. and fanning three times in a Sunday game against the White Sox? He did not think so then, but now, after years in the bushes, he knew.

He plucked slowly at his red nose, blinked his eyes, and began: "You may have heard, Vin, that Clipper Phillips of the New York Giants was on the campus this afternoon."

"Willie Klein mentioned it before practice."

"It's all over the campus," Davis said with a benevolent smile. "Anyway, Mr. Phillips called on me here after lunch. He's high on you as a big-league pitching prospect, Vin." He paused, almost for dramatic effect. "He'll be scouting you in the Illini game tomorrow."

Vincent left the coach's office and mounted the stairs to the field-house lobby, impatient to tell his father that tomorrow was the day. Tomorrow the big-league scout would be in the stands and he would throw that ball with every concerted ounce of muscle and brain.

For Vincent Sr. he would do it, that the father's sacrifice might be
vindicated in the son.

Stokes of the Illini, he thought. Low and inside, the slow one,
with two strikes maybe, after he has let a wild one go by. Those
others, Jankowski at short, a choke-up hitter to all fields. I have a
notebook in my head, not unlike Coach Davis's, and I will whip the
spitter at Jankowski and see what he can do.

In the entryway of the low, shambly wooden fieldhouse that used
to be a cow barn and had been remodeled for the athletes, he
blinked away from the old-gold blaze of the early-evening sun. He
noticed to his right a fresh white notice pinned to the bulletin board
and paused to read it:

May 26, 1906
St. Brendan, Illinois

ARCHBISHOP TO ADDRESS SENIORS!

His Excellency, Most Reverend Arthur V. Wagner, Archbishop of Lakeport and Chancellor of St. Brendan's College,
will address the senior class tomorrow evening at the Fieldhouse Auditorium. His subject: "The World You Face!"

Immediately after the address, Archbishop Wagner will pre-
side at a meeting in the Chancellor's Lounge for all students
interested in studying for the sacred priesthood.

Vincent pondered the announcement, thinking he'd like to hear
the Archbishop, who was widely celebrated as a public speaker.
It would be a good place to relax after the sweat and strain of the
game.

Behind him he heard one of the auditorium doors open and close.
Footsteps came on and ceased.

"You're just the guy!" said a voice, half gentle, half droll.

Vincent turned and saw the pale, thin face of Arthur Wagner, a
fellow member of the debating society.

"Hello, Art," he said, wondering at Wagner's abrupt statement of
recognition. There were in it the mirth and seriousness which made
Wagner both a good debater and an enigmatic personality. He was
perennially mirthful and, it seemed, perennially serious, the former
because of a tireless sense of humor, the latter, perhaps, because
he was the Archbishop's nephew. "Why am I just the guy?"

The tall, thin blond youth projected a deceptively shy smile out of his pale, delicate features. Then he brushed a lock of disorderly straw-colored hair away from his eyes and held up a three-page handwritten manuscript.

"It's all here!" he said with characteristic confidence. "All you have to do is read it at the convocation tomorrow!"

"Read what?" Vincent asked with an effort at geniality. One assignment was enough for tomorrow; namely, the undefeated Illini nine.

"I was supposed to deliver the address of welcome to the Arch," Arthur explained confidently. "But now Mother writes me that I'll have to go with her to Springfield. It's about my father's estate, and the lawyers say I must be there." Some of the lilting mirth surged back amid the sobriety of voice as he continued. "The Arch won't mind. After all, he'll be getting a good chunk of Dad's estate for his building fund."

Vincent felt the almost forbidden thrill of being momentarily on the inside of the Archbishop's private affairs. Yet this was the prelate's nephew; he could be excused for a sense of familiarity.

"I've got a ball game to pitch tomorrow," he said.

"You've got a bigger ball game than that to pitch—against yourself!" Arthur said with an engaging, yet insinuating smile.

"You can be real offensive when you want to." Vincent flushed with anger.

They stood there facing each other for several moments—Vincent angry, Arthur reserved and watching for a chink into which he could slip the sure edge of his charm. Then Arthur's shy-to-overwhelming smile came at Whelton from an apologetic approach and broadened into the irresistible projection of mirth.

Vincent found himself beginning to smile against his will.

"What do you mean, I've got to pitch against myself?" he asked good-naturedly.

The chink had opened. Arthur rushed to the assault.

"I mean you're good at something else besides baseball. You have the best public-speaking voice in the college, bar none. And if I weren't the Archbishop's nephew, Father Rector would have asked *you* to give this address of welcome."

"Thanks for the compliment," Vincent said coolly.

"It's no compliment, it's a fact!" Arthur held up the manuscript again and crackled it with a gripping motion. "And here you've got a chance to give the address anyway." He paused, smiled, and sighed. "New York Giants," he added, shaking his head slowly.

"Oh, you heard about the scout too."

Arthur nodded and looked at Vincent with piercing intensity. "Don't forget, my uncle is a sort of scout too—for a pretty big league."

"What's that got to do with me?" Whelton asked.

"You answer that question."

"I haven't even asked it," Vincent said, touching his hand to his forehead in a gesture of good-by and moving toward the door.

"You will," Arthur called after him with the engaging mixture of mirth and seriousness.

"Good *night*," Vincent said pointedly, pushing through the swinging doors.

In the soft sun of the late-spring evening, amid the green quiet of the campus, the chagrin kindled by Arthur's boldness subsided within him. He glanced at the tower clock soaring from the red tile roofing of Wagner Hall: six thirty-five. If he hurried to the railroad siding at the far end of the campus he could catch the six-forty Lakeport Limited coming from Dubuque. He could, as was his daily custom, jump off the train at Elm Park and take a streetcar east to Thirty-fifth and West Belknap.

He walked briskly along the cinder path that bisected the lawned, elmy campus. Tired and hungry, yet exhilarated with thoughts of the news for his father and the anticipation of his mother's richly laden supper table, he gripped his green sailcloth book bag and swung it pendulum-like beside him.

He fished his Ben Ben out of the watch pocket of his corduroy trousers and glanced at its bland face without arresting his pace.

Six thirty-eight. He peered at the western horizon and saw the sooty mushrooms of smoke. And then, across the lush Illinois prairie, came the forlorn, haunting whistle of the oncoming train, touching his heart with the universal loneliness of man.

Trains—the New York Giants—Philly, Cincy, St. Louis, Boston, Chicago. Ballplayers knew the mournful call of trains across America, shrill in the morning, chill at night. How would it be if he made the big show, maybe a quarter of his lifetime as a player, coach, manager—riding the continental singers of music as ancient as the heart of man!

He hurried down the staircase to the stilty siding where only a few students, late because of library work or some extracurricular activity, waited to board the Limited.

The train chuffed into the station. He climbed into the nearest day coach and found himself an empty seat. Settling onto the unyielding hardness of the shiny straw, he scuffed his feet against a newspaper. Hoping it was an afternoon edition, he picked it up and rearranged the pages on his lap.

He glanced first at the date line. It was the afternoon edition of the Lakeport *Herald*, open to the last page. In the upper left-hand corner was a two-column box in boldface type: "Death Notices. Carroll, Curran, Dumbrowski, Di Natale . . ."

He turned over to the news section, smiling at the thought of his father's phrase for the obituary section: "The Irish sports page!"

It would be the Lakeport *Herald* and his father smoking his pipe in the good leather comfort of his favorite armchair:

"Now this Laura Feeney . . . would she be the girl of Eddie Feeney who used to play shortstop for the old Logan Squares?"

"How old?" his mother would ask, guiding a needle through a thick woolen sock.

"Forty-five. Died of inflammation of the bowels."

"Too old," his mother would say. "Eddie Feeney's girl can't be more than thirty-five."

"Hmm!" his father would say through the heady, black furnace of his pipe as, undaunted, his eyes traveled down the "line-up."

"And what of this O'Brien fellow, Charlie O'Brien from Ashley Avenue? Didn't that Charlie O'Brien you used to go out with come from over north there?"

"It's not the same one," the lady would say without looking up from her darning. "Charlie—'Pudsie,' we used to call him—has been dead for about three years. It was the drink took him."

"Hmmm! Here's one. Miss Viola Duffy. Isn't she . . ."

"Vincent Whelton!" the lady would say, sighing. "You're bound and determined to go to a wake tonight. But if you do, you'll go alone. I'm not leaving this house."

"Hmmm . . ."

His elation at the prospect of telling his father about the big-league scout was subdued by the mental picture of his mother, damp with perspiration as she bent over her squat, black coal stove, doling out the steaming portions of stew and coffee and Irish bread.

What would she say about his possible tryout in the majors?

"Elm Park, Elm Park next!" the aged conductor called hoarsely from somewhere behind his high celluloid collar and handle-bar mustache.

Vincent gave the conductor his ticket, arose, picked up his book bag, and lurched toward the rear platform.

Soon he was aboard the rickety crosstown streetcar clacketing across the west side of Lakeport.

What would she say? What would she say?

Soon, leaving the streetcar, he saw two hundred yards ahead of him the flat, pungent cliffs of lumber piled up even higher than the ten-foot plank fence surrounding his father's lumberyard—the pine, the spruce, the oak were a pleasant sting in his nostrils. He heard the whinny of a dray horse, either Clem or Nellie, and he knew that Tom Judson, his father's teamster, was giving them their evening meal—a bag of oats, a bucket of water, a pitchfork of hay.

There were few children on the street, few adults, and the quiet of the late-spring evening was almost rural, almost holy in the moth-soft evening of west-side Lakeport.

Fifty yards from his house, the big green sign: Collins Tavern. A burly drayman in crusty denim coveralls rolling through the swinging latticed doors. And the glimpse inside—the thick, gray cloud of smoke—tired, grimy men leaning comfortably against the long, stout mahogany bar, smoking and talking over their tall or tiny glasses, or maybe just leaning there silently, savoring the pipe or the beer, the cigar or the hundred-proof, savoring thoughts of happiness or hurt, present, past, and future, staving off the supper hour for a little while, savoring time itself and holding it back for just a little while.

"It's still here, Vincent!" called a bold feminine voice from the narrow veranda of the residence alongside the taproom.

Kitty Collins. He could see her now, sitting on the banister in a tight-fitting green silk dress, her long, sleek auburn hair a lesser sunset, the fullness of her body and her smile charging him with the excitement of the first opening curtain at a long-awaited play.

In the instant before he answered her a series of lantern slides were projected in his mind. Kitty-the-tomboy goating about the sprucy eminences of his father's lumberyard. And her impish intrusion into the hide-outs he had arranged in the caverns formed by the outjutting of lengthy planks over shorter ones.

There had been the rainy fall day in his "clubhouse" amid the lumber, where in the lonesome afternoon she had come upon him as he whittled away at a ship model.

She was fourteen then, fragrant, fulsome, daring; and as she leaned over him to get a closer look at his work, he could feel the nozzle-pressure of one firm, full breast on his shoulder. Stormed by the fragrance of her hair, drugged by her insinuating voice, he had fled her, scrambling over the soggy cliffs of lumber until he was free and far away.

He had fled her, not because he was a sissy, but because he wanted her in some wild, deep chamber of his soul—wanted her long, deep, and lovely in the eternal rainy afternoon.

Then, later, her indefatigable strategy at birthday parties, school plays, and dances—always somewhere near him, the stroking of her voice, the brazen admiration. And lusty, beefy Mrs. Collins, winking boldly in his father's lumberyard office and lilting shrilly: "Niver be forgettin', Vinny, I'm savin' me Kitty for ye alone. . . ."

Now the woman again, the devilish power of her nearness, knowing he could have her by day or night, in wedlock or out. The woman!

"The cans are still here," she said. "Do you want to take them home?"

She meant the two pails of beer which Tom Judson usually picked up each evening—one for Mr. Whelton, one for himself. You went around to the rear of the tavern and stood in line with the women and the boys waiting with their pails. You waited your turn and Mrs. Collins filled them from a specially tapped barrel in the back room of the tavern. There was a bench for the ladies to sit on and have one while they waited, wiping the foam from their mouths with the backs of their hands and making whistly sounds of gossip about the man next door or the lady upstairs.

"Yes, Kitty, thanks. I'd better take it along with me."

"Well, come on through the house," Kitty said brightly. "It'll save you the trip around back and the waiting."

"That won't be necessary. I don't mind waiting a few minutes."

"Oh, come along, silly," she said, taking him by the arm and bringing all that buffeting fragrance close to him. "Besides, I haven't seen you since the parish reunion. How's school? I hear you may pitch against the U."

"That's right." He moved with her across the piazza in a state of pleasant unwillingness. "It's my turn to pitch tomorrow."

"Wonderful!" she said, pressing against him as she opened the door that led into a long, dark hallway. He hesitated.

Sensing his hesitation, she said, "Come along, silly. It isn't every boy I'd do this for."

And she said it with the double meaning she could put into almost all her words with men.

He pulled himself up short. There was trouble in that dark house for him—however enticing.

"Kitty," he said, backing toward the veranda stairs. "I've really got to get the cans and go."

"You high-toned Irish sonofabitch," he heard her whisper coldly from the darkness behind him.

He descended the stairs and turned into the alleyway, taking his place casually in a short line of women and small boys awaiting the nightly ration of beer.

Calmed after the emotional storm, he moved up slowly in the line. He smiled at the neighborhood mothers, ruffled the hair of a few urchins, while within him thunder rumbled distantly and lightning guttered to a flicker.

"Oh, Vinny-boy!" Mrs. Collins ogled him, handing him the brimming, foamy canister. "Have ye seen Kitty? She has a new dress on and all."

"Yes, I saw her, Mrs. Collins."

"Well, ye'll have to come callin' more, now that school is almost over."

He smiled politely, saying nothing. He took the two quart cans of beer, paid for them, and went out.

He walked toward home with the beer cans swinging on either side in a gentle, slapping rhythm. Ahead in the gathering purple of evening he could see his house lights competing weakly with the dusk.

And at the rear of the lumberyard another dull, yet persistent light—a lantern hanging on a spike in the stable wall where Tom, the drayman, would be feeding the quivering brown mare and the docile gray gelding, feeding them the multitudinous oats and the fragrant hay after the long, ponderous hauling of the day.

He turned into the yard and felt the rude, shiny cobblestones beneath his feet. He never walked on them without remembering the sparky clash of horseshoes against their flinty surface and the eternal clop-clop-clop of his childhood—lying in bed above the yard entrance or seated high on the springy leather seat beside Tom—and he remembered the ruthless kiss of the cobbles against his tender shins as he slid over them, sprawling after a baseball.

He paused near the small porch at the rear of his house, seeing his mother's slight, leaning shadow against the draw curtain of the kitchen. He placed one of the beer cans on the top step and walked toward the barn with the other.

When he had delivered the beer to Tom Judson and returned to the house, he could still see the slight shadow of his mother, leaning now over the kitchen table, leaning in service, ladling out hot, chunky stew from a deep dish to three figures who sat with lowered heads.

Mother's feeding the neighbors again, Vincent thought, lifting the latch of the screen door.

"Good evening, Mother," he said, stepping into the shiny kitchen —shiny oak floor, shiny blue paint, and shiny pots gleaming on the shiny black stove.

"Vincent!" his mother said, almost in suppressed fright. "I was beginning to worry. It's late."

"I stopped for the beer cans, Mother." He smiled at the threesome who had looked up at him, hesitant and a little anxious at their feeding.

They were the Crowleys, who lived in a flat by the railroad, just around the corner. Mrs. Crowley, a faded, wiry woman of forty, with a brave gappy smile and two unwavering blue eyes; Emma Crowley, thirteen, looking up from her stew shyly and with a flicker of feminine interest in Vincent; Willie Crowley, twelve, sullen, almost defiant in the presence of charity, yet avidly spooning up the stew. And Willie Sr., sodden in a tavern somewhere along Madison Street, gone with his railroad wages the previous evening—back in five days.

This was almost routine in the Whelton kitchen—a hot meal and a few dollars to tide the unfortunates over the weekend.

"Who in the name of God will help them if we don't?" his mother would exclaim whenever Vincent Sr. gently remonstrated about an oversize grocery bill.

Who in the name of God? Vincent thought, smiling at the Crowleys and receiving from their mother a greeting which painfully marshaled dignity.

Mrs. Whelton, tiny, dark, her coal-black hair tied back in a bun, poured steaming black coffee into thick white mugs and sliced up a huge, lumpy, raisin-studded loaf known as "Irish bread."

He went over to her and kissed her on her flushed, damp cheek.

"I've lots of news tonight," he said.

"Yes?" She looked up at him with small, snapping green eyes. "So has your father. You can bring him in a glass of that beer right now."

"Dad's back from the City Hall so early?"

"He's in the parlor pretending he's reading the *Tribune* but really waiting for you and the beer."

She picked up the canister he had left on top of the stone set tubs and poured part of the foamy contents into a large glass stein.

"Before you bring it in, stop for a moment in my bedroom. I've got something to tell you. . . . Now for some hot coffee and some Irish bread, Mother Crowley, and some milk for the children."

"You're too good to us, Mrs. Whelton," Mrs. Crowley said.

"You'd do the very same for me and mine."

"You'll be out of school soon, Vinny?" Mrs. Crowley asked, stirring her coffee. "What will it be, the lumberyard, I suppose?"

"Haven't quite decided, Mrs. Crowley."

"Well, you're a good boy all the same," Mrs. Crowley said.

Vincent picked up the stein and excused himself. He opened the door leading into the hallway.

The hallway was completely dark, but you do not need lights to maneuver in your own hallway. You pick your way along surely in a thousand familiar footsteps, the goings and comings of so many years in the same family house.

How different from the darkness of Kitty's hallway, he thought with immense relief—there the darkness and the hot, white light of furtive passion, here the darkness and the slow, even light of family love.

Halfway down the hall he could see the flicker of candlelight from his mother's room. He moved toward the dancing half-light, bearing the stein before him carefully.

In her room with the small brass bed, simple white dresser, lone, plain wooden chair, he was confronted with the vigil light burning before a statue of the Virgin which stood in a niche in the wall.

He placed the stein on the chair, slumped into a sitting position on the bed, and found himself looking at the sentimental plaster representation of the blue-gowned maid.

In the muted distance he could hear chairs scraping and his
mother's voice, gentle and firm. She was probably dipping deep into
the rainy-day money which she kept in her rose China teapot on the
top shelf of the pantry. Not even Mr. Whelton knew the extent of
its contents, even though he gibed at it as "the bank of Illinois."

Who in the name of God will help them? he thought, repeating
his mother's words. The Crowleys, hundreds of them in Lakeport,
thousands like them all over the country. Organized charity, yes,
but where was organized charity in time of immediate need?

Maybe I can make a lot of money pitching; maybe I can turn it
over to Mother to help folks around the neighborhood here, he
thought.

He was arguing with himself, he realized; he was arguing himself into a possible baseball career. It would make his father happy,
he knew, perhaps his mother too. It would bring the family fame,
bring in the money, too, plenty of it if he were good enough.

He watched the frail, sentimental blue virgin, benign in the
candlelight; he heard the kitchen door open and close, then the
gentle footfalls of his mother along the hall.

"Be especially nice to your father," Mrs. Whelton said when she
entered the room. "The boys downtown offered to run him for mayor
next fall if he'd go along with them."

"Go along?"

"They want him to sell lumber to the city at a big mark-up—
double the regular profit and give them half."

"He'll never do it!" Vincent said vehemently.

"That's what he told them," his mother said, her facial muscles
tightening. "They've threatened to run someone against him for the
Council here in the ward."

"Let them," Vincent said heatedly. "Dad can still win."

"You're your father's son. We'll go in now. He'll enjoy the beer
before his meal."

"Oh, Mother, before we go, I want to tell you my news," Vincent
said. "There'll be a scout from the New York Giants in the stands tomorrow. If I pitch well against Illinois, I may be offered a contract."

"Well!" She smiled with slow surprise, looking off into the shadows
almost inscrutably. "That's a fine tribute to your athletic ability,"
she added from what seemed to be a cool distance. "Your father
will be happy to hear this."

"And you?"

Sensing his discomfort, she kissed him, saying: "I do think it's wonderful and I *am* proud of you—only . . ."

"Only what?"

"Well, athletics are intended to refresh the spirit and strengthen the body. They shouldn't be the central occupation of life itself. But you talk to your father about it. Come on."

"Thank you for being frank with me, Mother." He picked up the stein and followed her down the hall.

They went into the parlor and saw him sitting straight in his plump brown leather armchair, the *Herald* limp in his lap. He was looking out into the darkness of the west side, across the black mass of tenement roofs to a soft, spring sky shuddering hugely with stars.

"Hey, Dad, here's your brew!" Vincent called airily. "I picked it up on the way back from school. How are you tonight, anyway?"

His father, a tiny replica of himself—broad of chest, short in the legs, turtle-head, thinning gray-black hair, and direct brown eyes—turned from his musing with the same transforming smile so typical of his son.

"Hello, Vin," he said brightly. "How did it go today?"

He took the stein and drank deeply while his son told him the big news.

"That's wonderful, wonderful!" he said with a geniality that did not require mustering. "I'll be there watching. Give them that spitter, especially in the clutch—give it to them fast and high."

"I will, Dad, when I can see a spot for it, I will."

"What do you think, Mother?" his father asked Mrs. Whelton, who had sat down unobtrusively on a horsehair chair under the wavering gaslight.

"It's wonderful—in some ways," she said. "You know how I feel, Vincent. I've told our son my attitude. It's up to you two."

"He'd mow them down in New York. Just like he'll do tomorrow," Mr. Whelton said. "Make a lot of money, too, Vin, honestly and cleanly."

"Mother told me about your trip downtown," Vincent said. "Don't be unhappy about it, Dad. You'll never have to be unhappy about that."

"I won't be for long, Vinny. It's just their arrogance—dictating to me after the way I've tried to serve the people of this town for over fifteen years."

"They'll never beat you in this ward, Dad."

"I don't know about that, son." Mr. Whelton shook his head. "They'll pour a lot of money in here and I just haven't got the cash to spend refuting their lies." He paused and sighed deeply. "But October's a long way off—let's talk about the big game tomorrow."

"You'd better do your talking over the supper table," Mrs. Whelton said, rising. "The stew will be cold."

"We'll be right along, Mother," Mr. Whelton said. "Tell me, how did Stretch Davis take all this?"

"He seems real happy—felt you'd be real pleased."

"I am. I am. Has Stretch got a line on the U's batters?"

"Some good angles. Says that Stokes can't hit a low inside slow ball."

"Feed it to him, Vinny!" Mr. Whelton said, rising and clamping his short, chunky arm around his son's shoulders. "He'll think he's playing golf."

"I'll try, Dad," Vincent said as they walked in to supper together. "I'll try."

After supper Vincent stretched prone on the snub white bed in his upstairs room, leafing through the pages of an American history text. He was trying to fix in his mind a sequence of important Civil War dates. He would need them for the quarterly exam on Monday and later for the final.

"'The Emancipation Proclamation,'" he quoted aloud, "'1863. Not to be confused with the preliminary Emancipation Proclamation in the fall of 1862.'"

He paused, rubbing his eyes after an hour of intense study. He let his head fall back on the pillow for a moment of relaxation. On the wall opposite him he could see the framed print of a painting of St. Vincent de Paul. His father was Vincent, too, but not "de Paul." The latter middle name for young Vincent had been Mrs. Whelton's suggestion.

And the inscription on the picture, written in his mother's delicate, disciplined hand: "To Vincent, that he may be mindful of his patron saint who served God faithfully in the service of the poor."

The lined, kind face of the great French humanitarian smiled sadly down on him. And he could not help recalling the lowered heads of the Crowleys, low with hunger and humiliation.

He heard the jingle of the doorbell in a muffled distance, his father's footsteps and an exchange of words. The door closed firmly and again his father's steps, moving up the staircase toward him.

"It's a package for you, Vin," his father said, rapping lightly on the door. "Special messenger brought it in from downtown—looks like some paper from school."

"Come in, Dad, bring it in." Vincent pushed himself to a sitting position on the bed.

"I'll just toss it to you," his father said, opening the door halfway and sailing the large brown envelope toward him with a gentle, underhand pitch. "How go the studies?"

"All right." Vincent focused his eyes on the address side of the envelope. In the upper left-hand corner he read the name: "Arthur Wagner," the address: "St. Brendan's College, St. Brendan's, Illinois."

"It's from that Wagner guy," he said with wry irritation. "He's the Archbishop's nephew—won't be around for his uncle's visit to the college tomorrow evening—wants me to deliver the address of welcome for him. This must be a copy of it."

"Seems to me you've got enough work cut out for you already," his father said. "Can't they get somebody else?"

Vincent opened the envelope, recognized the manuscript as the same Arthur had waved at him, and read the note enclosed:

Dear Vincent:

I explained my predicament to Father Rector without mention of your name as a possible substitute. Yet, so help me, he suggested you.

He said he'd speak to you in the morning, but I thought I'd presume to send over this biographical summary of the Archbishop's career. My original ten-minute address is also enclosed. Feel free to use one or both.

Why not take the job? After all, your flipper will be tired after the game, not your voice. And, besides, you'll like my Arch-uncle.

I'm off for Springfield. Good luck against the Illini and on the podium.

Pax et Dulcis,
Arthur

"Looks like I'll have to do it, Dad. Arthur's note says the Rector will ask me in the morning."

"He sic him on you?"

"Not according to this."

"Well, do what you think best," his father said. "But don't let it tighten you up for the game."

"I won't, Dad."

The shuffling, soft-voiced sounds of retirement in his parents' bedroom on the first floor, then the stillness settling over the entire house, broken sporadically by the creaking of dray wheels, the clatter and rush of a streetcar along Logan Avenue.

He finished his perusal of the Civil War section of the history text, marking with asterisks, in his notes, several dates about which he felt shaky. He snapped the text shut with a comforting sigh.

He lay back on the bed, one arm under his head, and glanced at the manuscript Wagner had sent him. It began with a quotation from St. Paul's first epistle to Timothy, Chapter 3:

" 'If a man desire the office of a bishop, he desireth a good work. It behoveth therefore a bishop to be blameless . . . sober, prudent, of good behaviour, chaste, given to hospitality, a teacher.'

"Such was St. Paul's blueprint for a bishop and the clergy in general," the manuscript went on. "Such is the Archbishop who sits now on this platform and honors St. Brendan's with his presence here this evening. . . ."

The script continued in detail about the Archbishop's career. And even though Arthur was writing about his uncle and namesake, the simple facts of a quarter century of service and dedication to God and human beings spoke eloquently and without stylistic embroidery.

It would read well if I could memorize it, Vincent thought.

His bedside alarm clock read eleven-ten. He could memorize most of the ten-minute passage by midnight and then get to bed. But where? His memorizing habit was to read aloud. That couldn't be done here with his parents sleeping downstairs. The stable, that was it! He could take a railroad lantern his father kept in the back hall and go out to the stable. He'd rest a few minutes and do just that.

At his bedroom window the curtains breathed softly, then billowed in a draft of cool spring air. Vincent inhaled the draft, cool but not without the sultry drug of early summer. Down Logan Avenue he heard the thick-brogued singing of a tippler stumbling out of Collins Tavern.

" 'That was the end of sweet Molly Malone . . .' " he heard the late-night tippler crooning along Logan Avenue. And, lying there, comfortably tired, summoning energy for the trip to the stable, he felt in the stirring of the curtains, the heady whiff of summer, the poignant song of the drunkard—he felt in all this the sweet, sharp, ephemeral sadness of youth.

" 'Alive-alive-oh-ho,' " the drunkard sang, more and more indistinctly, yet, it seemed, more sweetly, as he moved west on Logan, " 'cryin' cockles and mussels, alive-alive-oh.' "

Kitty Collins. She might be lounging on her front porch right now, the hungry red lips and asplike tongue, the pert breasts and leaning hips. The flame of her availability seared through him swiftly as the whole whirl of indecision dizzied his soul: the big league and the Archbishop beckoning in opposite directions, the hopes and frustrations of his father, the quiet resoluteness and dedication of his mother. For an instant the storm of youth and spring whirled wildly, ecstatically within him and he wanted to rise and seek the wanton one who could give him delirious oblivion.

He arose, crossed himself, shaking his head vigorously as after a vicious tackle in a football game. He slipped on his varsity coat sweater against the night air, picked up Arthur's manuscript, and tiptoed down the back stairs to the kitchen hallway.

After he had lighted the railroad lantern, he pushed out into the lumberyard and picked his way through the varied cliffs of pungent timber to the stable at the yard's extreme end.

"Whee-hinny-hinny!" the mare protested as he fumbled with the latch on the barn door.

"Easy, Flora, easy now," he called, letting himself into the barn.

He hung the lantern on a spike driven into the wooden pillar in the middle of the floor. And amid the stamping of hoofs, the snorts and switching of tails, amid the fragrance of hay, the sting of urine smells, the headiness of manure, he rehearsed the words of welcome to the Archbishop.

" 'If a man desire the office of a bishop, he desireth a good work,' " Vincent began in a resonant baritone voice.

And if, in Athens, Demosthenes declaimed against the roar of the waves, Vincent de Paul Whelton also had a discordant noise to test the strength and carry of his voice.

"Such was St. Paul's blueprint . . ." Vincent orated.

"Whee-hinny-hinny!" orated the restless brown mare.

CHAPTER II

Lost and Won!

STANDING by the third-floor window in the hallway of the Second Philosophers' dormitory, he wrung the creamy mud out of a mop, skimmed the sweat from his brow, and with a clenched fist watched for a few moments the progress of the ball game.

From what he could gather, mopping from window to window, his classmates, the Second Philosophers, weren't doing so well against their traditional rivals, the First Theologians.

Arthur Wagner, on first for the Philosophers, had let a sharp grounder knife through his legs with three men on; two runs had scored and there were still two on, with only one out.

Vincent had only one more hallway to mop and he would be free to go down there and get into things for the last two innings.

Bob Lambert, who shared a large, drab seminary room with Vincent and Arthur, was doing a good job subbing on the mound for Vincent. But the two runs loomed menacingly large—with Fraim of the Theologians cowing the Philosophers with a tireless fast ball.

Turning with a sigh of frustration from the sun-winking expanse of green, Vincent went at the grainy floor again, slopping and sloshing his way toward the last hallway bend.

He could have been out there, pitching all the way and shaking his big bat at Fraim. He could hit that Fraim, who was scaring those kids down there with a fast one. Hadn't he been clean-up man for St. Brendan's, even as a pitcher? He could have been down there if he had listened to Arthur, who wanted to get him excused from the routine mopping detail.

He leaned into the mop again, his stout neck and chunky arms glistening with sweat. Anger seared him, anger at his present athletic impotence—Fraim mowing those kids down, Lambert and his slow curves which the Theologians were hitting to all fields.

But he wouldn't listen to Arthur, who wanted to fix things. He didn't want it said that the Archbishop's nephew fixed things for him. He'd mop every floor in the sem first, yes, every damned floor!

That was profanity—he'd have to confess it, he thought, wringing out the mop at the last bend in the hallway. He hadn't said it, he had thought it—but it was profanation just the same. All right then, he'd confess it twice. Every damned floor!

He dumped the muddy water at an alcove sink. He turned on the faucet and pure, hot water rushed into the bucket. Purity, clarity flooded the bucket and seemed to flood his mind. His anger cooled and he twinged with remorse at his temper and profanity. He breathed a prayer to St. Peter, whom he looked upon as the patron of all hot-tempered people. He asked the intercession of the hot-headed Peter:

"Peter, wrathful in Gethsemani, indignant in the innyard as the cock crew thrice. Peter, who denied Christ vehemently, yet later died for Him," he prayed, "intercede for me in my moments of anger!"

He mopped again on the final length of hallway, hearing the thud of the catcher's mitt and the astringent thwack of the bat in the distance, hearing the jubilant jeers of the Theologians and knowing the game was almost lost.

Yet that final game of St. Brendan's against State, two years ago, had been almost lost. Whelton had had a one-to-nothing lead, with the big-league scout in the stands, and it all looked good until he tired in the first of the seventh. He had walked three men and then threw wild to first, trying for a pick-off. Two runs had scored on the wild throw, and State's one-run lead had looked awfully big going into the eighth and ninth, with his father grim on the bench and the big-league scout glancing at his watch and wondering about early-evening trains to New York City.

No score for St. Brendan's in the eighth, he recalled, his team-mates tense and swinging too soon and the one-run lead towering like Pisa and ready to topple on their heads.

He had one arm out of his jacket for the first of the ninth, when the student manager handed him a plug of Bull Durham wrapped up in a lumber invoice. On the invoice, a penciled note: "It's still a ball game, son. Feed them the spitter!"

He had looked down the bench to where his father sat with Coach Davis. His father smiled, punched his fist into his open palm, and Vin knew he had been talking with Stretch about the spitter.

He hadn't used it much until then, taking Stretch's advice about low-balling the big hitters. He hadn't used it much, thinking about the scout and knowing the spitter could make him look wild. Well, he had gone wild anyway, so use it he would, and to hell with the scout as two thousand pounds seemed to slide off his shoulders.

He swallowed a dipper of water, bit off a hunk of plug, and, with his jaw bulging like an infected tooth, headed for the mound. . . .

Now, mopping the floor in the hallway of the Second Philosophers' dorm, hearing the cheers and catcalls wafting in from the ball field below, the final game for St. Brendan's became all the more vivid and wined his memory deeply.

He had gone out and fed State the spitter, tonguing the ball amply before each pitch. He had set the Illini down: one, two, three, with two swift strike-outs and a pop fly to second.

And coming in for St. Brendan's last turn at bat, he had seen his father smiling calmly, confidently, and knew that the game, in a sense, could not quite be lost, no matter what the final score.

Someone said the scout was still in the stands, but it had been like a muted remark heard faintly in a crowded place. Willie Klein walked; Finnerty singled, sending Klein to third and bringing Vin to bat. The tying run was on third, the winning run on first.

Stretch signaled him to hit away.

He took his place in the batter's box, digging in with his spikes, taking his stance loosely, and riveting his eyes on Lefty Stevens, who, with lethal effectiveness, had been curving them inside and low all afternoon. He'd have to hit anything now, even the inside low one—but maybe, just maybe, he'd throw one outside.

He forgot the scout, his father, Stretch, and St. Brendan's. There were only three other people in existence: the pitcher, the man on first, the man on third. His universe now, all his being: the pitcher, the man on first, the man on third.

Stevens wound up and curved the first one low and inside for a strike. Vinny stepped out of the box, drying his hands on his pants legs, then in again, digging an anchorage with his spikes and swinging loosely. Stevens, a fast worker, seemed to take a little more time with the second pitch.

He wound up slowly and delivered what looked like a fast outside pitch that might break inside.

It might not break, it might not break . . . Vinny commanded behind tightly set jaws.

He checked his swing and brought his bat around late, connecting outside. The ball blurred low along the first-base line, well to the right of the first baseman. Vin dug for first and could see the ball careening into right field.

He pulled up at second as the right fielder retrieved and threw. The runs were in, the game was over, the fans were on the field.

In the locker room later he had been excited about the big-league contract, but he couldn't think, he couldn't decide. He wanted time to think it over, but there was little time. Clipper Phillips said he had to catch a train. Vin could sign the contract later and send it on.

"It's the excitement, Mr. Phillips," his father had said. "We'll send the contract on in the morning."

"I told you he had the stuff, Clipper," Stretch had said. "He'll ink it and send it on in the morning."

It, it, it! What was it for him? The big league or the seminary . . . It?

"Don't keep the New York Giants waiting, son," Clipper had said just before leaving for the train.

That evening, tired yet exhilarated, Vincent had delivered the address of welcome for the Archbishop in the college auditorium. He had gone over the speech again during his supper hour. He had dropped some of Arthur Wagner's literary phrases and substituted some simple ones more suitable to his own plain, strong style of delivery.

Speaking in the presence of the distinguished churchman, who sat on a royal dais which seemed in direct contrast with his lean, ascetic features, his meekness and gentle bearing, Vincent uttered young Wagner's vivid biographical words. He persuaded his audience to homage and a reiteration of belief in the apostolic mission of Christianity. And when he had finished, he wilted before the applause for the Archbishop and was overwhelmed at the persuasion he had inflicted upon himself.

Later Vincent attended the chambered conference, presided over by the Archbishop, for those interested in the seminary. The prelate took him aside after the conference and said: "I was hoping you would be here. That was a mighty good job out on the diamond this afternoon. Whatever you decide, son, ask the Lord's blessing on it."

Bumping home on the train that night, he recalled Clipper Phillip's admonition: "Don't keep the New York Giants waiting."

He wouldn't keep them waiting. He could wire from the railroad station in town.

The hall was finished. So was the ball game down on Seminary Field, judging from the yells of derision the First Theologians were inflicting on the Second Philosophers.

Vincent dumped the muddy water, wrung out the mop, and rinsed the bucket.

The staccato on the staircase, the yips of victory told him that the Theologians were climbing to their dormitory shower rooms on the floor below. And then the heavy clomping, the thud of the defeated, conveyed the approach of his classmates, climbing glumly, silently, to the third floor.

He went to his room, snapped a towel off the iron railing at the foot of his cot, and headed for the showers himself. He would get the whole sad story there.

He balmed his thoughts with anticipation of the Roman Bursary competitions in oratory and the essay in which the Second Philosophers would take part the following week. Perhaps they could make a better showing than the Theologians had made the previous year. There was still a chance to prove which was the better class. And he'd be in the competition with Arthur and Bob Lambert, among others; there'd be no mopping detail to keep him out of it.

He stripped and slipped into the shower. He blended the hot and cold water, letting it flood over him.

"Vinny, Vinny!" he heard Arthur call in the distance. "Where were you? We lost—we lost the game!"

CHAPTER III

The Bird Watchers

THREE seminarians at their books in the sultry May evening. Around them the rolling, wooded green of Illinois, and from the copses just above the athletic field, the clear, flutelike summons of a bird.

"Pho-phweet!" the bird insisted across the commingled green-and-purple dusk. "Pho-phweet!" the answer came from the other end of the wood.

Vincent lifted his pencil from the draft of the sermon he was preparing. He intended to deliver the sermon on Monday afternoon, in oratorical competition for the scholarship to the American College in Rome. But sweeter than the tongue of Cicero, he knew, and more beguiling, were the four notes of birdsong which had just burst out of the seminary dusk.

He heard the creak of a chair, looked up and saw Bob Lambert, lean, pale, and catlike, watching and listening at the window.

Art Wagner, too, looked up from the biography of Cardinal Newman, which he was studying for the essay division of the Roman scholarship competition.

"What is it, Bob?" Arthur asked.

Lambert turned slowly and looked at Arthur with the same controlled yet piercing shrewdness which never failed to irritate the Archbishop's nephew.

"This one you can call yourself, Art," Lambert said. "In fact, you've already recognized it."

He turned with a surprisingly warm, even benign aspect to Vincent and said: "Vinny can call this one." ("Even Vinny," he almost said.) "What is it, Vin?"

"Pho-phweet!" again clearly in the purple curtain fall of evening. "Pho-phweet!" the bird repeated, as if on cue from the bird watcher at the seminary window.

"Sounds like a bobwhite," Vinny said.

"Correct, Dr. Whelton," Bob said. "Life-first or year-first?"

"What does that mean?"

"Well, strictly speaking, you'd have to *see* the bird rather than hear it for the first time in your life in order to have a life-first."

"Or the first time in a year for a year-first?" Arthur asked.

Bob shrugged his shoulders. "Obviously most of us have seen and heard the bobwhites out in the woods there—while chasing a baseball or taking a walk."

"I've heard but haven't seen one," Vinny said. "I guess I'm still eligible for what you call a life-first."

"And a year-first too," Arthur said brightly. "Correct?"

"Correct." Lambert moved back to the desk at the foot of his cot.

"You ought to do all right with the Apostolic Delegate tomorrow," Arthur said, settling over Newman's *Apologia* again. "He's quite a bird watcher."

"Is that true?" Bob asked with more animation than usual.

"True it is." Arthur nodded, noticing Bob's interest and wondering whether he should have made the revelation. "Unk has been with him when he's identified feather folk around the chancery grounds."

Arthur, Bob, and Vincent had been selected from the Second Philosophers to accompany Father Rector and a group of priest-professors who were to escort the visiting dignitary, Archbishop Peruzzi, around the seminary grounds. The Apostolic Delegate and Archbishop Wagner would be on hand for the Roman Bursary competitions and would sit in with the panel of contest judges.

Bob had frowned when Arthur said "Unk." His roommate's understandable intimacy with his uncle, the Archbishop, was a source of constant irritation to Bob's conservative sensibilities. He could never quite abide such informality.

There was quiet again in the room as the three delved into their studies for the competition. Vincent pared and pruned at his sermon on his beloved St. Vincent de Paul; Arthur savored Newman, jotting down notes as he read.

Bob, who would compete in both the essay and the spoken

sermon, pondered the ascetic life of St. Francis of Assisi and, concentrating on the title of his sermon, decided to make a change. He resolved to make consistent changes in his six-thousand-word theme which would be both the subject of his essay and his sermon. He crossed out the original title: "Hermit in Brown." He dipped his pen, paused, furrowed his brow, and wrote down the new title: "The Bird Watcher of Christ."

Silence, silence, the eternal, sacred silence of study and night falling over them, the purple yielding to shades of soot, the soot to blackness. Three starkly illumined heads loomed over their desks near their respective cots. Three circles of light, three dedicated minds insulated against the world, boning, boning for the prize.

Arthur paused, feeling upon him the touch of the velvet spring night. Clever, retentive, agile of tongue and pen, he knew he'd do well in the essay, which would have to be written at one sitting, without notes. But would he do well enough? Would he do better than Bob, who, admittedly, was a more thorough if less spectacular student?

Credo in Newmanum . . . Arthur planned on using that phrase as an opener. *Credo in Newmanum* . . . *Credo in Deum* . . . It was always good to paraphrase a well-known and traditionally established phrase. It gave your own a certain classical solidity and grace, if only by association.

Arthur was drawing heavily on *Apologia pro Vita Sua*, Newman's autobiography, for background, thought, and phrasing which would spring him into a narration and analysis of Newman's life and spiritual meaning.

He looked across the room and saw the lean face of Bob Lambert, intent over the draft of his sermon. Long, lean, almost cadaverous in the ghastly light of the lamp, Bob suggested to Arthur's imagination Cardinal Manning, who at times had shadowed long and lean over the life of Newman. Newman the poet, intellectual, aristocrat, theologian; Manning the social actionist, reformer, champion of the laboring man and the underprivileged. Each was a giant —he must bring that out in his essay. The popular literary impression that Manning was the ogre in Newman's ecclesiastical life should be dispelled.

Such an emphasis would indeed be worthy of his entire theme. He thought about changing the dominant Newman theme to one that would give justice and balance to the roles of both Newman and Manning. But then he'd have to do added research on Manning and the time was growing short. So Newman it would continue to be: the gifted intellectual getting the emphasis over the gigantic social reformer: "Lead, kindly light, amid th'encircling gloom . . ."

There would be two Roman scholarships awarded for the essay. Arthur felt confident he could come up with one of them. Bob would probably get the other. It would be good to come through with a higher mark, however; it would be good to best the icy scholar in such an important test of mind.

But what about Vinny? He was in the oratorical contest with Bob. There was only one prize. Could Vinny tip him over?

Vincent had the best speaking voice in the class—a boom and a range and a relentless earnestness. He stood up like Daniel Webster, big and sure and good-looking. But Bob was in the contest too.

Why? Bob was a mild, careful, effective speaker, but there was no comparison. He might win on the basis of logic and subject matter. He was obviously in there for insurance purposes. If something went awry in his essay effort, he'd still have a chance at the Roman college in the oratorical.

Vinny was going to do Vincent de Paul and he'd do it well. But maybe he'd need a more original theme, a fresh and provocative insight. Cardinal Manning might be just the subject for him.

Arthur determined to talk with Vin about the matter. They could take a walk around the building after Compline services at nine-thirty. They'd have a chance to talk before lights out at ten.

Arthur thought about Bob again, seeing him there, skeletal and determined under the powdery light of the desk lamp. He sensed too well in what secret contempt he was held by the perfectly proper Lambert.

"Can I help it if I'm the Archbishop's nephew?" he had wanted to blurt out at Bob during the last two years. But he knew such conduct would manifest a silly preoccupation with his own vanity and would give public assent to the same opinion which Bob secretly held. So he had continued to try to get along with him—respectful of the peace of the room.

If it's a manipulator he thinks me, a manipulator I can be, Arthur thought. The Cardinal Manning theme, concerning his achievements in the field of social reform, would counterbalance the disfavor of his controversies with the more sympathetic Newman. Such a fresh and substantial oratorical presentation, coupled with Whelton's natural prowess as a speaker, might more than offset Bob's talent as a logician and researcher.

Arthur glanced at the alarm clock beside his bed: nine-fifteen. The student library closed at nine-thirty. He'd have time to go down and get some material on Cardinal Manning. Then he could talk to Vincent after Compline.

He pushed his chair back softly, slipped a cassock over his T-shirt and slacks, and went out of the room.

Arthur had the book. He paused in the vestibule of the library to examine it: heavy, formidable, bound in cardinal leather. There was a London book-review clipping pasted inside the cover. It chided the vast exuberance of the author, an English layman, who had tried to make himself a sort of Boswell to the living Manning and succeeded to a goodly extent.

". . . the study has inestimable value for its plethora of authentic material concerning Manning's ranging life and times. This, despite the author's arbitrary judgments and self-styled definitiveness."

Authentic material, Wagner thought. That's just what Vin will need, considering the lack of time.

Someone passed him as he leaned against the wall, browsing, waiting for the Compline bell to ring. He did not look up immediately but saw the shadow, long and lean. Bob Lambert. He glanced up several moments later and saw him speaking intently to Father Cahill, the librarian. Then the intense, reflective mien of the professional librarian, the pursed lips, the raised index finger. Bob followed into the stacks.

Arthur paged again through the volume, glimpsing in kaleidoscope the aesthetic Manning at Harrow and Oxford, Manning the country parson, Manning the lover ("Caroline, I have spoken to your mother . . ."), Manning the convert, priest, fortress of the poor in the London slums, Manning the adversary of Newman, Manning the bishop and social-action adviser of Leo XIII, Manning, Manning . . .

The long, lean shadow crossed the vestibule again and Bob Lambert passed with a quarto-size volume under his arm.

Then the Compline bell drilled through the seminary buildings.

"One moment, Wagner," Father Cahill said. "I'll walk through to chapel with you."

"Swell, Father."

"There's a fellow who knows how to relax," Father Cahill said as they scuffed briskly along the gaslit corridor.

"Who's that?"

"Your roommate, Bob Lambert."

"How so, Father?"

"Heavens above!" Father Cahill said. "Here it is practically the eve of the Roman scholarship competitions and he comes into the library looking for a work on midwestern birds!"

"Bob's quite a bird watcher," Arthur heard himself saying.

"Yes, but do you think this is the time for that sort of thing?" Father Cahill asked. "What would the Apostolic Delegate say, for example, if he knew that one of the chief contestants was studying bird watching this close to the contest?"

"I don't know," Arthur said, smiling wryly as they neared the hallway entrance to the chapel. "I just don't know."

"Pray, Lord, a blessing!" the seminarians on the right side of the chapel began.

Arthur and the others, to the left, answered:

"May Almighty God grant us a peaceful night and a perfect end!"

He could see Lambert and Whelton in the subdued light, could see their faces suppliant with the night prayer. What did the Roman scholarships really matter? Bird watching, the Apostolic Delegate, his uncle? The Lord's help against the powers of darkness was all that mattered here and now.

What if Bob topped the lists in both the essay and the sermon? What of it? What if he and Vinny didn't go to Rome? There would always be Compline, followed by Benediction, whether you were a prince of the Church or a simple lay brother. Compline in Rome, Compline in Illinois, Compline in Kentucky, Kansas, Iowa . . .

"Our help is in the name of the Lord," the opposite choir chanted.

Not in the name of the Roman competition winners, Wagner was tempted to answer.

"Who made heaven and earth," he and the choir beside him retorted.

Chanting the petitions for sweet, safe sleep in the Lord, Arthur grew contrite because of his irrepressible political guile. At bottom, he knew he was not here to engineer Roman scholarships for himself and his friend, and this was the time and the place to inventory

the strength of his religious vocation. He would forget about the
Manning theme for Vincent—he could return the book to the library
tomorrow—perhaps have a look at it for his own theme on Newman.
Vinny would do all right by himself.

"Convert us, O God our Saviour!"

"And turn away Thy anger from us!"

After Compline, Arthur found Vincent waiting for him in the hall.

"What have you got there?" Vinny asked.

"It's a life of Manning I've been browsing through. I thought I
might get a few insights on his relations with Newman."

"Did you see Bob? He was going to the library."

"I think I saw him as I hung around the vestibule. I thought his
material was pretty well up by now," Arthur said.

"I thought so too."

"Well, we'll escort the bishops around the grounds tomorrow,"
Vincent said. "Will you call your uncle 'Unk'?"

"Not in front of the Apostolic Delegate! The Arch would skin
me alive!"

"What will you call him?"

"I'll call him 'Archbishop'—what else?"

Vincent laughed, igniting Arthur to further laughter as they
climbed the hollow-sounding wooden stairs to their room.

In the auditorium the reception breakfast was almost over, and a
festive one it was. Pancakes and ham in honor of the Apostolic
Delegate and the Archbishop, who sat with Father Rector—all three
benign, smiling, and calm at the head table.

There had been a solemn Pontifical Mass in the chapel earlier,
celebrated by Archbishop Wagner, with Archbishop Peruzzi kneeling at a prie-dieu and the seminary choir singing the Mass and helping to send the whole majestic prayer spiraling up to heaven with
Rome and America intertwined in the love of God.

Vincent sat at a table with his roommates and three deacons from
First Theology who were to complete the student delegation accompanying the archbishops in their walking tour of the grounds.

Archbishop Gaetano Peruzzi was addressing the breakfasters in
his native tongue, bringing, it appeared, from the words *"Il Papa"*
interspersed through his remarks, a message to the students from
the Holy Father. He was a big man, inclining toward plumpness,

light of complexion, and raying forth a perpetual smile of delight.
When he had finished the liquid, musical flow of language, Father
Rector arose, waited for the applause to subside, cleared his throat
nervously, and sought to summarize the Delegate's remarks in
translation:

"His Excellency has brought so graciously to us a special message
from the Holy Father, who is fully informed of our work here and has
the deepest concern that you all may persevere as future priests of
God and bearers of the Christ to all the faithful in an increasingly
materialistic world. Archbishop Peruzzi has been empowered by the
Holy Father to grant all of us a plenary indulgence on condition
that we offer our next Holy Communion for the Pope's very special
intention. If you will all kneel, Archbishop Peruzzi will administer
the papal blessing."

The augmenting thunder of scraping chairs and bumping knees
filled the refectory as the Pope's emissary rose and, in Latin, admin-
istered the blessing.

When he had finished, he remained standing and rayed out again
his fixed and joyous smile.

"Now I speak in English," he began.

Father Rector, sitting to his left, cleared his throat almost apprehensively.

"I, too, have a special favor for you." The Delegate paused, and
the refectory was as still as an oasis. He raised one finger.

"After the scholarship competition, I give you *one* day off!"

The atmosphere was still hushed, although now charged with the
electricity of momentary confusion. Except for those involved in the
competition, classes were to have been in session as usual.

Father Rector cleared his throat briskly and turned his quizzical
features to Archbishop Wagner, who raised his eyes in a middling
way and shrugged his shoulders almost imperceptibly.

One of the seminarians in the rear of the hall began to applaud,
bursting the cloud of confusion and starting a lusty hand-clapping
round of approbation. Someone gave an Indian yell of jubilation,
and several cheers were added by the seminarians.

Father Rector rose strainingly on his dignity, cleared his throat,
and was about to add academic approval when the Archbishop
raised two fingers and spoke strongly again:

"I give you *two* days off!"

There was no pause this time. Wild applause and cheering swept

the auditorium, and Father Rector sank into his chair after one
hurried glance at the composed Teutonic features of Archbishop
Wagner.

"Rome is speaking," his features seemed to say, "let Rome be
heeded."

The applause continued gustily, the cheering swelled. The seminarians sensed the Roman Archbishop's festive mood and unleashed
all their pre-exam tensions and anxieties in a crescendo of approval.

The Apostolic Delegate smiled indefatigably, bowed his head in
courteous acknowledgment of their applause, and, oblivious to the
peremptory coughing of the Rector, stood his ground.

"I give you, I give you," he began again, raising three fingers,
"*three* days off!"

Then he settled into his chair with an affable sigh of finality as
the jubilation of the seminarians assaulted the ceiling.

It was the usual institutional sight-seeing tour.

"This is Brother Kevin, our cook," Father Rector said.

Brother Kevin, a round red Robin Hood friar, bumped the concrete floor with his knee and, after blessing himself, took the traditional "bite" out of Archbishop Peruzzi's ring.

Archbishop Wagner, standing to the right of the Apostolic Delegate, modestly subdued his rank.

"You, of course, know Archbishop Wagner," Father Rector said.

Down went Brother Kevin again, kissing Wagner's ring.

"How've you been, Kevin?" Wagner asked with familiar ease.

"Fine, very fine, Your Grace," Kevin said with a fudgy touch of a
Donegal brogue.

Archbishop Peruzzi looked about the roomy kitchen, his avid
black eyes flitting from the gleaming copper pots hanging on the
walls to the wide, low-slung wood stoves.

"I have a question," he said, touching the brother's shoulder gently,
almost affectionately. "You—you bake your own bread?"

"Yis, Your Grace," Brother Kevin answered, "'tis all done right
here!"

"Nice, very nice," Peruzzi said, smiling a sudden, wide smile.

"You had some for lunch, Your Excellency," Archbishop Wagner
said.

"*Si, si!*" Peruzzi said. "Very nice."

In the rear rank of the escort committee, behind the bishops, the

Rector, four priest-professors, and four seminarians from First Theology, Arthur Wagner stood between Vincent and Bob, pursing his lips like Archbishop Peruzzi, turning his hands in a small but expressive arc, and whispering, "Nice, nice, very nice."

Vincent choked off a laugh with a quick cough and hid a grin behind his hand. Bob frowned and looked straight ahead.

The retinue moved on, through the library, up to the dormitories, downstairs again, and out to the spacious, undulant campus, green-lyrical with lawns, trees, and birdsong.

"*Bellissima!*" Peruzzi said, pausing at the edge of the ball field and looking across the breathing loveliness of greensward to the dark tangle of forest beyond.

To the somnolent accompaniment of a muted conversation between the two archbishops, the retinue moved easily across the outfield to the batter's box at home plate.

Then a word came through strongly from Archbishop Wagner, a word intended for the hearing of all.

"Baseball!" Wagner said, enunciating the two syllables separately and emphatically. "Do you know of the game?"

"*Si, si.*" Peruzzi shaded his eyes from the sun. Then he mimicked the gripping of a bat, swung, and pumped his arms several times, as though running. A ripple of amusement went through the escort committee.

Archbishop Wagner increased the ripple to a wave with a stout guffaw of appreciation. His lean face red with merriment, he turned to the seminarians and called for his nephew.

"Arthur, will you come here?"

Arthur came forward with a shyness more decorous than self-conscious. He had met Peruzzi and other Italian dignitaries several times before.

"Yes, Your Excellency," he said.

Vincent found himself smiling—there would be no "Unk" here.

"Arthur, I would like Archbishop Peruzzi to know about our baseball player. Is Vincent Whelton here?"

"Yes, sir."

"Mr. Whelton," the Archbishop called. "Would you come forward?"

Vincent went cold with embarrassment, hesitated, then moved toward the prelates. He brushed against Lambert, looked up to excuse himself, and saw only the rigidly set features of one who looks and does not see.

"There you are!" Wagner said. "Archbishop Peruzzi, here is a young man who passed up a brilliant career as a professional baseball player to study for Holy Orders."

Peruzzi fixed Vincent with a startling look of interest, took his hand, squeezing it and patting it without relenting his penetrating stare.

Vincent flushed red, thought of kneeling down, but recalled that he had already gone through the line of ring-kissers with the rest of the seminarians at the auditorium breakfast.

"Coming here, Your Excellency, was no personal sacrifice," he managed to say.

"No sacrifice," Peruzzi said slowly, releasing Vincent's hand. "Very nice."

Then from out of the cool mystery of the woods behind home plate a bird warbled sweetly and swift.

Immediately Peruzzi was alerted, cocking his fine, bone-stark head and listening intently.

Again the bird warbled with brief ecstasy.

"You know birds?" he asked Vincent.

"Not very well." He thought of Bob Lambert but felt it might seem too forward to mention him.

The bird sang again, this time longer, sweeter, roost-settling, rid of anxiety, it seemed. Peruzzi listened, and Vincent saw with relief that Arthur was whispering to his uncle.

"Yes, yes indeed," Wagner said to his nephew. Then to the Apostolic Delegate: "We well know of your genuine love for the little singers of the forest. We have here among us a young man who is also quite a 'birder,' as they say. Lambert, Mr. Lambert, will you come forward?"

The birdsong again, a full, bright warble.

Lambert moved promptly to the foreground, cool, poised—almost, it seemed, rehearsed.

"You know this bird, my son?"

"Yes—yes, I believe I do, Your Excellency," he said with a nice reserve that was not without certitude. "It's a warbler—could be a hooded warbler. They like laurel thickets; they come up as far as the Great Lakes from the South in the summertime."

Peruzzi flashed his disarming smile and took Lambert by the elbow.

"It did seem to be a warbler. Come, perhaps if we move quietly we can see him."

"Gold with a black hood," Lambert said brightly to both prelates.

The retinue moved closely to the edge of the thicket—hushed, all eyes focused upward. They paused, straining eyes and ears, then the pert, sweet warble again.

"There, Your Excellencies, up there," Lambert whispered avidly.

The song ceased, twigs crackled, there was a flash of gold and black.

"There he goes!" Peruzzi said. Then slowly, approvingly: "The hooded warbler."

"Yes, yes," Archbishop Wagner said. "Up there through that twisted trunk."

"Life-first or year-first?" Peruzzi asked of Lambert in a direct comradely manner.

"Year-first," Lambert said. "I saw one last fall, Your Excellencies, heading South. That was my life-first."

"I must remember your name. What is it again?" Peruzzi asked.

"Lambert, Your Excellency, Robert Lambert."

"Robert Lambert," Peruzzi repeated slowly, benevolently.

Father Rector whispered something to Archbishop Wagner.

"Yes, yes," Wagner said, nodding. "Archbishop Peruzzi, young Lambert here is one of our finest young scholars, a first-rate student philosopher and theologian, Father Rector tells me."

"Nice, very nice," Peruzzi said, beaming.

Vincent had edged his way to the rear of the escort, rejoining Arthur.

"Ver-ee nice!" Arthur said, raising his eyebrows and tilting his head toward Lambert, who stood with admirable aplomb beside the Apostolic Delegate.

"Yeh, very swell," Vincent said. "He really *does know* them, though, doesn't he?"

Arthur nodded agreement.

"Shall we get on, Your Excellencies?" Father Rector asked. "It is almost time for Benediction."

The group walked back across the diamond toward the seminary buildings. In the woods behind them a bobwhite gave out with two notes of pure, whistly salute.

Arthur looked at Vincent and winked.

"You know it?" Arthur asked as they walked.

"Bobwhite," Vincent answered.

"Life-first or year-first?"

"Neither," Vincent said.

The Apostolic Delegate had paused to hear the bobwhite. Again the intense concentration and a rapt exchange of special bird-talk with Lambert.

This time Archbishop Wagner and Father Rector remained aloof from the conversation. Lambert seemed to sense this and drifted back to the seminarians as they approached the buildings.

"Make way for Monsignor Lambert," Arthur said.

CHAPTER IV

Man Proposes . . .

SUNDAY evening—cold corned beef sandwiches, tea, corncake, and the smell of boiled cabbage lingering from the heavy afternoon meal. Vincent finished his cake in the empty refectory, took one last sip of tea, blessed himself, and hurried away.

He crossed the campus in the soft, rosy light of the May evening. He felt the bulge of his sermon manuscript under the big scarlet B of his St. Brendan's varsity sweater, which he wore inside out during non-class and non-chapel hours.

He had finally committed to memory the entire twenty-minute text, and it was good to feel he did not really need the manuscript any more.

Father Steve Carney, his rhetoric professor, would be waiting for him at the auditorium to hear his practice delivery of the piece. It would have to serve as his dress rehearsal. The Roman scholarship delivery would take place at nine the following morning.

Vincent had tested his memory of the sermon in the presence of Arthur Wagner before lunch. When Bob Lambert had left to do some boning in the library, Arthur pushed a couch against the door, leaped on it, and cried: "Let's go, Cicero! Jump up there on the window sill!"

Then, for the first time, Vincent delivered the sermon on St. Vincent de Paul from memory—De Paul who could have played it safe as the clerical lap dog of the rich yet could not exist unless he was indefatigably in the service of the poor.

" 'The rich have their own defenses,' " Vincent had declared, quoting the great encyclical of Leo XIII and applying it to the life of St. Vincent.

Arthur had sat with folded arms and a purposely dead-pan face, which made it difficult for Vincent to continue smoothly. But continue he did, describing vividly how De Paul had been stoned by the very people whom he was trying to help. In this connection he had cited the famous Vincentian comment on the ignominy of accepting charity.

"You will find out that charity is a heavy burden to carry, heavier than the bowl of soup and the full basket. But you will keep your gentleness and your smile. It is not enough to give soup and bread. This the rich can do. You are the servant of the poor, always smiling and always good-humored. They are your masters, terribly sensitive and exacting masters, you will see. Then the uglier and dirtier they will be, the more unjust and insulting, the more love you must give them. It is only for your love alone that the poor will forgive you the bread you give to them."

On and on, the harvest of study, inspiration, and memory poured in plenty from the gourd of his spirit.

"Hail, Vincent de Paul," he concluded, "friend of the poor; hail and homage forever, friend of the friends of God!"

Arthur sat for several minutes without comment.

"Well?" Vincent asked.

"You've got it. Just give it that way—Lambert can't touch it. And the other two won't even come close."

"You really think so?"

"I really think so," Arthur said, his pale face spectral in the shadows of the room.

Vincent, walking now across the campus to meet Father Carney, felt a confidence in the sermon and his ability to deliver it which he had not known before.

He bounded up the wide sandstone steps to the assembly hall and went quickly through the door.

The hall was empty and the cool, majestic stillness seemed like an invitation to speak. Father Carney, he thought, would be along soon.

He walked down the middle aisle, his footfalls echoing. He climbed to the stage and went to the rostrum. He spread out his manuscript on the lectern, gripped the mahogany sides with both hands, leveled his eyes at the rear of the hall, and tried his voice:

"'The rich have their own defenses . . .'" strongly and with initial nervousness. He tried it again: "'The rich have their own defenses . . .'" firmly now, easier.

That's it, he thought, looking around the hall somewhat anxiously, noting by the big pendulum clock on the balcony that Father Carney was over fifteen minutes late.

Sensing the awkwardness of being on stage when not acting or speaking, seeing no chair up there where he could sit inconspicuously, he stepped down to the orchestra and settled into a first-row seat.

Recalling Arthur's confidence in his sermon, he allowed himself to savor his chances of winning the Roman scholarship. He thought first of the joy it would bring his parents if he should be sent to study in Rome—his mother warming to compliments from a neighbor as she poured an afternoon cup of tea, his dad trying to contain his pride as a colleague mentioned the news in the City Council chambers. But, above all, the Eternal City, the seat of the Faith, the Holy Father appearing on the balcony of the papal residence—above all, the books, the talk, the warm, lyrical people, the Roman church bells calling with the authority of factory whistles in America—all that and maybe heaven, too, if he could win the contest.

Arthur, he was sure, would go to Rome even if he did not win the classical essay contest. He had the money and could afford to pay his way; and, too, he was the Archbishop's nephew.

Together in Rome—Arthur with an art book in the Galleria or poking about the ruins of the Coliseum—hiking on pilgrimage to Monte Cassino. How good it would be! How very good!

Bob Lambert? Vincent felt no ill will toward him but could summon no warmth. Perhaps Bob would win the essay and even the sermon prize. Perhaps Vincent would win in the sermon category and Bob the essay. But the prospect of Rome with Bob Lambert for two years palled the excitement of the dream.

Steps in the foyer, quickly, lightly. Father Steve Carney entered, waved, and hurried down the middle aisle.

He was a spare, sandy-haired man of middle height, his face calm, open, incapable of guile, and as he approached, Vincent could discern he was summoning an apologetic smile out of some deep disturbance of spirit.

"Vin," he said, "I'm terribly sorry. It's our Legion of Mary friend,

Lucinda, she's very sick. I'm afraid she's going to die. I've just come from her and will have to go back right away!"

Lucinda. That was the fervid little colored woman who did the Legion of Mary work in Splinterville, the Negro community on the edge of town. She was one of a group of lay people who met monthly with Father Carney and several seminarians to map out and execute apostolic work involving fallen-away Catholics.

The seminarians were active in the group for the benefit of the experience later to be used in parish work.

Lucinda had been doing notable work in the Splinterville area but of late had been confined to bed with a chest ailment which had now been diagnosed as T.B. Father Carney had arranged for a doctor and had located her roving, ne'er-do-well husband.

"You'd better get on out there, Father," Vincent said, "this can wait."

Father Carney smiled—a sudden, confidence-building smile that made you feel you were at that moment the most important person in the world.

"Why don't you come with me—drive me over? The gig is outside. You can speak the speech from memory as we go along."

Father Carney would be taking Holy Viaticum to Lucinda—the consecrated wafer for the dying. He would give her, too, the last anointing—the blessing and symbolic purging of the senses that constitute the last rites of the Church. Vin, even driving the gig, would be helpful.

"Let's go," Vin said.

Outside the chapel, waiting in the gig while Father Carney got the Sacrament, Vincent could see the green, low-hilled beauty of the countryside. High over the lush rolling green, the brown mare sensed a predatory star, shook her belled harness apprehensively, and fountained a minute fireworks display with a stomp of rear hoof against the cobbles.

Vincent saw the cause of her unease circling over the low-lying hills to the west. He recognized the ominous black sailing and gliding as the turkey vulture. Bob Lambert would like to see this, Vincent thought, and would give detail and clue to the species as it hovered eerily over—yes, over Splinterville, west among the hills where the railroad junctioned briefly with hogs and beef for the stockyard empires of Lakeport.

The portent of doom and evil was routed in his heart by the

footfalls of Father Carney on the steps of the chapel. He took the
reins as the priest slipped deftly into the gig beside him. He clucked
his tongue, and the mare clopped briskly along the campus road to
the main highway.

With the ancient eyes of men's anxiety Father Carney searched
the skies and found the evil that must be routed with divine belief
and sacramental power. Only a moment apprehensive, he touched
the wafered Divinity at his chest, checking its physical security, and,
smiling, nudged Vincent to begin the memory trials of his prize
oration.

" 'The rich have their own defenses . . .' " Vincent began softly
yet surely amid the clopping metronome of hoof and sandy road.
He went through the entire sermon, secure now in memory, ready
as he ever would be for the climactic delivery on the morrow.

When he was done—raising his voice as he told the ultimate silver
beads of Vincent de Paul's unselfishness—the mare clomped on
briskly, the turkey vulture circled lower, and the soft spring dusk
flooded about them.

Father Carney spoke—softly, briefly.

"You'll do very well; substance, memory—the right mixture and
flow of both. But use that natural thunder of your voice wisely.
St. Vincent was a gentle man except when righteously aroused. Tell
that gentility in character, as it were, firmly, to be sure, but above
all, gently."

Vincent, seared now with grateful confidence, smiled at the priest
and said, "I will, Father; thank you."

The gig rattled primly over the low, lush hills into the valley of
Splinterville.

Down the hill, into the Swiss-like valley, coming, even as in the
city, on prosperous, burgeoning suburbia, knowing that the center of
town would follow, the bustle and the commerce of a small town
fat with grain and pork and steer. And Vincent knew with a sudden,
insistent chill how the other side of town awaited—the ramshackle,
the lassitude, and the stench of Splinterville. There hope was young
and strong and later wilted in the weeds, lifting its sorry petals
slightly to the sun but dying slowly every day.

And the trains shrieked past derisively, night and day, across mid-
America, hooting at the second-class race who dwelt within the
sooty purlieus of the coal dumps and the rails.

Among the neatly manicured lawns they clopped, bearing the
final sustenance to Lucy, the priest silent in the dust, the house
lamps winking on as locks snapped abruptly, sealing in the middle
classes against the fearsome and unknown.

Past the shops, the needle spire of the Presbyterian church, past
the Civil War colonel astride his greening bronze charger, past the
red brick town hall, on, across the tracks into Splinterville and the
lamp-flickering windows of tar-paper shacks.

"Lucy's place is in the third lane on the right," Father Carney
said.

Vincent nodded, tightening the reins for the turn. As they turned,
the age-old sounds of wailing and women-mewing filled their ears.
They proceeded about halfway into the lane, cautious about swaying
forms who knelt and stood about the entrance to Lucy's house.

"De Lawd giveth and de Lawd taketh away!" said a rich contralto voice in the darkness.

"Hallelujah!" responded a chorus of male and female voices.

This was followed by the mewing and the wailing again, articu-
lating into one clear lament by a male voice:

"She done good all her life and she goin' to the good Lawd now
—our Lucy goin' far away!"

"Hallelujah!" the chorus answered.

"Fourth house on the left," Father Carney said.

"Whoa, girl," Vincent said softly.

After helping the priest down from the gig amid instant silence,
Vincent knocked on the plain pine door, feeling the grate of bent
nails on his knuckles. An awakening of muted voices, footfalls, and
the door creaked open.

"You is the preacher?" asked the squat ebon lady who opened the
door. A slow, tired smile creased her features as Father Carney
nodded.

"Right in this way, Reverend," she said, stepping back.

She led Father Carney into the bedroom, which, with the kitchen,
made up the entire household. The door closed behind them, and
Vincent, sensing another presence, glanced to his right.

On a stool beside the cookstove a tall middle-aged Negro sat
slumped with his head in his hands. Every few seconds his head
convulsed slightly and he uttered a high-pitched sound.

Vincent moved to him and placed a hand on his shoulder.

The Negro raised his head, confronting Vincent with a scarred, unshaven face and bloodshot eyes that could not entirely be attributed to his grief. A sickly-sweet whiff of muscatel was on his breath as he spoke.

"You is a parson too?"

"Yes—that is, I'm studying to be one," Vincent said.

"Ah'm Lucy's husband, Jefferson Smith. I ain't been roun' heah much—but when Ah heard Ah came from Lakeport right away."

"I'm sure you'll be a consolation to her," Vincent said, knowing it was the nice thing to say.

"Ah've never been a consolation to nobody. Ah used to laugh at Lucy for changin' preachers like she did. Ah used to scoff at the way she'd run roun' the shacks helpin' the sick and guidin' the preacher and all. But she did a powerful lot of good roun' heah, en' the folks jist love her is all."

Vincent nodded slowly. The remorse in the husband's words almost crowded out the grief. And that, he sensed, is the most violent retribution of sin in the sinner—the inevitable realization that he or she has been a cause of misery in the life of a loved one.

Jefferson Smith sat in the heavy silence of the death watch, which was broken only by his convulsing sobs. Vincent slipped his rosary out of the leather packet which he carried in his side pocket and silently began the recitation of the Sorrowful Mysteries.

The minutes slipped by, twenty-five of them, before the door of the bedroom opened and Father Carney emerged, pale, wan, and calm.

"Vincent," he said softly, "come in and say hello to St. Lucy."

He called her a saint with a certain lightness that was not without deep conviction. He smiled at the husband, holding the door open as Vincent went in.

A child propped up on pillows.

That was the picture Lucy presented as Vincent crossed the threshold. Her body, tiny even in health, had shrunk to the proportions of a five-year-old girl. But the maturity and strength of spirit were still manifest in the burning smile which she projected on Vincent out of her coffee-colored face.

"Come in, Father Vincent!" she said brightly. "Have yourself a seat."

"Thank you," Vincent said. "How are you feeling?"

She smiled brightly again. "Since the father has come Ah's feeling mighty fine."

"I'm glad to hear that."

In the other room he could hear Father Carney buzzing firmly yet consolingly with Lucy's husband.

"Does you mind if Ah call you Father? Ah know you ain't a Father yet, but you will be and Ah might not be around to call you Father then."

"I don't mind at all, Lucy. In fact, I'll always remember you as the first one who called me Father."

Father Carney came back into the room and slipped quietly into a chair alongside Vincent.

"Vincent here is one of the best orators at the school," Father Carney said lightly. "He should be a fine preacher someday."

"Father Carney, what you say about this boy comes as no surprise to me. For the Lord is wise and He has given me a feeling of this young man's power!"

With a look of consternation Father Carney simply nodded at Vincent and exclaimed, "Well!"

Vincent's face reddened and he bowed his head, more with awe than embarrassment at Lucy's words.

"Young man," Lucy went on, fixing him with a tentacle of the death look, "listen to the words of a dying woman who has tried to serve Christ's poor with all her heart and soul! The Lord will raise you up high—and then raise you down. He loves you very much—dat's why he gave you so much."

As Lucy, closing her eyes in intense concentration, continued with a buffeting emotional power of speech, both Father Carney and Vincent slipped to their knees and bowed their heads in prayer. It was both the power of her speech and the sense that she might be slipping away that impelled them to do so.

"They say the Lord hurts most those He loves most. Ah do not believe dat is true. For the Lord is all love and lifts his hands only to heal.

"But it is true dat the few who learn of the power of His love make demselves suffer by doin' and doin' His work until dey lie dyin' at His feet.

"You is to know, Vincent, de power of His love. You is to know dat if you gets much, you gives much. De Lord will raise you up and raise you down. But you will love His poor, Ah knows you will, Vincent, Ah knows you will—whether you is up or down. . . ."

Lucy was taken then with a rocking, wrecking spasm of coughing which brought the plump Negro neighbor rushing from the shack next door. She seized Lucy in her arms and held her, motioning with her head for Father and Vincent to leave. They arose and left the room, crossing the kitchen to the outside door.

In the buckboard, rolling toward the center of town, Vincent broke the spell with a sigh.

"That was hard on you, son," Father Carney said.

"Yes, kind of. But even tougher for you. Is she a real mystic?"

"She just might be," Father Carney said. "I'm convinced she's a very holy woman, knowing her work among the poor and the intensity of her religious life. Whether you like it or not, you'll have to give serious thought to her words."

"That's probably the way the colored folk talk at these religious tent meetings," Vincent said, anxious to minimize the prophecies Lucy had uttered concerning him.

"It *is* their style," Father Carney agreed, "but it makes Lucy even more convincing; she's in character yet expresses the difference of perspective which her new-found faith has given her. So you'd better prepare yourself for the demands of the Lord—Monsignor Whelton!"

Vincent responded to this by snapping the reins. The mare jogged on out of town into the hills at a faster clip.

"Will she live long now?" Vincent asked.

"The doctor gave up on her yesterday. My guess is she'll die by early morning. You'll be busy with your oratory competition by then."

Oratory. The Roman prize! He had forgotten it entirely.

"Why don't you rattle off the speech for me once more? We have lots of time between here and the sem."

"I will, thanks, Father."

A full moon illumined the ribbon of sandy road that coiled over and through the hills. He thought for a few minutes and then began the familiar words about St. Vincent, unreeling them slowly, eloquently, to Father Carney and the eternal, moonlit hills.

It was after midnight when Vincent soft-shoed up the stairs to his dormitory room. The spell of the dying Lucy and her deep-striking words was still on him and seemed further sustained by the abyss of midnight in old St. Philip's Hall.

Walking close to the wall in the second-story corridor to avoid the creaking boards of mid-floor, he came to his room, paused, and heard the subdued breathing of Lambert and Wagner. The door was ajar and he slipped in, feeling his way to the cot.

He sank into a sitting position on the mattress, slipped off his sneakers, crossed himself, and lay back with a welcome rush of exhaustion. First the calm, white face of Lucy in dolor and the ominous singsong of her prophecy. Then the fading of her face and her voice, the fading, fading, fading . . .

Light and sound. The light of morning, dull and gaining-bright at the window to the east; Arthur's voice softly at his bedside.

"Vin, where were you? I've been sick with worry. Did the trip with Father Carney take all that time?"

"It did," Vin said, blinking the sleep out of his eyes. "It's a long way over to Splinterville by gig, and a long way back."

Across the room Lambert, too, was stirring, angling his long knees under the bedding, looking across at Vincent and Arthur with level gray eyes.

"Are you ready? Have you really got the sermon down?" Arthur asked anxiously.

"I've got it as well as I'll ever have it. I recited it to Father Carney, to and fro."

"You've got to win this thing, Vin. I'll go to Rome, win or lose, but you've got to win!"

"Supposing I don't," Vin said yawning. "The world will still turn."

"Yes, but not for you. For somebody like our pal over there." He nodded toward Lambert, who was now out of bed and pulling on a bathrobe.

Lambert slipped a towel off the piping at the bottom of his cot and left for the showers.

"I want you to listen to me, Vin, and listen carefully. This is my last chance to talk to you before the Roman competition. You've got a mark of destiny on you—whatever it is—and I don't know exactly what it is. But I know you've got it. And today is the *carpe diem* for you, Vin; this is the tide which leads on to fortune.

"You haven't got money, you haven't got influence. This is the only way you'll get to Rome while you're a student—and you belong there—you've got to be there, your future in the practical side of the priesthood is there!"

Vincent thought of Lucy. This was the second intimation of things to come hurled at his consciousness within the last twenty-four hours.

"I would like to go," Vin said. "But I really don't think failure to go would handicap me as a priest!"

Arthur's thin, handsome face became taut. "It would, Vin, believe me it would. It's got nothing to do with the spiritual life of a priest or his service to the faithful—I know that! But Rome is a club, a kind of social and political one among the clergy, if you will. The people you meet in Rome as a student will be of aid and comfort to you for the rest of your life. Nobody comes right out and says so—and I'd really be in dutch if my uncle heard me saying these things, but it's true—the highroads of the Church lead from Rome!"

Vincent was beginning to smolder. He wanted to go to Rome very much—perhaps more than Wagner knew. But it had nothing directly to do with his priestly vocation and he wanted Arthur to know it. The conviction welled to his tongue.

"I came here because of my interest in the highroads of the soul," he said sharply.

Arthur lowered his eyes, flushing with sincerity as much as shame.

"That's why I'm here too, Vincent, believe me. The interior life takes precedence and always will. But the interior needs the exterior—that's in the nature of things—our nature—the world's nature. The religious life needs the politics of Rome as well as its cultural riches and holiness. Don't be too hard on me. I—I—still believe in such a thing as a moment of history for certain people—and this may be your moment—you've got to bring it off."

Vincent warmed to Wagner's persistent concern for his success in the competition. He doubled up his fist and punched him easily, affectionately, on the arm.

"I'll give it my best, Art," he said. "Let's get to the showers, we'll be late for Mass."

Fifteen minutes to go. In a straight-backed wooden chair by the wide west window of his room Vincent intently perused the manuscript of his speech for the last time. He finished it, paused, slipped onto his knees and prayed for victory in the competition: ". . . if it is Thy will, O Lord." He prayed also to St. Vincent, his patron and the subject of his sermon. "Let my words give honor to you, win or lose."

He crossed himself, arose briskly, gave three strokes to his hair with a comb, took the manuscript off the bed, glanced at it drolly for a moment, and then tossed it with a touch of disdain on the study table.

Down the creaky hall, down the hollow wooden stairs. He wanted to whistle and did—the first few bars of "The Campbells Are Coming." He had the same strong, competitive feeling he had known when hiking out to warm up before the start of a baseball game. He knew he was right and ready—bring them on!

He hurried past the porter's lodge, had his hand on the brass plate of the swinging inner door, and paused. He had caught a glimpse of a dark, hunched-over figure.

Lucy's husband! The thought clanged through him like a fire alarm. She's dying, calling for Father Carney, this is the end!

"Jefferson," he called anxiously, turning and walking toward the crestfallen husband. "Lucy—is she—is she . . ."

"She's nigh gone, Mist' Vincent, she's nigh gone and callin' fo' de Parson Carney all de time."

Vincent turned to the seminarian serving his chore in the porter's lodge.

"Did you contact Father Carney?"

"Yes, Vin," the seminarian answered. "There's a note on his door. He took the early train for the city—he'll be gone for the day!"

"I wonder if we could get one of the other fathers to go."

"Fathers Kent and Sorelli, along with the Rector, will be judging the competition. They're the only three fathers on campus right now."

"Oh," Vincent said. As if he didn't know about the competition and its judges, as if he didn't know . . .

"Mr. Jefferson here tells me his wife received the Last Sacraments from Father Carney late last night. Is that true?"

"Yes, it is true," Vincent said. "I accompanied Father Carney on the trip—drove the gig, in fact. But this is different, she's different—Lucy needs somebody there, somebody official, maybe, from the new religion she's found and loved so much and served so well."

"She's been well provided for, Vin," the seminarian said with deadly accuracy.

"That's true, that's true," Vin said, biting his lip in thought and taking the slumping crag of man that was Jefferson by the shoulder. "Come on, Jefferson, come on."

"Are you going over there again?" the seminarian asked anxiously.

"I don't know. I might, I just might . . ."

The tower bell was striking nine when he got into an ancient lopsided buckboard behind a lank and bony mule. They creaked along over the cinders beyond the seminary grounds and into the low-lying hills as the bell was still. It had tolled for his scholarship to Rome, he knew, and Arthur Wagner would be apoplectic with frustration and rage. But Lucy was dying and she wanted Rome, too—the approximation of Rome he could try to bring her in Father Carney's absence.

"It's such a glory mornin', Mist' Vincent," Jefferson said, squinting into the roseate-and-silver hints of the west.

"Yes," Vincent said with the old acorn of childhood growing big and tight in his throat. A glory day, he knew, for Bob Lambert and Arthur Wagner, but most of all for Lucy beyond the hills where the railroad curved mightily to the west.

BOOK TWO

The Fight for the City

CHAPTER V

Off the Streets

WHAT happened to the big brewery horses?

Father Vincent Whelton, third assistant curate in the sprawling parish of St. Polycarp, framed this question in his mind on awakening from his after-breakfast nap. The nap privilege went with the sleepy, daily chore of saying the five forty-five workers' and widows' Mass each morning. The "chore" in St. Polycarp's and in many other parishes of the diocese went to "Junior," as the youngest curate was sometimes called.

He opened his eyes to a view of the great, wan brick brewery across the street from the rectory, where rickety, blunt-nosed trucks were harrumphing in and out of the garage-like entrance heavy with cases of "legitimate beer."

With the lid of Prohibition clamped on tight, the near-beer industry, augmented by the soft-drink line, was bravely, almost futilely, trying to endure. How, then, account for the relentless bustle and busyness of the trucking across the way? The big beer-wagon horses were gone, as were the kindly old plugs in his father's lumberyard. But the Acme Brewery—so busy, so bustly—who was drinking that much near beer; who, to sustain such industry, had that much enthusiasm for strawberry pop?

The answer, he knew, lay in the headlines of the unread Lakeport *Herald* on the night table beside his bed. INDICTMENTS SOUGHT IN POLICE BRIBING! the scarehead read. GANGS INFILTRATE BEER INDUSTRY, the subhead went on.

Just so they don't harm our little gray house, Vincent thought with a fond glance at the curtainless, single wooden house which stood out starkly between one end of the brewery and the beginning of a long line of shabby tenement houses.

The screeching brakes of a beer truck and the roaring profanity of a truckman as three little neighborhood urchins scrambled for safety were only another stark memo of the need for recreational facilities in the sunless tenement jungles of the parish.

Vincent, who had served as chaplain at the Pondview Naval Station during the World War, had visions of reproducing in miniature some of the recreational facilities that had made wholesome the idle time of young sailors at the base.

"Get the kids off the streets!" was his motto. And the condemned house across the street had high ceilings on the first floor which, with the room walls broken down, would lend themselves to some abbreviation of a basketball and volleyball court. The second floor for a library and sedentary game room, the cellar for making things out of wood and clay. Dreams, dreams, dreams . . . He had enough of dreams—he'd approach the pastor right now.

Up and out of bed with the sign of the cross. On with his cassock over the white collarless shirt and black trousers, into his shoes.

Down the long, narrow hall with the faded carpet to Father Regan's room. He'd be napping now or coming out of one—a bad time to call—but act now he must or the routine of the parish—services, confessions, converts, counting the collection—would sweep him away from the mocking challenge of the brewery and the little gray house. Father Regan, Vinegar Jack! "Don't try to save the world," he had said sternly in Vincent's first interview with him after his assignment. "Just do your job, carry your load around here, and leave the planning and the projects to the pastor. When you get to be a pastor yourself you'll appreciate my point of view. Now it's always a custom here that the youngest curate says the five forty-five Mass . . ."

But suffer the little children, suffer the little children playing in front of the brewery, under the wheels of the thugs and the mugs, suffer them not to suffer in the little gray house across from the rectory.

Vincent tightened his shoulders and rapped lightly yet firmly on Father Regan's bedroom door.

No answer. He rapped again, this time stronger, longer.

"Yes, yes!" answered the gruff, clipped voice. "That you, Bridey?

What is it now—a letter from the Bishop? What does he want now?"

The last, addressed to Bridey, the housekeeper, was uttered with a rising whine that is the protest of those who must constantly come up with money under difficult circumstances.

The pad-pad of slippers crossed the room and the door swung wide to reveal Vinegar Jack Regan, pastor of St. Polycarp's these long twenty years.

"It's you!" Father Regan said, arching his watery blue eyes and snorting out of a long veined nose. "And now that your nap is over, is it your pleasure to rouse the pastor from his?"

"Not at all, Father," Vincent said, "not at all. It's—it's just that I had to talk to you—now—before it's too late."

"Before what's too late?" the pastor trumpeted. "What have you been doing—mixed up with one of our sodality girls? Oh, my God, no! Have you been drinking on your day off? I WARNED YOU ABOUT PUNCH AND JUDY when you first came here!"

"No—no—no, Father Regan," Vincent hastened to assure him. "Nothing like that, nothing like that at all."

"Well, come in, come in—it must be something important if you had to derrick your pastor out of bed. You young curates—I swear I'll petition the Bishop to have you all gelded—you're up and bouncing about something all the time. Come in, come in . . ."

Into the pastor's bedroom, the widest, warmest room in the house, the rug wine-red and lawny-deep, the four-poster bed a sea of silken comfort, the stuffed leather chair and hunt-club lamps an invitation to romantic lostness in the buckram-bound volumes lining the walls.

"I won't detain you long," Vincent said.

"Sit down, sit down." Vinegar Jack was anxious to know whether it was mental, moral, or financial, sensing now the latter. "Sit there." He beckoned to a stuffed armchair which seemed incongruous in the handsomely appointed room and was obviously a calculated touch to discourage visitors from lingering overlong.

"It's just that I think we should do something more concrete to help the kids in the parish," Vincent said. "They're the sons and daughters of our parishioners and their playgrounds are the cobblestones. It's just a shame, Father Regan—and now with these trucks rampaging our streets—not to mention the hoodlums and their gunplay—the whole situation just cries to heaven for action."

"That's the city's problem, not ours," Vinegar Jack said, insinuating one lean finger deep into his veiny nostril. "Our job is to minister to the spiritual needs of the parish—which includes a big expensive parish school."

"But we have no schoolyard of any size where they can play," Vincent insisted, "and you know how slow the city moves. They'd have to tear down housing in order to make room."

"So—so-so, me young crusader, what is it you propose to your pastor now? Come out with it, boy. What would you have me do—and, mind you, how much would it cost?"

"It wouldn't cost too much at all, Father Regan," Vincent said eagerly. "If you could see your way clear to paying a modest rent for that house across the street we could renovate it with raffle funds. We could fix up the first floor as a gym, the second floor as a library, the basement as a workshop. The kids would love it—and they'd be off the streets in many of their after-school hours!"

"Ump!" Vinegar Jack snorted, reaching for a small oval tin box on the end table beside his stuffed chair. He slipped off the cover and offered a brown powdery substance to Vincent.

"Take a pinch, me bucko, it'll clear your head of some of these nonsensical ideas."

Vincent declined the snuff, and the pastor took a large pinch and sniffed it vigorously into both nostrils before speaking.

"In the first place, that old shack is condemned. The only way to acquire the property would be to buy it from the city on the promise that the building would be razed to the ground. Secondly, me boy—and you'll understand this better when you've been in three or four parishes—the Cardinal would have to approve the type of expenditure you suggest, and I know what he'd say beforehand."

"What is that, Father?"

"The same as I've already told you, lad. It's the city's moral and financial responsibility to provide adequate play areas for these children. They're the ones that should be awakened from their nap, not your poor old pastor."

"But I've already said, Father, the city moves too slowly—some child will die under the wheels of a brewery truck. Then all the playgrounds in the world will not make that child live again."

"God forbid such a thing, Father Vincent, but the first work of the parish must go forward, even if you and I, for example, were to meet an untimely death."

"Well," Vincent said in desperation, "at least grant me this—can I have permission to write to the Cardinal about this matter?"

Vinegar Jack drew himself up to the extremity of his sagging skin and his protesting bones.

"You'll do nothing of the kind. The pastor writes to the Cardinal for St. Polycarp's, and only the pastor—is that clear?"

Vincent sighed wearily. "That's clear."

"Very well," Vinegar Jack said, taking another pinch of snuff, "a very good morning to you."

Down the hall to his room, his lips the smoke-tight lid of a volcano of emotion. Out, out into the air; walk, walk, walk, something in him commanded. He had a fifth-grade religion class right after lunch in the parish school. It was almost ten. He swept a black topcoat off a hanger on the door of his closet and, hunching quickly into it, went out of his room and down the back stairs.

He hurried through the kitchen where Bridey Cleary nodded over her vegetable peelings. He acknowledged her nod with a tight-lipped grimace and headed out into the rectory yard.

In the air, in the sun of that cloudy spring morning, he let out his lungs in one great propulsion of frustration. Standing among the clotheslines, he could hear the roar of the brewery trucks out front, and a tracery of their exhaust fumes was slightly acrid in his nostrils.

"It's the city's responsibility. Don't write to the Cardinal. The work of the parish must go forward."

All the phrases of the pastor's reluctance to action clamored for aspirin in his head. But was the place condemned—he hadn't heard about that—was it really condemned? Why not find out for himself before religion class? Some one of the tenement neighbors must know.

If it weren't condemned, perhaps he could get at the Cardinal through Father Arthur Wagner down at the arch-diocesan newspaper office. After all, the Cardinal was still Arthur's uncle. The pastor wouldn't have to know his youngest assistant was involved.

Clanging the iron rectory gate behind him, he was confronted by Worsham Street and the tenement houses beside the brewery. Whom did he know in those grim, gray citadels of family life? Alice Walsh of the Mothers' Club, first floor, 109. He crossed to 109, just to the right of the intended "clubhouse."

The gloom and the soot of the neighborhood were relieved by clear windows, bright curtains, flower boxes adorning the gray tenement front.

Mrs. Walsh, alert at the front window, was on the porch to meet him.

"Good morning, Father," she said. "I saw you coming this way. Can I help you? Who did you want to see?"

"I wanted to see you, Mrs. Walsh. Can you tell me about the single house next door. Who owns it? Is it condemned, or what?"

"Oh, you mean the old Wilson place. It's owned by the brewery. There's talk they're planning to break through their own wall and build on."

"Oh," Vincent said, a note of disappointment rising in his voice. "Do you know who has the say on it?"

"Someone in the brewery," she said. "You can inquire in there. Are you thinking of doing something with it for the parish? We really need a place for the neighborhood kids something bad."

"The pastor might be interested in your sentiments, Mrs. Walsh," Vincent said wryly. "Thanks for the information. I'll go see the brewery people."

"Not at all, Father, not at all. It would be a fine thing indeed . . ."

It won't hurt to know the facts, Vincent reassured himself as he walked to the brewery entrance, even if the pastor won't go along. He knew it just might be that the pastor could be watching him from his bedroom window. He shook off the uncomfortable thought.

"I've got to know," he told himself.

He paused before a great green door marked OFFICE beside the truck entrance. He squared his shoulders and turned the huge brass knob.

A pretty, thin-faced brunette whom he vaguely recognized as a parishioner sat typing at a desk in front of the closed door of a private office.

"Good morning, Father," she said, rising and revealing the impress of her parochial training.

"Good morning, miss," Father Vincent said. "Would it be possible to see the manager?"

"Certainly, Father Whelton," she said knowingly. "Mr. Lorenzo has someone with him now, but I'm sure he'll see you if you care to wait."

He sat down and concentrated wryly on her identity. If she had been a student in one of his religion classes he would have known her right away. He had not been around the parish long enough for that.

But the high-pitched voice, the thin, sharp jut of her chin. Where had he known her singly and out of the blur of multiple parish faces? Could it have been the St. Patrick's play? He had pitched in and coached the musical concoction at the pastor's request—a prolonged series of skits and songs filled with Irish chauvinism and corny jokes. "The Hills of Erin," it had been called.

And she was? She was Joan Linehan, who sang "The Rose of Tralee" in a sweet if whiny soprano.

"You're Joan Linehan of the St. Patrick's play," he said with a hasty cordiality. "I thought I recognized you."

"Yes, Father," she said demurely. "We certainly enjoyed having you for coach this spring."

"I enjoyed doing it and I know the pastor was well pleased with the five hundred dollars net proceeds."

The subdued hum of voices in the private office took on a stronger timbre and he could not help hearing:

"You will!"

"I will like hell!"

in quick succession.

Lorenzo, Vincent thought, I knew a Lorenzo in the Navy.

"This Mr. Lorenzo—may I ask his first name?"

"His first name is Anthony, Father."

"Thank you."

The Lorenzo who had been his assistant as a naval chaplain bore the same first name. Tony Lorenzo, a dark Sicilian philanderer with high intelligence, swift shrewdness, and a fiery temper. He had been most orderly and reverent as assistant around the chapel but, paradoxically, was known as a crap-shooting fury and big-stakes poker player around the barracks. He was from the south side. Could this be the same Tony?

Vincent was about to ask when the inner office exploded.

"I don't need your help, you shake-down sonofabitch! get out of here!"

"You'll never deliver another goddamn barrel! I'll promise you that!"

The office door snapped open and a natty little man in a black derby and chesterfield strode out, glancing neither to left nor right.

Father Vincent heard the angry protest of a swivel chair and footsteps obviously to an office window.

Miss Linehan flushed red.

"I'm sorry, Father," she said. "This is—this is a highly competitive business," she continued in a lame, frightened tone of voice. She closed the door to Lorenzo's office. "I'm sure Mr. Lorenzo will see you in a few minutes."

It was obvious she wanted him to cool off before she announced Whelton's presence.

"How long have you been here, Joan?" he asked soberly.

"Almost a year. I was offered the job right after high school. It pays real well and Mr. Lorenzo is very nice to me. But you'll understand when I tell you I've been looking for another position."

"I understand, Joan."

She rose now, knocked on the door of the office, opened it, and announced Father Whelton.

"NOT MY OLD FATHER VINCENT!" announced the same bombastic voice, now without venom, which had trembled the door panels minutes before.

"Yes, yes, Anthony, how are you, how are you?" Father Vincent said, shaking hands warmly.

"Father, I'm fine—better than I deserve. Little did I dream, Father, when I was cleaning out your office as a gob . . ." He paused now, a trim, round man with a chiseled white face that only tardily would betray a stand of bristle. He still had about him, Vincent knew, weak or strong, obscure or famed, the same old cocksureness.

"Little did I dream, Padre . . ." Tony continued.

Little did he dream . . . Chaplain Whelton had not dreamed—he had known. Tony was heading for big things that dice could buy, and cards—he was successful at both. He had the brains and the personality to do other things—become an actor, a politician, perhaps even a lawyer. But never the patience, never the time.

"Little did you dream as you hurried out of the chapel, impatient for the poker game in Barracks Number 12, that you would someday be the general manager of Acme Beverages," Father Whelton said.

"That's it, Father," Lorenzo said. "That's it. Come in, come in."

Then to Miss Linehan: "I'm not to be disturbed, Joan—not even by Number One himself!"

Father Whelton followed him into the private office. Lorenzo closed the door tightly, and Vincent slipped into a chair near the broad, well-penknifed desk.

"But all this talk about me!" Tony exclaimed, running his hand through his seal-slick hair. "You across the street there—I know all about you—WHAT CAN I DO FOR YOU?" he demanded loudly and impulsively.

"You can tell me the status of the little gray house which the brewery owns," Vincent said with deadly directness. "You can tell me how I can get hold of it as a clubhouse for the young folks in the neighborhood."

"YOU WANT IT FOR THE KIDS!" Tony said, jumping up and opening a file cabinet to the right of his desk. He snapped out a folder and sat down again with a vibrant nervousness that seemed to send out a series of little electric charges. "Let's see here, let's see," he said more soberly, paging through the official-looking papers in the folder.

Vincent was sending out his own electrical charges now. This was one hurdle, the pastor another. But this must come first, then he could evolve some strategy or rather beseech the saints for a way to engage the sympathies of Vinegar Jack.

"OKAY!" Tony trumpeted, looking up and bringing his palm down flat on a legal-looking document. "You can have it rent-free for two years! We had it condemned so that we could build an annex to the garage. But this won't take place for at least two years."

"Did Number One say 'not for two years'?" Father Whelton asked in facetious triumph.

"Yes, he did," Tony said with appreciative wryness. "And Number Two—and Number Three—all the way down to me."

"Are you in the Big Ten?" Father Whelton asked, recalling the headline phrase about the beverage mob.

"No, I'm not!" Tony said with annoyance. "I only handle things here. But I'm not in the confessional box either. Do you want the house for the kids or don't you?"

"Tony," Vincent said softly, apologetically, "I certainly do want it—for the kids, Tony! If only to get them out from under the wheels of your trucks."

"I know it, Father, I know it," Tony said, radiant now with the power to give to someone whom he loved in his way and who had nothing to swap, nothing to give in return. "I was a kid around here myself and I know, I know how tough it is.

"But we'll have to *uncondemn* the place," he continued confidently. "It'll take about a week to push it through the building inspector's office. Then the lease is yours for two years. How'll that be?" he asked with a final glee that effervesced like jetting champagne.

"That'll be wonderful, Tony. God bless you, God bless you a thousand times!"

"Who shall I make the lease out to, Father? To you?"

Whelton thought about that one with a sudden calm.

"It will have to be made out to the pastor—Father Jack Regan. I'm having some difficulty with him. Can you—can you hold the lease until you get an okay on the building from the building inspector? In the meantime I'll do what I can to bring the pastor around."

"Sure I can hold it, and I'll put two of our janitors to work in there fixing things up. You just tell 'em what you want and how you want it. We'll pick up the bill!"

"Thank you, Tony, thank you! Now I've got to get back. I've got another religion class!"

He rose, reached over and squeezed Lorenzo's shoulder. "You crap-shooting little chaplain's assistant. You're wonderful."

"Happy to do it for my old padre!" Tony said in the big voice quick to glee and anger. "Let me know how you make out."

"I will, I will, Tony," Father Whelton said, opening the door. "And—Tony, for me, for anyone you love and respect—take care of yourself. Watch out for Number One and all the way down to Ten."

"I'll do that, Father." Tony laughed. "All the way down to Twenty would be more like it. I'll take care of myself so I can come and give the kids some time. You ought to see me play volleyball!"

"I'll hold you to that, Tony. I'll call on you when you're ready. Good-by, Tony. God keep you safe!"

Tony made a jovial pitching motion of dismissal, more boyish than disrespectful.

Father Whelton waved and smiled at the Linehan girl and pushed out through the great green door to the fevered, cobbled streets where the beer trucks lumbered explosively and agile urchins scrambled defiantly after baseballs close to the massive wheels.

Thinking amid the racket made by his footfalls as he descended the broad wooden staircase of St. Polycarp's school, Father Vincent debated which course to pursue with the pastor. Religion class was over and he'd be on call in the rectory until dinnertime. He'd better get it over with and go right to Vinegar Jack with the proposition which he knew would be unwelcome, despite Lorenzo's generosity.

He went out the side door of the school onto the narrow, rocky surface of the schoolyard. He fled from the grimness of his inevitable interview with the pastor and dwelt with a smile on fifth-grade Jackie Borland's recitation of the five Joyful Mysteries of the Rosary. Jackie had the first three right—the Annunciation, the Visitation, and the Nativity. The fourth Joyful Mystery, which asks for a meditation on the Presentation of the Child in the temple, Jackie had referred to blandly and with amusing accuracy as "the Circumcision."

I'll have to watch out or I'll be citing it that way myself, Vincent reminded himself, heading across the yard. What would the Married Ladies' Sodality say if I popped that one at them during the Rosary after Vespers on Sunday evening?

Through the wrought-iron gate, around the clotheslines, up the short flight of stairs to the kitchen. Bridey Cleary was basting a leg of lamb now and she almost let him pass before speaking.

"In case you're afther lookin' for the pastor, he's gone to see the Cardinal and won't be back until afther supper. He left a note for you under your door."

"Oh," Vincent said, "thank you, Bridey."

He paused at the entrance to the dining room, turned, and asked: "Is Father Regan upset about something?"

Bridey looked up from her cooking, tightened the muscles in her fiery red cheeks, and exclaimed:

"Whatever it 'tis, he's got a divvil of a mad on against you, me bucko. Ye'd better take a look at what's in that letter."

"Thanks, Bridey," Vincent said, moving toward the staircase. "I think I know why he's upset."

He took the stairs briskly, opened the door of his room, and saw the envelope, chaste and ominous, on the floor.

He pushed the door securely shut behind him and sank sharply down on his bed to open and read the letter:

Father Whelton:

　　While you've been teaching, I've had a little talk with Mrs. Walsh across the street and Joan Linehan at the brewery. I know what you've been up to this afternoon and it's out-and-out defiance of my wishes as pastor of St. Polycarp's. I'm going to ask the Cardinal to transfer you out of this parish and out of my hair. I'll have no truck with the favors of hoodlums for you or anyone else.

So prepare your mind and heart, young man, for a new assignment. I've no idea where he'll send you, but you won't get the chance to play the smart aleck with Old Jack Regan again.

Rev. Fr. J. R.
In J.M.J.

"In Jesus, Mary and Joseph," Vincent sighed, fighting off the bitterness and giving prayerful life to the pastor's closing initials of invocation.

He let the letter fall to the floor, put his head in his hands, and struggled to think clearly and control himself. What to do? What to do?

He had gone too far, undoubtedly. But it was not as brazen and defiant as the pastor made his inquiry about the condemned house seem. At first it had been curiosity; then the coincidence of meeting Tony Lorenzo, combined with Tony's generosity, had swept him off his feet.

Even so, even with the okay from Lorenzo on the lease, he had still intended merely to offer that possibility to the pastor with all due respect. Now this. What to do?

Arthur Wagner. Arthur might at least give him some advice. He was assistant editor on the archdiocesan weekly newspaper, *The Clarion*. He'd go down and see him early this evening, perhaps catch him for dinner. Arthur, dear, facetious, bold Arthur. He might even know a way to head this off.

He glanced at the clock in his room: four-twenty. His stand-by duty would end at five. Father Elkins, the senior curate, whose ulcers would not permit the heavy evening meal, would take care of any calls during dinner hour.

He got up off the bed briskly and opened a dresser drawer, anxious for the sight of a freshly laundered shirt and Roman collar, which, to his relief, were available.

But what about Lorenzo's offer of the house? He might still be able to salvage that for the kids of the parish.

Perhaps the Cardinal could be persuaded to take over the house as part of an archdiocesan project. It was hopeless to continue to buck the pastor, he knew. But he'd try, he'd talk to Arthur about it.

Yes, he thought wryly on his way down to get some hot shaving water from Bridey, he'd be able to do a lot about it out in some country parish in southern Illinois; he'd be able to keep real tabs on such a vitally needed city facility while he rang the bells and stoked the furnace in a country church. He'd be among the cows, and the little city gamins would be among the brewery-truck wheels.

"Your former curate," he whispered with a sigh of resignation, "in J.M.J."

CHAPTER VI

Out in the Sticks . . .

THERE were no bats in the church belfry and none, Father Whelton hoped, in his. But in the belfry of wide, barny St. Claire's church, snuggled deeply in the Tri-State Valley, the trouble was not bats. The trouble was doves, scores of them, which had settled and multiplied in the bell tower and now threatened to wreak their cooing and corrosive domesticity deep among the eaves and the rooftree of the church.

St. Francis, patron and protector of all birds, might not have approved, but Vincent had decided to send the doves back to the woods and neighboring barns by sealing up the belfry with double sheets of chicken wire nailed one upon the other across the window-like apertures.

Now in the hot August sun of late morning, attired in old black pants and a frayed white shirt cut for cool comfort at the armpits, he shooed and cooed at the birds who wheeled slowly in bewildered flight around him. He waved them away with one hand and hammered vigorously at the rectangular sections of chicken wire.

Far below him—for St. Claire's soared from the crest of a rolling green hill—he could look out to the railroad winding in an endless silver glint toward Lakeport. The farmhouses, barns, sectioned fields, the cows and horses seemed to have that toy-world sweep of peace and order so easily associated with the pastoral slopes of Switzerland.

He banged the last staple into place, having covered the east window. He paused, wiped the sweat from his eyes with a handkerchief, and let his thoughts dally far along the railroad to the great lake city from which he had been exiled by pastoral fiat only three months ago.

It brought back some memories, some association of ideas, this sustained cooing of the disturbed doves, which in its intensity and volume sounded like a bleating, now guttural and throaty, up the scale to shrill.

What was the association, the memory? Yes, the bird watcher, Bob Lambert, his roommate at St. Philip's Seminary. And the Apostolic Delegate, Gaetano Peruzzi, he too was a bird watcher and had been impressed by Lambert's shrewd identification of birds on the seminary grounds.

Father Bob Lambert. He was doing well in the Harbourton diocese. Arthur and Vincent had lunched with him in Lakeport a few weeks before. It was Vincent's first sight of him since Lambert went abroad on the Roman fellowship for oratory. He felt a nostalgic twinge now, knowing that fate and circumstances might have awarded the prize to him had he not taken it upon himself to minister to the dying Lucy in her railroad shack across the country-side from the seminary.

Sweet, loyal old Father Carney had pleaded with the seminary authorities to give a special auditing to Vincent the day after the competition. But rules were rules. He had not been present at the scheduled time and Lambert was the winner.

Who else had mentioned bird watching? Yes, the Cardinal in the interview arranged by his nephew, Arthur, on the day Father Vincent fled St. Polycarp's rectory for one last-ditch appeal.

"I remember you as athlete and orator," the Cardinal had said before confirming the final inflexible news of his transfer. "Yours was a memorable class. That fellow Lambert catching the fancy of the Apostolic Delegate because of a sharp eye with the feather folk. Where is Lambert now? I recall he went to Rome with Arthur and then didn't come back to this diocese. I'm under the impression he's attached to the chancery in Bishop Sliney's diocese at Harbourton."

"That's correct, Your Eminence. Father Lambert went on to further studies in Canon Law. They needed someone to work on marriage cases in the Harbourton chancery and he was sent up there."

"Yes, yes, now I recall," the Cardinal said. "I okayed the transfer myself. I did it for my old friend Bishop Sliney because he badly needed a bright young man for their marriage court." There was a touch of impatience in the Cardinal's voice, as if he should have known about Lambert without Vincent's reminder.

"Now about your own transfer," he said, clearing his throat and placing one long, lean hand tightly to his mouth. "I simply haven't got time to contact my young priests individually—and they need this interest and guidance more than the old ones. But I was happy you dropped by to see Arthur and I asked him to send you on in.

"Defying your pastor, Father Whelton, is, of course, a most serious offense in the life of a young priest or any priest. I've known Father Jack Regan many years. He was two years ahead of me at the seminary. He's not an easy man to live with and is almost astigmatic in his conviction that his way is the best way. And don't misunderstand me—often his way *is* the best way."

"But, Your Eminence . . ." Vincent said, feeling the hot blood of suppressed humiliation leaving a livid watermark at the nape of his neck.

"Allow me to finish," the Cardinal said with a quiet firmness. "I shall certainly try to anticipate your questions."

"I'm sorry, Your Eminence."

"Very well. Do you know—have you reflected at all upon the basis of the absolute power of a pastor, the head of a parish?"

Vincent shook his head slowly. He had reflected some, but this was not the place to volunteer his opinion. And he knew the Cardinal was asking a rhetorical question.

"The organization of the Church administrative, if I may use the term, is like a great orchestra playing an over-all majestic theme of divine organization from Christ and the Apostles to the papal succession, through the bishops, and on down to the parish priests and our Christian families. The organization of the Church is like multiple tableaux of Christ and the Apostles on different levels from the Holy Father down to the basic family unit."

The Cardinal paused and looked up at the awesome color reproduction of Michelangelo's *Crucifixion* which brooded in a large gold frame on the wall to the left of his desk.

Vincent sensed mischievously that His Eminence was straining somewhat to come up with informal, concrete thoughts that would not directly reflect the Church history course which the prelate had once taught as a seminary professor.

"St. Augustine himself," he continued, "echoed this idea when he referred to the fathers of families as 'bishops.' And in a more responsible sense, the pastor is the bishop of his flock—and that includes authority over his priests—a necessary authority.

"Think of it!" he said now with excitement, almost a fervor, which appeared at variance with his usually phlegmatic temperament. "Think of how marvelous it is for a world-wide organization to maintain a world-wide program of religion, which means maintaining authority and obedience to authority—a practical, inflexible oligarchy—and all this without armies, elections, secret police, or other external, formalized systems of government.

"Think of it!" he continued with the same ebullience, "all day long, twenty-four hours a day, somewhere in the world it is morning and Masses are being said, the corporal works of mercy performed, teaching, preaching, healing, praying, for the love of God and the love of man, all over the world, twenty-four hours a day.

"Something has got to hold all this together, Vincent, when you don't have armies, parliaments, police forces. We know that it is the love of God and the guidance of the Holy Spirit that holds us together and leads us forward. But when God leads we must know how to follow. And it takes obedience, constant, total obedience to proper authority throughout the entire Church, to clear our vision that we may see the ways and means of apostolic works that are revealed to us constantly by the Holy Spirit.

"And even when proper authority is wrong, which it must occasionally be, emanating from a weak human vessel as it does, we still must at least preserve the spirit of obedience.

"I tell you, when one young priest defies his pastor—and I am not directly accusing you of that—the world-wide warp and woof of the Church is strained and in danger of fraying. If many of my pastors are old, crotchety, hidebound, set in obsolete ideas, just remember that they have earned their golden decline. They have been impatient and rebellious in the time of their own hot-blooded youth. But they have learned over the years that the Church makes haste slowly, slow to accept, slow to reject. This prudence, be they bright or even stupid, has by some spiritual chemistry of the years become an organic element in their being—given to test the mettle of young priests, and, above all, to hold their flocks together and keep them moving toward the endless green pastures of heaven. Remember! No parliaments, no armies, no jails or policemen. Just the love of God and obedience to designated authority."

Vincent was moved but fanned one little coal of protest amid the shattered embers of his resentment of Father Regan's stubbornness.

"Your Eminence, I deeply appreciate the fine and articulate effort you have made to show me the importance of obedience in the work and the structure of the Church. I believe what you say deeply and I submit most humbly to whatever disposition you may make of me. But may I, before I leave, ask your opinion of the kind of under-privileged-youth work we proposed to do in St. Polycarp's parish? I know it was imprudently and too quickly proposed. But the idea itself—and the need for the project—surely that should not be minimized because of the impatience and disobedience of one young priest?"

Cardinal Wagner screwed his cool gray eyes to a shrewd focus on this tenacious clerical fledgling. And through his long, pale features a shade of mirth was suffused as he thought of Vinegar Jack sputtering into contact with this pert young mind.

"I am sending you out in the country to take the place of a sick pastor," he said coolly. "You will, in practice, be the pastor yourself—in full charge of a one-priest country chapel. I am not unmindful of your efforts to help the little gamins at St. Polycarp's, and a thorough effort will be made from this office to get Father Regan to provide similar facilities. But tell me this, Father Whelton, before I go any further—you seem most sympathetic to my remarks concerning the importance of obedience in fulfilling the work of the Church. Does this mean that you are prepared to apologize to your pastor before you leave?"

The Cardinal asked this question, fingering with slow grace the red piping of his cassock and with somewhat downcast eyes which nonetheless shed on Vincent all the intensity of a level gaze.

Vincent hesitated before giving the answer he knew he must give. He had been overzealous, he knew, and plainly disobedient in going over the pastor's head to make arrangements for the recreation center. But the lack of understanding, the lethargy of Vinegar Jack! He sighed perceptibly, blacked out the rebellion in his mind, and submitted.

"I am most willing to apologize to Father Regan, Your Eminence."

"Very well, you will take the afternoon train for Leestown on Sunday. That will permit you to assist Father Regan and the others with Sunday services. Another priest will replace you that evening."

The Cardinal glanced coolly up at a tiny, exquisitely carved cuckoo clock which ticked furiously in a shadowy corner of the gold, wainscoted suite. Vincent knew the interview was over.

"Good afternoon, Your Eminence," he said, rising, "and thank you for giving me so much time."

"One more thing, Father," the Cardinal said casually, opening a folder and perusing a letter. "Since you're bound and determined to be bleeding for suffering humanity, you can start right in at Leestown. The state prison is near you and I don't have a permanent chaplain down there. You'd better look after those penitent co-religionists of yours behind the walls. I'll send a letter out to the warden this evening."

Vincent wheeled, filled with joy and gratitude, and began to sputter his thanks. The Cardinal waved him on brusquely from behind the handy citadel of his authority, within which he could allow his humanity to be seen only a chink at a time.

CHAPTER VII

Death of a Friend

FATHER WHELTON's transfer to the Tri-State Valley was the farthest thing from Tony Lorenzo's mind when he entered his office at the brewery the morning after Vinegar Jack's wrath had achieved fulfillment.

The West Side Benevolent Asssociation, represented by Dapper Dan Lubell, the suave yet quick-tempered little hood whom Father Vincent had seen striding out of Lorenzo's office, looking neither to the left nor to the right, had delivered its ultimatum. No MORE BEER DELIVERIES TO THE WEST SIDE UNLESS WE ARE IN 50%.

That was the word, and Tony had trucks going out to speakeasies on the west side this very morning. And the Big Ten, his own southside bosses, had spoken: No SPLIT. WE'LL PROVIDE THE ESCORTS. YOU DELIVER. TO HELL WITH LUBELL!

So there was trouble ahead this morning, plenty of it. There was a .38 in the bottom drawer of the file cabinet where he also kept a bottle of scotch. He hated the thought, but he might have to use both before the morning was over.

Thus, when he saw sweet, little Joan Linehan sobbing at her typewriter, he was pricked with irritation. What the hell was she crying about at a time like this? Women will, he thought, women always will.

She upped her pert, moist nose, dabbed at the little red rims around her eyes, and bid him good morning.

"Good morning, Joan. What is it, what's wrong?"

"Oh, Mr. Lorenzo," she said, sobbing and bowing her head toward the typewriter again, "they've sent your friend Father Whelton away, and I feel—I feel I had something to do with it."

"You better come inside and get this off your chest," Tony said impatiently, beckoning to his inner office.

She followed him in and sat in the armchair to the right of his desk.

"Now what the hell is all this, Joan? I've got a lot on my mind today, and if you can't get hold of yourself I'll have to send you home. What's it all about?"

She looked so pretty and frail there as he asked her the question, something to cradle protectively in a man's strong arms. He had thought of her this way before. Any man does, but not your secretary, he cautioned himself. There were plenty of blond and brazen tomatoes down at the South Side Club to ease the tension. And she was the kind who would expect to get married after a little whirl or a big whirl. Sweet little Joan, the parish colleen, and all the Irish relatives in the background staring you into respectability—a job in the slaughterhouse looming in the treacherously close future, perhaps. No, no, not for him.

"It's just that the pastor, Father Regan, called on me after you left that afternoon Father Whelton was here. He wanted to know what Father Whelton wanted and what you said. He ordered me to tell him as my parish priest, and I did. I told him about the old brewery master's house and the plans to make it into a boys' gymnasium."

"For Christ's sakes!" Anthony said.

"Yes," Joan continued, "and the pastor spoke to Mrs. Walsh down the street. Father Whelton had been to see her for information too. I feel real bad about him leaving, real bad. Everybody liked him because he gave so much of himself to others. Everybody feels bad about him leaving, and I feel worse."

"It *is* too bad," Tony said, shaking his head in a compassion that was a relief from his own troubles. "That guy's loaded with ability; he's just too young, that's all. The old boys in the Church keep a tight hold on the young ones, otherwise they'll run too fast. But he knew how much the children needed a clubhouse of their own. He knew something had to be done right away to get them out of the way of the trucks.

"I'll tell you what I'll do, Joan. If you'll stop this crying and get out there and get to work on those consignment orders for the west side, I'll get the janitors to go to work on the old house. We'll have it fixed up in a week or so. I can get City Hall to send out some playground equipment—basketballs, indoor games, and handicraft stuff. We'll do it for Father Whelton and the little kids. Okay?"

"You will!" Joan exclaimed, her red-rimmed eyes widening. "You'll do all this for Father Whelton!"

"Not for him—for the kids on the streets. That's the way he'd want it!"

Joan jumped up and kissed him on the cheek. "You're wonderful!" she said, turning and heading for her desk.

"Hey, I wish I had a few more houses to fix up so you'd do that again!" Tony said. "Get ahold of the janitors and have them clean up and paint up the joint. Tell them to use anything we've got around here and get the rest from Zwinker's Hardware on the brewery account."

"Right away, Mr. Lorenzo, right away."

"I'll give you a letter to Umbrella Jack Doyle at the City Hall later."

"Umbrella Jack Doyle?" Joan said, pausing at the door. "The president of the City Council? He's been in here, hasn't he? The fat red-faced man with the umbrella. Why does he always carry an umbrella? I remember it because the sun was shining brightly that day."

"You figure it out, Joan?" Tony said, chuckling at her seeming naïveté, which really was a reflection of inner shrewdness. She knew well that Umbrella Jack got his contributions that way. Pop! Into the umbrella with the greenbacks! Maybe it was a good thing the brewery had been taking care of Umbrella Jack. Now maybe he'd get someone out here at the city's expense to handle the kids and the equipment.

"On your way to the janitors' room, see if that west-side truck is being loaded. I'll have to go along with this one."

"Oh," Joan said apprehensively. She was talking like a wife or a girl friend already.

What would it be like to have a wife or a steady girl? he wondered with momentary indolence as he sat at his desk watching her thin, sweet presence become an absence as she left on her errands.

A girl friend, that is, a sweetheart you had big out-in-the-open plans for—home and babies, pushing the carriage on Sunday where

everyone could see you and you could see them. Peanuts and pop-
corn at the ball park, maybe, with a little replica of yourself.

He'd never really had a steady girl, a real love affair, a girl on
whom he was completely gone and from whom he would not be
gone in the morning with the ten-spot left under the boudoir lamp.

He had the charm, the gab, and the quick recognition of who
could be had and who couldn't ever since he was sixteen, running
to the bank for rolls of quarters and nickels for the boys in the back
room of the pool hall.

He didn't have to leave them a dime, he knew, but it was best,
Dapper Dan had taught him. "Leave a sawbuck under the lamp and
they can never come back at you. You can always say they did it
for money."

And now Dapper Dan Lubell was on the other side—the west
side, where Tony himself came from and where Dapper Dan had
taken him under his wing around Gypper Kelly's Pool Hall. It was
Lubell, in fact, who had recommended him for this job with the
south-side crowd just after the war. Everything was sweet and rosy
then, a new deal and lots of money to be made for both factions.

Money. Too much of it. Too much success. Why split it up when
you can have it all? Thus the breakup of the partnership between
east- and west-side mobs. Thus the trouble now and his old patron
Dapper Dan gunning for him if he took the truck to the west side
this morning.

Well, he would, damn it. He'd have an escort too. And if Dan
wanted trouble he'd get it—plenty.

He slipped his gold watch out of the pocket of his white checkered
vest and glanced at the time—nine twenty-five. The delivery was
due at ten-thirty. They'd have to leave in about ten minutes, as
cross-town traffic would be slow. He fingered the fine-spun gold
chain and again thought of Lubell. He had won the watch and chain
at a club prize fight sponsored by the West Side Benevolent Association when he was a sailor stationed at Great Lakes. Knocked out a
Polack named Grunsky from the packing house and broke a finger
doing it. It was all hail fellow then, and Lubell had wanted him
to keep on with boxing. But the broken finger and puffed eye were
warning enough, and Chaplain Whelton, too, had talked him out of
keeping on with it.

"Amateur boxing, yes," the chaplain had advised with more than a little prejudice, "but don't turn pro, Tony. You just might end up shadow-boxing in some barroom."

Nine twenty-eight. I've got to go. He rose, slipped into the black leather jacket which hung beside his blue serge suit coat, reached for the dark brown wool cap with the snap-button open at the visor. He shoved the cap on, pulled it down a bit to one side, looking like the hood he would have to be for the next hour or two.

He leaned deep into the file cabinet, pulled out the bottom drawer, and lifted both the scotch and the unholstered .38 from their resting place amid some old picture folders. He had no use for shoulder holsters—never had occasion to use the gun anyway—and if he had to, he could always throw the gun down some sewer without worrying about getting rid of the holster. He'd stick it in his jacket pocket, and if he had to use it, it would be just as handy there.

He pulled the cork off the scotch, poured a healthy dollop into a water glass, and tossed it into his gullet, shaking his head and grimacing. The mellow yet fierce concoction warmed the tight-knit nerves of his stomach and kindled warmth in his blood. One more. Another dollop—a larger one—down, down, with the grimace and the shake of the head.

"Ahhhhh!" he sighed as the warmth seemed to muster his courage. Now he was ready to go.

He took out the revolver, broke the barrel, spun the drum, which was oiled and in good order. He put the .38 back in his jacket pocket and went out into the brewery.

He walked down the long dark salvage area with the stacked empty wooden barrels looming like warty mountains all around him. He opened the door to the central brewing area, was momentarily blinded by the assault of flickering overhead gas lamps, and went in.

He passed at first unrecognized among the great, bellying vats foaming and steaming, making the atmosphere thick and heady with a yeasty, malty oppressiveness.

On a catwalk circling the greatest vat of all, an apish creature stripped to the waist and covered with orange tufts of hair beckoned a clublike arm at him amid the billows of sweet and yellowy steam.

It was Teedee Quinlan, the brewmaster, and he had recognized his boss. "MALT AND HOPS GOD PROVIDES!" Teedee bellowed at him. "COME HERE, I WANT TO SEE YOU!"

Tony hurried to the vat and squinted up at Quinlan through the steam.

"What is it, Teedee? I'm in a hurry!"

Teedee cupped the back of an orange-tufted hand to his lips. "We found a dead rat at the bottom of Vat Number 3!"

"Christ!" Tony said. "Get rid of the brew."

"We'd already got rid of it!" Teedee yelled mischievously. "You shipped it out to the city councilors' clambake at the dunes last Saturday!"

"Jesus, no," Tony said.

"Jesus, yes!" Teedee yelled.

Tony sighed and shrugged his shoulders. "Nobody sick, I guess. I was out there myself and had a few glasses. I hate to tell you this, but the stuff tasted better than usual."

"Never fear, me boy," Teedee hallooed with a burst of ribald laughter. "There's enough denatured alcohol in Quinlan's brew to kill all the poison in a sonofabitch like that."

"Maybe you're right," Tony said, fighting off a queasy feeling. "But boil the vat out before you use it again and get some more cats around here, right, Teedee?"

"Sure I will, Tony," Quinlan gruffed, "and take care of yerself this mawnin'! I hear there's more than beer brewin' this fine day!"

"You hear correctly, Teedee. I'll do the best I can. See you after lunch."

Before going out on the shipping platform, Tony glanced back just once at the sawed-off orange giant looming through the steam like some awesome guardian of a sulphurous pit of hell.

Flush with the ramp in the garage-like shipping pavilion was a big snub-nosed lorry, its engine rasping and burbling evenly like a lioness prone. Two dark, heavy-set men in leather jackets were sitting in front, their caps pulled down in stylized fashion, their visor buttons unsnapped. To one side of the lorry purred a sleek, long black sedan with one tight-suited man at the wheel, also with the stylized cap, and two tight-suited men in the rear—one wearing a black derby, the other a light gray homburg.

Tony waved at the watchman tending a huge roll-up sheet-metal gate. He jumped into the front seat of the sedan beside the driver.

"Hi, fellas. Here we go," Tony said.

"Here we go," said Mr. Derby, fondling a double-barreled shotgun between his knees. Mr. Peaked Cap had a bulge at the chest, as did Mr. Homburg.

As the gate squeaked open Mr. Homburg said, "You got a rod?"

"In my pocket," Tony said, adding, "You guys are dressing pretty fancy for a possible funeral."

"Big Al wants us always to look good!"

"Okay, Jake." Tony waved to the lorry driver. "Get going, we'll follow."

"We don't have trouble till the west side," the sedan driver said as they pulled out into the cobbled street now dazzling with reflected sunshine.

"That's right." Tony glanced at St. Polycarp's rectory, wishing he could pray or had a right to. To his right he caught a glimpse of Joan Linehan at the office window, and maybe she was crying again for a different reason. She'll do the praying for me maybe, he thought. And he was scared deep and cold, the way it used to be in the dark of his childhood bedroom when he woke feverish from a nightmare in the small hours of the morning.

On his right the old gray house that Father Whelton wanted for the kids. Joan had done her job well, for two brewery janitors were already measuring the frames of the shattered windows on the front side.

If I get through, Tony found himself thinking almost as a prayer, if I get through I'll give some evenings to the kids myself—teach them to box, maybe, without learning at a pool hall, teach them to jab without getting off balance and keep that guard up when bringing around the right . . .

Now through the railroad yards, heading west, among the great dingy walls of tenements, children, fat women leaning on window sills, peddlers hawking shrilly, iceman, ragman, the cop on the beat suspicious at their passage, knowing, yet almost happy in the knowledge he would not be involved.

The peace of the town and the peaceful people called forth a twinging echo of longing in Tony's head—to be no one and thus someone, to come and go on the transit system and read about these things, clucking one's tongue at the bold black print and the high resolves of the mayor and the police commissioner, who were getting their cut for high resolves after the highjacking and the murders had taken place.

Across the wide viaduct now to the west side—slowly, the black

creature of swift dispatch and high maneuverability behind the
creeping lorry.

Beneath him the network of silver ribbons bearing the traffic west
to Kansas City, Denver, Phoenix, San Francisco, and on the same
rails bringing the beef and corn from the wide western plains.

At the corner of Corinth and Bellrose avenues on the west side,
by prearranged signal the lorry pulled over to allow the sedan to
take the lead. The guns in the sedan were handy now—the shotgun
lying lightly across the lap, the pistols gripped with safety catches
off, the lumper in the truck beside the driver fondling an automatic
rifle.

Forward slowly again along wide streetcar-tracked Bellrose
Avenue, toward the Bellrose Club and their first delivery. Now the
high, vertical sign: BELLROSE SOCIAL CLUB.

"They may be at the windows in the second-story poolroom across
the street," Tony said, his olive features now gone completely white,
his lips so tight, his throat so dry, he found it difficult to speak above
a whisper. "Pull over to the right and signal the lorry to do so. We'll
get out and walk up on the poolroom side so we'll be right under
them if they're there."

They got out of the sedan, leaving Mr. Peaked Cap at the wheel
with motor idling. Tony walked over and spoke to the lorry driver,
who had pulled up behind the sedan.

"Stay here until we give you the come-on. They may be at the
poolroom windows, second floor, across from the club. When I wave,
give it the gun and turn into the alley by the club as quick as you
can. There's no way they can hurt you there—brick walls both
sides. If they fire, just duck and keep going."

"Oke," the lorry driver said, the little diamonds of perspiration
on his forehead signaling the terror of the big man as well as the
small.

Tony moved along the sidewalk, close to the store fronts, followed
by Mr. Homburg with his hand poised inside his coat and Mr. Derby
with shotgun brazenly cradled, like a hunter alert for the flushing
of grouse.

Walking on foot bones where there seemed to be no blood, his
head heavy with the strain, Tony asked himself: How can I know,
how can I tell if they're up there in the poolroom ready to use us
and the street as a shooting gallery, making us and the street like

fish in a rain barrel and Bellrose Avenue the Khyber Pass with the woolly-woollies shooting down on the Bengal Lancers and all that?

Under the overhanging bay windows of the second-story apartments, tailor shops and social halls. Keeping close in under, they could not look out and up without risking detection.

Behind him, as they clipped along, he knew the other two were asking questions as nervously as he. He had to make the decision quickly.

Two doors away from the pool-hall staircase entrance and now within full sight of the Bellrose Social Club, he led them into the portals of a Yiddish delicatessen.

The sharp admixture of salami, pickle, and dark rye bread smells, calculated to prick an edge of hunger, now only stirred a pang of nausea in his stomach.

"There's only one way to find out who's up there," he said. "I'm going up. Check your watches with mine—ten-fifteen. The delivery is due at ten-thirty and we're going to be on time if we have to carry the barrels in from back there!"

Mr. Homburg and Mr. Derby checked their watches against Tony's.

"Give me fifteen minutes. If I don't come down, wave the truck on and shoot it out with them—if you have to. Okay?"

"Oke," Mr. Homburg said. "Will they have a Tommy?"

"They might," Tony said. "There aren't many around. Big Al's supposed to have the only one in town. The Army keeps a check on that stuff."

"You don't mind if we come up after you, once the truck is rolling?" Mr. Derby asked.

"Do anything you like if I don't come down. But get the truck rolling first. Clear?"

"Clear," said Mr. Derby as Mr. Homburg nodded.

"Here I go," Tony said, taking one look up and down the street. "Don't get itchy until you have to. And remember—fifteen minutes —ten-thirty."

"Oke," said Mr. Derby.

Tony walked, whistling a lively tune now, "I'll be down to get you in a taxi, honey, and bring the ambulance too . . ."

Into the entrance now, up the stairs, lightly; a little eight ball before lunch, a beer, a horse or two at Cicero Downs . . .

The wood tattoo of feet, the blithe whistling, and he was on the top landing.

The green-curtained glass door was open and he was before them. Dapper Dan, poised for a corner shot at the six with a rebound to the twelve at the side pocket, looked up coolly.

There were three at the window with the guns, and one had the "piano."

"Tony," Dan said with the old suavity which grew smoother under tension. "We've been expecting you, come in."

The three at the windows wheeled sharply, and safeties clicked in swift series like the crackle of knuckles.

At the other two tables, cues froze, and a shot, already launched, was a hollow, mocking echo of doom.

Lubell looked at him steadily with level gray eyes, his thin silken face emotionless but his hands gripping the cue.

"Anybody else coming up?"

"Not right away," Tony said.

"Sure?"

"Sure," Tony answered.

"Okay, Hothead," Lubell said, waggling his cue stick without turning toward the windows. "Put them down. And, Ziggy, you better get out in the hallway."

Ziggy, a broad-shouldered hood whom Tony remembered as an ex-fighter, walked over to the entrance landing, .38 in hand. Hothead, a pasty-faced ferret of a man with a pimple-scarred neck, lowered the Tommy and turned again to the window, as did his partner, automatic rifle in hand.

Hothead was Lubell's bodyguard, his entire fulfillment in life reaching its repeated focus only when he was behind a blazing gun. It was said that Lubell sometimes lent him out on special jobs for Big Al—and maybe that's why both he and Lubell were still alive.

"You better get in on this game—Jackie, give him your cue," he said to a silk-shirted pool shark who couldn't have been more than twenty years old. "You used to be pretty good, Tony—before you went across town. I remember, I taught you all you knew, and then you started taking me."

Tony glanced at the stripling pool shark and knew a twist of memory. Dapper Dan always had a young guy around him, bringing him along, some bright kid with lots of moxie and drive—it fed something in him that should have been fed by children of his own.

"I haven't got time, Dan. I want to talk to you."

"You can talk while we clean off the table," Dan said firmly. "There's only a few balls left."

Tony took the cue from the young hood who was standing by.

"I had this shot all figured out just before you came in," Lubell said. "Watch that side pocket."

Tony could see the wall clock as Lubell skillfully connected: ten-nineteen. The six plunked into the corner pocket; the cue ball angled off the cushion toward the side and, with both the eternity and inevitability of such a shot, caressed the twelve home.

There was one ball left, the eight, snug against the back cushion, mid-point between the corner holes.

"This shot is yours—for me—for old times, Tony," Lubell said, softening just a little. "Put it in there." He motioned to the side pocket near Tony.

Tony hadn't played pool for a long time. He had been too busy for the kind of schedule needed for such a casual, time-consuming game.

"I'm rusty, but I'll try it," he said. "Then we'll talk—eh?"

"Then we'll talk," Lubell said. "You're still a fast-ball man."

"Still fast," Tony said, leaning to line it up. Ten twenty-three. What to do? Run for it? No! Keep them talking—let the time run out. The trucks will be moving then—run for it. The guys at the window will be busy. Use my gun? No—not with Ziggy at the door.

He concentrated, then shot, hard, plenty of spin; the eight angled to the side cushion across, back, across—in!

Lubell smiled and spoke to the wide-eyed hoodling standing near him. "That's my boy—I taught him everything he knows."

"It was lucky," Tony said. "I'm as rusty as a gate."

They handed their cues to the youngster and stood by the table.

"You bringing the stuff in this morning?" Lubell asked, lighting a cigarette and puffing suavely.

"Right on schedule," Tony said.

"Right on schedule," Lubell repeated. "You shouldn't do that to me, Tony. Anybody else I wouldn't mind so much."

"I've got to do it. It's my job."

"Give up your job. You can always come back with me—right now, in fact. Give it up now—while there's time."

"While there's time?" Tony asked, glancing at the clock: ten twenty-seven. "It's coming through, Dan, I wouldn't lie to you. You taught me to go through without flinching—that was one thing you taught me."

"I did." And now the softening was more evident in Dan's voice. "I treated you like a son."

"You did, Dan, I'm sorry."

"I'm sorry too, kid—sorry it has to be this way."

Ten twenty-eight. Maybe he ought to go now, try to get out before the violence started. He couldn't stand being there with Dan when it was going on.

"Okay, Dan, I've got to go now."

Ten twenty-nine.

"Go?" Dan said, firming again, going cold. "You'll have to stay here, kid. There's less chance of getting hurt if you stay here—over in the corner, maybe, where there's no windows. I like you a lot, kid. But business is business!"

"I've got to go, Dan," Tony said, knowing he'd have to run from Ziggy now and maybe get it in the back, but not from Dan, not from Dan in the poolroom twelve years ago, giving him one every time he ran across to the bank for a roll of quarters, not from Dan paying his mother's hospital bills, angling a job for his father on the city, not from Dan in the corner of the ring as he was about to quit and the Polack was grinning between rounds, not from Dan sending money and creature comforts to him in the service, not from Dan who got him his job at the brewery—not from Dan.

Ten-thirty.

"You better stay, kid." Dan dropped his cigarette, crushing it out with a deft dance motion of his patent-leather shoe.

Tony heard the lorry harrumphing into gear and he knew the time was now. He broke for the door and ran flush into Ziggy, grabbing the pistol-whipping arm and hustling him against the wall.

"They're coming!" he heard Dan shout. "Cut them to ribbons. I'll get this kid!"

Ziggy's pistol spurted out of his grip under the impact and clattered down the stairway as Tony, holding with one arm, scuffling and kneeing, went for his own.

The firing started with a fusillade of shots, then the stutter of the Tommy as the motor roar increased in volume.

Dan was on Tony's back now, grabbing for the gun, with Ziggy clawing for the .38 too.

"Drop it, kid, drop it!" Dan said, putting the strangle on Tony's neck.

Ziggy had his fingers on the gun now, and it was all three straining in a unity of writhing flesh until the gun went off. Now it was only two in the struggle, with Dan down, bleeding in the face and gasping his last.

Tony got the gun and brought it down on Ziggy's skull with all his ebbing strength.

Behind him the firing, the stutter and reports—now the shattering of glass and a wild, whimpering moaning. Beneath him, prostrate, Ziggy rolled crazily down the stairs.

Now the caterwaul of sirens, the waning of gunfire, and the full gory sight of Dan dead at his feet. He slumped to his knees and took him in his arms.

"Dan, Dan, not Dan . . ." he said, trying to wipe away the blood that ebbed from his temple. "Dan, Dan," he whimpered, burying his head in the dead man's checkered vest.

When the police arrived they found Tony, inert and slowly weeping, over the dead body. They lifted him up, snapped on the cuffs, and led him doglike away.

CHAPTER VIII

Life in the Death House

EARLY evening in the state penitentiary.

Father Whelton was on his way to the warden's office, where he customarily called after finishing his religious chores with the inmates of his own faith and sometimes with those of other faiths, or no faith, who simply needed a man of God with whom to chat.

From the second-story corridor in the Administration Building he could look down through the open door of a guard's balcony post and see the gray-clad men in the dining hall silently wolfing down their evening meal.

What an after-dinner prospect for them all, he sighed, seeing much of the quiet desperation in their faces as they made the almost futile gesture of holding body and soul together in order that body and soul could be held behind bars.

One of his penitents, a young manslaughter convict who had killed a man while drunk in a barroom brawl, had told him of the pressures now being plied upon him to plan and project a future life of crime beyond the walls. His cellmate was a fifty-year-old thug serving out his second term for armed robbery.

"The guy's driving me out of my mind. After lights out he's constantly scheming ways to make easy, fast money when he gets out and constantly invites me to go in with him. He keeps telling me I'll never get a decent job again because I'll be an ex-con when I get out of here four years from now. At first I laughed at him and told him to lay off. But he keeps on, and now maybe I'm beginning to believe him, maybe now I'm beginning to listen. He even wants me to sleep with him. I'm scared, Chaplain, real scared, and I don't know what to do."

He had promised to do something. Warden Phelps would know the man's record here and outside. If what the convict said was true, perhaps he could be reassigned. But it should be done from top to bottom in the whole prison, Whelton knew. He would see Warden Phelps right now.

But he'd have to be careful. His frustrating experience in St. Polycarp's parish had taught him something: the road of the crusader is fraught with alarms which get to ringing loudly and frighten key people away.

He'd just resume the pleasant chats he'd been having with kindly old Warden Phelps about city politics—he was a former state senator from Lakeport who had been slightly acquainted with Vincent's father. Then there were the mercurial fortunes of the Lakeport Blue Sox. He was an avid baseball fan. There would be an "Any problems?" sequence somewhere in the dialogue, and he'd have his chance to spring the one about who should be having whom as cellmates.

He turned into the reception room of the office, greeted the guard at a bare desk just inside the door, and asked to see the warden.

Phelps, a good-looking gray-haired man of slacking rotundity and a rather unhappy face, was looking broodingly out the window in the direction of the gray-towered death house at the far end of the quadrangle.

"Good afternoon, Warden," Whelton said.

"Good afternoon, Chaplain." The Warden swung around in his chair, brightening the unhappy lines of his face with a smile. "I'm glad you came in. How did it go this week? Are you beginning to get the swing of things here?"

"I am, thank you, Warden. I'm getting on fine."

"Sit down, sit down here," the warden said, rising and twisting an office armchair toward the priest. "Tell me, have you seen what Ty Cobb did to the Blue Sox the other day?"

"I haven't seen a newspaper in weeks, Warden, but I'm interested. Is Cobb still burning up the league?"

"Is he ever!" the warden exclaimed. "Two doubles and a single off Walsh yesterday, three stolen bases, and five batted in. He's completely demoralized the Blue Sox in this last series, I can tell you!"

"He's a great ballplayer," Father Whelton said. "As a pitcher, I know he can be completely unnerving—watching him dancing about at first and then trying to keep your mind on what to throw to the plate."

"That's it, that's it!" the warden said with the exuberance of the rabid baseball fan. "He jitters up so many—the pitcher, the catcher, the second baseman—that they're inclined to make errors and help along the cause of the Tigers that way."

"What was the final score?" Vincent asked, anxious to get on to his own problem.

"Nine to one. And the Sox were lucky to get off that easy. There's just no stopping this Cobb. Say, before I forget it," he continued, "there was an old sidekick of your dad in the City Council who passed away yesterday. Wicky Nolan from the near north side—did you know him?"

"I heard my father speak of him many times. God rest his soul," Vincent said. "I remember my father telling us they called him 'Wicky' because he always had a stogie in his mouth which he never smoked but chewed until it was limp."

The warden chuckled richly. "You've got a good memory, Father —that's the fellow—that's the fellow!

"Well, now, Father," he said, getting almost abruptly back to business, "how did it go today? Any problems?"

"It seems to be going fine. We had a good gang at general services for all faiths after lunch and I'm grateful to you for letting the Catholic men get to confession this evening before dinner."

"Well, I had to close all the shops down half an hour earlier. You see, I just couldn't give time off to the Catholics alone or I'd have a riot on my hands."

"I understand and I appreciate it very much, Warden."

"Of course we have the rabbi and the minister in here for Sunday services, and you come Fridays as well, so we're doing what we can for the spiritual welfare of the inmates." The warden concluded this statement almost smugly, as if there were no other difficulties, and Vincent sped quickly to his special inquiry.

"You're always kind enough to ask me every week if I have any problems," he began. "Up until this week I've really been too unfamiliar with an institution of this type to recognize a problem. But I do have an inquiry to make this time."

"What is it, Father?" the warden asked almost apprehensively. "Fire away."

"Well, Warden, to be perfectly frank with you, I had a conference with an inmate not of my faith who complains that he's in the same cell with a person who's really out to teach him how to beat the law once he gets outside again. The victim is a first-termer and I believe he's sincere in his objection to such an influence. I feel it's my responsibility as a spiritual adviser to many of these men to call such a state of affairs to your attention."

"I'm aware of the problem, Father Whelton," Phelps said with a weary sigh. "Any warden is. And I know what you're going to ask. You're going to ask why we put these new fellows in with the incorrigibles. And the answer is a simple one. We try not to, but we just haven't got enough cells to go around on that basis. Believe me when I tell you this, little Father; we go down the line and couple them up as best we can according to their records, but we just run out of cells, and the good end up with the bad."

"I'm sorry to hear that for two reasons," Vincent said. "One, because of the inmate involved, and two, because you clearly imply we need bigger state prisons."

"Unfortunately we do need more adequate living facilities in our prison," the warden said, "and the appropriations just aren't forthcoming. But in this instance, and perhaps in just a few more, I can help you. Leave the name of the convict with Miss Cochran and I'll have him transferred to what we hope will be a more congenial cell. I may be able to handle four or five more as you come across them in your weekly rounds."

"Thank you very much, Warden."

The warden swung his chair around and looked again in the direction of the death house.

"Have you been over there today?" he asked with a touch of melancholy.

"Why, no," Vincent said. "I thought the place was empty."

"It's not empty now. The Lakeport deputies brought in one Anthony Lorenzo shortly before dinnertime this afternoon. He's the young hood who knocked off Dapper Dan Lubell in the west-side brewery gang war. They caught him on the scene right after the shooting. The Lakeport newspapers aroused the public and the district attorney and they brought him right to trial."

"Tony Lorenzo!" Vincent whispered through dry lips. "My God, I know that boy! When did all this happen?"

"You mentioned you haven't been reading the papers," the warden said. "About two months ago—shortly after you started coming here!"

"He's guilty of murder?" Vincent asked incredulously. "He's here in the death house?"

"Guilty in the first degree, and we'll put him away early in September."

"I'd like to see him, Warden—please!" Vincent said. "I'd like to see him right away."

"I thought you might. You say you know the boy?"

"He was my chapel assistant in the Navy," Vincent said. "And later I met him in St. Polycarp's parish, where he was running a brewery for the mob. But I always believed he had good stuff in him, a fresh kid, but intelligent and unselfish. I always thought he'd grow up and get away from the wrong people; I just knew he would. I can't believe it, Warden, I can't believe he'd willfully kill a man!"

"Seeing is believing," the warden said gently. "He's across the yard there. I'll have the guard take you over if you like."

"Thank you, you're really very kind."

"The boy probably needs someone like you right now," Warden Phelps said. "Get on over there."

"God bless you!" Whelton said, rising.

The warden buzzed for the guard and asked him to take the priest to see Lorenzo in the death house.

There is no gray like the gray of the death house. It is in the light, in the shadows, the walls, the ceilings, the faces of the guards, in the blue of their uniforms, and thick in the air of the place with almost the taste of gray—a damp, mouth-drying alum.

Father Whelton sensed all this as he was led through the vaultlike walls of bars and up the stairs to the second floor where dimly a row of cells with one bulb burning in one cell alone could be seen. If the place had been painted in the gayness of red and yellow, the gaiety would be gray, he knew, for death is gray and death is king here, master of all, as always, but here explicitly so, with none of the bromides or escapist pleasures to make it seem almost nonexistent and far away.

"Right down here, Father, to Cell 7," the floor guard said, clanging the cell-block door authoritatively behind them.

"Thank you." And he went eagerly forward now to Tony alone with Mr. Gray, Tony alone, all alone on a wide, wide sea of gray.

"The chaplain is here to see you," the guard said, inserting a great steel key in the lock of the cell door.

On the tight, gray blanket he lay, his hands pillowed under his head, an open book flat down on his chest, beside him an almost empty tray of supper dishes.

"I didn't send for the chaplain," he said quietly, without averting his eyes from the ceiling.

"You sent for me a long time ago," Father Whelton said gently. "You sent for me the day you applied for the job of chaplain's assistant so that you could get out of k.p."

"Father Vincent!"

Tony leaped to his feet and rushed to the bars, devouring the priest with his sad, open face.

"Father Vincent!" he repeated in a choked whisper, the tears welling for an instant in his dark-circled eyes.

"It's just me, Tony," Father Whelton said, smiling and touching his hand. "May I come in?"

"You certainly can!" Tony said with a touch of the old cocky exuberance. "Any time—any place!"

The guard swung the gate open and let Vincent in, following him to pick up the supper tray.

"Sit down, sit down right here in my favorite armchair," Tony said, sliding a low wooden stool out of the corner to the foot of his bed.

The guard moved out with the tray and clanged the door tight behind him.

"The warden said you could have half an hour."

"Thank you," Vincent said.

They were alone.

"Tony, Tony," the priest began, "what *is* all this? I just heard it now! I'm part-time chaplain here. Tony, forgive me, I didn't know!"

"That's all right, Father. Joan Linehan told me you'd been shipped out. She wanted to contact you, but I said 'No'—you've had troubles enough for a young priest. It all happened real fast, Father—Lubell's death, the newspapers, the trial—and I'm here now. Maybe this will happen fast, too, and it will be all over!"

He let Tony talk, not wanting to ask him if he was guilty, believing he could tell by the way Tony talked—and it figured already;

the bewilderment was there rather than the weight of guilt. Maybe, dear God, he wasn't guilty, maybe there was still a chance.

"That was foolish of you, Tony," Vincent said. "I would have come to you, I would have come . . ."

" 'I was in prison, and you came to me.' Remember that, Father? I found it in this book they gave me in the county jail." He touched the open Bible beside him on the bed. "I was looking at it again before supper, Matthew 25:36, eh, Father?"

He gave the citation with the glowing pride of a small boy who has learned his lesson well.

"That's it, Tony, Matthew 25:36," Vincent said, sensing what was coming next.

"Remember the time you said the special Christmas Mass for the boys in the brig? You used this passage and you had them all in tears, remember?"

"I remember, and you remembered. You served my Mass. But tell me, if you feel like it, did you have a good lawyer and all that? What kind of a defense did you put up?"

Tony was reticent, looking out through the high barred window at a trace of rose in the evening sky.

"You can tell me, surely, Tony?"

"Yeh, Father, I can tell you, I guess," Tony said, turning again to the priest. "The mob didn't send any high-class mouthpiece over. Big Al must have been sore about the shooting because it turned on the heat. The brewery was raided and closed and everyone's lying low. They let me stew—to the lions with Tony—I got it from the public and the mob both. And I guess I deserved it—I killed Lubell, a guy that was like a father to me. I just drifted along through it all and let them say what they wanted all through the trial."

"And your lawyer?"

"Joan got me a lawyer—a nice young guy from the Loop, named Bill Ryan. He did his best, but Ziggy lammed it—they couldn't find him—neither Ryan nor the D.A."

"Ziggy?"

"Yeh, Ziggy. He was in the scuffle when Lubell got it. The D.A. said it wouldn't have made any difference because Ziggy will get the heat, too, when they find him. Maybe Big Al's given him the heat by this time."

"Are you sure it wouldn't have made any difference?"

"I don't know, Father, all I know is Lubell is dead and I—well, I had a lot to do with his death."

He didn't kill him—he didn't kill Lubell. A scuffle—an accident, maybe, or maybe Ziggy did it. But Tony didn't kill him—he knew now; thank God, he knew.

"Maybe we can still find Ziggy," Vincent said with an attempt to restrain the excitement in his voice.

"No, Father, no." Tony buried his face in his hands for a moment and then lifted his head. "Leave things as they are, Father. I'm getting what's coming to me. I should have got out a long time ago —I wanted to—but the living was easy. Now I'm going to pay. Leave things as they are."

"Will you do one thing for me, Tony?" the priest said softly. "It's got nothing to do with finding Ziggy."

"What is it, Father?"

"This is confession day for most of the Catholics in the prison. Would you want to make your peace with God? I can bring you Holy Communion on Sunday if you do."

Tony's olive features were white now, his lips taut and bloodless.

"Yes, Father," he said, "I want to go to confession."

"Kneel down, Tony, and bless yourself," Vincent said, slipping a small purple stole out of his inside coat pocket, kissing it and placing it around his neck. Tony knelt down in tears and crossed himself.

"Bless me, Father, for I have sinned. It is four years since my last confession . . ."

"The warden's car is waiting to take you home," the guard at the gatehouse said when Father Whelton entered.

"Fine," he said, sensing the peace of evening as the prison lights twinkled on behind him in the waning old-rose sunset of the countryside, sensing the peace of evening in the calm, moist eyes of Tony as he bid him good-by, promising to return on Sunday. And he knew now what he'd have to do—tonight, in fact. He'd have to take the nine o'clock train to Lakeport from Plainville. He knew what he'd have to do tonight and tomorrow—find Ziggy Plansky, that's what he'd have to do.

He could try to get someone, maybe Arthur Wagner, to go up to the mission for Saturday-evening confessions or get back himself in time. But he must go now. Find Ziggy, find Ziggy. St. Anthony, patron of lost things that must be found, help me find Ziggy!

He climbed into the rear seat of the warden's black Packard sedan parked inside the gate and spoke to the guard at the wheel.

"Will you be kind enough to take me to Plainville? I've got some business in Lakeport and would like to catch the nine o'clock train."

"Whatever you say, Father," the guard said, touching the shiny visor of his blue cap.

The heavy iron gate creaked open, and they rolled out onto the dusty road that circled the prison and led to the main highway.

The powerful sedan spun along beside the bastionlike walls, and Vincent knew an involuntary relief being outside of them. For even when you didn't belong behind them you knew you were imprisoned there, however temporarily. Guards, he thought, must know that feeling, too, and long for their days off. And in the swift driving of the chauffeur, speeding away from the vast tomb for the living, he sensed that lightness of release.

Ahead now the highway, arrowing east and west, east to Lakeport, west to the Tri-State Valley, and beyond to the rich granaries of Iowa and Kansas.

Ahead at the crossroad, in lone, dark silhouette, a figure standing beside a suitcase. Closer now. It was a woman, a young woman, slim and with skirts glad-furling in the sassy evening breeze.

"Why, it's a young lady," Vincent said to the driver.

"Yes," the guard said. "Probably waiting for the Plainville bus. It'll be along in about half an hour."

"She must have been visiting the prison," Vincent said. "Has she walked all this way from the prison gates?"

"She must have, Father. The bus does go in and out before and after regular monthly visiting hours. But this is no visiting day. She probably showed up to see some new inmate and was refused entrance. She knows now."

They were close to her now. She turned, wind-whipped, a wisp of silk brown hair tangled in her lips.

"We'll have to give her a lift," Vincent said.

"It's against the rules, Father. I'd be glad to, but the warden . . ."

"I'll explain to the warden. Good God, we can't leave her there after this ordeal. Do pick her up."

"Well . . . all right," the guard said, bewildered. "I may get blazes for it, though."

"I'll take full responsibility," Vincent said. "Please stop—now!"

The chauffeur slowed the vehicle and drew up alongside her. Vincent rolled down the window and called to her.

"Beg your pardon, young lady. Can't we give you a lift to Plainville?"

She nodded quickly, gratefully, out of a face streaked with tears, and stooped for her suitcase.

He got out of the car and hurried to her, and recognition shocked him as he drew near.

"Joan!" he said. "Oh, day of surprises! Whatever are you doing here?"

He knew then what she was doing, but the words came out of him anyway.

"Father Vincent! Is it you? Is it really you?" she asked, the tears coming again.

"It's really me, Joan. Jump in. We'll take you to the station."

"Oh, Father, this is so wonderful," she said, smiling now and drying her tears. "I really came here to find you and tell you about Tony. Now you must know all about him. Have you seen him? They wouldn't let me in. Only relatives, they said, and at special times."

"I've just come from him, Joan. He's in fine spirits now—went to confession and all."

The Packard sped along the highway now, nearing the environs of Plainville.

"You've got to help him, Father—he's innocent of murder, I'm sure of it. His attorney is convinced the gun went off accidentally in the fight. But we couldn't find Ziggy Plansky. He's disappeared, and no one who was there will talk. The district attorney wouldn't help much. Bill Ryan says he was under pressure from the mayor and the commissioner to get a conviction real fast. Their hands aren't clean and they're afraid of a city-wide investigation."

"I'm convinced Tony is innocent too, Joan. In fact, I'm going in to the city tonight and see what I can do. Where can I contact this Bill Ryan?"

Joan fished in her bag and gave him Bill's card.

"Now about yourself . . ." Vincent said. "I may be able to get you in to see Tony on Sunday. You can help me a little bit if you'll take over catechism classes at the mission tomorrow. Why not stay at the Plainville Inn tonight and go up to St. Claire's in the morning by bus? There's one at 8 A.M."

"I'd love to, Father. And do you really think there's a chance for me to see Tony Sunday? They're very strict, you know, and I'm not a relative."

"Not yet," Vincent said with a sympathetic smile.

Joan blushed deeply but did not flinch.

"I love him very much, Father. My family thinks I'm absolutely crazy for coming up here. But with my job at the brewery gone and Tony with only a few weeks to live, I'd rather be near him and take a chance on seeing him."

"I understand, Joan. I think he loves you too. And I think we can do a lot with him if we can get him off."

"We've got to, Father, we've got to!"

"We'll drop the young lady off at the Plainville Inn, driver, if you will, please."

They were in the town now, among the tidy houses and winking gas lamps.

"Joan, who could I try to contact besides Ryan that might know something about the fight and about Ziggy's whereabouts? Somebody who was there, I mean."

"Let me think," Joan said, wrinkling her pale brow attractively. "Yes—yes," she continued as a little light kindled in her mind. "Tony told us about a young hood nicknamed 'Silkshirt' who was a poolshark protégé of Lubell's—just like Tony was when he was a kid. Tony says he might be able to tell where Ziggy is, since they were both so close to Lubell."

"Couldn't the district attorney locate this kid?"

"They said they tried, but he took it on the lam, as they say. He might be around now that Tony's been convicted."

"That's very possible. Where would I look for him?"

They were parked in front of the inn now, an old white frame house with a large veranda dotted with wicker chairs.

"Bill Ryan's been trying to spot him at Kelly's Pool Hall on the west side. It's way up on Bellrose Avenue, directly across from the Bellrose Social Club."

"I think I know where it is," Vincent said. "Let's get you into the inn now. You'll need a good night's sleep before setting out in the morning. I want you to have lunch with my housekeeper and tell her you're to handle the catechism classes. She'll give you the books and things. I'm sure you've done this sort of thing at St. Polycarp's."

"I have, Father."

He took her into the lobby and bid her good night, shaking her hand, warmed by the gratitude in her blue eyes.

He got to the station, boarded the train, and later, bulleting toward Lakeport through the blackness of the countryside, he read his breviary and listened to the relentless tap dance of the wheels and the rails, saying "Silkshirt, Silkshirt," over and over again.

CHAPTER IX

Hide and Seek

THE early-morning sun was deceptively mild and cool when Father Vincent stepped out of a Lakeport taxi directly in front of the cathedral rectory. He paid his fare as the cathedral tower tolled out the hour of six across the cavern calm of the city and the eternally sighing sameness of the lake shore.

Arthur Wagner, he knew, often celebrated the quarter of six Low Mass in the cathedral. He decided to take a peek into the vestry before heading up the long three-story climb to Wagner's room. If he could catch Wagner there, tell him of his intended search for Silkshirt and Ziggy, he'd be able then to say his own morning Mass before going elsewhere.

He would offer his Mass this morning for the success of the search. *Introibo ad altare Dei* . . . I will go in to the altar of God and find Silkshirt . . .

He moved briskly to the rear side door of the cathedral, took hold of a brass ring on the heavy oak door, and pulled it to him, hearing, above its sonorous creak, the sure, refined accents of Father Arthur as he recited the prayers after Mass.

"St. Michael, the archangel, defend us in the battle . . ."

And as he entered the vestry, he could hear, too, the dominantly feminine voices, thin yet fervid, joining in with the priest—widows and washerwomen, spinsters, teen-agers, elementary-school nuns— and here and there the gruff yet shy accompaniment of a policeman, trainman, newspaper reporter—all beseeching the protection of the great archangel Michael while the city slept.

Vincent set down his hat and sat on a folding chair by the entrance to the sanctuary and altar, and opened his breviary to the morning prayers.

On the altar, Father Arthur finished the Divine Praises and, preceded by an altar boy, entered the sacristy, covered chalice in hand. Vincent glanced up at him, seeing him still rapt in the ritualistic drama of the Mass, more heady with the flesh and blood of God than the bread and wine of man which he had consumed in the ritual of transubstantiation.

Arthur saw Vincent now and smiled, creasing with warmth the tight, waxen lines of his face. Vincent rose and helped him disrobe, talking with reverent touches and smoothings on the priestly garments, mutually reticent in the majestic wake of Holy Mass.

Finally Arthur spoke, quietly, as one who wakes from love.

"Did you pop out of the sky or something, Vin? Gosh, it's good to see you! What brings you here?"

Vincent smoothed the vestments in their deep, fragrant cedar drawers and pushed them shut.

"Who do you know in the district attorney's office?"

Arthur Wagner smiled and, looking tall and austere in his black cassock, turned and put both hands on Vincent's shoulders.

"I thought we had you snugly out of circulation for a while," he said. "Why can't you just be the simple country pastor—calm, stable, blessing the crops and helping with the harvest? I've been trying to build up this image of you around the chancery for the last three months. And I was just beginning to succeed. Now"—he began to laugh, a mirthful yet subdued laugh—"now he shows up all of a sudden and asks if I know anyone in the district attorney's office."

"Well, do you?" Vincent pursued, smiling wryly.

"Yes, I do. I know *himself*, Edward Patrick Carroll, shining defender of the law and district attorney for all Lakeport County."

"Good," Vincent said. "I'll talk to you about him after I've said my Mass."

"Use the main altar," Wagner said. "There'll be nobody out there until seven except a few devout scrubwomen who'll be happy to hear another Mass with you.

"Lefty," he called to the altar boy who, lingering like an after-school pupil fond of a pretty teacher, was hanging up newly laundered altar-boy cassocks in a wardrobe.

"Yes, Father," Lefty said, showing a pure, pert face that would look the same in the archdiocesan newspaper about fifteen years later in the section where the annual pictures of newly ordained priests were printed.

"Father Vincent, this is Lefty Woods, who struck out seven midgets from your old parish on the South Side. He pitches for the cathedral midgets and likes to serve early Masses. Father Vincent was quite a pitcher himself, Lefty, before he got involved in 'politics.' While he was in college, in fact, he received an offer from the New York Giants."

"Pleased to meetcha, Father!" Lefty said, wide-eyed. "Did you really get an offer from the Giants?"

"I really did, Lefty—once. But that was quite a while ago. What's your favorite pitch?"

"I try to throw a curve a lot, Father, but sometimes it just doesn't break and becomes a fast ball," Lefty said, wrinkling his brow and bringing all his freckles into a blurring blend of brown.

"Lemmee see your pitching hand." Vincent took hold of his small but callused left. "Show me what you do with your fingers when you throw the curve."

"I just use t'ree," Lefty said, absorbed in the exhibit of his pitching hand. "The first two and the thumb. I try to snap it off the thumb."

"You're a pitcher!" Vincent said, grabbing Lefty's biceps with quick appraisal. "It's the snap all right—off the thumb—the wrist snapping, the arm following through. But don't use the curve too often—too hard on your arm!"

Arthur watched now with intent gray eyes, sensing the poetry of Vincent's absorption in the boy. The D.A., Tony, the state prison were forgotten now. A boy, a boy, learning something fine. If there was music in the spheres, it sounded now.

"Tell me this," Vincent said. "Do you think a lefty has a natural curve?"

"Everybody says so, but I don't believe it."

"Why don't you believe it?"

"It's just that there's so many right-hand batters and they think the ball's comin' at 'em when a lefty pitches—no matter what he throws."

"You're a pitcher, a real pitcher!" Vincent said.

"Thanks, Father. Would you like me to serve your Mass?"

"I'd like that very much."

"Okay. Now that's decided," Arthur said. "Two pitchers on the altar. The national pastime has merged with the Catholic Church. Wait'll the Protestant brethren find this out."

"I'll see you upstairs at breakfast," Vincent said.

"Yes, and this is my day off. Maybe you'll go to the dunes with me. Think of it: sun, sand, surf—*peace!* And all within fifty miles of Murder Town, U.S.A.!"

"We can't go to the dunes today, Art," Vincent said firmly. "We've got to see the district attorney."

"The district attorney!"

"That's right. I'll tell you all about it at breakfast."

"Okay, we'll go to the dunes this afternoon then," Wagner said with tentative enthusiasm.

"We've got two more errands to do in the afternoon." Vincent's bland reply was muffled as he pulled a black cassock over his pants and shirt.

"Two errands—where?" Arthur said indignantly. "This is my day off!"

"I was hoping it would be when I left the Tri-State Valley," Vincent said coolly. "Say, by the way, do you know a young lawyer named Bill Ryan?"

"Sure I know Bill . . ." Arthur paused now, the light of understanding flaming in his mind. "Oh, I get it now! But *no!* Oh, Vincent —*no!* Not Tony Lorenzo! Really, now! That case is all cut and dried! *You're* not really going to try to save him from the chair, Vincent—really, now!"

"I'll tell you all about it at breakfast," Vincent said calmly as he adjusted his vestments. "You ready, Lefty?"

"All ready, Father."

"Vincent! Vincent!" Arthur sighed, his hands limp at his sides.

"I'll see you upstairs," Vincent said, placing his biretta firmly on his head, lifting the covered chalice, and following Lefty out into the sanctuary for the Mass.

"Oh, my poor day off!" Arthur Wagner looked glumly after him. "He'll be up before the Cardinal again!

"Tony Lorenzo," he said, shaking his head, yet smiling as he opened the door to the staircase leading up and across the yard to the rectory. "Tony Lorenzo! What next? What next?"

Silkshirt was tired of smoking cigarettes and reading magazines. He was tired of sandwiches and coffee, too, and bored with the little slatternly blond waitress who lived down the hall and lounged around his furnished room at night. She was slim, supple, and fiercely ardent with her kisses, but her skin had a slack drabness about it that was the color of the faded, water-streaked bedroom wallpaper, and she had an unwashed smell about her that couldn't quite be suppressed by the cheap perfume with which she daubed her armpits and her hair.

The papers said Lorenzo was in the death house at the state pen now, and he wondered if it might not be all right for him to come out of hiding and maybe play a game of eight ball or two at the Bellrose Social Club or—maybe—maybe even across the street at Gypper Kelly's Pool Hall. No, not there where Dapper Dan got it when the gun went off.

When the gun went off . . .

He mustn't think it or even say it. There had been a fight between Ziggy and Lorenzo over the gun and it went off, killing Lubell. But he mustn't say so; he was told not to say so by Hothead, who brought him his meals. Big Al said he and Ziggy would go for a ride if the D.A. found out what actually happened.

It had to be this way, Big Al said, so that Lorenzo would go to the chair and the public would be happy that crime does not pay. The heat would then go off and the breweries could reopen. The D.A. wouldn't go looking for more evidence, but he'd have to prosecute if he got some. That's what Big Al said. It was either Tony or the two of them—Ziggy and Silkshirt—so take it or leave it, Hothead told him, and that's what Big Al said.

Ziggy was hiding in a room like this somewhere in the neighborhood, but Silkshirt didn't know where. Maybe he saw the papers, too, about Lorenzo in the death house. Maybe he wanted to get out and shoot a game of pool, drink a cold beer in an open, airy place, and sit down beside a girl that took a bath once in a while and smelled all fragrant like the grass out in the infield at Cicero Downs.

Hothead said so many scary things when he brought the food and the magazines that Silkshirt didn't get scared any more. It had got so that if Hothead said something nice it might scare Silkshirt, because you get used to things and it's the new and unexpected things that scare you.

So he wasn't so scared when Hothead said that the only reason Big Al didn't have Silkshirt and Ziggy taken for a ride was because the heat was on and there just couldn't be any more killings right now. That didn't scare Silkshirt so much now because he had heard Hothead talk about killings and rides so often it was like the baseball scores.

But Big Al had sent Hothead to Detroit this week to do a job on a guy who was trying to muscle into Lakeport. The waitress had brought him his breakfast and lunch and he wondered if he might now sneak out for supper and maybe a game of pool. He could wear a pair of dark glasses, part his hair the other way. He could stay out of sight as much as possible, and Lorenzo would fry in early September, so what was the danger now?

But not Kelly's place. Maybe Dumbbell's place on Carrot Street near the railroad yards. There'd be a few niggers playing there and some bohunks from the packing house drinking beer. It ought to be safe there after sundown, and he could tell Nellie, the waitress, to come and let him know if someone came to the room looking for him.

He lay back on the lumpy mattress and accepted the sweet sharpness of the thought, dulling it pleasantly with a self-induced sense of security now that Hothead was out of town.

If only Lubell hadn't stopped that slug, things would be different. Lubell . . . Silkshirt felt a pang of loss more selfish than affectionate. Lubell had lifted him to a higher level of purgatory, rescued him from an apprenticeship in the slaughterhouse, where he had the savory job of mopping up the hot red blood of steers and pigs after the bohunks had wielded their deadly clubs and knives.

"Why not come and work for me?" Lubell had asked him one Saturday night when Silkshirt had pocketed three balls in a tight game for a pair of silver dollars.

And to Lubell he went as club runner and general coat holder for the mob, telling his careworn immigrant mother that he had taken a job as club janitor—Lubell's suggestion—which in a way was true. After all, he did build fires and often kept the keys to the place when Lubell and Hothead were not around.

Oh, how the jack rolled in after that! Lubell had taught him a lot of tricks with a cue stick and would plant him in a series of money games with older players. Shy, sweet-faced, immaculate in a white silk shirt open at the throat, he would team up with Lubell and gather in all the heavy sugar bet on the game. Lubell gave him twenty per cent of the winnings, and this was rarely much less than five dollars at a time.

It was getting so that no one would play him, when Lubell was knocked off. Silkshirt had been itching to take on that wise guy Lorenzo. Lubell said he'd been one of the best with a cue stick. Well, he wanted to prick that big windbag that day, but the shooting started before he could challenge him to a game.

There'd be no game now with Lorenzo, and if Lubell had to go, it was good enough for that smooth-talking wop from the west side. "The big brewery executive" had a new "office" now, and if he stood up suddenly he'd bump his head against the ceiling of his cell. He had a nice new place to sit down now, too—the hot seat!

Lubell had said he'd break Lorenzo, but it took Dapper Dan's death to do it. "I put him in there—I can throw him out!" he had said more than once. "If you were a little older I'd move you right into his chair," Lubell had promised Silkshirt. "I take care of all my boys, just like I took care of him—and what does it get you?" he had said in his typical quiet manner, which, when bitter, was deadlier than a rattlesnake's venom.

It had got him a bullet, Silkshirt now knew. And maybe it would have got him a bullet eventually anyway. For Silkshirt now knew that Big Al, not Tony Lorenzo, had blocked Lubell's former attempts to deal with the brewery.

Maybe, Silkshirt thought, toying with the grimy tassle of the window shade near his bed, maybe it's good I wasn't old enough to move into Lorenzo's job. Maybe Big Al would have had more reason to unload me than he has now.

He sighed, rubbed his eyes, shook his head, seeking to obliterate the burden of too much thinking. He closed his eyes and sought sleep.

The rasp of long fingernails against the outside panel of his bedroom door startled him.

"Silkshirt, it's me," the thin, sweet whine of Nellie's voice called in a quick whisper.

"Fer Crissakes," he mumbled to himself. "What does she want? It's three hours till supper."

"Silkshirt, Silkshirt," she persisted, "open up, it's me—Nellie."

"I know goddamn well it's you," he said with the arrogance of complete possession. "What the hell do you want?"

"Open up," she insisted, "it's important!"

The bedsprings moaned as Silkshirt lurched morosely to the door, slipping the bolt and turning the key.

He opened the door a little, holding it firmly with his foot. There stood the faded, wiry wisp of a girl, Nellie, holding a cold bottle of beer in her small brown hands.

The sweet, whiny voice spoke out of a being that seemed complete in a faded hank of yellow hair and a wan, green work dress.

"Let me in, Silkshirt. I've got some news for you and I brought you a beer."

"Oke," he said condescendingly. "Come in."

She slipped in, closing and bolting the door behind her. She puckered her mouth and, knowing no flicker of desire, Silkshirt shrugged his shoulders, ignoring her lips and taking the beer from her hand.

"What is it? Spill it. I was takin' a nap."

He slumped down on the bed, again taking a long pull on the beer. She sat down beside him, resting her hand lightly on his knee.

"Wait'll I tell you!" she said, her hazel eyes livelier than all the rest of her life-drubbed presence.

"Tell me what!" Silkshirt said casually, taking another swig.

"Ziggy was in! Ziggy was in for a drink!"

He snapped upright into a sitting position and grabbed her thin elbow viciously.

"Ziggy!" he said. "When? Whu'd he say? When?"

"Silkshirt," she mewed plaintively, "you're hurting my arm. He was in about twenty minutes ago. He had a shot and a beer down at the corner of the bar and didn't talk to no one. I smiled at him, but he pretended he didn't know me. He came out for a drink, Silkshirt, now that Lorenzo's in stir, just like you've said you'd do yourself."

"Where'd he go? Which way'd he go?" Silkshirt demanded.

"I knew you'd want me to find out. I waited a while after he was gone, then slipped out the back way. I hurried to the corner of Carrot Street and saw him go upstairs above the Dumbbell's pool hall."

"He's livin' *there?*" Silkshirt said. "I knew he was around here somewhere. And he came out. He's figurin' just like me, figurin' it's safe with Hothead away and Lorenzo in the death house. Whu'd I tell you, Nellie, whu'd I tell you!"

"That's what you said last night, Silkshirt, that's what you said," Nellie responded with admiration.

"That settles it!" he said confidently, taking another drink of beer.

"I'll go down to the Dumbbell's myself today and shoot a game or two. Maybe I'll see Ziggy."

"It'll do you good to get out of this hole. But be careful and don't stay too long."

"I won't, Nellie," he said with self-comforting wisdom. "I can't afford to be seen around. There's too much at stake," he added, not quite realizing what he meant by that strong and mature phrase unless it was his own hide that might be at stake.

"See? Di'n I tell you I wuz yir gal?" Nellie said coyly, leaning forward and kissing his neck with a depth of feeling unmistakably sincere.

Even Silkshirt was moved, perhaps because of involuntary gratitude.

"You're not a bad kid at all. When the heat goes off I'm gonna get you some clothes and take you around—fatten you up, maybe, over in China Town. And fer Chrissakes," he exploded, "take some time off and go down to the city baths. Scrub off that goddamn ten-cent perfume with sand soap and maybe you won't stink half bad!"

"I will, Silkshirt, I will," Nellie whined, leaning closer.

CHAPTER X

Inside the D. A.

It was just another routine morning for District Attorney Edward Patrick Carroll, or so he implicitly believed. Carroll was graying handsomely but rapidly, like most big-city D.A.s in the year of Big Al.

His assistants were at court, handling the routine trial business of the office, the mail was neatly stacked on his desk, and the list of morning appointments was centered on his desk before him to be perused, maneuvered, juggled quickly or leisurely indulged, depending on the political import of the caller.

"Remember, you're to see your wife and boy this morning," Miss Mara had scrawled at the top of the appointment list.

Alice! Tommy!

She was talking about going to California with the boy. She had her fill of his staying out nights on "political business." She had heard about Sally Womack, the show girl he was keeping in one of Big Al's apartment blocks on the north lake shore. There would be no divorce, she said, because of their religion, but she was going off to California with Tommy.

Carroll sighed with involuntary bewilderment and regret. He had just begun to enjoy the peace that had come over his office with the quick conviction of Lorenzo and the resulting letup of pressure from the papers and the public regarding the sway of organized crime in the town. In some quarters he was beginning to be looked on as the great prosecutor and guardian of the public peace. He was just beginning to enjoy all that when Alice hit him with this.

And of all things! Tommy in the movies! Alice really was ambitious for the boy. Tommy had been soloing in the choir at old St. Agatha's, and some visiting celebrity had seen him and heard him. They were going to try him out for the role of Little Lord Fauntleroy along with maybe a hundred other kids with mothers like Alice whose sons soloed in choirs all over the country.

"Little Lord Fauntleroy," Carroll muttered aloud. "Jesus! Not Tommy, not my boy Tommy! Hell, why don't they try him out for Huckleberry Finn or something like that? Little Lord Fauntleroy!"

But he knew he hadn't given enough attention to Tommy during the past eighteen months of his term in office, nor to his mother. It wasn't just the dame, although she relieved the tension and was handy for recreation late at night when his work was done and he needed leisure most. "You can't take your wife to a night club at three in the morning." He sighed bitterly.

He pushed the buzzer on the right side of his desk and Miss Mara popped in, looking like a movie star herself with bobbed hair and red knee-length dress.

"Yes, Mr. Carroll."

"Peg, I note that my wife and boy will be in later. Call them and tell them I want to take them to lunch. And get hold of Sally over at her place. Tell her that lunch with a mutual friend is out. I'll contact her late this afternoon."

"Yes, Mr. Carroll. You want some flowers for your wife?"

"Good, Peg. Send her over a single red camellia, as usual. Anything else?"

"Only one thing, Mr. Carroll. Maybe we'd better call that mutual friend if you're not having lunch with him. I recall he wanted to come over here and you suggested lunch at the apartment. Don't you think we'd better contact him directly?"

"Yes, I think it's a good idea. I don't want him busting in here. Someone on the papers would get hold of it and we'd be filling up the editorial pages again. Try to get him now. He's an early riser."

"Will do. Oh, still one more thing . . ."

"Yes?"

"A Father Arthur Wagner called—very nice—said you'd know him?"

"Yes, he's over at the archdiocesan newspaper. He's the Cardinal's nephew, by the way. Where'd I meet him? Oh, I gave a talk at a press luncheon. What did he want?"

"He wants to duck in for a few minutes between appointments if it's all right with you. Says he has a priest from upstate in tow who would like to meet you."

The fame of the Lorenzo case again—the public defender—this was good for confidence, good form, too, the clergy reassuring their brethren that Lakeport had a Christian vigilante. Big Al would like it; he was always talking about the statehouse. Maybe, maybe it could be done if they could keep things bottled up.

"Upstate, eh?" Carroll said, patting a wisp of silver hair that covered a thin spot on the side of his head. "That's good stuff, Peg. By all means shoot them in whenever you can."

"Will do," Miss Mara said, nodding and turning, clicking on out like an F. Scott Fitzgerald dust jacket suddenly come to life. Lean and lacquered she was, leggy and lissome, but with no champagne glass, fur coat, no Illini pennant. Maybe that on a fall weekend, but now all business, gay but relentlessly so for the D.A. and his secrets.

He opened his correspondence folder—a letter from Warden Phelps at Plainville— "Prisoner docile, seems resigned to his fate. If you think there is any chance of his appeal being upheld, let me know, as it would save me a lot of trouble here as to arrangements for the execution in September."

The appeal. It wouldn't be upheld as far as he could tell. Ziggy and Silkshirt wouldn't be found—Big Al had assured him of that; and they wouldn't be sought very diligently—Captain Hardy of Division 6, where they'd probably be hiding, had assured him of that.

He scrawled a note on the letter: "Peg, remind me to dictate confidential letter to Warden Phelps this afternoon—prospects for the success of the Lorenzo appeal late this month—dim, etc.—public rightfully demands action and cleanup, etc. E.P.C."

There was another crudely scrawled note from Lorenzo's mother of the type he received about once a week, beseeching him to renew his efforts to find the others "involving in thees creem—God and Bless'd Mamma will help you find . . ."

She had been in one day, a sweet, stooped little woman with her bowed head in a kerchief. She had been in the outer office many times, but he had let her in this once and had been patient and kind with her, assuring her that everything was being done.

That fresh little bastard Bill Ryan was probably behind all this —the letters and the visits. There was a note from him, also, in the folder.

"I deeply resent your complacent attitude in assuring me and everyone that the police are constantly on the lookout for the two missing witnesses of Lubell's death. If Lorenzo dies before these witnesses are roused from hiding I shall devote my career to the proof of your deviousness and negligence in this case, even if I have to enter the political lists myself."

The D.A. chuckled involuntarily. "Now Ryan wants to run against me . . . another morning-glory . . ."

There were several donation requests for charity balls and a handful of chance books from various parishes. There was also one more poison-pen letter threatening his life if he didn't come up with "Ziggy and Silkshirt."

Ziggy and Silkshirt—maybe, maybe it would have been better if Big Al had gone ahead with his original plans. After all, what Big Al did, he did on his own. But Carroll had asked him to lay off. The town was still tight with concern and smoldering tension over the arrogance and license with which the brewery crowd had defied the police. Al had assured him he could get rid of the evidence, but there was always the chance that someone would find out and tip off the papers. Then there'd be more killings, more and more . . .

His buzzer rang and he lifted the phone.

"It's your landlord, Mr. Carroll," Miss Mara said.

"Put him on."

"Al," he said vigorously. It was always good to take the initiative with Al or he'd want you eating out of his hand. It was always good to be urgent and brief. He could be less urgent and less brief than most because he was D.A., but still, he knew, people were the same no matter whom they were dealing with; they were diplomatic for a while, but eventually they'd revert back to themselves. And himself? He knew that he couldn't face Al if he didn't have the upper hand. How long would it be? How long?

"Al, I'm sorry, but lunch is out. . . . No—no other business. It's my wife and son, Al. . . . Oh—Sally told you. . . . Yeh, they're going away—that's right, Al. . . . Yeh, the movies—what do you make of it? . . . Yeh, Little Lord Fauntleroy. Why don't you try out for the role—heh-heh-heh! . . . Yeh, the Big Bad Wolf—that would be better. Tommy's good though, Al, he's real good. . . .

"Yes, you can talk. No one gets on this line. . . . Yes, yes . . . No, I don't think Ryan will come up with anything before the appeal, do you? . . . No, no, Al—if you want my co-operation, no! Let them be until after the execution. . . . No, no, Al. I don't want any part of anything like that, Al. . . . That's right, Al, let them be. . . . No, Al, the cops won't find them unless they walk in and sign the blotter. Just let Division 6 alone, Al. . . . Oh no. I don't need anything—maybe in the fall. . . . Still think I could do it, eh? . . . We'll see, Al, we'll see. . . . Yeh, maybe at the club late tonight. . . . Yeh, I'll be with Sally. . . . Okay, Al. . . . Yeh, thanks, Al, good-by."

That was it again. Keep it revved up from the time you start talking about him—keep sure of yourself, talk fast and loud—that was the way to handle Al, or he'd handle you, he'd have you waiting on him hand and foot. But where now, what now? The appeal rebuttal, he'd have to get one ready. Start it this afternoon, after the letters; not a chance, Ryan, not a chance.

Ziiii-zit!

"Yes, Miss Mara?"

"Father Wagner is here and his guest."

"Send them in."

He straightened his papers, gave his hair another pat, settled back with the brief open in his long, pink, manicured hands.

County of Lakeport *versus* Mildred S. Black.

SUBJECT: Alleged conduct of bawdyhouse on South Side . . .

They were usually well protected under Big Al's system but there had to be prosecutions—a drunken disturbance or a stabbing was bound to bring them to court periodically. And it looked good in the papers—law and order. Al had a fund for that too.

"District Attorney Carroll!" Miss Mara announced, swaying charmingly at the door. "The Reverend Clergy have arrived."

Carroll looked up. It was Father Wagner and another priest, short, thick-limbed, serious of mien.

"Father Arthur!" Carroll said resonantly, rising and hurrying cordially around his desk with outstretched hand. "So good of you to come by."

"You were nice to fit me in, Ed," Arthur said, shaking his hand and nodding toward Vincent. "This is Father Vincent Whelton, who's toiling in the vineyards upstate."

"Awfully good you could come in, both of you," Carroll said, shaking Vin's hand. "Come, sit down, sit down."

He motioned them to armchairs making a V in front of his desk.

"Vincent Whelton . . ." Carroll mused fetchingly. "Now that sounds like a familiar Lakeport name."

"You may have known my father," Vincent said. "He was in the Council for some years."

"Of course I knew him!" Carroll said heartily. "We served in the Council together fifteen years ago. I was just a kid then and he was very kind to me, very kind indeed!"

"Dad was like that," Vincent said.

"He certainly was! You know what he did for me—and every other new councilman when he was chairman? He got the whole crowd to applaud my maiden speech, that's what he did. I wanted to build a new world and all that—the kind of thing that makes everybody yawn—and he got everybody to give me a big hand. I thought I was really somebody then, I really did, and it was your dad's doing."

"Did you ever build that new world?" Vincent asked him with a wryness that did not entirely conceal the bluntness of his intent.

"Eh?" Carroll said, his cordiality fading for just a moment. "New world?"

Wagner coughed and interposed hastily: "Father Vincent means were you able to accomplish any of the objectives you mentioned in your maiden speech? He's quite an orator himself, and I imagine he's curious as all get out about what you said in front of his father."

"Oh," Carroll said with a certain tight-jawed recovery of his composure. "Maybe I did . . . maybe I got some of my objectives. I wanted a new playground in Ward 9 and I got that before the year was out."

"That was something good," Vincent said.

"It was, it was." The old cordial note returned. Pointedly turning to Arthur, Carroll asked, "How is His Eminence these days?"

"He's fine, just fine. Busy and aging, but robust as ever."

"I'm happy to hear that! He's simply the best-loved man in this community—and by all faiths, too—that's the big tribute to his life and work."

"Thank you, Ed," Arthur said. "We don't want to tie you up, we know you have a busy calendar of appointments."

Carroll nodded pleasantly, as if he didn't mind having them use up his time. And in a way, he didn't. He was in the presence of men of pure motives, and he fed on their presence a little, knowing they would not shoot him or slander him if he did not comply with their wishes.

"Father Vincent here has among his other duties in Plainville the assignment of chaplain in the state prison," Arthur said tentatively.

Vincent, sensing that Carroll was on edge, watched his reaction closely. The thin veil of cordiality in Carroll's features was rent asunder by Arthur's revelation. Lorenzo, Lorenzo, the Lorenzo case. He knew now the real purpose of their call.

"That's very interesting," Carroll said lamely. He picked up a gold letter opener with downcast eyes that sought the disguise of serious thought and mustered himself to go quickly on the offensive. "I—I—as you may know, Father Whelton, I had to send a young fellow up there recently."

"Yes, Tony Lorenzo," Vincent said. "I know I must confess, as a prison chaplain, having talked intimately to the boy, I must confess there seem to be some enigmatic aspects to the case."

Carroll had control of himself now and masked firmly the wise, sure, yet sympathetic demeanor.

"You're absolutely right, Father! There were aspects of the case that could not be given the searchlight of direct inquiry. Not that it would have impaired the verdict substantially, but—are you familiar with the case?—it might have implicated one or two others seriously."

"Yes, I am rather familiar with the case," Vincent offered, braking his impulse to mention his familiarity with Lorenzo, sensing it as the more prudent course not to show all his cards. "You apparently refer to the inability of the police to find two key witnesses of the tragedy."

"That's correct," Carroll said coolly. "We've searched high and low for the parties nicknamed Silkshirt Williams and Ziggy Plansky. We are still searching, in fact. And unless they're dead, we'll find them eventually and bring them to trial. You may be sure of that, Father."

"If you won't think me too presumptuous, Mr. Carroll, it might be the humane thing to locate them before Lorenzo takes the long walk."

"That's just very possible, Father. Let's see—Lorenzo is scheduled to die about mid-September—if his appeal is denied. I must reiterate, however, that our position is a solid one. We will prosecute the others—or at least one of them—for possible murder, but that will in no way change our case against Lorenzo. He went to the pool hall as the armed leader of a bootlegging mob, determined to get his shipment through. In the struggle Lubell was killed. My first duty is still to the public and, human sentiments aside, we've got to stop the lawlessness and killing in this town."

"I'm glad to hear you say that, sir, but, as you know, Lorenzo's defense attorney has an entirely different point of view. He believes that the witnesses are hiding and are being protected."

"By the police?"

"Perhaps," Vincent said.

"There are absolutely no grounds for such a position. And if you weren't wearing the cloth," Carroll said, going beet-red, "I'm afraid I would have to use much stronger language in repudiating such an implication on your part."

Vincent's face was also red with anger, and he said coldly and measuredly:

"It is because I wear the cloth that I am taking this position. I know this boy. I know that he has done wrong and deserves punishment. But he has not, I believe, committed murder, and it would be a crime against heaven if he were executed while the pivotal witnesses for his defense had not the opportunity to testify for him or against him. This, too, comes under the heading of duty to the public. Is not a miscarriage of justice a sin against society as well as the lawlessness of hoodlums?"

Arthur coughed, trying to catch Vincent's eye, but the words were out of him and the air was tingling with tension and challenge.

"I have stated the position of this office, Father," Carroll said coldly and with unconcealed rage. "It is irrevocable."

"Very well," Vincent said, rising. "I do thank you for giving us some time. It was courteous of you."

"Yes, Ed," Arthur said, trying to strike a lighter, more cordial tone. "Thanks very much. Hope to see you around."

"It was nice of you both to drop in." Carroll reached over the desk this time and shook Arthur's hand quite genially. He then offered a cold fish to Vincent, who clasped his hand briefly as they nodded at each other through the arctic air.

Carroll buzzed for Miss Mara, who showed the priests out in the midst of a tomblike silence.

After they had gone Carroll stared with frozen mind at the portrait profiles of his wife and son—sweet, open, honest—the priests gone —all the good against him, he sensed, wife, son, leaving—priests leaving. Sweet, open, honest faces—leaving, leaving, left.

He shook his head, blinked his eyes. Anger seared and soared in him.

That fresh little bastard! I'll fix his wagon. Who do I know over there at the chancery? Who do I know besides young Wagner? Monsignor O'Hara—that's his name—fixed a bunch of tickets for his friends and relatives—tipped his lawyer brother on a few juicy accident cases.

He pressed the buzzer at the side of his desk.

I'll fix that fresh little bastard!

"Yes, Mr. Carroll?" Miss Mara popped in, whitely now, flustered, the F. Scott Fitzgerald cover girl no longer.

"Get me Monsignor O'Hara at the chancery."

"Yes, Mr. Carroll."

CHAPTER XI

Into the Cage

TAXICABS were honking like wild geese awry where the two priests stood, in respite, on the sidewalk outside the courthouse.

"Of course you've gone and done it again," Arthur sighed. "And this time I'm in it with you. How can I possibly intercede for you with Unk if I'm involved myself?"

"You won't have to intercede," Vincent said, calm now after the altercation with the district attorney, calm but thrilled in a slow-glowing way with the increasing scent and excitement of the chase. He was more positive than ever that they were onto something. They'd just have to find Silkshirt and Ziggy—today—now! "We've done nothing wrong."

"Nothing wrong in one way," Arthur said, "if you mean trying to help that poor boy in the death house. But you're on French leave from your upstate mission—remember!"

Vincent was mock-indignant. "I certainly am not on French leave, Art. This is my day off—just like yourself!"

"Yes, your day off—I recall. Do you always do things like this on your day off?" Arthur asked with a resigned smile. "And who, pray tell, is ministering to the faithful while you're up here bearding the district attorney in his lair? That slip of a girl from St. Polycarp's? How will you explain that one to the Cardinal?"

"Why do I have to explain it to His Eminence?"

"Ohhhhh . . ." Arthur sighed wearily again. "Call one of those cabs while I again point out the facts of life to you. Do you think for one minute that Carroll is going to take your interference in this case lying down? His whole career would be ruined if you are able to locate those witnesses. To Carroll you're a brash, immature busy-body cleric from upstate. He may be on the phone to Monsignor O'Hara right now."

"You're probably right, Art." A shade of apprehension crossed his features. "But I've still got to go through with it."

Vincent signaled for one of the raucous, boxlike taxis which were nibbling relentlessly at traffic all along Tri-State Boulevard. A yellow checkered cab squawked and jolted to a halt alongside them.

"Where to, Reverends?" the cabdriver said, leaning one tanned arm back and snapping open the door.

"To the cathedral," Father Arthur Wagner said, stooping and climbing in.

"Oh no, Arthur," Vincent said hastily. "Take us to the Rice Building on Upper Lake Drive. We've got to see Bill Ryan."

"*Not me!*" Arthur exploded sullenly. "I've gone as far as I'm going! Driver, stop this cab!"

The driver, bewildered and darting his head and eyes in indecision, pulled over to the curb. He'd been through this sort of thing before, but it was usually a lovers' quarrel or a pitched battle between husband and wife about who was late or who was going where. The feel of this was the same, however, and the air just as torrid.

Vincent flushed more with sympathy for Wagner than irritation. It was true, he *was* imposing on Arthur's friendship more than was discreet, and it could put Arthur in a bad light at the chancery—his job at the paper—his relationship to the Cardinal—his previous pattern of intervention for a former roommate at the seminary.

"Very well, Art," Vincent said with a compassionate smile as Wagner pressed on the door handle with one hand, pushing a dollar bill at the cabdriver with the other. "By all means go along. I'm sincerely sorry if I've got you into hot water."

"I'm all right, Vin, if I get out now. Do what you like, but——"

Arthur was stinging with the first flarings of remorse now but had enough momentum to carry through his act of self-jettison from the situation. "But, for heaven's sake, I'll be of no help to you if I'm also involved. I'll see you back at the rectory tonight—okay?"

"Okay, Art, I'll see you then," Vincent said gently.

"Good luck." Arthur grabbed his shoulder briefly and hurried out of the cab.

Vincent smiled and asked the driver to continue on to Ryan's.

The cab pestered the traffic again, burbled and honked along Lake Drive. Vincent knew a pain of loss at Arthur's going. He was positive the search had to be conducted, and he had looked forward to Arthur's comradeship and cleverness. Perhaps he had presumed too much in expecting Arthur to go along with him, but their friendship had never been something he had to think about twice and he had believed that Lorenzo's life-in-the-balance would have challenged Arthur into seeing the adventure all the way through.

But, no—but, no—gone, now, gone . . . alone, now, alone . . .

He closed his eyes in the cab and mustered his strength. Two roads of the mind were open now: darkness and discouragement or light and faith. Christ was alone for truth's sake. He hung there alone, alone, and the truth prevailed.

"Rice Building," the cabdriver said, pulling up.

Father Arthur Wagner decided not to take another cab back to the cathedral. It was only a five minutes' walk back along Lake Drive and then one block to the left. He felt anew a pang of remorse at leaving Vincent, sensing his need and belief, but still, he was doing the right thing to protect them both.

What to do now? He could perhaps still salvage the afternoon as part of his day off. He was under considerable pressure each week as the newspaper deadline came and went and usually needed this free time to unwind. He could get some lunch back at the rectory and play a game or two of tennis on the Lakeport University Courts. Tennis? Tennis shoes. Vincent had the tennis shoes.

No matter then. A nap. Some reading. A walk along the lake.

He swung briskly along the wide sidewalk across from the lake front in the astringent sunshine of high noon. He acknowledged at first the many greetings of passers-by, then decided to adopt the role of solemnity, signifying almost that he was on sick call.

He did this because his thoughts kept turning to Vincent and the dangerous situation he was in. He was, as he had told Vincent, almost positive that the D.A. would retaliate in some way through the chancery office. After all, to Carroll, Vincent was just a pip-squeak cleric sticking his nose into something that did not directly concern him.

Turning off the drive at Cathedral Avenue, he decided to duck the front door of the chancery and slip in through the basement chapel and up the back stairs to his room. If Carroll had contacted the chancery, he didn't care to be summoned on the carpet.

At the fringe of the lawny cathedral grounds he turned left, encountering no one. Thankfully he knew that all would be at lunch, the sextons and the curates.

He walked to the rear of the cathedral and opened the heavy door to the basement chapel. Down into the cool, candle-flickering gloom, across the bisecting aisle, genuflecting at mid-point, and on up front to the vestry staircase leading up and across to the sleeping rooms on the second and third floor of the rectory.

He moved briskly but as quietly as possible up the carpeted stairs and down the hall to his room. He opened the door and saw a note on the carpet.

He picked up the note and closed the door behind him:

Father Arthur:

I told Monsignor O'Hara this is your day off and you're probably down at the dunes. If you get this tonight, contact him right away. Is Father Whelton in town? The Monsignor seems to think so.

Hastily,
Fr. Jack Egan

That was that. Carroll had popped off to Monsignor O'Hara. Now what?

He sighed and slumped on his bed. Now what, now what?

He might as well have stayed with Vincent and gone along with him. They'd probably both have to go on the carpet before Monsignor O'Hara tonight, anyway—and better to explain things to him than to the Cardinal!

Where would Vincent be now? At Ryan's. He might as well go with him. They were both in dutch now, anyway.

"Go with him! Go with him!" his mind tolled involuntarily.

Why not? If they could locate the two hoods and uncover some evidence on the Lorenzo case, they'd have a much better explanation for the chancery. Besides, why be afraid of Carroll? It does look as though he's been playing along with the hoods. He'll get his comeuppance sooner or later, if that is true. . . .

"Go with him! Go with him!"

He could slip right out the way he came in and get some lunch with Vincent. He arose, brushed his hair, adjusted his collar, and hurried down the hall.

The Rice Building was big, old, and ornate. There was the marble lobby, Corinthian columns, and the slow, caged elevators strumming slowly up and down.

Father Vincent checked Ryan's office number and took the elevator to the tenth floor, noting by the lobby clock that it was a few minutes after noon. He hoped he'd be in time to catch Ryan before he went out for lunch, as it was urgent for him to make his west-side excursion right away so that he'd have a chance to catch the midnight back to Plainville and his duties at the mission. Ryan could give him some advice and perhaps moral support if he could only catch him in.

He got out of the elevator and went looking for Suite 1038.

There was no one in the tiny reception room, but there were two size-twelve feet on a wide expanse of black desk in the office beyond. They belonged, he could see, to a hefty black Irishman in an unpressed salt-and-pepper suit who was leaning back in a swivel chair, munching on a sandwich and absorbed in a thick-sheafed manuscript balanced deftly on his thighs.

"I hope you're Attorney Bill Ryan," Vincent said.

The big black-haired Irishman looked up with a start.

"Come in, come in," he said, unlimbering, rising and dropping the brief down with a thump. "I hope you're Father Vincent Whelton."

"I am. And I'm lucky to catch you in."

"I'm usually here," Ryan said heartily, reaching across the desk and shaking his hand. "Have a seat, Father. Joan Linehan called from some little jerk town upstate and said you might be in."

"Joan's a smart girl. Did she say how things were going at the mission? She's teaching catechism today."

"She said to tell you everything's fine and your housekeeper is treating her like a long-lost daughter."

"I knew they'd get along."

"I hear you're going to help me crack this thing wide open. Tell me how I can help you," Ryan said with a booming confidence and aggressiveness that made Vincent wish Ryan were the district attorney.

He related his reaction to the visit with Lorenzo in the death house and told him of his call on the D.A.

"I'm convinced the boy is innocent of the murder," Vincent said, "just as I presume you are. And the district attorney looks like a man who's doing a big cover-up job for someone and at the same time making himself look like a knight in shining armor before the general public."

"You've got the package," Ryan said, beckoning to the brief. "I've just been rereading the minutes of the trial. The appeal will be a waste of time without new evidence."

"Precisely," Vincent said. "We've got to help the police—and there must be some honest policemen in this town—we've got to help them find this Ziggy and Silkshirt combine."

"If they're not dead," Ryan said. "What do you suggest?"

Vincent told him of his plan to go into the area in old clothes that very afternoon and do some snooping around.

"I've done the same thing already myself," Ryan said, "but it won't hurt to try it again. If they're not dead, they're still in hiding in the Division 6 area. That's where Big Al's patronage is heaviest. You've probably heard that Captain Hardy does pretty much what he's told. Hardy isn't called the 'richest cop in the world' for nothing."

"Isn't there someone we could contact there if we located one or both of these witnesses?"

"Yes, there is," Ryan said. "There's a Sergeant Donovan who'd make the pinch for us. Connors has tried to have him transferred for years, but he's been on the force too long and, while he doesn't go bloodhounding against Connors' will, he nonetheless does his duty when confronted with duty. I could call him for you at home during lunch hour. I'll tell him you're going to be in there and to give you full co-operation if you call on him in a hurry."

"That would be fine," Vincent said. "Would he respect the confidence? I don't want the chancery to know too much about this until we can make some headway. They probably know enough already. I'm sure Carroll must have called in and complained about me."

"Donovan's my godfather and an old friend of my dad's. He won't talk."

"Yes, I recall," Vincent said. "Your dad was on the force, wasn't he?"

"He certainly was. For thirty-five years, God rest his soul, and he wouldn't take a salty cracker."

"I recall hearing my father speak of him. He was an honest man."

"There are a lot of them left in this town and we've got to pull some of them together or Lorenzo is going to fry."

Vincent nodded. "You wouldn't want to come along today?"

"I'd like to but couldn't for two good reasons. One, I've got to go to court this afternoon on a tort case. Two, I've been in there already and they'd recognize me. You'll probably want to mosey around the Bellrose Social Club a little. Shoot a game of pool and have a beer. They're coming and going all the time. You should have someone with you, though, who can steer you around. Some teen-age kid, maybe, that knows his way around."

"I thought of just that," Vincent said. "I thought of asking Father Phil Redmond, a seminary classmate of mine, who's a curate at St. Raphael's on Bellrose Avenue. He could probably corral some older boy to take me around."

"Good," Ryan said. "And you'll want to visit the Dumbbell's place on Carrot Street near the railroad yards. That's quite a hangout for the small fry in the mob."

"Dumbbell's on Carrot Street. I'll remember that."

"If you get something hot, call the sergeant or me, Father. I'll be either at Municipal Court or here."

"Very well, Bill. I can get into some old clothes at St. Raphael's. Thanks a lot and keep pitching for Tony. You've got a lot of courage. God bless you."

"God bless you, Father. And good luck."

They shook hands again, and Vincent went out into the hallway. He pressed the elevator buzzer and looked into the cavern of cables, spotting an ascending car down about four floors. The car whined into full view and jolted to a stop.

"Up or down," a familiar voice greeted him as the grated door opened.

"Art . . ."

"Yes, let's get going. I was afraid I'd miss you," Arthur said with a warm smile.

"Art, you shouldn't have come back. I really don't want to involve you," Vincent said, flushing with gratitude as he entered the car.

"West side, please," Wagner said facetiously to the elevator operator.

The car dropped down and down into an abyss of the unknown, caging two young curates in a lions' den more fearsome than Daniel's.

CHAPTER XII

Tackle Rush

"YES, I know who you mean, Father. Jackie Williams, he's the one, the one they call Silkshirt. He's disappeared. He hasn't been seen for weeks."

"That's the one," Vincent said, lacing up a pair of Arthur's tennis shoes in Father Redmond's upper-story rectory room.

Father Redmond had got hold of Nickie Saunders, who, tall, gangly, quick-minded, looked as suited for the role of pool shark as he was for his actual service as head altar boy in St. Raphael's Church on Bellrose Avenue.

Father Redmond, a short, mirthful redhead, prickled by wonderment at the nature and scope of the excursion into neighborhood pool halls planned by his former classmates, now confronted Arthur Wagner, who looked like a playground instructor in gray pants, short-sleeved shirt, and low-cut sneakers.

"You decidedly do not resemble Sherlock Holmes," he said in mock disapproval, "neither of you."

"We'll get the job done," Arthur said, "especially with Nickie here to steer us around."

"Oh," Redmond said almost disdainfully, "Nickie knows all the sporting places in the neighborhood—by observation only, he tells me—an entirely circumspect excuse, diplomatically offered by St. Raphael's head altar boy."

"Honest to Pete, Father," Nickie said, flushing with teen-age earnestness, "the first time I was in the Bellrose Club was with my big brother Stocky. And I've never been to the Dumbbell's, although

I've passed it many times and did a lot of peekin' goin' by. That doesn't mean I don't know most of the guys that go in those places. After all, I either grew up with most of them or went with their young brothers."

"Stop being so self-conscious about pool halls, Nickie," Vincent said, rising and smoothing out the wrinkles in the gray cotton trousers. "And you, too, Father Redmond! You know as well as I do there's nothing wrong with a game of billiards. It's where the pool tables are and who runs them that cause most of the trouble. If I could get a boys' center going in the diocese, I'd have a whole big section filled with pool tables for the kids!"

"That, I believe, Father Sir Galahad," Father Redmond said soberly, "but you'd still have the problem of lice-ridden places like the Bellrose Club and the Dumbbell's."

"There wouldn't be much problem," Vincent answered, "if we could get the future Silkshirts to go play their pool at an organized center."

"Splendid, noble!" Arthur said. "But let's get going before my nerve runs out. After all, we didn't go to a school for Pinkertons; we went to a sweet, pure little seminary. I'm getting more jittery by the minute. Let's get this over with."

"I'm ready," Vincent said. "So, Father Phil, if we sniff out anything, we'll send Nickie back to you on the fly. You'll take care of the rest. Right?"

"Right. As soon as Nickie does the Paul Revere act I'll contact the sergeant and Attorney Ryan."

"That's it. Off we go."

"Godspeed," Father Redmond said. "If none of you shows up, say, by nine tonight, we'll come looking for you. Right?"

"Right," Vincent said. "Thanks for everything, Phil, and see you later."

Father Redmond watched them descend the back stairs of the rectory, seeing them as three striplings in sneakers going out perhaps to toss a football around. He felt at first a pang of terror, then a surge of faith in Nickie's knowledge of the neighborhood and its denizens.

He watched them go, shaking his head and sighing, a little terror, a little confidence.

On Bellrose Avenue now, the three walked lightly amid the clang and the clamor of streetcars, taxis, the cough and the roar of trucks and teamsters plying in and out of the freight yards. The two steeples of the world between them: behind, the red brick spire of Saint Raphael's; ahead, the high, sooty, rectangular sign of the Bellrose Social Club.

"Your brother Stocky won't be in the pool halls today, will he?" Father Vincent asked Nickie.

"Not a chance, Father," Nickie said, "he's gone from Lakeport a long time. He married a girl in Milwaukee and settled down there. Works in the Cudahy plant."

"Good," Vincent said. "You might have too much explaining to do if he were around."

"Carrot Street is down by the railroad yards about one block from here," Nickie explained. "Should we take a turn by the Dumbbell's? Then you'd know where it is if we should get separated or something."

"Yes, let's go by there once," Vincent said. "What do you think, Art?"

Arthur Wagner nodded his agreement. He didn't know what to think. He had Monsignor O'Hara on his mind, thinking the worst— that this was a wild-goose chase—wondering what he could say. Maybe Phil Redmond would go along with them on an alibi. They were helping him check on errant youngsters in the parish, maybe; helping him make a survey of where the fresh kids were hanging out. How did that sound?

"Father Vincent was in town on his day off, Monsignor. We called on Phil Redmond and he had this project going. Just a little survey of where the young parish toughs were hanging out. Pass the butter, Monsignor."

"Down here, Fathers," Nickie said.

They turned left on a short narrow street lined with gloomy railroad tenements, thick with the soot of the engines, thick in the air, thick in the walls and the skin and the souls.

"There's Carrot Street," Nickie said after they had walked a short block. "We turn right here. The Dumbbell's is ahead, and we'll still be moving in the direction of the Bellrose Club."

Ahead, too, was the vast, shimmering steel network of the yards with traffic parked or moving slowly, the freight cars chiming and rattling in an over-all symphony of haulage; the meat, the machinery, lumber, farm produce, oil giving sustenance to a nation, undisturbed, untouched by the barroom and tenement squalor surrounding the yards.

"That's the Dumbbell's," Nickie said, "that crumby two-story shack on the corner."

Vincent saw the place, a double store front with rooms upstairs, the plate-glass windows painted opaque green and the shades tightly drawn in the rented rooms above.

The pool-hall door was open as they passed, the stench of smoke and stale beer wafting out and the hollow clocking of pool balls in the midafternoon somnolence marking a kind of eternity of indolence in rude contrast with the vast and relentless industry of the neighboring plants and yards.

Vincent squinted a look through the strong sunlight and into the shadowy depths of the pool hall but could see only the dim bulbs hanging over the tables and a few shadowy figures leaning against the walls or crouching for a shot.

Rounding the corner, he looked up briefly at the rooms overhead and exchanged quizzical glances with Arthur.

"Might be," Arthur said with a grimace as they moved on toward Bellrose Avenue.

Purgatory must be something like this—or maybe even hell, Arthur thought, sitting on a bench in the Bellrose Social Club, sipping a bottle of ginger ale and watching the shadowy figures of Vincent and Nickie huddling over the green felt under a shaded gray light.

Arthur looked around and saw the others leaning and lounging here in the darkness of midafternoon while the sun blazed down outside and most human beings were engaged in the productive pursuits of the day.

Nickie was pretty good with the cue stick and had already beaten Vincent, who perhaps was too alert concerning who came and went to concentrate on his game.

Nickie said he'd bang his stick three times on the floor if Silkshirt or Ziggy was around the place or happened to come in.

They had taken a good look around the bar downstairs before coming up here to the second floor and the pool hall, but no sign of their quarry.

Nickie was shooting for the eight ball now, crouching patiently and calling the shot for the corner pocket. There were footfalls on the stairs as he shot, and Arthur found himself looking at the entrance to the hall as the eight ball plunked softly into the leather net pocket, assuring Nickie of another win.

A squat dark man in a worn leather jacket appeared at the door and entered. Arthur coughed abruptly and Nickie looked up intently, then shook his head.

"You have a go at him, Art," Vincent said. "He's too slick for me."

Arthur finished his drink, rose, took the cue stick from Vincent.

"I'll take over as the sacrificial lamb if Nickie will answer one question," Arthur said.

"What's that, Father?"

"Who brings you up here now that your brother Stocky is in Milwaukee?"

"Nobody," Nickie said, laughing. "I come up myself. After all, I'm almost seventeen and there's not much to do evenings around here."

"See what I mean?" Vincent said. "Now you can tell the Cardinal why we need recreational facilities for these boys."

"You can tell him yourself," Arthur said, chalking up his cue. "You'll probably be haled before him real soon. Rack 'em up, Nickie."

Nickie racked up the balls, and Arthur broke them well, pocketing the two and the six.

Vincent took to the bench and kept his eyes on the door.

Arthur went for the one ball and missed a side-pocket shot.

"There's lots of room for you to sit down here," Vincent said. "Nickie will take over now."

And he did. He set about cleaning the balls off the table methodically until the footfalls sounded on the staircase again.

This time a tall young man appeared in the shadows of the doorway. His shirt collar was up and it could have been silk. He paused, drawing on a cigarette, looking the place over. His eyes fell on the strangers, taking in also the familiar figure of Nickie, and he was quickly gone.

Nickie thumped his stick three times.

"Silkshirt?" Wagner asked, squeezing the question out of a taut throat.

"That's him," Nickie said. "Let's go."

They clattered the cue sticks on the table. Vincent tossed a half dollar on the felt surface, and they were after him.

Vincent caught up with the other two at the bottom of the stairs and saw Silkshirt flash for an instant in the sunburst of a quickly opened door.

He ran through the bar, bumping an old man and knocking down a chair; he was at the door and out as Silkshirt rounded the corner toward the yards.

Thank God for the sneakers, he thought as he cut sharply to the right, hearing the running and shouts behind him and the quick patter almost faintly before him.

The street was a dead end now, with a high brick fence dividing it from the railroad yards. He saw Silkshirt gain the top of the fence with a leap, and he knew he'd have to do the same.

He ran easily now, puffing, and hoping for that second wind. Silkshirt must be puffing, too, he told himself; easy now, save what's left for later.

Now the wall, and springing without breaking stride. The tiled wall top seared both his arms, but he had it and hung on, swinging his legs up and over.

Silkshirt was already on the tracks, running across to an armada of parked freight cars.

It was a long drop down from the wall where a breastworks of wooden ties and packed earth sustained the wall at the lower depth of the railroad bed. If he leaped he might sprain an ankle. He'd have to hang down as Silkshirt had probably done. He turned and looked back, seeing Arthur and Nickie rounding the corner into the dead-end street.

"You and Nickie go get the cops!" he yelled. "I'm going after him."

Twisting to hang down the sharp drop to the inclined tiles, he saw Wagner wave and stop Nickie in full flight.

He dropped and broke his fall with his hands, landing luckily in the packed black dust between the railroad ties. He scrambled on hands and knees, ape-fashion, down the slant of the ties and was running again across the wide network of tracks.

Silkshirt was nowhere in sight, but he must have ducked through where a yellow freight car was the only one uncoupled in the first long line of cars.

He got to the freight car and slowed to a walk, knowing that speed was no longer the advantage. Now the jungle of freight cars, he knew, the stalker and the stalked.

"Silkshirt!" he called, stooping under the next line of cars, searching and calling. "Silkshirt, I'm a Catholic priest. We won't do you any harm. We just want you to talk to the police. Silkshirt, do you hear me? I'm a priest! It's a matter of life or death. We must talk to you."

No answer. The strumming of cars moving far down the line, the rattle and the chiming, then the stitch of a cricket on some grassy siding amid the rutty, oppressive heat of the ties and the rails.

"Silkshirt! Where are you?" Vincent called. "We've got to hear your story. An innocent man may go to the chair if you don't talk."

No answer. He determined now to check the open cars. He looked far down the line to the right and the left. He could see one far to the left, the door half open with wisps of hay awry on the floor. Silkshirt wouldn't have had time to make that one. He ducked under a coupling on the next row of cars and heard the squeak of a sliding door in the row ahead.

What to do? Silkshirt could slip out on the other side. Better to duck under the next row and perhaps catch him coming out. Under a coupling again, out of the hot sun, perspiring and puffing heavily now. No longer the strong-armed pitcher who could run and throw with the best of his age. This was a rugged way to get back in condition. There in the shade of the car which was little less warm than the sunlight, he waited and watched.

Lurking there, his heart pumping heavily with exertion and the sweat rolling and sooty upon his entire body, he breathed a Hail Mary for the success of the pursuit.

Minutes went by, an eternity of minutes. The calling had done no good. He would have to catch him now or pen him in until help came. He wiped the perspiration out of his eyes. The squeaking again, the squeaking and the swinging clatter of a freight-car door.

Silkshirt peeked out, looked to right and left, then leaped from the car directly above Vincent. He saw the long lean legs pistoning by him and threw all his weight upon them in a flying tackle from his squatting position.

"Lemme go! Lemme go!" Silkshirt squealed, flailing Vincent's head with his fists. "I ain't done nothin'—lemme go!"

Vincent was up and on him now, pinning his shoulders down and straddling him with his knees.

"Calm down, son, calm down," Vincent gasped. "I'm a priest, I won't hurt you."

"You're a goddamn liar!" Silkshirt said, writhing like a beached trout and with the great round tears of youth in terror welling in his eyes.

"Calm down, son, calm down," Vincent said, pinning his shoulders and arms even stronger now. "The cops won't harm you—on my word. They just want to ask you some questions. You must believe me."

He looked down into the weak, dissipated, yet handsome face and saw what he thought was submission there, submission and tears and tension breaking.

"Calm down now, son, and I'll let you up," Vincent said.

"Okay, Father, okay," Silkshirt said, going inert under his grip. "Let me up. I'll do anything you say."

Vincent relaxed his grip but retained an authority of pressure. "I'll let you up right now if you'll come over to the stationhouse with me. You know you're wanted as a witness in the Lorenzo case, don't you?"

"Yes, Father," Silkshirt said limply. "Just let me up. I'll go with you."

Vincent stood up, reached him a hand, and yanked him to his feet.

"See *you* later!" Silkshirt snorted, bolting out of the priest's relaxed grip and breaking into a sprint.

"Hey!" Vincent yelled, but wasted no time in taking off after him.

Silkshirt loped steadily now, across a wide cinder area away from the tracks and in the direction of several warehouses and a series of alleys. Vincent knew he'd have to catch him before he reached the warehouses, where Silkshirt could conceal himself and work his way out to the street.

He was a fool to trust him, he thought, puffing but settling into a stride that at least did not lose him any ground. He gave a quick glance to right and left. No sign of Arthur, Nickie, and the police.

Silkshirt was puffing, too, and the priest began closing in on him. One more tackle, one more. But, oh, those cinders.

Closer now, closer. He pumped his elbows and legs harder, feeling a flash of flame inside his chest. He leaped, caught Silkshirt's ankles for an instant. His hands slipped to the raspy kiss of the cinders.

Silkshirt was down, and Vincent was on him again, all over him, pinning him safe with knees and hands.

"This time you'll stay right here until the police come, Mister

Fleet-feet!" Vincent said, spitting the acrid cinder dust from his mouth and gagging strongly at the pit of his stomach.

"Okay, Father, anything you say," Silkshirt said, sobbing in uncontrollable gulps which seemed to rise in waves from his chest.

He straddled the boy, panting and heaving, for what seemed like a long time. He heard the low moan of a police-car siren and sighed with profound relief.

BOOK THREE

The Red Necktie

CHAPTER XIII

Time Passes

". . . To PLACE in nomination . . ."

The radio horns were blaring outside the cigar store beneath the second-story suite of rooms called the Christian Youth Center. There were multiple noonday knots of people gathered there at the corner of Alleghany and Senate streets as Father Vincent paused, fascinated, before ascending the stairs to his youth-center office.

All across the nation people were standing near the loud-speaker horns, cocking their heads intently in a wryly independent native American manner, more of them around loud-speakers in cigar stores, radio shops, and barber emporiums than in their own homes. For radios with loud-speakers were still a comparative luxury in 1928.

" . . . the man in the brown derby, Alfred E. Smith, governor of the great Empire State of New York . . ."

Father Vincent stepped back from the youth-center entrance, relaxed, folded his arms, leaned against the entry wall, and pleasantly resigned himself to a respite from the fund-raising and housekeeping problems of his office upstairs.

He thought of his father, recalling his passionate devotion to his duties as a regular Lakeport delegate to his party's national convention. How he would have enjoyed this moment—Al Smith, a Roman Catholic, being nominated for President.

And the fine, open normalcy of the atmosphere at the convention this year: "Bring Back Prosperity! We Want Beer!"

It intrigued Vincent to think that Smith, if elected, would repeal the Volstead Act and thus deal a knockout blow to the racketeer brewers and vendors of rotgut whiskey.

It was hard for a clergyman to say it publicly—even though Vincent felt he would not hesitate to do so—but there was just as much beer and whiskey available under Prohibition as previously. But now most of it was inferior, much of it actually poisonous, and it was often consumed to the staccato accompaniment of Chicago "pianos."

He knew this fact of life more intimately because of his association with Tony Lorenzo, but it was just as obvious to any citizen in any large city or town in America who read the daily newspapers or slipped into a speakeasy for a drink.

Through the swinging doors now, the rhythmic tattoo of a punching bag, the hollow clock of billiard balls filling his ears. There were about twenty teen-age boys in the gym taking conditioning exercises and sparring around. At the two pool tables in a walled-off corner six young men were plying their cues. There was no fast money here, no silk shirts, no beer, no wisecracking adulation of the hoods. They were boys being boys in this cool, converted second-story suite of rooms, out of the swelter and monotony of big-city streets in the dead of summer.

"Hi-ya, Father Vincent!" a rapierlike colored youth hallooed, pausing at the punching bag and shimmying the sweat from his glistening torso. Vincent waved amiably in acknowledgment of the barrage of halloos and salutes set off by the bag puncher.

The colored boy was Bicky Brown, a gifted young athlete from the south side whom Father Arthur Wagner had sent to the center. There was no question of his acceptability in Vincent's mind, but he had hesitated because of the predominance of white boys from the rest of town. But Arthur had urged him to take Bicky in right at the start.

"Let people know what the guiding principle of your center is without labeling it. The center is for all boys, right?" Arthur had importuned. "Then get off on the right foot. Take in the colored, too; take in Bicky Brown. He'll win a lot of amateur fights for the center boxing teams. Then, later, you can take in more colored fellows."

"Look," Vincent had countered. "I'm very sympathetic, but I've got to get this center off the ground first. And don't be trying to make a liberal out of me, a great bleeding heart for the new masses, like yourself. I'm for the old masses and mostly for the Mass. I'm for the old parish spirit on this subject; we've got to go along with Vinegar Jack on this problem and take things slowly, gradually."

When the boys showed up for their first program of training for the boxing team, Bicky Brown had been among them, isolated, resented by the others, but game and with a trusting look in his eyes.

Before turning them over to Kenney O'Byrne, the boxing coach, who was nervously looking to Vincent for guidance, the priest gave a little talk on the true meaning of the center. His theme was brotherhood and in complete recognition of Arthur Wagner's position. He had centered his talk around Bicky Brown and his equality as a dignified human being in the eyes of God.

"Besides," Vincent had concluded with a smile, "Bicky's just about ready to take on anybody who aspires to represent the center in the welterweight class. That right, Bicky?"

"That's right, Father," Bicky had answered, flashing a stunning white smile out of his inky features.

"Okay, step right up," Father Vincent had challenged amid general laughter. "Who's going in there with Bicky first? You take over, Coach O'Byrne!"

There had been several rugged specimens from the west side ready to try their mettle with Bicky, and the program was on.

Later Arthur, whose temporary estrangement had been quite calculated, informed Vincent with elation that a new star of the liberal outlook had risen over Lakeport.

"Yes, the star has risen," Vincent had agreed glumly, "but the center may fall. Who's going to kick in with the money now? All these conservative businessmen downtown here will be afraid I'm going to try to marry their fashionable daughters off to Negroes and all that malarkey."

"I'll get you the money through the archdiocesan newspaper," Arthur had reassured him. "Just keep operating on the idea that the center is both a profoundly Christian and American institution. It's for all the kids, no matter what their background—right?"

"Right."

"You'll have so much money coming in eventually that the Cardinal will be tapping your funds for other projects. They'll make you a monsignor in self-defense."

"Stop talking about the money and bring some of it in here. You can start right now." Vincent had held up an invoice. "Here's an equipment bill from Spalding's for six hundred dollars."

Walking down the long corridor to his office, he reflected, too, as he had so many times during the past five years, on the vision and generosity of Cardinal Wagner, who had assigned him permanently to youth work in Lakeport after the Lorenzo case had broken wide open. The capture of Silkshirt, then Ziggy, and their inevitable testimony concerning the accidental nature of Dapper Dan Lubell's death had obtained first a stay of execution, then a reprieve for Tony Lorenzo.

Two new trials had eventuated, one for Lorenzo, culminating in a ten-year sentence for manslaughter, the other trial exposing District Attorney Carroll's connivance with the mob and sending him behind the same bars with Lorenzo for malfeasance in office.

It was then that the Cardinal had ordered Father Vincent in from the Tri-State Valley to his assignment in youth work throughout the archdiocese.

He entered his office, and Joan Linehan was there at her desk, perusing a telegram raptly and, obviously, for the third or fourth time. There was a hint of roses in the natural pallor of her features which indicated that this was happy news.

"Remember what I told you, Joan," he said, breaking in on her. "If we could read all correspondence the way we read love letters, no meanings or implications would ever be lost."

"Father!" Joan said, the tea roses in her pale cheeks heightened with both fright and surprise, "this is no ordinary telegram. They're letting him out on parole, Father Vincent, do you understand? Tony's going to be free—free!"

"I do understand," Vincent said, "and I'm most happy. I must confess that I knew a parole was in the works. Bill Ryan told me there was a good chance that Tony might get four or five years off for good behavior. I hadn't intended to buoy up your hopes until I had more definite information."

"Well, nothing could be more definite than this," Joan said, waving the wire. "He was paroled yesterday. He'll be in on the seven forty-five tonight."

"That soon! Marvelous!" Vincent said. "I'd love to meet him at the station, darn it, but the Cardinal is calling department heads together tonight. There'll be a big ado about how much we can spend and where we'll get it for the coming year. But that shouldn't stop you from leaving here right now. Get going, go buy a new hat or something, get out of here!"

"Now?" Joan said, glancing at her watch.

"Now!" Vincent said. "Get going! And tell Tony to come around and see me as soon as he can. I'm dying to see him."

"Oh, Father," Joan said, rising, "I could kiss you!"

"If you weren't an Irish-Catholic puritan you probably would. Tell Rita at the switchboard to shoot all the calls in on my private line."

"I'll do that," Joan said, grabbing her hat and bag from the bottom drawer of her desk. "See you tomorrow, Father, I've got a real heavy date."

He watched her go, the footsteps fading and being gradually supplanted with the thud of a basketball, the sock-sock of billiard balls, the tap dance of feet on canvas.

He thought of Tony trying to get a job, an ex-con, a former inmate of the death house, an underling of Big Al. And Joan in the picture, sweet, good, deathlessly loyal.

"God help them!" he whispered, sighing and pushing through a small, wooden gate to his inner office.

At his desk he wrote a note to himself as a memo to call Father Arthur Wagner at four-thirty to learn where they were to have dinner. Monsignor Bob Lambert was to be in town as guest speaker at the department heads' conference and was going to have a dinner with his former seminary roommates.

Monsignor Lambert! It hadn't taken him too long, a papal chamberlain in his thirties. "Just an old bookworming roommate with a sharp eye for birds!" Vincent had exclaimed when they received the word of his papal appointment. "Especially cardinals!" Art Wagner had added tartly.

Vincent hadn't seen Lambert for over ten years, but the word from the Harbourton diocese up on the lake was that he had done a brilliant job as secretary to the chancery, and his papal designation was no great surprise.

Now after ten years to see him, the tall, lean Lambert, a bird watcher not only in inclination but in physical aspect. Would he have grown stout now? Hardly, not with that bony nature, not with all that alertness and guile.

Time passes, time passes . . . Vincent reflected mellowly. Tony out of jail, the youth center a reality, a Roman Catholic running for President, Bob Lambert a monsignor, and Arthur Wagner editor in chief of the archdiocesan newspaper, *The Clarion*.

Time passes, time passes . . . and within, Vincent knew, we are the same. The same dreams, schemes, longings, frailties, and strength. Time passes, but we are still the same. At twenty the same, at thirty, sixty, eighty—the same drives and dreams, the same unique soul God made.

He glanced again at the memo reminding him to call Art Wagner. And thinking of Wagner as new editor of the archdiocesan weekly newspaper, he could not resist a smile.

Arthur had set about to transform *The Clarion* completely and abruptly since he had become editor less than a year ago. Formerly the paper had been variously referred to as "The Diocesan Fly Swatter" and "The Cardinal's Bulletin Board."

The smile became a chuckle as Vincent thought of Arthur's first crusading editorial which only the Cardinal's nephew could have printed without being shipped bag and baggage to the Tri-State Valley.

"Everybody loves the Pope but nobody listens to him . . ."

Arthur, brimming with social and political ideas gleaned during his long sojourn in Rome, had become a passionate advocate of former Pope Leo XIII's encyclical on the rights of the laboring man, *Rerum Novarum*. He had reorganized and restyled the stuffy, pious old weekly within a fortnight after assuming chief editorial responsibilities.

He had ripped out the old "Ball and the Cross" banner and substituted a cut of the Holy Father reading one of his encyclicals to a mass of people. Underneath the banner was the New Testament quotation: "Be ye doers of the Word and not hearers only."

"Readers of this publication must be doers of the Word, not just hearers," Father Wagner had declared in his maiden editorial, which he published in boldface type on the front page of the weekly. "Being doers of the Word, we suggest, also means heeding the words of the Holy Father in his papal encyclicals. For is not His Holiness, Pius XI, the official interpreter of the Word of God for many millions of Christians throughout the world?

"Let us also, then, be doers of the Holy Father's words of advice through his and his predecessors' great encyclicals on the social order, the liturgy, and all matters that affect our religious life.

"We must help, by editorial and journalistic exposition, to emphasize the practical value of the Pope's written and oral utterances and to reiterate that the Word of God is for doers, not hearers only.

With the Cardinal Archbishop's approval and counsel, this, then, will be the editorial policy of *The Clarion* as long as I am editor."

"He won't be editor long!" Vinegar Jack Regan had cackled when Vincent had last seen him. "Nephew or no nephew, he'll be out in the bushes with the cows once His Eminence ties onto the kind of bolshevistic nonsense his brother's son is dishing out!"

Vincent had changed the subject to a plea for some co-operation from Vinegar Jack on his youth program, which he wasn't getting from his irate former pastor.

"I promised the Cardinal I'd help you and I will."

"All we want is the collection at one Sunday Mass. That was the Cardinal's specification, I believe," Vincent reminded him coolly.

"Would ye preach at the six-fifteen?" Vinegar Jack retorted impishly.

Vincent smiled wanly. "Father Regan, you know very well there's only a handful of old widows and night workers at the six-fifteen—even on Sunday."

"It all depends," Vinegar Jack snapped. "I think I know my own parish better than some that hardly had time to unpack here. In the summer months ye'd get a good piece of the crowd that leaves early for the beaches."

"Very well," Vincent countered quickly. "I'll take the six-fifteen on Labor Day if it's available."

" 'Twould bring you in a good hunk," Vinegar Jack agreed, involuntarily impressed by Vincent's astuteness. "I'll look into it and drop you a line. But ye'd better tell your brave writer friend to stop stuffing the Holy Father down our necks or he won't sell a paper around here. We revere the Pope greatly, but we don't need a whippersnapper to be telling us the meaning of what he says. We have eyes to read ourselves, and *The Clarion* could use some news of our whist parties and building-fund drives instead of all that blather about labor unions and changing the world overnight."

"I suggest you tell Father Wagner himself," Vincent had said, reaching for his hat. "Good afternoon, Father Regan."

Behind Vincent now in his office at the center, he heard the clash of a mop and pail. That would be Stringbean Lincoln, the lank, shuffling darkie who did janitor work around the center. The door at his back separated him from the locker room, beyond which were the showers and a short-cut entrance to the gymnasium.

Kenney O'Byrne, his gym instructor might be in his office now.

Vincent glanced at the latest bill from Spalding's and decided to show it to O'Byrne. There was that new punching-bag item and new velvet sleeves for the ropes around the ring. Was that latter necessary?

He rose and unsnapped the lock on the door leading to the gym.

"Good afternoon, Stringbean," he said, entering the locker room.

"Yassuh, Father Vincent." Stringbean looked up from the pail with a grin.

"Is Kenney in his office?"

"Ah b'leeve he's in the ring with the boys."

Father Vincent continued on to Kenney's office, deciding to leave the bill on his desk with a note for Kenney to drop by later. He hurried through the lockers to the rubbing room, where Kenney had a desk in the corner. The sweet and astringent smells of mint and liniment filled his nostrils.

Above Kenney's desk he noticed a gallery of glossy pictures featuring Kenney, who was a real camera bug, with various sports celebrities who had visited the center. Under each picture was a green ink scrawl expressing various and intimate thoughts which linked the celebrities with Kenney. And they were all in the same handwriting.

The vast, puckish blandness of Babe Ruth's profile beamed out of one shot in which Kenney had managed to squeeze between Babe and Father Vincent. Underneath this picture the inscription read: "I understand that when you were light heavy champ of the 3rd Fleet, Kenney, you didn't have much time for baseball. But you still look like you could hit a baseball a mile. Always your friend—The Babe!"

Kenney had been a successful boxer in the Navy during the war and was now communicating this skill to the boys in the center. He was still a little punchy, but he loved children and was a good trainer as well as an instructor.

Vincent had noticed the "forgeries" before and found them highly amusing. He glanced at another one: Knute Rockne with his arm around Kenney and the inscription beneath: "To one of the greatest competitors I've ever known."

Though amused by Kenney's publicity hunger, Vincent was irked by the ease with which he ordered expensive equipment for the gym. Raising money for the center was an increasingly difficult problem, and he resolved to talk seriously to Arthur about his offer of help through *The Clarion*. Which reminded him, he'd have to call Arthur right away.

He hastily scrawled a note to Kenney and left the athletic-equipment invoice with it. As he was leaving for his office he glanced up at the self-adulation department of the great Kenney O'Byrne.

Under a picture of the Cardinal and Kenney was the following epitaph forged in Kenney's deft sweeping hand: "Blessings to Kenney O'Byrne, a noble son of the Church—His Eminence, Arthur Cardinal Wagner."

Father Vincent shook his head and quelled the wild surge of mirth within him as he walked toward his office and the telephone.

CHAPTER XIV

The Making of a Monsignor

AT THE department heads' meeting in the Hotel Urban everybody wore a name tag but nobody read the names. The priest delegates had all gone to school with each other or had served together in the parishes, and at such a gathering the phrase, "I didn't get the name," was a joke, and a bad one at that.

In the middle of the room, in the informal pattern of folding chairs, Vincent sat with Arthur, intent on what the panel was discussing from the platform. Monsignor Lambert had the floor and was commenting on mixed marriages.

Cardinal Wagner presided with the astonishing simplicity that certain public figures can maintain despite the ornate trappings of their official attire. Blighted by the wearing williwaws of his seventy-odd years, yet still lean and alert with the handsome hawkishness of a medieval Roman prince, he slumped somewhat against the broad-backed brocade armchair and with chin cupped leisurely in hand drew in the measured words of the young Monsignor from the up-state Harbourton diocese.

Arthur nudged Vincent as their former seminary roommate spoke. "Unk is really giving him the once-over."

"Yes, and he loves it," Vincent whispered. "Remember the bird-watching performance he gave at the sem for no less than the Papal Delegate?"

"I remember," Arthur acknowledged softly. "Now the bird is watching him—the hawk, I mean."

The young Monsignor continued his discourse, his face fuller, touched with the rich red sustenance of the Bishop's table, the darting alertness in his manner having given way to ease, calmly exuding a confidence that he was well on his way to the top of the ladder.

"I do not think we are overly rigorous in insisting that marital ceremonies between Catholics and those of other religions be denied the sacramental surroundings of our churches. Requiring mixed couples to take their vows in the parlors of our rectories has a salutary effect on both parties as well as a preventive effect on others of our brethren who might be contemplating a union with one of another faith. It is obvious to all of us that Holy Mother Church discourages mixed marriages because of the inherent dangers to the religious faith of both the Catholic participant and the offspring of the mixed marriage."

He paused and coughed modestly, touching his lips with immaculate fingers that Vincent thought might have been worked on by the hotel manicurist.

"The pledge of the non-Catholic party to co-operate in rearing the offspring in the Catholic faith is too often looked on as temporary expedience. I say, since the spirit of the Church is to discourage such marriages, we should continue to maintain the atmosphere of discouragement—namely, the rectory parlor as the necessarily cold locale of the ceremony."

The Cardinal languidly lifted his chin and nodded slowly. There was little need to nod among the other members of the panel and in the audience. What Monsignor Lambert had stated was a fresh presentation of established policy in the dioceses of America.

Lambert bowed politely to the Cardinal and took his seat.

"Very apt, very apt," the Cardinal muttered in tones hardly discernible to the audience. Then louder: "Is there any further comment from the panel?"

The panel, consisting of three rotund, sleepy-eyed clerics in various stages of middle age, conveyed their willingness to curtail the discussion with consecutive smirks, shrugs, and archings of the eyebrows.

It was not hard for Vincent to discern that all three of them had had other plans for their weekly day off before the panel summons came from the chancery office. Officiating at mixed marriages was quite a regular routine to them, and they emitted no icy blasts at the principals even though the vows were taken in the rectory. The simple truth was, Vincent knew, that rectory parlors were a lot better heated in wintertime than were the sacred confines of the sanctuary, if one wanted to get literal. But Vincent was irked at Bob Lambert's tone of intolerance—even though his position was a respectable one.

"'The atmosphere of discouragement,'" Vincent repeated glumly to Arthur. "He sounds like the Grand Inquisitor."

"Why don't you get up and protest?" Arthur urged. "Wake this joint up! It would give them all an appetite for dinner."

"I just might," Vincent said.

The Cardinal, alert to their whispered restlessness and himself torn between mirth and miff at the somnolence of the panel members, cast his line out into the audience.

"Do the two young fathers in the middle of the hall have a contribution to make? Even if it is a considered opinion on the Lakeport Blue Sox it would help at this point."

Laughter warmed the chamber and eased Vincent's tension, which had risen from his resolve to counter Lambert's high-handed presentation of an established policy.

"Go get him, Vin," Arthur hissed.

Vincent got to his feet, gripped the folding chair in front of him with both hands until his knuckles went white, cleared his throat, and began to speak.

"It is not in the spirit of criticism of my accomplished classmate, Monsignor Lambert, that I rise to speak. But rather in the spirit of charity.

"Although the diocesan regulations require at present that mixed marriages take place in the rectory rather than in the church, I beg to remind the panel that this is a local, a predominantly American regulation; it is hardly an ex-cathedra pronouncement of the Holy Father, nor is it integral to the deposit of the Faith, if I may hazard that opinion.

"As a matter of fact, I would dare to suggest that bringing these mixed couples into the church for the wedding ceremony is closer to the spirit of Catholicism than keeping them out."

Vincent paused, clearing his throat again. The panel was prickling with life now. Monsignor Lambert's features had gone completely white with mingled rage and surprise. Cardinal Wagner leaned forward, his chin cupped again in his hands and a half-smile of amusement on his face.

"Let us not forget that the parable of the Good Samaritan is a permanent item in the deposit of Faith. Christ Himself sent his

Apostles to the gentiles. And we are apostles to those outside the Faith just as surely as the original twelve.

"America, with its peculiar and numerous native Protestant religions, perhaps is not ready for the full application of this spirit to the mixed-marriage ceremony. But the Church and our physical churches are a home to all men, because Christ is there incarnate in the Blessed Sacrament, and we cannot, in good faith, emphasize an exclusive mixed-marriage policy too strongly!"

All eyes were on Monsignor Lambert now, including the cool, intent gaze of the Cardinal. There was no more cat-napping on the part of the clergy sitting on the panel with Lambert; gone temporarily, at least, were the daydreams of getting in a good hotel dinner before the waning of the day off and the early rising in the morning for six more days of routine parish duties with tough beef and boiled cabbage waiting in the rectory dining room.

Lambert rose, taut before his old adversary of seminary days, nodded gracefully at the Cardinal, saying with steely politeness: "If I may, Your Eminence?"

The Cardinal nodded, unable to conceal a thin smile of delight as he savored the turn of events which had inflamed the wooden texture of the entire panel performance.

"By all means, Monsignor."

"I should like first to thank my old seminary roommate, Father Whelton, for emphasizing the Pauline counsel of charity as being important above all things. But as Father Whelton has so astutely recognized, the American church is still relatively a missionary church in a predominantly Protestant nation, and our cautions against mixed marriage and the dangers to the nurture of the Catholic faith among the offspring of such marriages are all too obvious. We must certainly be charitable, but the practical restriction of mixed marriages to the rectory is a caution to our young people. For certainly there are enough available young Catholics of marriageable age, and we must encourage our young to marry their own kind."

"Very well said." The Cardinal nodded. "An afterthought, Father Whelton?"

"Only that I agree substantially with Monsignor Lambert on things that seem rather obvious to me. We have always had mixed marriages and undoubtedly always will. I still think we should warm them with a little more welcome in the spirit of Christ and the Church."

Vincent took his seat, and Arthur elbowed him in the ribs with vigorous affection. "That's my boy—hold your ground!" he whispered.

"Mmmmmmm!" the Cardinal said, clearing his throat for comment. "P'raps you're right, although present policy seems to be in Monsignor Lambert's favor. I like your emphasis on the spirit of Christ and the Church in these matters, Father Whelton. It is all too easy to just go along with authority." He paused and eyed the members of the panel sardonically. "Christ did send the apostles to teach *all* nations—a priest is a priest for all men. There is no question about it, and there never will be in the mind of the Church.

"This has all been most stimulating. Let us thank both these young men for seizing the heart of the issue and worrying it about. I think we'll have more of these panels in the future, and I do hope that Monsignor Lambert will come back soon again. Let us pray."

The entire assemblage followed the Cardinal's recitation of the Our Father, the Hail Mary, and the terminal "Glory be to the Father and to the Son and to the Holy Ghost. As it was in the beginning, is now, and ever shall be. World without end. Amen."

When the closing prayer was over, Vincent wondered if Monsignor Lambert would still be well disposed to dine with his former seminary roommates. It had not taken him long to sidle over beside the Cardinal. But that was normal enough. He was the only other Monsignor present besides the Cardinal's aide, the rubicund, bald Monsignor O'Hara now making his way through the knots of chatting clerics among the disarranged folding chairs—the same who had berated Vincent for visiting District Attorney Carroll.

"Do you think he'll still have dinner with us?" Vincent asked.

"Of course he will," Arthur said with a wry smile. "Just because you threw a javelin at your old roommate, don't think you wounded him mortally. Your independence impressed Unk; thus Lambert is de facto impressed. I know him well. He'll join us, feed with us, feed on us, and use what he can back in Harbourton to help boost himself up the ladder."

"Why does there always have to be that kind of a ladder?" Vincent mused. "After all, there's really only one ladder that amounts to anything—Jacob's."

"You poor boy!" Arthur said. "You'd still be out in the Tri-State

Valley presiding at the birth of peasants and Hereford cattle if you hadn't brought a certain corrupt district attorney to an accounting. You got hold of a ladder that led to your present assignment in youth work, did you not?"

"Maybe I did," Vincent conceded, "but that wasn't my primary objective."

"Truly, truly!" Arthur cooed. "But I've got to get some news for the paper and say hello to Unk before he leaves, if the good Monsignor will let me get a word in edgewise! Don't run away, we'll get to dine with that man in the red necktie yet!"

"I'll be here," Vincent said, looking over Arthur's shoulder and sensing that Monsignor O'Hara was seeking him out.

Arthur was up on the platform taking notes from the panel members when Monsignor O'Hara spoke to Vincent.

"Father Whelton, His Eminence wants to see you in Parlor B. He'll visit you there on his way out of the hall."

"Thank you, Monsignor."

Monsignor O'Hara nodded coolly. He had not forgotten, nor would he ever forget, Vincent sensed, his impertinence in smelling out the district attorney scandal. Was he still a friend of Carroll's as he mildewed away in the state penitentiary? Perhaps the doughty old Monsignor was still Carroll's friend. And perhaps now, Vincent thought with a pang of charity for both, perhaps now he was a friend to Carroll as he never could have been before, a priest who could console the mighty brought low. "I was in prison, and you came to me . . ."

And now the Cardinal wanted to see him. About what? The budget, of course. The youth program was costing the Lakeport diocese too much money. Fifteen thousand a year from the Cardinal's office and whatever he could beg from the parishes by preaching annually at a series of masses. Was it that fifteen thousand was too much? Perhaps the Cardinal thought so or had been led to believe so.

Vincent, walking toward Parlor B in the hallway, panicked for an instant. Perhaps Vinegar Jack or even Monsignor O'Hara had convinced His Eminence that the athletic budget should be split up among individual parishes.

"But the parish priests haven't the time for these kids," Vincent could hear himself arguing. "And eventually we'll be able to train leaders to go out into the parishes and perform that function for the pastors. But we've got to learn the problem in one central point, a clinic, a laboratory, Your Eminence. All we need is time, Your Eminence. We're learning, we're growing, all we need is your continued generosity and time, time, time . . ."

He entered Parlor B, took a chair and waited, clearing his throat with nervousness and shifting his feet.

What else could he tell the Cardinal? Income, that was it, ways and means to raise money. No matter how holy or generous, that was what American bishops needed most: money coming in, and plenty of it—without strings attached.

He could tell him about his plans for an annual boxing tournament to which he hoped to attract at least ten thousand people in the Lakeport indoor stadium. Kenney O'Byrne had about twenty young boxers ready to go as the CYC team, and there would be many other clubs throughout the city and state eager to enter such an event. It could clear five or six thousand dollars and cut down the appropriation by that sum.

He was ready with all these arguments, tense and nervous but ready, when the Cardinal rounded the corner, followed by Arthur and Monsignor O'Hara.

Vincent went down on his right knee and kissed the Cardinal's ring.

"Get up, get up, Father Whelton," the Cardinal said. "This must be brief. I'm already late for an appointment."

He rose just in time to catch a wink from Arthur, who was standing by the door behind stern, roseate Monsignor O'Hara.

"I liked the way you spoke up at the panel meeting. You gave it life, you and—ahem—Monsignor Lambert. You'd better do more of these things for me—speaking things, that is. I get terribly exhausted going about to ceremonies, and Monsignor O'Hara isn't getting any younger either. I want you to take a desk at the chancery office and be available afternoons and sometimes in the evening. You'll have to do some appearing and talking for me here and there."

"Monsignor will arrange a desk for you, eh, Monsignor?"

"Yes, Your Eminence."

"But—but, Your Eminence," Vincent sputtered, "begging your pardon, sir, the youth center . . ."

The Cardinal gestured casually, his hand heavy with the rubied signet ring of his office. "Oh yes, the center, Father Whelton. You're doing good work over there, I hear; giving the colored folks a sense of belonging and all. Keep it going, keep it going, but see that you're available for me in the afternoons and on occasion in the evening."

"Yes, Your Eminence, thank you, Your Eminence . . ."

The Cardinal gave a small flourish of his jeweled hand, turned, and headed for the door. He paused at the exit, turned, and with a mischievous twinkle in his eye said:

"And from now on, let me handle the district attorney!"

"Yes, Your Eminence," Vincent said, dizzy with surprise and joy.

CHAPTER XV

The Ghost of Lucy Walks

"How can I handle it?" Father Vincent asked Arthur in bewilderment as they stepped out of the elevator into the staid old lobby of the Urban Hotel. "I mean where will I find time for both the Cardinal's business and the youth center too? Either assignment is a full-time job."

"Don't be thinking of all that," Arthur said impatiently. "Just tackle it. The Cardinal tapped you on the shoulder, didn't he? Be glad you're destiny's tot. Just plunge into it—you'll manage it."

"It's not as easy as that," Vincent said. "I'm just beginning to see the light over at the CYC, and it's been a night-and-day operation of planning, manipulating, and scheming. You probably won't believe me, but I wanted to turn down the Cardinal's request for my services."

"Vincent, Vincent," Arthur said in mock disgust, peering through the revolving doors at the sudden sheets of thin summer rain which were raising clouds of steam from the sun-baked pavements and the lakeside boulevard. "Apparently you don't recognize a command performance. Do you think you'd get adequate co-operation on your youth-center projects if you turned the Cardinal down? You opened your big, eloquent mouth against the solid, careful utterances of Monsignor Lambert and now you're unwilling to go along with the consequences. But don't bother me with that now. We've got to get over to the Senate Hotel for dinner with Lambert. And there isn't a cab in sight."

They pushed through the revolving doors and stood under the

awning as the rain thrummed mightily down on the parched hide of the vast metropolis.

"I've got to drop by the office and check things for a minute. I can pick up an umbrella while I'm there. You take a cab on over to the Senate Hotel and I'll join you both right away."

"But you'll get wet!" Arthur said anxiously, still peering through the rain.

"I'm just a block down the street and there are awnings almost all the way. I've got to see how things are at the gym and in the office."

"All right, Reverend Administrator," Arthur said petulantly. "Don't keep us waiting too long."

"I'll be there," Vincent said, squeezing Arthur's arm and dashing for the next awning, a long one shading a series of fashionable women's shops along the boulevard.

He was anxious to see if there was a message from Joan. She must have met Tony by now and would have called back about it. Perhaps he could see them both for a while after dinner. What would he be like now? What would it have done to him? Five years in a cage, five years in which to resist dry rot and bitterness, five long years.

Now he ducked, running through the rain into a narrow, cobbled alley that snaked in behind the shops and led to the back entrance of the gymnasium. Darting close to the brick walls, he absorbed only a few scattered drops of the steady, shimmering rain. With one jump he was in the back stairway of the youth center and let out a triumphant sigh.

"I made it!" he said aloud, closing the door behind him.

"Yassuh, Parson," said Stringbean Lincoln, who was wringing out a mop in the back hall. "It's a real wet one."

"Oh, Stringbean," Vincent said, pausing on the stairs, "I didn't see you at first. Everything all right upstairs? Is Joan in the office?"

"Yassuh, Parson, she done come in jest a few minutes ago."

"Anybody with her?" he asked, resuming his climb.

"She all alone up there, Parson—ain't nobody in the gym nuther."

"Okay, Stringbean."

All alone. Where was Tony? He quickened his step on the stairs until he reached the second flight and hurried down the hallway to the rear private door to his office.

The door at the other end of his office was closed, but he could hear the sporadic staccato of typing from the outer reception room. He opened the door to the lavatory, hung up his suit coat, washed his face and hands, combed his hair.

The typing stopped completely for several minutes and then resumed, now more sustained. Joan knew he had arrived.

He put on his suit coat, fished out a black umbrella and an old felt hat from the clothes closet next to the washstand, and opened the door to the reception room.

Joan was at her typewriter, a forced, polite smile on her face as he greeted her. Her features were wan and drawn and he could see the reddish eyelids and tracery of tears on her cheeks, now hastily concealed by dabs of powder.

"Joan, you're here," he said gently. "How come? Where's our boy? Where's Tony?"

"Oh, he wanted to be alone," she said with a hurt sigh. "I thought I'd better come back here and type up these financial statements for the chancery office."

"Well, tell me something about him?" Vincent asked. "What's he look like? How is he?"

"Oh, he's thin, a little gray at the temples," she said. "He doesn't say much, Father. I couldn't rouse him out of it. He's bitter and a little cynical. He keeps saying he wants to be alone. So I—well, I—just left him alone."

"Where is he now?"

"Well, I left him in the restaurant at the railroad station. He said he needed a drink. That would mean he might have headed for the Bellrose Social Club. And you know who hangs around there. His old buddies—that's who! It's the one place he shouldn't go to after what he's been through."

"You're right," Vincent said, his features tightening with determination. "I'd better take the chance he'll be there and go talk to him. I have a dinner engagement with my seminary roommates, but this is more important."

Joan's face was alight now with renewed hope.

"Do you think you should see him, Father?" she asked dutifully, almost apprehensive that he would change his mind.

"You know I should, Joan," he said. "Now here's what I want *you* to do. Take five dollars out of the petty-cash box and cab on over to the Senate Hotel. You'll find Father Arthur Wagner and Monsignor Bob Lambert in the dining room there. Tell them I'll be tied up for a while and I want you to be their guest for dinner. Arthur will pay, but it's raining out, you'll need the five dollars for cabs and odds and ends."

"Do you think it will be all right, Father?"

"Of course it will be all right. They'll enjoy you and it will do you good. Tell them I'll be along as soon as I can. Now get going—they're waiting for me."

"Very well, Father," she said, rising, a pretty, blushing smile on her face for the first time since he had returned. "It's so good of you to look after Tony."

"I'll give him a hit on the head if he doesn't snap out of it," Vincent said with mock aggressiveness.

"You'll probably have to."

He went back into his office and sat in a swivel chair for several minutes after she had gone. What to do about Tony? What to do? He'd love to bring him right into the CYC as executive assistant. He had all the ability. He had run the brewery—bootlegging, it was true, but the same administrative office and business problems as any factory, like those of a legitimate brewery, for example. He could bring him in here, but there was no money available for that type of salary.

He'd have to have some job along the organizational line. Labor, maybe . . .

He had read only that morning in the Lakeport *Herald* that the paper workers' union was conducting a city-wide drive to organize giant utility paper-box companies and all the smaller box shops throughout the city. Who would know about contacts? Arthur, of course; he was all fired up with the social-action stuff and had been running stories in the diocesan weekly about the activities of labor unions. He'd talk to Arthur about it later.

First he'd have to find Tony and, if he was drinking, straighten him out. Then maybe they could talk about a job.

He stuffed his pipe with the aromatic contents of a humidor on top of his desk, lit it, signed several letters Joan had placed there for his attention, then picked up the phone and gave the operator the number of the Lakeport Taxi Company.

Through the gym now, where only one colored teen-age boy, a study in pantherish suppleness, was whopping at the big canvas bag.

One colored boy whopping at the bag in the drowsy, sticky summer evening. But that was progress, thank God. And there were more of his race coming to the gym; but, like the white boys, they were off swimming somewhere, seeking relief from the steaming mantle of humidity that had enveloped the city.

"Bicky!" he called, waving, as he crossed the volleyball floor. "How's it coming?"

Bicky paused, steadied the bag with one leather-mittened hand, blinked the sweat out of his eyes, and flashed a smile.

"Very good, Father. I'll be ready."

He meant the CYC team trials in late September, when the "varsity" squad would be picked for inter-city and inter-state ama- teur boxing competition.

"I know you will be, Bick. I'm counting on you to really go places in that welterweight division." He waved again and, proceeding to the swinging doors at the front entrance, paused for a moment and looked back. Bicky was still taking a breather, leaning against the bag and looking at the priest with almost doglike affection. "While I think of it," he called back to Bicky, "have you got soap, clean towels, and bandages?"

"They're all locked up, Father. Kenney's gone swimming with the others. I've got an old towel from yesterday."

"No, no, that won't do at all. I'll go out the back way and catch Stringbean. He's got the keys and will take good care of you."

"Thanks a lot, Father," Bicky said, flashing the sun again from be- hind the black cliff of his face.

The priest waved one last acknowledgment and pushed through the swinging doors. He turned right and went back through the suite of offices again. He noted Joan had gone as he hurried through to the back staircase.

Below, he heard the mop pail knocking and the plaintive sing- ing of Stringbean.

> "Dere's a gal Ah know in Macon,
> Wid eyes like balls of twine,
> Dat wind and wind about me,
> But Ah can't say she's mine . . ."

"Stringbean."

"Yassuh, Rev'ren'!"

"Give Bicky the treatment after he gets through up there. Open up Kenney's locker. Get out some towels, new bandages, liniment.

Give him a rubdown after he showers. Give him the works now. Here's a dollar for the extra trouble."

He stuffed a dollar bill into the bony, white-skinned palm as he hurried out into the alley.

"Yassuh, Rev'ren', yassuh. Good as done, sir, yassuh!"

The rain was still falling steadily as he snapped open his umbrella and hurried down the cobbled alley to the front of the building. The cab was waiting at the main entrance. He jumped in, mentioned the Bellrose Social Club, and was whisked away into the infinite sequined curtains of rain.

At first the cab browsed patiently in the downtown traffic, padding its way toward the viaduct leading to the west side. What to do? What to do? Vincent thought. He won't be drunk, he won't be, the priest told himself. He wants time to think, he wants time to clear his mind for a decision. Joan, however desirable to him, was a decision Tony did not want to face. But women don't understand those things, especially when they're young and living almost wholly on their emotions.

But the Bellrose Social Club wasn't the place for him to be making decisions. It was right across the street from the scene of the shooting which had sent him to prison. And Big Al's boys would be around there, telling him of the latest regrouping, the latest racket scheme. What to do? Just go in there with the collar showing and see if he was there. Sit with him awhile and try to get him out of there quickly. Where to go? Get him a good, clean room and line him up a job. Arthur's mother would have a room for him in her spacious duplex apartment near the cathedral. She gave hospitality to many rectory visitors from out of town. Arthur would persuade her to take Tony in until he could calm down and get his thinking straight. Down Bellrose Avenue now, along through skid row, where it was always a holiday even in the middle of the week. The pool halls with cheap speaks in the rear, the chestnut and hot-dog vendors, the ragged, dejected figures sitting or lying drunk in doorways and under awnings. It always seemed to him an earthly extension of hell where there was no time, just endless hopelessness and night that could hardly be distinguished from day. Even in the pelting rain a few were slumped or reeling on the curbstone, and there welled up in Father Vincent a prayer of both compassion and gratitude, sorrow for the derelicts of city society and gratitude for the chance to head off a few future skid-row denizens through the work of the youth center.

The high vertical sign of the club loomed up a block away. The cabdriver pulled alongside an entrance marked "Billiards."

"Shall I wait, Father?"

"Yes, will you? I'll leave the umbrella here. I shouldn't be too long."

"I'll shut the meter off," the cabdriver, a snub-nosed Irish type, said. "I know you wouldn't be coming out here unless you were trying to help somebody."

"God love you," Vincent said with an involuntary sigh of relief. Unlooked-for kindness in time of trial always had that effect on him—a lifting of weight, a balming of soreness. "I'll see you in fifteen or twenty minutes."

"Check."

Climbing the steep stairs to the billiard hall above the clubhouse chambers, he opened and smoothed out his raincoat lapels so that the Roman collar would be clearly visible. He wanted no shifty looks regarding who he was or what he was seeking. He was a priest, and many of the well-dressed loafers in a place like this were slipshod members of his own church. The hollow clocking of the pool balls brought back stark memories of the successful search he and Arthur had made for Silkshirt. Silkshirt . . . He'd be a grown man now. Where was he? In jail? Here, maybe. Poor Silkshirt blabbing the whole business to the police, a frightened, weak-kneed boy who had thought he could play the role of one of Al's toughest hoods.

He achieved the top landing and rounded the corner to the billiard room. There, under green-shaded hanging lamps, several games were in progress.

The muted hum of conversation ceased, cue sticks froze, and a few rolling balls mocked the silence.

"That's all right, boys," Vincent said strongly, pushing his old black-green felt hat to the back of his head informally, "go right ahead with your games. I'm looking for a friend."

He blinked his eyes, peering through the coils and billows of blue —chalky cigar and cigarette smoke. Tony wasn't at the tables. He glanced along the folding chairs where several players were sipping bottled beer or smoking, awaiting a table.

Near him a slim, one-armed figure in a green visor finished racking up a triangular complement of balls, snatched at some silver coins tossed on the worn green felt.

Father Vincent recognized him and waited for him to turn. The head, the thatch of yellow hair struck a responsive note which was confounded by the stump at the right shoulder.

"Hi, Father Vincent," the pinched, wan face of Silkshirt greeted him from under the cracked visor.

"Silkshirt!" Vincent exclaimed. "Come over here and let me see you! What's happened to you?"

Silkshirt shambled over to the priest, and the others, relaxing, resumed their play.

"Guess you didn't recognize me at first," Silkshirt began with a thin, self-pitying smile. "I lost the arm about six months after the cops let me go. I lost it in the same place you found me, the railroad tracks. Only this time I wasn't runnin' from the cops."

"Oh," Vincent said. "I'm sorry, Silkshirt."

"It's awright, Father. They let me alone after that. Guess they thought I had punishment enough for spillin' my guts to the cops. They even let me take this job up here without squawkin'. I like it, too; you know how I like to play pool."

"We've got a table over at the CYC. You're welcome to come over and use it. And there are no strings attached, just try to be a good kid, that's all."

"I might do just that. I've seen the fights and you sitting down in the front row. I remembered yuh. You're doin' a lot of good work for the neighborhood kids, although I don't go for nigger-lovin' myself."

Father Vincent reddened, and anger rose within him which he restrained. Silkshirt lowered his eyes and turned toward the back room.

"If it's Tony Lorenzo you're lookin' for, he's in the back room. Don't look bad after five years in stir, either."

"Thank you, Silkshirt."

He walked along the wall toward the back room, which really was only a space at the rear of the hall walled in by a green beaverboard partition. There were several ice-cream-parlor tables with imitation marble tops and twisted wire legs. A few old tads sat in pairs or alone, smoking and drinking ale. At a table in the corner, puffing on a cigarette, a half-empty beer in front of him, sat Tony Lorenzo, silent and alone.

"Tony!" Vincent said, standing and looking at him for a few moments with his hands on his hips. "Tony—Tony, you're a sight for sore eyes!"

"So are you, Father," Tony said, rising and extending his hand. His once glossy-black hair was gray at the temples and shot through with the same color. His olive skin was haggard and off-white. But the jut of the chin was still there, the snapping black eyes and roguish smile. He was to Father Vincent the same Tony who had hurried from the naval chaplain's office to the barracks dice game on payday, the same Tony who had offered to give the parish a house for recreational purposes while administering with brisk efficiency a hoodlum brewery. The inner flame of his spirit was still glowing within him, unquenched by five years of animal captivity. Vincent saw this and was glad.

They shook hands and sat down together.

"Not bad, not bad," Father Vincent said. "It must have been that pure-grain alcohol in the infirmary that kept you going."

Tony laughed. He had been an orderly in the prison hospital during most of his term.

"You've got a point there. Many an evening when I was finishing up my work, a shot of the prison doc's alky in a cup of black coffee was the difference between facing a night in the cell and not facing it.

"You know, Father, I was thinking of you about the time you walked in. I was thinking you might be sore about me walking out on Joan in the railroad station after all she's done for me. I was hoping you'd understand it right. I just wanted to be alone with myself in this town for a few hours. I wanted to see you eventually —you know that? I want to see Joan too. If I love anybody in the whole world, it's her, even though I don't know just where she fits in my life."

"I think Joan understands now. And I want to leave you alone too, Tony, believe me. But why here? Why right here?"

"I don't know," Tony said. "I was just drawn back to this place where my troubles all began. I just had to see the place again and see who is around."

"Silkshirt's around," Vincent said glumly. "He's the only one I noticed."

"Yeh, he's about the only one around here, and he never was much but a punk kid errand boy. They tell me most of the big guys went to Detroit when the town got hot. There's a few of the guys running a truck protection racket on the south side right now, I heard."

"I read about that in the papers," Vincent said impatiently. "But tell me, Tony, what are you going to do? Where are you going to stay tonight, for example?"

"I thought I'd get a room down near the railroad depot. I've got enough money to keep me going for about two weeks while I look for a job."

"What kind of a job?"

"Anything, Father, just anything. I can do hospital orderly work now, you know."

"You can do better than hospital work. You've got loads of organizational ability and you proved it, despite the dubious auspices. I'd like to take you in with me down at the CYC, and I will as soon as our income improves. In the meantime—well, have you ever thought of the labor movement? There's a big organizational drive on among the paper workers right now."

"Say, I read about that in the paper this morning," Tony said with a quickening of interest. "The AFL is really going after Utility Press and these small-fry paper sweatshops around town. Yeh, I'd like something like that. You know, Father, I like to get people working together for something constructive. I had a group going right there in the prison during off hours."

"What did you have them doing?"

"Oh, we put on debates, minstrel shows, and things. It wasn't bad at all. Murderers and highjackers speaking the lines of the immortal bard. You won't believe it. I played Mark Antony in *Julius Caesar*. A guy played Calpurnia. Remember her lines:

"When beggars die, there are no comets seen;
The heavens themselves blaze forth the death of princes . . ."

"That's wonderful, Tony." Father Vincent said. "You could do that for my kids down at the CYC."

"Think I could, Father?" Tony asked with a wistful note in his voice.

"I know you could. And you can do something for me right now. I've got a cab waiting downstairs."

"What is it, Father?"

"I can get you a nice room tonight, right downtown near the cathedral. It's simple, clean, private; come and go as you please.

Will you move into it now for a couple of weeks while we see what can be done about this labor organizing job? Father Arthur, whom you'll remember, is practically a Bolshevik on the labor question. He knows all the union officials, and I'm sure he'll try to put you next to these people who are organizing the paper industry. Will you take my advice this once? Will you come downtown with me now?"

"Okay, Father. But one favor," Tony said anxiously. "Don't tell Joan about it. Tell her you saw me and I'm fine, but let me think her out awhile, okay?"

"Okay. Whatever you and Joan do is your own business. I'll stay out of it."

"Good. Let's go."

"Right," Vincent said, sighing and rising. "Where's your bag?"

"It's over at the depot. We can pick it up maybe on the way down."

"Fine. I'll hurry ahead and hold the cab for you. Why not join me in a couple of minutes?"

"Thanks, Father," Tony said with a grin. He knew that Father Vincent was trying to save him the embarrassment of walking out of such a place with a clergyman. It would have looked as though Tony had been about to blow his pay check and had just been saved from perdition while the wife and babies waited in terror back home.

Vincent walked out through the billiard hall, a pleasant smile on his face, but hardly looking to the left or right. When he reached the exit, he saw Silkshirt behind a glass candy counter in which there were a few boxes of cigars and assorted cigarettes. Silkshirt waved tentatively, as if he wanted to talk, but Vincent returned the wave and hurried on.

He was a pitiable little wretch but young enough, maybe, to straighten out. He can't be more than twenty-three or twenty-four, the priest thought as he stepped briskly down the stairs.

Then another thought occurred to him as he glanced at his watch: eight thirty-five. He would have to phone his apologies to Bob Lambert and Arthur at the hotel. That was one dinner engagement he'd never make.

Outside it was almost dark and the rain was still falling. The cab was still there, but the front right door, peculiarly enough, lolled open. There was a crowd knotted at the entrance to the alley beside the club, and he could see the cabdriver gawking on the fringe of the gathering.

Father Vincent opened up his umbrella and hurried over.

"What is it?" he asked the cabdriver. "What's happened?"

"An old nigger fell off the club's loading platform and bumped his head. He was loaded with wine, I guess, but he's almost done for. They've sent for the police ambulance."

"Let me through," Vincent said, tapping a big man in coveralls on the shoulder. The big man hunched off Vincent's hand in indifference to someone whom he thought wanted a better look. Vincent handed the umbrella to the cabdriver. "Follow me with the umbrella if you can."

"Check, Father."

"LET ME THROUGH! I'M A PRIEST!" he commanded this time, spinning the burly man in coveralls around and plowing through the wall of people. He could feel the ribs of the umbrella at his back as he moved forward.

Under the pale light of a battery torch held by an onlooker, a lank gray-haired old Negro lay in the mud, gasping within a heaving circle of the curious, his skull covered with blood, which the rain diluted down his face in continuous streamlets.

"Hold that umbrella over us," Vincent said to the cabdriver, stripping off his coat and placing it over the old man. "AND IN THE NAME OF HEAVEN, STAND BACK AND GIVE THIS POOR OLD MAN SOME BREATHING ROOM!"

The crowd inched back with the slow, serpentine reluctance of the mob, and Vincent knelt in the mud beside the dying old man.

"Are you a Catholic, sir?" Vincent said, tying a large white pocket handkerchief around the wound in the back of the man's head.

He stared at Vincent starkly, moved his lips, trying to speak, but no sound emitted.

"Anybody got any whiskey?" Vincent asked the crowd.

A partly consumed pint of alcohol was passed into Vincent's hands.

"Raise him up, please!" he asked of no one in particular.

"Okay, Father, I'll get him."

It was Tony, there in the mud with him now, and it brought a wan smile to the priest's anxious face.

Tony got his arms under the man and lifted him to a three-quarter sitting position. Vincent gave him a healthy swig of the bootleg alcohol, which he swallowed gratefully. Again Vincent asked him the question:

"Are you a Catholic? If not, would you want me to say any special prayer for you? Or would you want me to contact any special clergyman after you get to the hospital?"

"Ah's not a Cath'lic, Parson," he said in a hoarse, rattly tone, "but Ah knows you."

Vincent took the flashlight from the onlooker above him and held it to the man's face.

"Good God!" he said. "I know this man. He's Jefferson Smith!"

"Yassuh, Parson Whelton, you 'member you took care uh my Lucy. You come from the priest school to see my Lucy. Ah 'member, Ah 'member!" He caughed up blood now rackingly, which Tony wiped from his mouth.

In the distance the whine of the police ambulance could be heard.

"They're coming for you. Can you hold on a little while?"

"Ah's done, Parson, Ah's done. But Lucy sent you to me, Parson, Lucy done sent you. She sent you to look after little Lucy. She's home now—ask the boys upstairs—Ah work there to try to be 'spect-able for mah Lucy. Look on her, Parson, and Ah'll jes' shuffle along. Big Lucy wants you to, Parson . . ."

"I will," the priest said. "Hail Mary, full of grace . . ." he prayed, making the sign of the cross over Jefferson.

"He's gone, Father," Tony said.

"God rest his soul!" Vincent's eyes were misty as he recalled the saintly death of Lucy Smith in Splinterville years ago.

In the background two policemen bearing a stretcher were shouldering their way through the crowd.

"Are we too late, Father?"

"Yes, but I think he would have died en route to the hospital. He fell against that loading platform and did an awful job on his skull."

"We'll take him to the hospital anyway. Who is he?"

"His name is Jefferson Smith. They know about him upstairs."

They unstrapped the stretcher and loaded him onto it.

"ALL RIGHT, CLEAR OUT OF HERE. YOU'VE DONE ENOUGH GAWKING FOR ONE EVENING!" the policeman commanded.

The crowd gave way before the stretcher-bearers.

"Here's your coat, Father," a voice said gently as Vincent arose from his mud-spattered knees.

He looked into Silkshirt's face, and there was a gentleness in it he had never noticed before. Death softens us all, he thought, even this twisted, hard little boy.

"Thank you, Silkshirt."

"I'll take it, Father," Tony Lorenzo said.

"Jefferson lives at 4708 South Maple in Browntown," Silkshirt explained. "He did odd jobs for the club upstairs. He drank a little too much, that's all. Everybody liked him, though," he said mistily. "He always had a joke on his lips—everybody liked him."

Tony nodded to the cabdriver, who was standing glumly by.

"I've got the address, Father. We'd better go now."

"Yes, take me home first. I'll clean up, then we'll go see Lucy. I knew her mother a long time ago," he sighed wearily, "a long time ago."

They sloshed through the alley toward the street and the cab. The rain had let up, but the sky was still starless and heavily overcast.

Tony helped Father Vincent into the cab and glanced up at the skies.

"*When beggars die,*" he said bitingly, "*there are no comets seen . . .*"

He slumped into the cab beside Father Vincent, who smiled wanly and threw an arm around Tony's shoulders.

"Let's go home, Tony, let's go home."

CHAPTER XVI

Tour of Inspection

It was no morning to be entertaining his former seminary room-mate, Monsignor Robert Lambert, chancellor of the Harbourton diocese. But there were Monsignor and the reverend editor of *The Clarion* sipping coffee in front of him and basking in the morning sun which showered through the CYC office windows.

Arthur Wagner had persuaded Lambert to stay overnight and at least see Vincent for a while in his "home" setting at the Christian Youth Center.

"Vin, you've got to show him the works this morning," Arthur had remonstrated over the rectory phone at 7 a.m.

Vincent's eyes were red and burning with exhaustion; his nerves were fitted with innumerable electric triggers, the bequest of the previous night's ordeal.

After securing a dry change of clothes for himself and Tony, they had traveled far south to Browntown in search of Lucy Smith.

Deep in the sodden tenement jungle, their cabdriver had ferreted out the Smith address. There was no one there, no light, no answer to their knocking.

A cricketlike old lady in the tenement across the hall fastened her black talons on the frayed lapels of her faded kimono and chaffered a message in the weird dust-light of a fly-flecked bulb.

"Lucy ain't here. De police wuz here 'bout ole Jeff, but she ain't here. She gone to de camp where dey tell us-uns how to git out from under you-uns. She gone up dere in de woods and she be back tomorra."

"Did the police say they'd get a message to her, ma'am?" Vincent had asked, yawning to cover up an involuntary smile.

"Yassuh, Parson, dey did, sho 'nuff."

"Thank you, ma'am, thank you. We'll be going along."

Sipping coffee now with his former roommates as Arthur talked of Al Smith's chances in the coming presidential election, Vincent combed his memory for the name of that Socialist labor retreat camp in River Woods. That must be the place she went to. Lucy, a radical, a revolutionary! What would her mother think of that? Yet the child must certainly be wide awake intellectually—going to meetings like that.

What was the name of that camp? Actionville—that was it—Actionville! He found himself warming to the name, thinking drolly that it would look well tacked over the entrance of the youth center, without the long-haired revolutionaries and ponderous dogmas, of course!

Tony would find out what she was like. He was on his way out to see her now. He'd see her himself, perhaps, tonight at old Jeff's wake. Lucy's daughter a Bolshevik! Lord help us!

"You haven't heard a word I said," Arthur exclaimed petulantly, sensing the absence of Vincent's concentration.

"I certainly have," Vincent exclaimed. "You said the price of coffee is showing a sharp decline in Brazil!"

"Bravo!" Monsignor Lambert chuckled. "You've proven conclusively you have thoughts of your own. In the seminary you seemed to hang on Arthur's every word."

"Did I?" Vincent asked, arching his eyebrows.

"I said," Arthur began again, "that Al Smith won't make it because he's a right-hander, that's what I said!"

"So we'll have Hoover!" Monsignor Lambert exclaimed triumphantly. "He fed the refugees during the World War, now he can apply his skill to feeding us—especially if money gets tight."

"Well said," Arthur observed. "I do believe you've acquired a sense of humor since you became an expert at fixing up bad marriages in Harbourton."

"Thank you," Lambert acknowledged coolly.

"Finish your coffee, Arthur," Vincent said. "Then we'll go show Monsignor our gym. Tell me, Bob, what are you people doing by way of a youth program in the Harbourton diocese?"

"The usual parish thing. There are balls and bats, there are boxing gloves and lots of other paraphernalia in the school-basement lockers. There's always someone around to supervise—a young priest, a member of the alumni.

"We don't go for this center sort of thing. We're a small diocese. We don't have the money, and many of our parishioners live on farms and are spread out all over the place."

"You say you don't go for the center idea." Arthur pursued the hint of condescension in Lambert's tone of voice. "Would you go for it in a big city diocese?"

"I don't think I would," Lambert said, sensing the challenge and assuming the aloofness he used to summon so readily in the seminary. But there was polish to it now and a little charm. There was a change of pace, too, as he quickly showed with a more genial tone of voice.

"I'd have to see Vincent's setup here thoroughly, of course, before I'd come to any conclusion. But I just don't think it's good to pull the kids away from the parish- and parochial-school environment. When they're under twenty I think they're just a little too young to be centering their recreational activities in a downtown marshaling point. Also, you have a different problem here, Vin, on the inter-racial thing. We're much more provincial, of course, and it would never work in our little place. In the first place, the population is predominantly German and of German descent. There are Negroes, yes, in our little industrial towns and in Harbourton itself, but not in great numbers."

"Do their children attend parochial schools?" Vincent asked.

"Uh—some of them. But you know, most of these folks are from the South and have that Sunday-go-to-meeting type of religion."

"Do the colored boys play with the white boys at the parish schools?" Arthur probed.

"Well, don't write an editorial on it, Arthur!" Lambert said with a touch of mirth at the corners of his mouth. "But they seldom do —except in the instance of one or two exceptional baseball or football players, who, by the way, are extremely popular around Harbourton."

"See!" Vincent said, pumping one fist into his open palm. "It could work. It's working here and it could work there!"

"Oh, Vin, I'm not sure of that—the center idea, anyway," Lambert objected mildly, his cool, gray eyes indicating the true firmness of purpose behind his remark.

"Other than the difficulty of the inter-racial thing," Arthur said pointedly, "I know you couldn't possibly be against the Christian principle of social justice involved in giving the Negro his inheritance as a child of God——"

"Now wait a minute!" Lambert said. "I came over here to see Vin's project. Don't be hitting me over the head with the Popes the way you do to the readers of *The Clarion* every week."

"No, no," Arthur said politely. "I won't, Bob, I won't. But tell me what your real practical objection is to a setup like Vincent's."

"Well," Lambert began, "it's no reflection on you, Vin, but I just can't see putting that kind of diocesan money into one basket. We're still building churches and schools in the diocese, and the need is especially great in the rural districts. I just can't see putting substantial blocks of our money into a downtown center—and the Bishop can't see it, which is the important thing."

"Glad you got that in there," Arthur said facetiously. "I thought maybe the Bishop might have gone to his eternal reward shortly after you started talking."

"He's still bouncing," Lambert said with his appraising smile.

"May he bounce a long time," Vincent said. "But you still don't have anybody to look after the special problems of those kids in the parishes. You may not have inter-racial problems among the kids, but I'll bet there are other problems."

"Yes, and I know what one of them is," Arthur said impishly. "Don't forget, Bob, we read the Harbourton papers up here."

"Are you referring to the high percentage of our boys who attend the YMCA gymnasium and the Lutheran Athletic Center? We've just stated policy on that—there's no taboo or ban on such attendance. All the city and town leagues play their games in those centers. We've simply alerted our boys and girls to the possibility of proselytism. I'm sure the Protestant and Jewish brethren would do the same if their children were to attend Catholic gymnasia."

"I seem to recall that you expressed yourself in much stronger terms than that in the Harbourton press," Arthur said. "Hints about excommunication and the like."

Lambert lost his veneer and went completely red in the face. Without moving a muscle he then asked icily:

"Father Whelton, did you invite me here to see your center or to have me tossed and turned on the griddle by our gentle-voiced friend here?"

"Indeed I did, Monsignor. Arthur, lay off! Let's go see the place. Right this way, if you will."

"Sorry, Bob," Arthur said as they moved through the back-office entrance to the gym. "I was just trying to clear the air."

"That's quite all right, Arthur," Lambert said with polite glumness. "But do you always clear the air with a fusillade of rockets?"

Vincent opened the door that led into Kenney O'Byrne's combination rubbing room and office. "This is Kenney O'Byrne's famous gallery," he said, waving at the solid wall of glossy prints of boxers and other athletes which filled the space above O'Byrne's desk. "Would you like to take a look?"

"Yes, you'll enjoy this," Arthur said. "Kenney, whom you'll meet out in the gym, is a study in colossal yet lovable ego. I'm going to drop a hint to him that you're quite an important Harbourton church dignitary and he'll have a photographer around here in about five minutes."

"You mean I might land up here with all these athletic notables?" Monsignor Lambert said, squinting amiably up at the echelons of unframed autographed prints. "Some of them have personal messages on them. Isn't that Babe Ruth?"

"Yes," Vincent said. "That's Kenney with his arm around the Bam, and that shy little cleric on the right should be familiar to you."

"Yes," Lambert said. "You look like the cat that swallowed the canary."

"What could I do? Kenney took the Babe completely over. Got him to come up here and autograph balls for the kids."

"Note the inscription," Arthur said.

Monsignor Lambert read the inscription aloud: " 'Father Vincent, you're doing a great job with those kids down at the center! And you too, Kenney! Babe Ruth.' That's very nice."

"Take another look at the handwriting," Arthur urged.

"What's this?" the Monsignor said with a droll smile. "Why, the writing is different in that last phrase—similar, but different."

"That's Kenney O'Byrne, the handwriting expert, batting for Babe Ruth," Vincent said, chuckling.

" 'And you too, Kenney,' " Monsignor Lambert repeated wryly.

They looked at the other pictures on the wall—Red Grange; the trainer of Reigh Count, the Kentucky Derby winner; Jack Dempsey— all autographed in similar fashion.

"One more thing," Vincent said as they proceeded through the

locker room to the gym floor. "Kenney likes to be addressed as
'Kenney the Great.' That's what he was called when he was light-
weight champ of the Pacific fleet, and you'll simply have to go along
with it."

"You'd better go along with it if you want your picture in the
gallery," Arthur quipped.

"I'll go along," the Monsignor said. " 'Kenney the Great.' Tell me,
Reverend Editor, how come your classic features are absent from
the gallery of champions?"

"*I* am persona non grata with Mr. O'Byrne. *The Clarion* has not
published his picture as yet, so he will not 'publish' mine."

"Why don't you oblige?" Lambert asked.

"How can I?" Arthur pleaded facetiously. "I run at least three
pictures of the Cardinal every week, and the rest of my pictorial
space is taken up by shots of parish activities. I simply have no
room left for camera lice."

"You'd better be careful what you say about my boxing coach.
Here he comes now!"

Kenney O'Byrne bustled into the locker room, carrying an armful
of sixteen-ounce boxing gloves and grinning out at the world like
a small black bear. His bearish appearance was accentuated not
only by thick, unmanageable black hair which he continually
brushed away from his eyes but also by the tufts of hair that could
be seen through his T-shirt and all over his clublike forearms.

One of the boys in the locker room had alerted him to the presence
of "visitors" in the rubbing room, and of course he was hurrying
about his business.

"Kenney, come over here," Vincent said. "I want you to meet an
important visitor."

"Sure, Farduh, sure!" Kenney said, plumping the gloves down on
a locker-room bench.

"This is Monsignor Robert Lambert from Harbourton. Monsignor,
this is Kenney O'Byrne, our boxing coach."

"Yes, yes, how do you do, Kenney?" the Monsignor said, shaking
hands with the grinning, hairy creature in front of him. "I've heard
a lot about you. They call you Kenney the Great, do they not?"

"Say, where'd you hear about that?" Kenney exclaimed while
shaking hands. "Up in Harbourton? I wouldn't be surprised. I been
there. I been there!"

"I'm sure you have," Monsignor Lambert said. "I believe you've put on some boxing matches up there."

"You heard about that too, Monsignor, eh?" Kenney said blandly. "See that, Father Vincent? They know all about us up there!"

"That's right, Kenney," Vincent said. Then he averted his head toward Arthur, who was standing by with a genial yet patient mask on his face. "You've met the editor of *The Clarion* before, I presume."

"Yeh—yeh," Kenney said coolly, "I know Farduh. He's gonna give the kids some publicity soon in *The Clarion*, ain'tcha, Farduh?"

"Well—yes," Arthur said, reddening, "I will. Just as soon as you give me a good story and some good pictures, not setups. You must realize, Kenney, I can't use the same kind of picture that fits into your gallery so well."

"Oh no?" Kenney shook his head slowly in consternation and pushed the hair out of his eyes. "You want something newsy, eh?"

"That's right, something everybody will be interested in."

"I got it! I got it!" Kenney said enthusiastically. "Right here—today—now!"

"What is it?" Father Vincent asked rather anxiously. He wondered what was going on that could be so momentous and he, the director, unaware of it.

"Bicky Brown and Julie Rodriguez, that's what. They're going at it again this morning for three rounds! Whoever wins it will be captain of the boxing team next fall."

"What's all this?" Monsignor Lambert asked.

"Bicky and Julie are two of our most improved young boxers," Vincent explained. "Bicky's a Negro boy and Julie a Puerto Rican by descent. Whenever they box it's blow for blow, and we still don't know which is the better. I wasn't aware they were boxing this morning, Kenney."

"Sure, Farduh, they got eight votes each for captain of the varsity team, and both of them said they'd like to settle it this way. No matter who wins, I'm gonna make 'em co-captains if it's all right wit' you."

"It's all right, but don't let them hurt each other badly."

"Aw, there might be a little blood, but they're both rugged, Farduh. I'll watch 'em close," Kenney promised.

"Blood?" Lambert asked tentatively, arching his eyebrows sharply. They were approaching the ring, where Brown and Rodriguez, in their respective corners, were prancing and dipping, waiting for Kenney, who would act as referee.

"They sometimes draw a little blood, Monsignor—a split lip, a sensitive nose—it's rarely anything serious. These kids get themselves in excellent condition and they know how to protect themselves," Vincent explained.

"Blood is blood, my dear classmate," Monsignor Lambert said with a sustained hint of disapproval. "I was under the clear impression that we Christians are traditionally contra the Roman arena for more reasons than one."

"I agree with you, Bob," Vincent said, "but boxing can certainly be rigidly supervised—as it is here—there's no need for the type of brutality occasionally seen in the professional ring. Isn't that so, Kenney?"

Kenney had one hand on a ring post and was about to climb the steps into the ring. He kept looking over his shoulder toward the front of the gym, as if anxiously expecting someone.

"Isn't that so, Kenney?" Vincent repeated firmly. "We don't tolerate brutality in the ring, *do we?*"

"Oh, yeh—yeh, Farduh, dat's right—no rough stuff. Nobody gets hurt, Monsignor, nobody gets hurt."

Around them the lean, lithe ones and some too fat, some too thin, were going through various stages of gym routine, pounding, dancing, yipping, or quietly doing push-ups or bends. In the far left corner there was a volleyball court, with much hullabaloo from a wedge of urchins leaping and batting in the gray cotton jerseys and trunks which Vincent issued as standard equipment.

Kenney was checking the boys' boxing gloves now. They were wearing the "pillows," Vincent noticed, the sixteen-ounce gloves that would cushion the impact against the eyes, chin, nose, and midriff.

Kenney kept glancing toward the front of the gym as all activity gradually ceased and an avid, eager audience of about sixty boys and several men from the building gathered around the base of the ring.

A runty man in a dark suit and smoking an oversize cigar appeared at the front entrance carrying a square black suitcase.

Kenney raised a paw to his mouth and shouted:

"IGGY, BRING THE CAMERA!"

"Now comes Iggy Klutznick," Vincent explained. "He takes pictures for the boxing crowd in town here. Not a bad photographer, either. I haven't been able to figure out what Kenney's hold over the fellow is, but he takes pictures for Kenney all the time."

"I've got an idea," Arthur said. "But I won't reveal it in front of the Monsignor. I can see he is already aghast at how we carry on in the big city."

"Thank you for sparing me the details," Monsignor Lambert said. "It must have something to do with some form of blackmail. Kenney probably has something on Mr. Klutznick."

"Perhaps," Arthur said with a sly smile of assent.

Kenney sent the boxers to their corners and waved Iggy on, pointing toward the clergy.

"First, one right here"—he pointed—"I'll be down!"

Kenney introduced Iggy to the priests and proceeded to arrange the pictures.

"No picture of me," Vincent demurred, "but I would like you to take a shot of the Monsignor. Perhaps in the ring."

"No, no, no," Lambert said quickly. "Not in the ring. Take a shot here if you like, but not in the ring."

"Okay, whatever you say, Monsignor. You wanta get in this, Farduh Wagner?"

"No, thanks, Kenney. I'm not very photogenic," Arthur said, exchanging a look of sympathy with Vincent.

"Okay, Iggy," Kenney said. "Take a shot of me shaking hands with the Monsignor. Okay, Farduh Vincent?"

"If it's all right with the Monsignor," Vincent said dryly. "But let's get it over with and get on with the match. The fathers and I have other business today."

The two priests stepped aside, and Iggy moved back for the shot. Kenney grabbed hold of the Monsignor's hand, a limp, reluctant fish.

"I'm welcomin' him to the center, get it, Iggy?" Kenney said.

"Yeh, I get it," Iggy said from behind his furiously champed cigar. "Just smile, please; smile, Monsignor Lambert."

The Monsignor, responding pleasantly to Iggy's courtesy, flashed a pleasant smile and the camera clicked.

Vincent climbed into the ring and spoke to both Bicky and Julie.

"You're both my boys—remember that. Hit hard and clean and remember we're here to help each other, not to hurt each other."

"Okay, Father," Julie said, flashing a smile out of his dark features.

"You bet, Father," Bicky added, rivaling his opponent's smile out of the ebon background of his face.

Kenney was in the ring now, bringing them together.

"One more, Iggy, one more," he called down.

Iggy spidered up on the apron of the ring and angled another shot.

Kenney called them together, crunched their gloves, making them meet, and directed them back to their corners.

"Okay, three three-minute rounds, with Iggy, the timekeeper, and myself as the judges. Let's go."

He raised his hand, dropped it, and the timekeeper, an older boy, tugged on the bell rope.

In they weaved toward each other, with Kenney dancing between them. They were both fast, Julie showing himself the quicker of the two with a series of rapier left jabs which were swiftly blocked by Bicky.

"Weave and circle, weave and circle," Kenney called, putting his best ringside manner forward for the guests.

Monsignor Lambert watched, cool but fascinated, the osmosis of human physical combat permeating his consciousness in spite of himself.

Bicky took several more jabs, blocking all but one, which stung him on the side of the nose. Julie came on now, jabbing.

"Bicky wants him inside," Vincent said.

"Inside?" the Monsignor asked.

"He wants him in close where he can use that good right of his."

Julie's jabs were aimed at the colored boy's face now, but still Bicky held his punches, blocking and circling, blocking and circling.

"Keep 'im comin', Bicky chile," old Stringbean Lincoln called from Bicky's corner. "You has the big surprise for dat boy!"

Bicky kept him coming, and Julie was in there boring low at his opponent's midriff, whopping rights and lefts against the chocolate washboard in front of him.

Bicky made his move. He took one step back and unleashed an uppercut that caught Julie on the point of the chin, stopping him sharply. He followed with a left to the middle and then a full uppercut that lifted the Puerto Rican off the canvas and dropped him with a thump to a rolling, sitting position out of which he eased, sprawling, to the land of whistles and skyrockets.

They cat-called, whistled, and screamed for Bicky as Kenney hovered, kneeling, over the inert Rodriguez, motioning for the bucket and rubbing his cheeks.

"You has just been elected captain, man!" Stringbean Lincoln said as he climbed through the ropes with the water bucket.

Vincent hurried up the stairs to the ring.

"This is disgusting!" Monsignor Lambert said, his face gone livid with anxiety and irritation. "That boy may be seriously hurt."

"He'll be all right, Bob," Arthur said.

"I hope so. I simply can't see why Vin can promote this type of thing. There are so many other forms of recreation."

In the ring Vincent rubbed Julie's wrists while Kenney applied a wet sponge to his face. He stirred now and moaned gently into consciousness.

"Kids like to box, Bob. Better that they do it here where their souls and minds might get some attention than in the streets and alleys with bare knuckles."

"Well, I've had enough," Lambert said with an impatient sigh. "I've got to catch that noon train to Harbourton."

They had Julie on his feet now.

"You all right, Julie?" Vincent asked.

"Yeh, yeh, Father, what hit me?"

Bicky was there, his sense of triumph scattered by sympathy.

"Didn't mean to hurt you, Julie. You all right?"

"Okay, Bicky, okay. We gonna keep goin'?" Julie asked, shaking his head to eject the cobwebs and gamely trying to ready himself for the other two rounds.

"Whud'yuh think, Farduh?" Kenney asked eagerly.

"That will be all," Vincent said sternly. "You two kids shower up and get dressed. If you feel any pain, Julie, I want Kenney to take you right over to Doc Andrews. Do you understand, Kenney?"

"Right, Farduh, right. I'll fix them up in the rubbin' room, both of them. They're my aces—they're my co-captains. That's what you both are now, co-captains! All right with you, Farduh?"

"All right, all right," Vincent said, patting both on the shoulder. "I've got to get back to the office."

They went back to the office in silence, the Monsignor cool and noncommittal in the presence of Vincent.

"I'll take Monsignor to the train," Arthur said finally.

"Very good," Vincent said. "It was nice of you to come over and see things here, Bob. I really didn't anticipate putting on such a show for you, however."

"A show indeed," Lambert said shortly.

Vincent left them in the hallway after getting their hats. He took one last look over his shoulder at Monsignor Lambert walking down the corridor with Arthur and breathed a prayer of thanks that Julie had not been hurt.

In the reception room Joan was busily typing. She looked up as he entered.

"Did you see the match?" he asked.

She nodded and smiled slowly. "Aren't you glad we're not in the Harbourton diocese?"

Vincent could not resist a healthy, steam-valving laugh.

"Just let's hope the Cardinal lives to be a thousand," he said, walking into his office.

CHAPTER XVII

The Congress of Vienna

WHEN Tony arrived at Jefferson Smith's tenement in Browntown, the cricketlike neighbor told him that Lucy hadn't yet put in an appearance.

"She maybe go right to work from de country camp. De police been dere too, so she know 'bout her farder if she dere."

The neighbor gave him the name and address of the factory, a plant called Roma Paper Box Company near the railroad yards about six blocks south of the Smith tenement. She also gave him the name and location of the funeral home where Jefferson was laid out.

He could walk it from here, deciding to look in on the Four Square Gospel Funeral Home on Merchant Avenue, the nearest main street. Lucy might just be there, and it would save him a trip over to the factory.

That was quite a name for a funeral home, he thought with a smile. It was probably tied in with a gospel mission that did up the whole job for a modest fee, the minister being both preacher and undertaker, a shrewd little meeting between heaven and earth.

He walked along South Maple toward Merchant Avenue, seeing continuous signs of the way in which these impoverished colored city folk expressed flourish and fanfare in their lives, belying the squalor of their surroundings and the rigorous, unwritten laws of their ghettoed lives.

Pushcart vendors hawked boiled crabs, slices of watermelon, moundlike shavings of ice colorfully dyed with fake fruit juices. Flamboyant signs proclaimed the presence of numerous social clubs and secret societies for both men and women. And parked sporadically along the curbs in front of the dingy, smelly tenements were long, shiny automobiles that seemed dislocated from the fashionable apartment cliffs of the swanky north side.

The presence of the expensive automobiles made him remember the maunderings of Willie Scofield, a high-pressure secondhand automobile salesman he had met in prison who had pulled off one shady financial deal too many. One remembers everything that is said in prison because there is so much time to remember.

"When those folks get prosperous—even momentarily—they buy fancy cars because it's hard for them to put their money in real estate," Willie had said. "Course it's hard to collect the rest of the payments. But they're like anyone else: once you get them on the hook, you can keep after them for the money."

He reached Merchant Avenue and the Four Square Gospel, a large white store front with dusty gray curtains. The door was open and he entered. He noted the whitewashed walls, the folding chairs arranged to left and right with an aisle in the middle.

The open coffin was propped up in front of a raised, sheeted table which served as an altar. The hall was empty but for a tall Negro girl who sat straight and immobile in a chair near the coffin.

He went up to the coffin, glanced at the long, powdered face, so ravaged formerly, now peaceful in death. He knelt down on the knotty hardwood floor, blessed himself, whispered an Our Father and a Hail Mary, crossed himself again, and stood up. He took a good look at Jefferson. This man had meant nothing to him, but his death had touched Tony's being in a crucial hour. For when Father Vincent had burst in on him like an angel of mercy at the Bellrose Social Club he had been contemplating death himself. Over the viaduct would go the ex-con at midnight, or maybe some provoked and bloody finale with the police as one last gesture to the old brawly hoodlum life on the south side.

He turned to Lucy, tall and gaunt like her father, her face pockmarked, but in her piercing green eyes the low, smoldering rumble of a stirring volcano.

"You must be Lucy Smith," he said. "I'm Tony Lorenzo. Father Vincent, an old friend of your mother's, sent me to find you. I imagine he'll be in touch with you later, but the guy is simply exhausted. I know he had to keep an important engagement at the youth center this morning. Then he probably collapsed into bed for an hour or two."

Lucy nodded in a quiescent, noncommittal manner.

"I know who Father Vincent is," she said in a rich, disciplined contralto voice like that of an actress. "My father often urged me to go and see him, but I never could. We just don't speak the same language."

"How do you know that if you've never met him?" Tony said gently but firmly.

Lucy ignored the question.

"It was nice of you to come way out here," she continued, a slow smile in her homely angular features showing a fine set of white, strong teeth. "And it was darned nice of you and Father Vincent to try to help Daddy in his extremity."

Her manner of speech stamped her as an educated woman. What was she doing working in a paper-box factory?

"Not at all," Tony explained. "I never knew him, but Father did. It was a moving coincidence, your mother and everything. I was thinking as I looked at him that he touched my life at a very crucial time of my own and helped, with other things, to bring me back to an appreciation of being alive—and free."

"Free?" she said, moving a minimum of facial muscles. "None of us are free."

"Your neighbor said you might be at the Roma Company. I was on my way over and decided to check here first."

"I no longer work at the Roma Company."

"Oh?" Tony said. "Did you leave?"

"I was asked to leave. When they gave me the news of my father they said they couldn't let me go until 3 P.M. We had ten thousand soapboxes to strip and they said they couldn't spare me until then. So I just left."

"That sounds outrageous. Maybe they'll take you back after the funeral."

"They had other reasons for letting me go. They knew I was trying to organize a union," Lucy said.

Union! The idea touched off a small grass fire in his mind. That was what Father Vincent had suggested. And that might be the group, too, the printing trades.

"I've been thinking of doing some organizing work myself. Perhaps I can call on you for some help."

"I'll be available," she said with a flicker of interest. "I know most of the workers in the plant. But I'm not home on weekday evenings. I'm taking courses in the social sciences at City U."

That explained the polish. She took speech and dramatics also, Tony guessed.

"Father Vincent wants to know if we can help out financially."

"Thank you just the same, but the insurance will bury Daddy. We're poor, but that's one advantage of being a member of the proletariat. Only the bourgeois have substantial debts. That's because they live largely on credit."

The proletariat and the bourgeois! So that was it, that was the burning dedication! She was a Socialist or maybe even a Communist.

"Okay, Lucy," he concluded, extending his hand. "I'll be running along now. I'm sure Father Vincent will try to make the funeral tomorrow. And I'll be in touch with you on that organizing thing."

"Very well, Mr. Lorenzo," she said calmly. "Thank you again— nice of you to come by."

"Not at all, Lucy. So long now."

"So long."

He left her, feeling much of her calm and even certitude. A spell, it seemed, a kind of absorption of her quiet.

"Only the bourgeois . . ." she had said. "A strange girl," he muttered, walking to the downtown bus stop. "A very strange girl."

At the corner of Merchant and Wanda Place he saw the downtown bus slowly pulling away, went into a spurt of running for several yards, then realized he could not hail it in time.

He paused, sighed, lit a cigarette, and pondered his next move. He sucked in the heady mildness of the weed, blew it out, and with it some of his smoldering indignation over the firing of Lucy Smith.

"Those bastards!" he muttered savagely. "So that's how they operate. No wonder the unions are conducting this drive. Father Arthur had the connection."

It was now twelve-thirty. There wouldn't be another downtown bus along for at least twenty minutes. He decided to call Father Arthur at the office of *The Clarion*. Father Vincent had said he'd be there after twelve.

On the corner, near the bus stop, he stepped into a cigar store where several flashy-looking Negroes were scanning the tout sheets and racing form. They gave him the once-over quickly. He smiled, breaking the spell of police possibility, and they went back to their drawling, dawdling speculation on the afternoon's winners at the nation's race tracks.

He looked up the newspaper number in the book, penciled it on the back of a match cover, and called.

Arthur was soon on the line, hearty as ever in his flippant yet serious manner.

Tony explained where he was and why.

"Good, good," Arthur interrupted him. "Father Vincent is hiding for the afternoon, dead asleep. We had quite a session with Monsignor Lambert at the gym this morning."

"I thought he'd want to get some sleep. That's why I haven't called."

"It's all set for you over at Mother's place," Arthur said. "Just get your bags and go over there any time you're ready. That's Mrs. Lorraine Wagner, 219 State Boulevard, around the corner from the Cathedral."

Tony copied down the name and address. He had stayed at a cheap hotel near the depot last night and could pick up his luggage there later.

"Thanks, Father," Tony said. "It's very kind of you."

"Not at all. Mother will make you perfectly at home. She has all sorts of people wandering in and out—university people, transients, and such. Just move in and take a seat at the dinner table as if you've always been there."

Lorenzo laughed. He made it all seem so informal.

Tony told him about Lucy's troubles at the Roma plant, and Arthur's mood changed to biting yet restrained anger.

"*They* did that!" he exclaimed in sheer unbelief. "I can't believe it, Tony. Why—why, her father—dead and all!"

Tony mentioned the union accusation and her revolutionary leanings.

"Bourgeois!" Arthur said, meaning "baloney" or "tommyrot."

"She's against the bourgeois!" Tony said facetiously. "Maybe that's the real trouble."

"Bourgeois again! Why, I know the owner of the plant very well —Nino Venezzia. He's a very gracious Italian gentleman and utterly devoted to the Church. His daughter Rosa, an art student, stays with my mother. She's an older girl—a widow. You'll see her around the apartment probably tonight. Who did the firing? I simply can't believe it!"

"Lucy didn't say who actually did the firing, but maybe this de-voted Catholic friend of yours fired her because of her radical ideas. She thinks that's the real reason she was canned. Do you think Father Vincent could help her?"

"Maybe," Arthur answered. "But he can't be disturbed. And to-night he's representing the Cardinal at a fund-raising banquet for the new seminary wing. His Eminence has gone to Washington."

"What'll we do?" Tony asked.

"I'll come out there and we'll try to see Mr. Venezzia. I'll be by in about half an hour. Why don't you check again with Lucy in the meantime and find out who actually fired her?"

"Right. By the way, can you get your union friend to turn me loose on that place? Lucy says it's ripe for organization."

"I'll try. I'll call him right away. He's Tommy Naski, business agent of the Allied Paper Workers. He's got plenty of guts and is honest as the day is long."

"Sounds good to me. I'll see you in half an hour or so, right here."

"All right, Tony, I'll see you."

Wheeling along in a cab with Father Arthur, who was nervously alert for his first view of the Roma plant, Tony expressed his puzzle-ment at the seeming contradiction in Venezzia's devotion to religion and his ruthless handling of Lucy.

Tony had slipped back to the gospel center to find Lucy sitting as calm and impassive as ever.

She had informed him that it was Venezzia, the multimillionaire paper-box tycoon himself, who had done the firing. But his plant manager, a nosy, distrustful brute named Zangora, had really put the bug in the owner's ear about her crusading and revolutionary ideas.

When Tony had told her about Father Wagner's intended inter-cession, she laughed out loud.

"Venezzia's a Knight of Malta and one of the heaviest contributors to the Cardinal's charities. The vastness of his paper-mill holdings in Italy have placed him in a position of power and influence with both the government and the Vatican. What," she asked with an eerie chuckle, raising her long, graceful hands, "can Father Wagner do in the face of all that? Besides, I am committed to certain political and social beliefs that run contra to those of the Church—and Venez-zia knows it. Father Wagner would do well to stay downtown and continue to write editorials which please the Cardinal so that he, too, can someday become a wearer of the royal purple."

"He's not that kind of a guy, Lucy," Tony had said irritably. "He's constantly in hot water for editorially expounding ideas on things social, political, and economic."

"Give me a 'for instance.' "

"For instance, he has accused the pastors of the diocese of ignoring the papal encyclicals when they advise their flocks on various social and political matters."

"Hmmm!" Lucy had conceded with an adroit crinkling of her brow. "That's a big 'for instance.' Well," she had concluded with a sigh. "He sounds okay—like to meet him, in fact. But he's butting his head against a stone wall if he hopes to prevail on Mr. Venezzia."

Now in the cab padding along the railroad embankment toward the plant, Lorenzo pondered these things and was tempted to try to dampen Arthur's seeming foolhardiness.

"Do you think you really ought to do this?" Tony asked hesitantly. "Maybe we can get her on the union payroll with me while we organize this place."

"Of course I ought to do it," Arthur said firmly, his pale face tightly drawn, his strong yet delicately molded hand clamped tightly on the window handle beside him. "If Father Vincent were available he'd do the same darned thing."

"Okay, Reverend," Tony said with a grin. "I'm with you."

The cab pulled alongside a long two-story brick building dotted with dust-laden windows.

"There's the office entrance over there, Father," the cabdriver said, pointing to a staircase that led up to the second floor.

They could hear the presses pounding and thrumming in relentless rhythmic beats. Beneath them as they climbed the stairs they felt the mild earthquake tremors of the entire building. The clouds of swirling cardboard dust were ticklish in their nostrils and had, like a locust plague, dimmed and grayed the light of the sun.

Tony took a quick look into the plant and saw the sweep of the presses, great black flat-beds lined up along opposite walls in two series of fives like heavy artillery, with their attendants crawling above and around them like ministering insects.

Immediately to his left he caught a glimpse of a pitlike room at the bottom of which, blanketed in a rising cloud of gray cardboard dust, some thirty people, men and women, colored and white, were stripping the waste material from separate blocks of cartons. They worked with little clawlike knives, in silence and steadily, endlessly, up and down, stripping and piling, stripping and piling.

"That's where Lucy worked," Tony whispered to Arthur. "Get a load of that snake pit."

Arthur leaned over the balustrade and took a good look.

"My God!" he exclaimed. "Are those human beings?"

"They sure are, at about thirty cents an hour. And they think the coal miners have it tough!"

"Lucy's better off out of here," the priest said, shaking his head wearily.

At the top of the stairs they entered a small enclosed reception room with a kind of open porthole behind which a plump, middle-aged woman sat at a switchboard.

"Father Wagner to see Mr. Nino Venezzia," Arthur said. "He's expecting me."

"Very well, Father. I'll ring him right away."

"Want me to wait here?" Tony asked.

"No, no!" Arthur said vehemently. "You come in with me. I want you to get all this firsthand. It'll be useful later."

Tony laughed spontaneously at the priest's unvarnished partisanship.

"You and Father Vincent, you're really a pair."

"Don't associate me with that—that—boxing promoter!" Arthur said with sneering facetiousness.

Again Tony found himself laughing. There certainly was a challenge in this kind of life, just as big and exciting as the one he had known in the rackets. And the cops weren't after you here—yet—he added mentally.

"All right, Father, you can go right in," the switchboard operator said, appearing at a door to their left.

They followed her through a series of dusty wooden partitions in which girls were typing and men in green visors were at drawing boards or working over ledgers.

At the end of the hall she pressed a button and received an answering zit which released the lock on a heavy mahogany door.

"Go right in. Miss Amassa will meet you down the hall."

They stepped from a wasteland into a deeply carpeted and wainscoted oasis, sweet in atmosphere and cooled by a series of hidden

fans whose soft whirring was a benediction after the incessant pounding of the presses below.

In a cubicle at the end of the wainscoted corridor a slender, olive-
skinned woman of unidentifiable age and wearing a long black dress
of severe design was waiting for them with a tired yet welcoming
smile.

"Welcome, Father," she began in a cultured Italian accent. "Mr.
Venezzia is expecting you."

"Nice to see you, Miss Amassa," Arthur said, shaking her hand.
"I've talked to you on the phone. This is my friend, Mr. Lorenzo."

"A pleasure to meet you, Mr. Lorenzo. Will both of you come
right this way?"

She knocked perfunctorily on a door marked "Private" and turned
a long bronze handle which was cast as a serpent and looked like
a Renaissance antique.

They were ushered into the throne room of the master, a lush,
rococo setting replete with deep, ruby oriental rugs, wine-colored
wallpaper, a bust of Dante Alighieri on a marble stand, and behind
the wide mahogany desk of Nino Venezzia hung a magnificent reproduction of Raphael's *Madonna*.

Venezzia, a tiny, bald bird of a man with large, incendiary blue
eyes and a stern cleft chin, seemed to flounder a bit in a loose-fitting
black silk suit. He had a gold-plated French telephone to his ear and
waved them with almost hissing cordiality into handsome red leather
chairs to the right of his desk.

"Sit down, Father," he said. "Sit down, my friend," he said to Tony.
"Let me get rid of this call."

The scratching and shrilling of a man talking excitedly at the
other end of the phone resumed while Venezzia gazed steadily, with
the coldness of a Doge of Venice, at a small, exquisitely carved
wooden statue of St. Benedict which stood on the shiny expanse of
desk to his left.

"Mr. Steinkraus," he interrupted slowly, with the coldest arrogance of authority Tony had ever heard, "I have guests here waiting
and I do not wish to discuss this matter any further."

More scratching and shrilling at the other end of the phone.

"Oh, unions, unions, I know," he said with an impatient sigh. "They
want one here in my plant also, but they will not get it. I am master
here, you are master there. Give them a bigger price than the union
teamsters and they will come licking your hand."

Father Wagner threw a wink at Lorenzo, who yawned to suppress a smile of recognition.

"Give them the money and they will carry more for you. So then you will not have the unions nipping at your heels and the money expended will be less in the long run. . . . Yes, yes, bill me for the extra haulage but get all that cardboard stock off the ship tonight. We have obligations here. . . . Yes, yes, call me tonight at home. Good-by, Mr. Steinkraus."

He rose now, leaning to the left a little because of some present or former ailment of the side. He looked like a little Renaissance dwarf who had somehow come into vast power and opulence.

"Father Wagner," he began slowly, extending his right hand, on which glowed a large, fervid ruby set in a wide burnished gold band. "Father Wagner," he repeated in the same leisurely tones, "priest and journalist, nephew of a great prince of the Church. How are you and how, may I ask, is His Eminence?"

"I'm fine Mr. Venezzia," Arthur said, taking the limp white hand and gripping it lightly. "The Cardinal is in excellent spirits but is now out of town on ecclesiastical business."

"Is he?" Venezzia said, arching one dark eyebrow drastically and giving Tony a hint of a diminutive John Barrymore. "That is a matter of grievance to me, as I had hoped to see him at the fund-raising dinner for the seminary tonight. But the work of the Church must go on. All the Knights," he added with an opulent gesture of his hand, "all the Knights of Malta will be there."

"Indeed," Father Wagner said with studious respect. "And the Cardinal will send a very special personal messenger, you may be sure."

Venezzia paused now and turned to Tony, bestowing his bony, birdlike countenance full upon him.

"And who is this young man? Let me see. Napoli—no?"

Tony shook his head slowly, a careful smile on his lips.

"Sicily—yes?"

"Yes, that is to say, my parents, of course," Tony said politely.

Nino Venezzia looked at him intently, and Tony could almost read his mind. "Bandito," his face was saying. "Siciliano—bandito."

Tony blushed deeply and Father Wagner was quick to fill the breach.

"This is Anthony Lorenzo, a protégé of Father Vincent Whelton of the Christian Youth Center. Mr. Lorenzo served as naval chaplain's assistant to Father Vincent during the war."

"Ah, a warrior of the sea," Venezzia said graciously. "A true son of Mare Nostrum," he added pretentiously, and took Tony limply by the hand.

Now he sat down again, opened an embossed red leather box, and offered them both long, aromatic Havana cigars.

Arthur took one and Tony, thinking drolly that he might not get the chance again, also accepted one with thanks.

Flame was dispensed from a silver lighter molded to resemble the leaning tower of Pisa, and the master settled back, the rituals of welcome ended, ready to assimilate the purpose of their call.

"Now, what is it Father?" he began. "What is it I can do to help you?"

"Mr. Venezzia, I come way out here today on an errand of mercy. An employee of yours, a Miss Lucy Smith, whom your firm terminated today, is an old friend of ours. Both Father Vincent Whelton and I knew her mother while we were in the seminary."

Arthur knew he was stretching a point somewhat on that. But he had met old Lucy once or twice and he knew that in Vincent's absence this was the most effective presentation he could make.

"Yes, yes, yes." Venezzia nodded with slightly impatient fatigue. "I am sorry to say I had to let the girl go. I am sorry, too, about her father's death, but her desire to be with the deceased was not the true reason for her dismissal."

"I am aware of that, Mr. Venezzia," Father Wagner said pleasantly. "But I cannot believe that such a young girl who is striving so diligently to get a college education—and who might one day prove to be a credit to her poor, harassed race—could be quite as subversive as your action would seem to imply."

"It is entirely possible that you are correct," Venezzia said graciously with a tired, opening gesture of his fish-limp little hand. "But it has been impossible for me as a devoted son of the Church and as a practical businessman to ignore the reports of my foreman, Mr. Zangora, regarding this girl. I will get him up here so that we may review this information at first hand."

Tony looked as if he were about to say something, but the priest shot him a warning glance. It was obvious to Arthur that Lucy herself should be present when the foreman spoke his piece, but this was no shop-committee meeting, there were no bargaining rights here, no union. And Arthur wanted to keep it on the level of Venezzia's benevolence, where there was just the chance he might decide to make the grand gesture and allow Lucy to come back.

Venezzia pressed a buzzer on the right leg of his desk, and Miss Amassa appeared.

"Miss Amassa, have Mr. Zangora come up here. He's down on the production floor somewhere."

"I'll phone him right away, sir."

"Father Wagner," Venezzia began musingly, "let me say something to you about all this before my foreman arrives. I have read with deep interest, and some alarm, your vigorous editorials on the writings of the Popes as they should be applied by the clergy and faithful in terms of American life."

"I'm grateful you've taken a serious interest in them—not too many have," Arthur said.

"How could I do otherwise? I am at once an Italian immigrant and a loving son of the Church. My roots and connections are European and will always be. From the great forests of Germany and the Alps comes much of the pulp which is used as an end product in this very mill. I control interests in paper mills and box factories throughout Italy and I purchase vast quantities of paper board in Canada, the great Northwest, and in New England for both foreign and domestic use.

"The world-wide Kline Brothers Soap Company, which is my largest client, has its strongest mercantile roots in Europe. But we Europeans have an entirely different understanding of social problems than yourselves. In Europe a Socialist, and even a Communist, is in many instances socially and politically acceptable. We are realistic about those things in European commerce. If the Socialists are in the majority, we do business with them. We accept their silly nationalization and collectivism, and it simply becomes a vehicle for our capitalistic practices under another guise. This is true of unions in Europe, where socialism is strong. We accept them, we live with them in friendly fashion, and often we conform them, however subtly, to our desires. However, these things are not true of the United States of America."

"I appreciate your frankness," Arthur said, "even if it does seem a rather ruthlessly pragmatic attitude for a Catholic businessman."

"My dear Father," Venezzia said quite firmly, "may I say that I am a Catholic as a Catholic and a businessman as a businessman. These two credos do not always agree."

"That's precisely what Pope Leo XIII argued in his encyclical *Rerum Novarum*," Arthur insisted. " 'The rich have their own defenses,' but the workers must organize to protect themselves."

"In Europe, yes, little Father," Venezzia said. "And I speak as a Catholic now. Socialism and communism seek to master the spiritual as well as the material. The Holy Fathers, then and since, have recognized this and are calling for Christian trade unions which will resist the godlessness of collectivism while retaining its most valuable elements of social justice. Correct?"

"Correct, Mr. Venezzia," Arthur said, leaning forward intently and summoning the big question. "But what of the United States? Is not the Church the same here and are not the problems of exploited workers substantially the same?"

"The Holy Fathers are not, in my opinion, speaking to the American workers in their pronouncements on the social order," Venezzia insisted. "Here is a land of abundance, even in these years of unreasonable inflation. Here capitalism is supreme—Socialists and Communists are outcasts of society and are invariably subject to arrest as anarchists and criminals. It is a different climate. Here, the stability of free enterprise; in Europe, constant change and revolution. I know, my boy, I know these things."

"I need not remind you of my editorial position on these matters," Arthur said coldly. "The Holy Father speaks to us all."

"Tell me, my son," Venezzia said, shifting into cordial and avid curiosity. "Does His Eminence explicitly countenance your constant editorial crusades in behalf of organized labor? Surely you must realize that the great bulk of his financial support for his most worthy archdiocesan projects comes from sources of great wealth and industrial ownership?"

"His Eminence has most graciously allowed me to interpret the writings of the Popes in terms of American social problems as long as I do not misrepresent the Holy Fathers," Arthur said flatly.

"That is typical of the Cardinal's broadness and depth," Venezzia said shrewdly. "And now, Mr. Zangora."

Miss Amassa escorted a giant, muscular Italian in shirt sleeves, dungarees, and black high-top shoes into the room. His head was huge and inanimate but for two piggish little eyes that danced electrically in thin rims of red.

Venezzia introduced him and asked for an explanation of his reasons for firing Lucy Smith.

"Well, Mr. Venezzia, Father, Mr. Lorenzo," he began in a heavy, nervous voice, deferring even to Tony, whose role in all this he could not yet identify. "As you may know, Miss Smith's father died at a time when we needed her very much in the stripping room for a job which we had to get out by three o'clock. I asked her to stay until then and she refused. So I took her upstairs to this office."

"What happened then?" Father Wagner asked.

"Tell him, John," Venezzia said.

"I think Mr. Venezzia was going to let her take the time off, but she gave him a lot of guff about working conditions here and the need for a union. He told her to pick up her pay and leave, which she did."

"That is true," Mr. Venezzia said. "What else did she say, John?"

"She said she'd be back with a union organizer."

"There you have it, gentlemen," Venezzia said. "That is the truth. I would have let her go to the wake out of respect to the dead. But she was insubordinate and threatened me with a union."

Arthur, a little taken aback by this revelation of what actually happened, hastily improvised a different tack.

"Well, may I ask, Mr. Venezzia, why couldn't Mr. Zangora, her foreman, have honored her request for time off under the circumstances?"

"Answer that, John," Venezzia said.

"We always give time off for emergencies except where there's a rush job on. Those are my orders from the boss here."

"Well, was she a good worker?" Arthur asked.

"She worked hard," Zangora admitted. "But she was constantly stirring up the women, especially the colored ones, against the separate toilets and things like that. And she gave them pamphlets to read, about labor unions and socialism."

"Yes, this was all reported to me by Zangora," Venezzia said. "I will be perfectly frank with you. This girl is brilliant. She does not have to do menial labor in a box company. I am convinced she is a plant—either of the labor unions or, even worse, the Communists. I did not fire her for this, as I had no evidence. I fired her for insubordination."

"I can't argue with you on that, Mr. Venezzia," Arthur said. "But what about these separate facilities, may I ask? Do you really segregate the races?"

"We do," Venezzia said. "We have both northern and southern white workers here who strenuously object to that kind of intimacy with the colored."

Father Wagner restrained an impulse to anger, realizing they had gone as far as they could go with Venezzia.

"Well——" the priest said as he arose to go. "Business is business, I guess."

"Business is business," Venezzia repeated coldly. "I will not turn my plant into a social battleground. We are here to produce paper boxes."

"There's an old Italian proverb," Arthur said, "with which you are undoubtedly familiar, Mr. Venezzia. It goes like this: 'Si non è vero, è bien trovato,' meaning, 'If it's not true, it's a good story.'"

Venezzia's face was cold, impassive.

"Thank you for giving us so much of your time," Father Wagner concluded, shaking hands casually with the boxmaker. Tony Lorenzo nodded slightly as they moved toward the door.

"It was my pleasure," said Venezzia with penetrating graciousness. "Surely, at times we can be agreeable in disagreement."

Arthur made a slightly genial face and walked out of the room, followed by Tony.

Out of the dust, out in the sunshine, coming up for air, they stood for a moment, stunned.

"Turn back the clock to the nineteenth century!" Father Wagner said, grabbing his forehead comically. "I feel as if I've just attended the Congress of Vienna."

"Let's go get a cab," Lorenzo said, shaking his head in sheer unbelief. "And bring on that union job!"

CHAPTER XVIII

Father Vincent and the Red Necktie

"You've got about an eight-inch hole in the editorial section this week," Father Ed Saulnier, assistant to the editor of *The Clarion*, said, leaning over Father Wagner's shoulders and pointing to the "hole" in the make-up sheet under the lead editorial.

"That much of a hole, Ed?" Arthur said, turning from his typewriter and squinting at the dummy page.

"Sure, don't you remember?" Father Saulnier reminded him dryly. He was a dark, round little priest who could sit at a rewrite desk longer than any newspaperman Arthur had ever known, having been city editor on a small Indiana daily before entering the seminary.

"You followed my suggestion to pull out those extensive quotations from Franklin Roosevelt's nominating speech at the convention. After all, you did intend to make it clear that Al Smith had been nominated rather than Roosevelt. Right?"

"Right," Arthur said with a little laugh.

"That leaves you room for another fairly good-sized editorial."

"What do you suggest?" Arthur asked.

"Why don't you do a piece on women's hats at the cathedral fashion show and give the editorial bloodhounds a rest?" the assistant editor suggested in his characteristic dry manner.

"I really should, I guess," Arthur conceded. "We've got enough people mad at us as it is."

"If this were a secular newspaper I'd say that was a good thing, because you sure have made this sheet readable. But with things as they are in the Church militant, I'm afraid both our heads are going rolling down those stairs one of these Fridays."

"Do you really think His Eminence would do that to us?"

"If he comes up with 'accidie' some dark misty Friday morning you may be in trouble."

" 'Accidie,' what's that?"

"That's an ancient monastic complaint which we probably identify today as plain old ulcers. Anyway, you'd better do me an eight-inch, two-column editorial if you want a newspaper this week. We go to press in an hour."

"I'll do it right away, Ed. Thanks for the philosophy."

"It's not St. Thomas, but it works," the priest said, sidling back to his desk with his eyes fixed glumly on the dummy page held before him.

Arthur settled at his typewriter again, rolled out the filler squibs he had been typing, dropped them in the out basket, and inserted a fresh sheet in the writing mill.

Why not fire a shot across the bow of Venezzia and the Roma Paper Box Company? That would make a tangy little fillip as the second editorial of the week. The Lucy Smith case and the unjust and unchristian working conditions at the plant were a natural for the application of papal principles on social justice.

In the enthusiasm of the moment, and in the flare-up of his indignation at Venezzia's smooth, smug ruthlessness, he was ready to start firing away when he caught Father Ed Saulnier's baleful eye on the other side of the office.

"Women's hats," Father Saulnier said glumly.

That let the air out of the balloon.

Ed was right for more reasons than he knew. He couldn't do it. Father Vincent would be making the fund-raising pitch for the Cardinal at the seminary dinner that evening. He just couldn't jeopardize that—too many things would get hurt—Vincent, the building fund, and, last but not least, the surge of "accidie" when the Cardinal returned from Washington over the weekend.

He glanced at his watch—6 P.M. He'd have to be at his mother's house for dinner in an hour. Tony would be there and he wanted to help put him at his ease.

"Okay," he sighed, nodding at Father Saulnier and grinning sheepishly. "Women's hats."

This would come under the heading of a summer editorial—lightly

and politely. He went at the keys with his fingers, paused in thought
for several minutes, then starting tapping away:

"The modeling of fruited and flowered feminine straw hats," he
wrote, "at the Cathedral Married Ladies' Sodality Fashion Show
this week brings welcome summer relief from political hot air, raids
on speakeasies, and the dizzying fluctuations of Wall Street ticker
tapes . . ."

Half an hour later he hurried down Cathedral Street in the hope
that he could still catch Vincent at the rectory and possibly spur
him over to his mother's for a cocktail.

The paper would be on the press in an hour and Father Ed would
be there to handle last-minute details. He walked briskly past the
cathedral and clanged through the wrought-iron gate that separated
the church from the rectory.

On through the side door now with the pungent smell of fried
haddock and boiled potatoes strong in his nostrils. Up three flights
to Vincent's room and a knock on the door.

"Come in, come in," Vincent said cheerily.

He found the priest, wan yet refreshed from his afternoon nap,
penning some notes on index cards at his desk.

"How you coming?" Arthur greeted him. "Have a good nap?"

"The arms of Morpheus," Vincent said, looking up from the notes
and turning in his chair. "How'd you and Tony make out with Lucy?"

"It's a long story. I'll tell you on the way over to Mother's if you'll
come by for a drink. Tony's there now."

"Oh, good," Vincent said, making one last note and jogging the
cards evenly together. "Funeral arrangements satisfactory and all?"

"Yes, the old guy's insurance took care of that. Come on, now,
throw on a collar and your coat. I don't want to make you late for
the fund-raising dinner."

"Right you are," Vincent said, rising. "I've got some notes here.
The Cardinal gave me a message for them and asked me to make
a few pertinent remarks."

"It's the chance of a lifetime for you," Arthur said with a little
twinge of envy that was quickly engulfed by a surge of deep affection. "Everybody that's anybody will be there, from the mayor
down."

"That's what the papers said this morning. I wish I could get a

few dollars out of them for the youth center, but this is the Cardinal's
show."

"And you are his spokesman. What are you going to say?"

Vincent was snapping on his Roman collar with one hand and
reaching for his black linen suit coat with the other.

"Oh, the usual, I guess—the endless, omnivorous need for priests
—'going therefore, teach ye all nations,' et cetera."

"Good. Comb your hair, grab your straw, and let's go."

In a side bedroom of Lorraine Wagner's long, cool, tastefully furnished apartment Tony Lorenzo lay clad in T-shirt and trousers,
with his hands clasped at the back of his neck.

This was the life, he thought, looking at the cool whiteness of the
venetian blinds and feeling the deep sweetness that comes with
awakening from a two-hour stretch of completely abysmal slumber.

What was it that had awakened him? The merry, yet enervating
splashing of a shower and the low, rich crooning of a young woman's
voice, one of the most seductive moments he had ever known.

He could still hear her stirring about in the big bathroom which
adjoined his room and another, probably hers. That must be the
Venezzia girl, Rosa.

Mrs. Wagner had told him she had the room on the other side
of the bath and to be sure to lock both doors when using the place.

If Father Arthur had not cabbed him right to the door with his
bags he probably would not have taken up the offer of hospitality.
But the tall, youngish matron with shining, bobbed white hair had
swept him into ease with her informal friendliness and the sureness
with which she immersed him in the commodious comforts of her
home.

Oh, what a heaven of softness and light after all that iron and
concrete at the state pen! The tension oozed out of him like an
interminably slow sweat and would for a long time to come, he
knew.

Father Arthur had introduced him to his mother and rushed off
to the newspaper office.

Lorraine—and she insisted he call her that—gave him a big splash
of gin and tonic and sat him down in her big cozy living room,
which was dominated by a grand piano and a series of religious oil
paintings from Italy.

"Dinner's the big meal here," she told him in her brusque yet kindly way. "You take a good shower and a nap, then'll we stoke you up good with haddock and potatoes. There'll be people coming and going here all the time—Arthur's waifs, I call them. But you get the best room—that's Arthur's orders—and besides," she added with a shrewd, penetrating tilt of her silver head, "I think I like you."

He had sat opposite the piano in a soft brocade chair which, along with the drink, held him a complete prisoner for over half an hour. Before going to his room, two of "Arthur's waifs" had come in—a blind university student from Germany and a curvy, honey-haired Norwegian girl who was studying music and ballet.

Now he could hear the other girl, the one he had not seen, crooning and moving about quietly in the lavatory. The daughter of the master of the Roma Paper Box Company.

He'd have to be discreet once the organizing drive got under way. Maybe by that time he'd be in other quarters, which would be best for all concerned. He certainly would not want to bring tension or discomfort into this house of peace and kindliness. But Father Arthur had known the possible implications of all that when he invited him here in his delightful friendly way; it had not bothered him in the least.

Now the lock on the door to the lavatory snapped and she was gone. He glanced at his watch: six-fifteen. He'd better get up and dress for dinner. Father Arthur had promised to be here at six-thirty with Father Vincent if he could snare him before the fund-raising dinner.

He swung off the bed in his stockinged feet and groped in the half-light for his trousers on the chair. As he dressed, the telephone rang insistently. He heard Lorraine's footsteps and her bluff voice as she answered. Soon she was knocking vigorously on his door.

"Tony, Tony," she called, "are you awake? It's Joan from Father Vincent's office. She wants to talk to you."

"Tell her I'll be right there."

Joan. He had been wondering about calling her. He had known that sooner or later he would have to contact her, face up to the fact that he thought the world of her, was deeply grateful to her but didn't love her in the way she wanted and deserved to be loved—the halter at the altar and the cottage and babies. It was not for him, not for a long time, he knew. That would be a kind of prison, and he had just got out of a prison. Dear, sweet, generous, loving Joan . . .

"Hello, hello," he said, picking up the phone. "This, you, Joan?"

"Yes, how are you, Tony? How're you getting along?"

"Fine, Joan. It's very nice here and I think I've got a job with the unions. I report to a fellow named Naski tomorrow."

"Oh, that's swell. I'm so happy for you, Tony, honestly."

"Thanks, Joan, you've always been such a peach."

"Tony, I called because Cardinal Wagner is trying to get hold of Father Vincent from Washington, D.C. I just called the cathedral and he and Father Arthur are on their way over to you. Have Father Vincent call Operator 7 in Washington as soon as he comes in. Will you do that, Tony?"

"I sure will—Operator 7."

"That's right. Well . . ." Joan said, pausing painfully, "it's been good talking to you, Tony."

"Same here, Joan," he said, stormed for a moment with confusion and regret. Then he felt a little terror that he was letting go of something real big and wouldn't get another chance at it. His grip on the phone tightened; he calmed himself. "We'll have to get together soon, Joan. Soon as I can get a toe hold on this new job."

"That would be nice, Tony."

"All right, Joan, all right, I'll give Father the message," he said nervously.

He dropped the earpiece onto its hook, and it clattered a little, mocking him.

It's best this way, he told himself, adjusting his tie in the mirror at the phone table. I'm not ready for what she wants. She'll thank me later for it.

"Ton-ee!" Lorraine called. "Come out here in the kitchen and keep me company. The fathers will be along any minute now."

"Okay, Lorraine," Tony said, and started down the hall.

There was one door to the left just before the dining room. It swung open, and she came out with a large, square portfolio under her arm.

He was taken aback for a moment, thinking a teen-age boy had walked out of the bedroom. She was a statuette of blackness: black boy-trimmed hair, black gabardine jacket and slacks, black sandals, and dark, burning eyes shaded by long jet eyelashes.

"Excuse me," was all she said in a soft, shy voice. But there was no shyness in the look she gave him, holding his face with her black eyes and boring deep into him.

"That's quite all right," he said, backing against the wall.

She moved past him and he caught the scent of some expensive perfume. She clocked down the hall, let herself out, and was gone.

"Who's that?" Lorraine called from the kitchen. "Is that Rosa? I want you to meet her. Rosa, is that you?"

Tony walked through the dining room to the kitchen.

"She's gone, Lorraine, gone off with a package of sketches or something."

"That's her, that's her," Lorraine said brusquely, waving a paring knife at him from over a colander of potatoes at the sink. "She comes and goes—like a little black cat—comes and goes."

That described her, Tony thought, a little black cat, a Siamese, maybe—if there were black Siamese cats—with all that comeliness.

"Lovely girl, lovely girl," she said, peeling away. "Sit down at the table, Tony. I'll get you a drink in a minute. You like that gin?" she went on, answering her own question. "I'll give you more of it. The Archbishop of Mexico City sent a case of it to His Eminence and he sent it over to me.

"Lovely girl, lovely girl. Isn't it a shame—so young and a widow —married some fellow in Rome who got killed in a racing automobile. Lives here and goes to art school—won't stay with her father. Could have a castle to herself on the lake, but doesn't want it. Likes to be alone and paint. Just comes and goes, comes and goes . . ."

"Like a little black cat," Tony said.

"That's it, that's it exactly," she said, drying her hands and reaching for the gin in a cupboard under the sink. "Here now, I'll give you one before the others come. You haven't had much of this lately, have you? That's why I'm sneaking you a little extra now. We'll make it up to you, boy, we'll make it up to you somehow."

That was a nice thing to say, Tony thought, stormed with grateful emotion. He got up and kissed her on the forehead.

She stepped back, at first a little aghast.

"That's for being so nice to an old jailbird," Tony said.

"Well—I never—— Well!" she said, putting her hands on her hips. "Why, I haven't had a kiss from a man since my husband died."

"You could do a lot better than Tony Lorenzo," he said with a laugh.

"Yes, and a lot worse, too," she said snappily, splashing some gin into a glass and adding quinine water. "Here, get this down, the boys will be here soon."

Tony sat contentedly at the kitchen table, sipping his drink while Lorraine peeled the potatoes and mused on the Cardinal's phone call.

"It's something very important, otherwise he'd have talked to me," she said. "He's got something big on his mind or he'd chit-chat awhile. I wonder what it is," she mused.

Tony didn't press her, but he could tell from the tone of her voice that she had a good idea what it was. She'd been through these things with the prelate off and on for twenty-odd years and she was sensitive to every nuance. Something was in the wind—what? He took a sip and turned from the problem to the more pleasant memory of Rosa.

Rosa, he thought with a chuckle, the lady next door.

The doorbell drilled through the cool, dim silence of the apartment. Lorraine wiped her hands on her apron, put her hand deftly to her hair, and hurried down the hall.

Tony wondered at her as she left, feeling the cooling warmth of the gin. The mother of a brilliant young priest, the sister-in-law of a great cardinal, as zippy and chic at fifty-odd as a young flapper, yet having the depth and sincerity that fitted her background.

He set his half-empty glass down, rose, and waited for them. Voices and footsteps, welcome faces; what a contrast to the waiting in the cell for food, for someone to let you out, the cold, indifferent faces of the "screws" in the state pen.

"Here's your wandering boy, Father Vincent," Lorraine said, leading the priests into the kitchen. "Arthur, you mix the drinks. Father Vincent must call the Cardinal immediately."

"Hi, Father," Tony said. "Joan called. She said you were to get Operator 7 in Washington, D.C. It's the Cardinal."

"So I understand," Vincent said, grabbing him strongly by the arm. "How are you? Quite a hassle out at Venezzia's place, eh? Art was telling me about it on the way over. I'm no little shocked at the whole thing—not Lucy so much—she probably was insubordinate —but the conditions at the plant, the sheer pragmatism of the man. He's one of the outstanding sons of the Church here and even more so in Rome."

"Don't be too shocked," Tony said consolingly. "If we can put the union clamp on him he'll be all right."

"That won't be easy. Perhaps I'll get a chance to chat with him tonight."

"You'd better be careful about chatting with him," Arthur said. "Leave the editorials to me. You've got money to raise for Unk tonight, remember. And get going on that phone call."

Lorraine turned the gas higher under the potatoes.

"Father Vincent," she urged anxiously, "get going, the Cardinal may be waiting."

"I will—right now." Vincent headed for the hallway.

Tony and Father Arthur followed him and went on to the living room. Once in the large room, Tony let his curiosity get the better of him.

"What's hot?" he asked the priest.

"I'm not sure," Arthur said, closing the door to the hall. "At least now we won't have to go through the agony of trying not to eavesdrop." He sat down and sighed.

"What do you think it is?" Tony asked.

"I can only guess. It just may be something wonderful for Vin, that's all."

Tony could see that the priest was under considerable strain. He was beginning to pay a price for his editorial candor. And if he was able to get away with it rather because he was the Cardinal's nephew, it was also true that his editorial crusading spirit, diplomatically speaking, could not be the easiest thing in the world for His Eminence to accept. There were the advantages on the one hand and a certain roadblock to higher echelons on the other. And this, as his closest friend talked to Washington, the Cardinal's nephew knew.

He sensed the possible significance of the call on the eminently important fund-raising dinner coming up that evening. He loved Vincent with all his heart and wished him well, but the potential sanction of his editorial freedom clanged like a death knell with every accentuating beat of his heart.

Queen of Humility pray for me, he pleaded silently as he paced up and down, while Tony tried not to look apprehensive. For he had grown fond of this brash, brilliant young priest and, even amid the tension of the moment, was deeply cognizant of the riches of friendship he had in both Father Arthur and Father Vincent.

Lorraine swung open the door.

"Arthur, come quickly," she said. "The Cardinal will speak with you now."

He hurried down the hallway to the telephone, where Vincent was still talking to the Cardinal.

"I'm simply overwhelmed, Your Eminence," he was saying in a voice hardly above a whisper, "but I will try to do a good job for you tonight—and always."

"I'm sure you will," Arthur heard his uncle say vigorously. "Now will you put Arthur on, please?"

"Here he is, Your Eminence," Vincent said, handing the phone to Arthur.

"Your Eminence, how are you, sir?"

"Splendid, splendid," he said heartily. "I saw the wire-service story on the fund-raising dinner. You've done a good job."

He always complimented Arthur before giving him a big, bitter pill of some kind to swallow. It made the gulping a little easier, Arthur knew.

"I've just given Father Whelton some interesting news and I know you will rejoice with him. At the instance of myself and the Apostolic Delegate, the Holy Father has appointed Father Whelton a papal chamberlain with the title of Very Reverend Monsignor."

"That's wonderful," Arthur said huskily, feeling the lump in his throat growing. Vincent leaned back against the wall, his head in his hands.

"I simply felt we had to do it anyway because of his fine work at the center. And I'm doing it informally so that I can send him to the dinner tonight with a little added authority. There'll be so many important people there and I want him to make the right impression all around. I'll be back Sunday with the letter of appointment from Rome. Vincent can put on his red necktie then."

"Yes, Your Eminence," Arthur said, the tears of joy welling in his eyes as he smiled at Vincent. "Do you want me to give it to the press and radio?"

"Yes. We'll be too late for the evening papers, I know, but give it to the radio people and send a story to the morning press. Also, get hold of the mayor, who's acting as chairman tonight, and give him the story so he can make the proper introduction."

"I'll do that right away. Anything else?"

"No, be a good boy. I'll see you Sunday," the Cardinal said gently. "Put your mother on now, please."

"Mother!" Arthur called, and Lorraine was there, leaping out of the hallway darkness, bursting with excitement.

Arthur took Vincent by the elbow and led him into the parlor. Tony stood there soberly, his hands at his sides.

"It should have been you first," Vincent said with deep emotion. "It should have been you."

"No, no, Vin," Arthur said, blinking the mist out of his eyes. "Tony, come over here and look at our brand-new Monsignor."

Tony grabbed Vincent's hand, and with his stout right pitching arm the new Monsignor gripped Tony affectionately by the elbow.

"Will you give us your first blessing, Monsignor?" Arthur said, smiling happily.

"I will. I most certainly will."

"Can we wait for Mother?"

"Yes," Vincent said, feeling for the first time a surge of both humility and pride at the bestowal of the rank. A papal chamberlain! The mention of Arthur's mother struck him deep with longing for his own parents, the little dark saint in the lumberyard kitchen, the scrappy ward boss, now gone.

"Father Vincent! Father Vincent!" Lorraine called wildly, hurrying down the hall.

She threw herself upon him and hugged him strongly.

"I'm so happy for you, so happy." She pushed herself away from him and turned to Arthur. "Isn't it marvelous? Thank God! Thank God!" she said.

"Thank God!" Arthur repeated. "Mother, Monsignor wants to give us the first blessings!"

"Yes, Mother Wagner, you first," Vincent said.

Lorraine knelt in front of him, the other two on either side of her.

Very Reverend Monsignor Vincent Whelton, papal chamberlain to His Holiness, Pope Pius XI, placed his hands over her forehead and bestowed his first blessing as a prelate.

"I ask God's blessing for you, dear, for the first time as a monsignor, and I ask you to receive it, not only for yourself and my dear friend, your son Arthur, but also in place of my mother and father who cannot be here but would rejoice at the great honor which the Holy Father and His Eminence have bestowed upon me. *In nomine Patris, et Filii, et Spiritus Sancti.* Amen!"

Lorraine kissed his hands, her face moist, and blessed herself.

Vincent crossed over to Arthur and placed his hands over his forehead in the same manner, intoning the blessing.

"My dear, dear friend," Vincent said as Arthur kissed his hands reverently.

And then to Tony, whose head was bowed almost in comalike depth.

"And you, Anthony, how good that you should be here at this moment."

"*In nomine Patris, et Filii, et Spiritus Sancti. Amen!*"

There was a moment of keen silence which Vincent suddenly broke.

"I'm so sorry that I have to go now," he said. "But we'll rejoice together at another time."

Arthur got to his feet quickly with the others.

"I'll go with you," he said, grinning mischievously. "The whole wide world is waiting for the news!"

BOOK FOUR

Closer to the Throne

CHAPTER XIX

Bidding It Up!

WALKING along Lakeport Boulevard at five minutes of nine that evening, Tony Lorenzo blinked in pleasant bewilderment at the events of the day and still felt a deep glow of happiness over Father Whelton's new rank and title.

"Monsignor Whelton," he whispered, involuntarily attracting the attention of a matronly woman who had emerged from a swanky apartment house with a Pekinese at the end of a leash.

"What's that, young man?" she inquired, eying him shrewdly. "You must be looking for the cathedral—three blocks down the boulevard there and to the left."

"I beg your pardon, ma'am," Tony said. "I was just thinking out loud."

He stepped up his pace and hurried away from her toward the brightly winking marquee of the Senate Hotel a block to the south. As he moved closer, the hotel entrance drew him like a magnet.

The Monsignor and Father Arthur would be in there, the dinner just about finished now, and the "victims" would be settling back for the speeches.

He had a strong yen to hear the Monsignor's remarks, his maiden speaking effort as a papal chamberlain. If banquets were still the same, the doors would be open and he could go in, lean against the wall, and hear the speeches.

He ignored a cool, rather suspicious glance from the gold-buttoned doorman at the hotel entrance and entered the busy lobby, where he spotted the calendar of events mounted on a triangular stand. He went up to it and found the listing:

ARCHDIOCESAN BUILDING FUND DINNER, 8 P.M., OVAL ROOM, MEZZANINE.

He climbed the heavily carpeted stairs bordered with potted rubber plants. The doors to the Oval Room were wide open and he could see the head table looming in the distance amid rolling billows of gray cigar smoke.

From the telephone booths against the wall to his left he heard a gruff voice that struck an odd, familiar note in his memory.

"Of course it's near beer!" the voice said defiantly. "So what if one of your customers did get drunk on it? Maybe he spiked it with a shot of ether or something. There's less than two per cent alky in Red Ball Ale, so take it or leave it."

He glanced over at the booth, the door of which was standing ajar and was not surprised to see big Teedee Quinlan, his old brewmaster at the Acme plant. He paused, hearing the conversation out before addressing him.

"He wasn't drunk," were the words Teedee snarled into the telephone. "He was bloated from drinking too much of the stuff. You could get that way on orangeade. . . . All right, all right, send the stuff back. I'll send a new case out in the morning if it will make you feel happier. But all the stuff is the same, it's all the law will allow."

The huge, aging, yet immensely vital redhead slammed down the receiver, popped his cigar back in his mouth, and stepped thumpingly out of the booth.

"*Red!*" Tony called, grinning from ear to ear.

The cigar came out of the mouth and the jaw dropped as the red giant squinted at him with intent, almost piggish green eyes.

"Tony!" he said in amazement. "Is it really you?"

"It's me, Red," Tony said, striding forward and shaking his hand, pounding his shoulder.

"I'll be a wall-eyed bastard!" Red said. "It's really you, and you haven't changed, you haven't changed much at all."

"And you haven't changed either!" Tony said. "Was that the batch of beer with the rats in it?" he asked, chuckling. "I'll bet your near beer is twenty per cent alcohol by volume, at least."

"Waaal," the brewmaster said, snorting contemptuously, "there is a little kick to it at that. But you know me better than anyone. I'm

a brewmaster. I can't make that dishwater, Volstead or no Volstead!
But when-ja get out, Tony? What are you doin' here?"

"I just got out a couple of days ago. I came over here to listen
to the new Monsignor. You know him—Father Whelton. He used to
be in the parish across from the brewery."

"I know, I know," the redhead said, taking him by the arm. "You
got a table? Why not sit with me? I brought a whole table to help
the Cardinal—a great man—a great man. Come and sit with me! I
got a little something under the tablecloth too."

"I'd love to, Red," Tony said, accompanying him into the dining
room.

The waiters were bustling about with ice cream and coffee when
they entered the room. Tony took a look at the head table in the
distance and could see Monsignor Whelton chatting with an aristocratic white-haired man whom he recognized as Mayor O'Leary.

There were two overdressed middle-aged men seated at Teedee's
table with their wives, one a sedate gray-haired matron and the
other a heavy-set blonde who was working very hard at being a forty-
five-year-old beauty.

"You remember T. P. O'Neil," Teedee said, gesturing toward the
older of the two men. "You met Tony Lorenzo at the Acme brewery
some years back, Tip."

Tony shook hands with Tip. They always called you Tip if your
name was O'Neil, Tony thought, just as they call you Soupy if your
name is Campbell or Terrible Terry if your first name is Terence.

"Hello, Tip," Tony said. "It's been a long time."

"Good to see you, Tony," Tip said laconically. He knew all about
it, remembering Tony when he used to go out to the race track.
Many of Tony's former associates had been "clients" of his, and
Tony had made a bet or two himself in the old days.

"And this is Mrs. O'Neil," Teedee said, nodding at the matronly
one. "Here's Mr. and Mrs. Eddie Nye. Eddie's a sports writer, but
mostly about horses."

Eddie Nye, a sharp-eyed, plump little man prickling with nervous
energy, shook hands and nodded pleasantly. His big blond wife gave
Tony a wide, inviting smile as he sat down.

"I'm anxious to hear the new Monsignor sound off," Tony said.
"He's quite a speaker, you know."

"He's a wow!" Teedee said, biting the head of a new cigar. "He'll
shake down every dollar in the joint for the Cardinal."

"I hope so," Tony said. "The Cardinal hand-picked him for the job."

"We'll see that he gets a good piece of change, eh, Eddie?" Teedee said knowingly.

"We'll do the best we can."

"How does it work?" Tony inquired. "How do they go about raising the cabbage?"

"They bid it up," Teedee said. "Most of these people are business-men and politicians, all friends of the Cardinal. When things get popping they compete with each other—pledging and outpledging. That's why I brought Eddie. He'll liven up the bidding if it gets dull. Right, Eddie?"

"I'll do what I can."

Tony took another look at the head table and saw the Monsignor talking now to a slight, stooped figure dressed in a costume that made him look like a Spanish admiral. It was Nino Venezzia. There were others up there dressed that way, Knights of Malta, Knights of St. Gregory, plumed and banded in their uniforms of ancient papal privilege.

His eyes roved to the end of the table on the right, and he saw Father Arthur sipping a glass of water and alertly watching the speaker, a notebook and pencil on the table in front of him.

The mayor was calling for attention now, making little authori-tative tinkles with a spoon against a pitcher of water.

He introduced the guests at the head table: Venezzia, the other Knights, the governor's military aide, the president of the Chamber of Commerce.

"And of course you all know the Honorable John I. Doyle, presi-dent of the City Council and my strong right arm."

"Hey, that's Umbrella Jack Doyle!" Tony said. "I haven't seen him for years."

"I'm surprised you haven't," Teedee said with a knowing wink, passing Tony a shot of whiskey and soda which he had maneuvered into a paper cup underneath the overhanging drape of the table-cloth.

Tony laughed at the joke, which evoked a polite chuckle from Eddie Nye, who got the point all right.

"He ought to be good for a couple of thousand."

"I'm not so sure of that," Eddie Nye said. "It goes into the um-brella easy, but comes out hard."

"We'll shame the bastard into it—if we have to," Teedee said.

The mayor was introducing the Monsignor—"well known for his charitable work at the Christian Youth Center, et cetera. One of our very own, the son of the late city councilor, Vinny Whelton, whom we all remember so well on the west side, et cetera, et cetera."

There was polite applause as Monsignor Whelton rose to speak. Everyone was giving him a sharp-eyed once-over, perhaps a little miffed that the Cardinal himself had not shown up.

Vincent sensed all this, cleared his throat nervously, and drove his powers of articulation up through the seething sea of thoughts and emotions within him:

" 'I am the voice of one crying in the wilderness,' " he began. "Those, as you know, are the words of St. John the Baptist, who went before Christ, proclaiming His coming. Our visual symbol of Christ in the archdiocese of Lakeport is, of course, His Eminence, Arthur Cardinal Wagner, so beloved by all of you here. And in his absence I have been given the duty and the privilege of addressing you.

"The Cardinal is crying out to you in the wilderness of immortal souls. He needs priests to minister to his people in the wilds of a city and its environs which are torn by the unrest of post-war adjustment and all the social ills which have been visited upon us by easy money and the utter folly of the Volstead Act.

"Our growing boys, secure in the faith of the old parishes, are still coming forward with vocations to the holy priesthood, but, alas, there is no room in the inn. Our seminary is overcrowded, understaffed, ill equipped. We must build, expand, remodel—and we must do it now!

"You, the leaders of the community, many of whom are also devoted Catholics, have signified your interest in rallying to this cause. Giving forth with the money you have earned in commerce and the professions is not an easy decision. The extent of your giving can only be made easier by the realization that a seminarian, a priest, must give—with his whole life and all his life—in order that there may be one fold and one shepherd.

"Consider the words from St. Luke when Jesus asked a disciple to drop everything that was important to him in his life and come follow Him. Consider the answer in terms of the sacrifice of young men who will become sacred dispensers of the sacraments for the rest of their lives because of your contributions here tonight. 'I will follow Thee, Lord; but let me first take my leave of them that are at my house.' "

Monsignor Whelton paused. They were with him now, lifted by his eloquence, wondering and reverent at the ringing baritone of his voice and the unself-consciousness with which he spoke of sacred things, as though the hotel dining-room rostrum were a pulpit in the cathedral.

"This is what the Cardinal is continually asking many of your sons and brothers to do: leave their families, their mothers, their fathers, their privacy and possessions, that the command of Jesus to his Apostles might be continually fulfilled: 'Going, therefore, teach ye all nations, baptizing them in the name of the Father, and of the Son, and of the Holy Ghost . . .'

"I am as the voice of the Cardinal crying out in a wilderness of souls," Vincent intoned, repeating his theme. "He calls upon you to reward sacrifice with sacrifice. Give in fullest measure, according to your means—give tonight—so that new towers of truth will rise above the seminary grounds, higher than the Babel of ticker tape, with bells of peace speaking out sweeter than the staccato of hoodlum machine guns. Let this be the symbol of our times—rather than the canyons of Wall Street and the stutter of illicit guns—the towers of peace rising above the seminary.

"Give, my friends, give tonight that the Cardinal may give. 'I am the voice of one crying in the wilderness.' Hear ye Him!"

Monsignor Whelton bowed his head and turned his hands in gentle, dignified supplication. A pall of awe had descended on the audience and he took his seat in silence.

Teedee Quinlan planked his cigar into an ash tray and brought his two great palms vigorously together, sparking a huge, rolling round of applause.

"How about that! How about that!" Tony said, bursting with love and admiration for the Monsignor. "I'd give him a million—if I had it."

"He's got the blarney," Eddie Nye said. "The Cardinal knew his man."

"My, my, my!" Mrs. O'Neil said with misty eyes.

"What a doll! What a perfect doll!" the big blonde said, hitching up her girdle a little.

The mayor had arisen and was calling for attention again.

"If such golden-tongued eloquence cannot move us," he began a little stiffly, "we are beyond the pale," he added. "You are to be congratulated, Monsignor," he concluded, exchanging courteous nods with Vincent.

"Now we'll start the bidding, gentlemen," the mayor said. "You have the bidding procedure outlined there on your programs: a minimum of one hundred dollars, starting and progressing. The time limit on highest bids will be three minutes, and we hope to get about ten such bidding periods in during the next half hour. And remember, the highest bidders in each three-minute period will have their names inscribed in bronze on the cornerstone of the new seminary building.

"I'll start things off right from the head table here by offering my personal check for five hundred dollars, a sum which has been matched by contributions from my fellow workers at the City Hall. This means we are contributing one thousand dollars to the Cardinal's Seminary Building Fund! Any competitive bids—and we'll donate the thousand anyway."

There was a burst of applause while the mayor called for a competitive bid.

"What do you say? Anyone want to top it? It will take eleven hundred to do so." The mayor glanced over at Umbrella Jack, who was loosening his collar and avoiding the issue as blandly as possible.

Teedee was on his feet, waving his cigar.

"I'll take half of the bid—five hundred fifty clams—if Umbrella Jack will take the other half."

There was a roar of laughing approval. Everybody knew how close Umbrella Jack was with a dollar, regardless of how much he was able to shake down.

"What do you say, Jack?" the mayor said affably. "You speak so well of the Cardinal all the time!"

Jack mopped the perspiration off his ruddy, flabby features, rolled his eyes in considerable desperation, glared at Teedee, and nodded vigorously.

"There you have it," the mayor said. "Eleven hundred dollars for the building fund, plus our thousand from City Hall, making a total of twenty-one hundred dollars."

More applause as two short-skirted, short-haired flappers rushed to Teedee and Umbrella Jack with pledge cards.

The mayor resumed his toastmastering and got the bidding going again. Tony watched Eddie Nye, who observed the second round of bidding in a shrewd, noncommittal manner.

Teedee, who was still chuckling over his success in putting Umbrella Jack on the spot, bit off another cigar and sensed Tony's interest in Eddie Nye's strategy.

"He's waitin' for a big bid, then he'll go into action. We can get the big cabbage if we get stuck with the bid. There's a lot of these fellows like the Cardinal but can't come out into the open in his behalf," Teedee explained.

"They'd better not," Tony said. "They'd do him more harm than good. And I'm positive he wouldn't take their money."

"That's so," Teedee said with a diplomatic shrug. "Nonetheless, we're going to try and get him some extra money here, and it's nice to have a little protection."

"How far do you think Nye can go?"

"You'll see," Teedee said.

The mayor continued through several more bidding periods, averaging about fifteen hundred dollars each.

"You now have contributed approximately fifteen thousand dollars in total bids," he revealed. "Taken with individual pledges here this evening, this brings our total to over twenty-five thousand dollars from this dinner alone. But we did tell the Cardinal that we would try to net him at least forty thousand dollars. So there you have it—one more bidding period and fifteen thousand to go. This will have to be the biggest three minutes of all. Let's go!"

"Mr. Mayor." It was Nino Venezzia calling for the floor, standing and holding his plumed hat like an overdressed monkey.

"Mr. Nino Venezzia, president of the Roma Paper Box Company and a Knight of Malta," the mayor said, acknowledging his request for the floor with a gracious wave of the hand.

"Mr. Mayor," Venezzia said calmly, with one talonlike hand fastened on the back of his chair, "Very Reverend Monsignor, honored guests, all gathered here like myself to help our own distinguished prince of the Church. May I say that I have been deeply moved by the eloquence of this young Monsignor here—Monsignor Whelton . . ."

The Monsignor nodded acknowledgment with a smile but was thinking of Lucy and the Roma plant with the segregated toilets. Perhaps he'd get a chance to speak to him privately about all that, as he had promised Tony he would do.

"The words of this young prelate veritably lifted me out of myself, and for the first time in my life I acquired a glimmer of understanding of what it must be like to leave one's family and embrace the magnificent loneliness of the religious celibate's life. I had intended to make a contribution of five thousand dollars in behalf of myself and my family . . ."

There was a drone of admiration and awe at the mention of the figure.

". . . but having heard this plea from the Cardinal's emissary and wishing to assist the mayor in reaching his quota, may I say that the Venezzia family is now prepared to offer the building fund the entire fifteen thousand dollars."

A gasp split the guests and stunned them into silence.

Fifteen grand! Tony thought. And he won't do a thing for his employees.

Teedee threw a wink across the table at Eddie Nye.

"We can't go a helluva lot beyond twenty gees," Eddie said apprehensively. "But I'll try and get him up there."

Eddie stood now and rolled a wave of confused delight over the diners by addressing the toastmaster.

"Mr. Mayor, Mr. Mayor," Eddie Nye said. "The West Side Improvement Association, in co-operation with the Red Ball Beverage Company and the Fairgrounds Raceway, realizes the civic importance of clergymen in our community and wants to help the Cardinal build his new seminary. We are prepared to top Mr. Nino Venezzia's offer of fifteen thousand dollars with a competitive bid of sixteen thousand greenbacks."

The mayor rapped for order amid the gleeful waves of ebullience that this counterbid had generated.

"Ladies and gentlemen, order, please—your attention, please. This is wonderful, truly wonderful."

Nino Venezzia wrinkled his brow and gazed shrewdly down at Eddie Nye. He shrugged his shoulders and smiled drolly.

"I am in competition with this kind of money?" Nino muttered. He shook his head.

Monsignor Whelton, anticipating the approval of the Cardinal at the thumping success of the affair, looked down the table at Arthur and nodded happily. What would Venezzia do? Go higher? Yes, yes, he would, Vincent believed. He wants to be top contributor at the dinner. Shrewd, yes, but proud also, proud of his plumed hat, proud of the financial muscles which he could show before the Cardinal and the entire archdiocese.

"To make things interesting," Nino announced slowly, "I will go to eighteen thousand."

Eddie Nye did not hesitate a second. "Nineteen thousand," he said tersely.

The onlookers were tense now; conversation had ceased.

Nino Venezzia cleared his throat, and with two hands tightly grasping the back of the chair leaned forward with cold, inflexible features.

"You leave me no choice," he said. "Twenty thousand dollars."

All eyes were on Eddie Nye now. He glanced at Teedee, who shook his head slowly.

"We concede the bid to Mr. Venezzia," he said, breaking the tension. "But we are still prepared to add a substantial contribution to the present total."

Applause broke out like thunder, and the mayor wound up the dinner, announcing the approximate figure to be fifty thousand dollars.

"A princely gift for a prince of the Church," he said pompously. "Heartfelt thanks and good night to you all."

CHAPTER XX

Over the Papal Wine

ALL that can happen in a couple of days . . . Tony thought as he said good night to Teedee Quinlan and his friends in the Senate Hotel lobby.

He declined an invitation from Teedee to go to a speakeasy for a nightcap, longing for the cool quiet bedroom at Mother Wagner's. Over the fatigue deeply rooted in him there lingered a mellow glow of shared triumph at the Monsignor's fund-raising success.

After the usual good nights and promises of future get-togethers, he hurried across the lobby to be out, gone, away from crowds and noise. He'd get a chance tomorrow to call the Monsignor and tell him how much he had enjoyed the speech and fund raising. After the dinner, Venezzia, the mayor, and many others had crowded around Vincent and eventually taken him upstairs somewhere for a moment of relaxation. It had been no time for Tony to intrude, especially with Venezzia there.

Passing the coffee shop to his left, he heard his name called in the hale, hurried voice of Father Arthur.

"Tony, Tony, just a minute," Arthur said. "I've been looking all over the lobby for you. I caught a glimpse of you down back during the bidding. What did you think of our boy? Wasn't he great? Just great! Look, I've got to make some more calls to the papers and then go upstairs and join our new prelate! But come in here first for a minute. Tommy Naski is here and a couple of others you happen to know."

"Couldn't I see him in the morning, Father?" Tony said wearily. "I'm just done in now."

"You do look tired," Arthur said, slowing the urgency of his voice. "But go in and see Naski for a few minutes and then go home. You may not catch up with him so easily in the morning. He's all over the place all the time."

"Okay, Father," Tony said with a sigh. "You coming in?"

"No, I've got to run. They're over there in the right-hand corner. I told him I was looking for you." He paused now and added slowly, "Joan's with him and the district attorney. You know him, Bill Ryan, the guy who handled your case—remember? Go in there and say hello. Then you and Tommy can sneak off somewhere and talk a little bit. Okay?"

"Okay."

Joan was there. She had been at the banquet? Of course. There to see her boss in a moment of triumph. And Bill Ryan was D.A. now. He hadn't known that. And what of the former D.A., outwardly a public defender, inwardly a tool of the mob? He had been exposed, busted, sent to jail, all largely due to Father Vincent and the present D.A. The spell of whirring time dazed his mind; the years, the years, the fleeting, kaleidoscopic years . . .

She sensed his entrance. Their eyes met as he strode toward the table where she sat with the two men, the powerful Pole and the lean, alert public servant.

"How are you, Joan? Wasn't he something tonight? You must have been very proud of the new Monsignor."

"I was. How are you, Tony? You must be exhausted. So much has happened since you've been home. You'll remember Bill Ryan. He's a big shot now, Tony. We knew him when."

"How are you, Tony?" the D.A. said, rising and extending his hand.

"I've been lookin' for you!" Tommy Naski said, getting up quickly. "We gotta have a talk—tonight. I hear you've already cased the place for us. Father Arthur thinks we can really knock it over. How about this guy?" Naski continued gruffly as they all sat down. "He's just back in town and he's in business already."

"I'm glad to hear it, Tony," the D.A. said. "I really think you'll do well in the labor movement."

Joan smiled deeply, warmly. She thought so too. She knew so.

Tony noticed that the D.A. was looking him over shrewdly, having sensed Joan's warmth toward him. He was a bachelor, fond of Joan, and perhaps surveyed a rival. Well, he'd be disabused of that fast. He'd be just right for Joan, someone high class and going places big, with her connections in the Monsignor's office to help. Old Tony wouldn't stand in the way.

They reminisced a bit over coffee—the trial, the trouble, the exposé.

"Where's Carroll now?" Tony asked. "He must have served his time by now."

"Yes," the D.A. answered. "He got time off for good behavior—went to California—Los Angeles, I believe. He's practicing law there and doing very well, they tell me."

"I'm glad to hear it." Tony stifled a yawn. "He's got a lot of ability. Too bad he got loused up the way he did."

Joan, sensing his fatigue, said she had to be going. The D.A. said he'd drop her off, and they left, she with a smile and a brief but steady look at Tony that said so much more than words.

"Okay, I'll make it short," Naski said boomingly when they had gone. "You're on the payroll, thirty a week and five a day expenses. You're an official organizer for the Allied Paper Workers as of now."

"Thanks a lot, Tommy. What's our first move?"

"Get ahold of this girl they fired—Lucy whatever's-her-name. We'll pay her whatever she made at the plant to help you out—maybe a couple of bucks extra besides.

"We'll circularize the place Monday morning. See if we can whip up some interest and get the old man to call us upstairs. We'll hit them with some printed stuff, and you and this Carrie Nation dame can work out some specific stuff later on—names and numbers of all the players, segregated toilets, great churchman, twenty thousand dollars to the Cardinal—we'll use everything."

"Right," Tony said. "Hit him with everything."

"Okay, I'll meet you out in front of the Roma plant at six-thirty Monday morning. Get home now. You look as if you're about to fold. But see if you can soft-pedal this Lucy dame. We don't want a revolution; we just want to organize the joint. If she says, 'Workers of the world, unite!' you say, 'Under the American flag!' Get it? Wave that flag all over the place. We don't want any mounted police over there right away."

"I get it," Tony said with a smile. "The Stars and Stripes forever."

"That's it," Tommy said, rising in his minor earthquake manner. "I'm grabbin' a cab right now. I'll drop you off."

"Thanks a lot, Tommy. I really want to get home."

"Suite 11-B," Father Arthur said to the elevator boy. It was a good feeling to have got the story of the fund-raising dinner off to all the local papers and the wire services. The two local morning papers would give it a pretty good play and maybe the AP, UP, and INS would give it a couple of inches nationally.

He could visualize the heads in the local morning papers. If he were writing the headlines himself they'd say:

BRAND-NEW MONSIGNOR

PINCH-HITS FOR CARDINAL

RAISES FIFTY GRAND

AT FUND-RAISING DINNER

It was a good feeling, too, to have sent that telegram off to the Cardinal, who was aboard the Lakeport Express from Washington. Those five figures harvested at the dinner would dust off some ancient gleam in his tired old eyes, bringing back warm and mellow memories of his own fund-raising sorties as a young Monsignor. Well, the old boy had done it again, Arthur conceded to himself with complete admiration; he had picked his man at the right place and the right time. That was one of the reasons he was a cardinal— the precisely right move at the precisely right time in the supreme interest of Mother Church. The Church makes haste slowly, and so do cardinals, but with such swift slowness and such deadly aim!

And Venezzia! Twenty thousand dollars! Arthur thought of the encounter of the afternoon and chuckled. A noble son of the Church and a son of a so-and-so also, if he could judge from his policies at the Roma plant.

He rapped at the door of the suite eagerly. He was anxious to witness the interplay between Venezzia and Monsignor Whelton. Vincent had promised to mention Lucy and conditions at the plant. Would he do so now with all that money at stake and the Cardinal arriving tomorrow to applaud his triumph?

When the door was opened by a white-coated waiter, Arthur saw a spacious, gilded suite filled with uniformed dignitaries, priests, and monsignori. He walked over to a gold brocade sofa where Monsignor Whelton was seated between Mayor O'Leary and Nino Venezzia. Directly in front of the sofa was an ivory coffee table on which rested several shimmering champagne glasses.

Venezzia stood up and beckoned to one of the waiters, who advanced with an ice-filled silver bucket holding a regal, unopened, white-and-gold magnum of champagne.

"Let me show you this bottle, Monsignor and Your Honor, before the gentleman opens it for us."

He made a ceremony of uncovering then a gold-leafed label on which was printed the papal coat of arms.

"The others are drinking Mumms—the very best at that—but in honor of the Cardinal and the new Monsignor, we shall drink from an overstock of the Holy Father's personal vintner. This, good friends, is papal champagne."

"Marvelous," Vincent said, the naïveté and wonder of the westside seminarian still strong in him.

"You will note the motto on the label around the bottle neck," Venezzia said pompously, rocking back on his patent-leather shoes.

"*Servus servorum Dei,*" Vincent read reverently. And to the mayor, who nodded in pseudo recognition, he translated: "Servant of the servants of God!"

"Precisely," Venezzia said. "Now we will taste of this heavenly nectar." He handed the magnum to the waiter and resumed his seat to the right of Monsignor Whelton.

"I do wish His Eminence were here," Vincent said a little anxiously. "This should really be his pleasure, Mr. Venezzia."

"Put your fears at rest, Monsignor," Venezzia said graciously. "I have saved him a bottle of the same, which will be at his residence on his return."

"You think of everything, Nino," the mayor said with a chuckle.

At that moment Vincent saw Arthur. He rose and called attention to his presence.

"Father Arthur is here. Now we have a member of the Cardinal's family present."

"Father Arthur!" Venezzia said with his ever-recurrent graciousness. "Priest and crusading journalist, champion of the downtrodden, nephew of His Eminence, welcome to our party!"

"Thank you, Mr. Venezzia," Arthur said. "How are you, Monsignor? Greetings, Your Honor."

"Did you get your chores out of the way?" Vincent asked.

"Yes, all of them. You'll be all over the papers tomorrow, and a telegram has gone rattling off to the Cardinal."

"Fine," Vincent said. "I assume you gave His Eminence the big play. After all, this is his affair, not mine."

"The papers do things their own way," Arthur said. "They know where the emphasis should be in a story. And the Cardinal will understand."

"I hope you're right," Vincent said apprehensively. "After all, I'm not 'official' until Sunday."

"You are 'official' now forever," Nino said. "Come, Father Arthur, be seated and partake of the papal champagne."

"Lovely," Arthur said as the waiter poured the bubbly liquid into their glasses. "I heard your little homily on the papal vintner as I approached."

"Let us drink to His Eminence," Venezzia said, raising his glass. "How close he does seem in the wine of the Holy Father. To his success in the new seminary building project and in all things."

They sipped in tribute to the Cardinal, and Vincent, drinking champagne for the first time, felt the sparkling gases prickling inside his nose.

"Now to our new Monsignor," Venezzia said. "To his eloquence and, as I understand it, to his charity for underprivileged youth."

"Thank you, Mr. Venezzia," Vincent said. "And may I, in the name of the Cardinal, toast your generosity toward Holy Mother Church?"

They drank to that, and the mayor proposed a toast to all who had contributed that night.

"Now we must hear from our editor. Surely his poetic and rhetorical sense as expressed so fluently in his editorials will be productive of some appropriate phrase at this time," Venezzia said.

This was getting too gracious for Arthur, gracious to the point of grimness. He thought for a moment, smiled facetiously, then uttered, lifting his goblet, " 'O for a beaker full of the warm South!' "

"Ahhhhhhh . . ." Venezzia said, smacking his lips. "You have the makings of a true connoisseur. You have toasted the wine itself."

"That was a *noble* thought, Father Arthur," said the mayor, a little heady now and anxious to match the grace of Venezzia's comments. "It hit the spot—especially after those other more formal toasts. Is the phrase your own?"

"The phrase is John Keats," Arthur said.

"It is at that," the new Monsignor said, feeling the glow of the wine growing pleasantly throughout his blood stream.

"Another, Monsignor?" Venezzia said, nodding his head slightly at the waiter.

"That's all for me," Vincent said. "The warm South is one thing, but the equator is another."

They all laughed, and the entire suite had a pleasant, subdued gaiety about it. There were no women present, Arthur noticed. It was not hard to guess that Venezzia had prudently arranged the party to exclude the distaff guests at the banquet. The visitors in the suite were predominantly Roman-collar. While it was highly improbable that anything untoward would be said or done if women were present, Venezzia knew the sense of prudence in the Church and felt a deep responsibility toward the absent Cardinal. So the wine flowed moderately well among these dedicated males, both clergy and lay, orchestrated by the outgoing talk and laughter of men among men.

Vincent was nibbling at mixed nuts and potato chips now, throwing a dam up against the trickles of headiness he was beginning to feel.

Arthur, noting Vincent's concern for his decorum, smiled and tossed off the remnant in his goblet. He offered his glass to the attendant waiter as Venezzia nodded invitingly.

"I simply must have one more. It is such a rare opportunity."

"It is indeed," Vincent said. "And you have worked hard tonight. As for myself, I am still the simple west-side boy weaned somewhat on strong tea and good brown ale. Champagne is the drink of princes."

"You will sip champagne many times in your life," Venezzia said, "if only in ceremony. The call to higher echelons has been given you, and you must accept it."

"Thank you, Nino," Vincent said. "I will go where I'm sent and do what I'm told. But I still prefer the pure, yet sometimes dirty faces of my kids at the center."

"You must talk to me about your work at the youth center," Venezzia said. "I have read of it, and your approach to the idea of a centrally located recreation center for boys intrigues me. Do you not feel that such work can be done separately in the parishes?"

"Speaking of parishes," Arthur said, glancing at a group who were laughing at the remarks of a wry old father who was holding forth on a sofa to their right, "there's your old pastor, Vinegar Jack. He had some strong ideas about independent parish activities, eh what?"

"He certainly did have strong ideas, and we went round and round many times when I was his assistant—and afterward!"

Arthur caught Vincent's eye meaningfully. He had purposely mentioned Vinegar Jack because he knew Vincent would associate him with Tony Lorenzo and the brewery. If he was going to say anything about the Roma plant to its owner, now was as good a time as any.

"Your Honor," Arthur said to the mayor, "why don't we let these two world visionaries compare notes while you and I quaff a little of Vinegar Jack's wit over there?"

"An excellent idea!" the mayor said, rising. "Father Regan, by the way, has been a faithful supporter of mine on the south side for many years."

Arthur threw another look at Vincent, who nodded slightly, then he and the mayor sauntered across the room to the hilarious fringe of Vinegar Jack's "court."

The group saw the mayor and opened up so that he could get close to the effusive Irish cleric.

"Father Jack," the mayor said in his warm, pompous way, made more cloying by the rise and surge of the champagne, "how are you, old friend, how are you?"

"Sure and I'm fine," Vinegar Jack said quickly, shaking his hand with a finger grip only. "And I see," he added with a sharp glance at Arthur, who nodded and smiled at him, "that you haven't changed a bit. You're still in disreputable company, same as when I saw you last at the boxing matches in the Hippodrome."

There was a gust of laughter at this, as Arthur laughed, too, hearing the good-natured banter of the younger clerics gathered around, some of whom were classmates of Vincent and himself.

"Sure, His Eminence has many crosses to bear," Vinegar Jack continued, "God help him. And not the least of these is that tower of Bull-shevism which we call our newspaper."

"Did you say Bull-shevism?" the mayor asked, amused.

"Yes, I said Bull-shevism. And ye all know what I mean!"

Arthur flushed this time, but the general mirth took the sting out of the remarks, and he could not help joining again in the laughter.

"May I quote you on that, Father?" Arthur said when the laughter subsided.

"Ye can quote anything ye like. But leave me own good name off of it. Ye're a little too good at 'quotin,' me fine bucko. Every nut in Europe that thinks the Pope is out to beat the Russians at their own game has a by-line in your paper. And the Married Ladies' Sodality in me own parish gets nary a line."

"I'll print anything they send in, Father, any time. I never get any news from your parish, and we simply haven't got the staff to get out there and get it ourselves."

"Come on now, Father Jack," the mayor said with pleasant firmness, "lay off this lad. Do me a favor and tell these good fathers about the Cardinal and the Irish whiskey."

"Ye remember that one, d'ye?" Vinegar Jack said, his sharp, bony features softening. This was his vulnerable spot, Arthur now knew. He was a pushover for a good audience and for the bolstering of his repute as a storyteller at private gatherings. Perhaps he had tried the same role at public dinners or church missions and retreats and had failed. Perhaps this was the canker at his breast. Too, there was no "red necktie" for him at his advanced age. He had cut at the deserving as well as the undeserving with his tongue, and while he was a good priest and an able pastor, old wounds had throbbed all the way to Rome in curtailing the natural privileges and honors of his age and station.

What must his thoughts be at seeing the new Monsignor—his former errant assistant whom he had jettisoned into the sticks and for whom he had predicted a sorry future? Arthur winced at the thought. "Sufficient unto the day is the evil thereof," was the thought he nailed on the screen of his mind as Vinegar Jack brogued in leisurely manner into the warp and woof of his story.

"Well, ye'll recall His Eminence makin' the pilgrimage to Lourdes and the mayor himself goin' along for the Irish end of the trip. Well, I couldn't go meself, as I'd been to Limerick for me sister's golden wedding anniversary only the summer before.

"Now His Honor here persuaded the Cardinal to visit Ireland with him on the return swing. And so we were all down to the train with the big boss himself and, as is his way, he singled me out sharply on the platform before he stepped into the train."

Vinegar Jack's features softened again and he went into a wistful mood, a sort of story within a story. With the utter fearlessness of the old and virtuous, their lives largely behind them and the moral barricade about them, he laid his life completely open for a moment to this group of predominantly young priests.

Father Arthur's heart went out to him and he wished that Vincent, deeply absorbed with Venezzia at the other end of the room, could have shared this golden moment.

"I don't know why His Eminence always does this," Vinegar Jack mused softly. "A way of pulling me into his close surroundings and out of the crowd as if I was someone special to him. Sure I'm just another shepherd in the field, but the Cardinal seems to be makin' somethin' up to me all the time as if I should-a been a bishop or at least wear the red necktie like young golden mouth over there." He digressed, nodding toward Monsignor Whelton. "And he once me own sassy brat of an assistant with all sorts of Bull-shevist ideas that I thought would land him up in the loony house. But he's over there now with our gracious Eye-talian high mucky-muck, and I must admit he's come a long way."

There was a tear in his eye at this admission, remorse and a little pride, too, Arthur sensed, in the rise of his former rebellious assistant.

"But anyway, His Eminence has this way about him that makes him great and makes you feel great too, that when he's talkin' to you and concerned with you, 'tis only you in the whole world that's on his mind.

"So he tells me from the train steps, drawing me close up while the monsignori fidget and fuss trying not to listen, he tells me he's goin' to Ireland with the mayor and if he gets to Limerick he'll go see me sister and pass the time of day at least.

"'Now is there anything you'd want me to bring back to you from the Old Sod?' he asked me as sincerely as you'd please. Now you know, you young gossoons, I'm quick on the draw for a laugh even when half serious, and I am what I am because I've always spoken out, whether with the low or the high.

"'If ye will, Your Eminence, bring me back a good quart of Irish whiskey,' I said, half in jest. 'And if ye do get there, me sister Kate will tell ye where to get the jug in the village and she'll give ye a good feed of corned beef and cabbage in the bargain.'

"'I'll do that, Father,' the Cardinal said, bringing that hawk face down like the grand seal of the Pope upon a bit of parchment. He shook my hand and was up the stairs of the train and gone.

"Well, he was gone the whole month of July and part of August. And divvil a thought I gave to the whiskey again, but only that he might get home safe and all with him by the help a God. 'Twas on the Feast of the Assumption and a lot of us who couldn't get into the procession were waiting in the vestry of the cathedral for the Cardinal to start High Mass. Down the middle aisle he came, under the canopy, fresh and as chipper as he could be with the reverence in him as ever, but him not hesitating to nod at those he knew and loved along the way. The procession swung into the vestry, and we stood aside to let them proceed to the high altar. And while the altar boys fussed around the sanctuary lighting the candles and arranging the chairs, the Cardinal caught me eye and motioned me over.

" 'I saw your sister Kate,' he said. 'The corned beef was fine and so was she.'

"I was nodding and thanking and full of blushes, when what does he do but reach under his robes and slip out the package of Jameson's, all done up in its fancy seal. 'And here's your Irish whiskey,' he said as the procession moved forward to the altar.

"Well, there's me story and it's as true as I'm standing here. You shoulda seen the great red beef face of Monsignor O'Hara go white when he saw the Cardinal hand me the whiskey, and you'd know the truth of me tale."

"Now I begin to understand," Venezzia said, nodding slowly. On the other side of the room they could hear the laughter that followed Vinegar Jack's story about the Irish whiskey.

"My old pastor is really wowing them over there," the Monsignor said.

"He's an extraordinary old man," Venezzia said. "The Irish combination in the extreme—sharp tongue and warm heart. But I am not to be distracted."

He continued to probe Monsignor Whelton's theories and program for the youth of a sprawling, crime-ridden metropolis.

"You are not professionally trained in social work, I take it," Venezzia observed as Vincent nodded. "You are utterly and completely a man of action, and yet you are conducting a successful experiment in your youth center which must make the professionals blush.

"To take all races and all creeds in this seething city and bring them together in peaceful athletic pursuits! I see, I see now why you have tried to take the emphasis off the purely local or parishional activity. This way the north gets to know the south, the east the west."

"Exactly, Mr. Venezzia," Vincent said, appreciative of his understanding. How can this man be so rigidly practical in his plant and yet so liberal of mind? Vincent asked himself. How can he?

"Come, tell me now, Monsignor," Venezzia chided gently, "do the white boys really accept the colored in your center?"

"They do, they do," Vincent insisted. "At first there was aloofness and tension, but athletics under Christian guidance is the great leveler. There's nothing like competitive sport to put young people at their ease and make them appreciate each other's qualities."

Venezzia paused in thought, noticed Father Arthur deep in private conversation with the mayor, and Vincent sensed this must have urged some association with the afternoon's dispute at the Roma plant.

"I rather wish I could achieve the same conditions at my paper-box plant on the south side. But it would be most impractical, most impractical."

"What are these conditions, may I ask?" Vincent pursued, taking advantage of the opening. "You see, I am deeply interested in some type of adult recreational and educational work along the lines of my center. We are not established yet with the young people's program and simply do not have the funds for further expansion. But in time to come perhaps we will be able to set up some evening schedule for adults. It would be of inestimable help to me if you would tell me of the conditions at your plant."

Venezzia smiled wisely. "You are a diplomat as well as an actionist, I see," the benign, alert old Italian aristocrat observed. "Such a balance will serve you well in the years of violent change which most certainly lie ahead for Americans—and, yes, the entire world. Perhaps the Cardinal's nephew has informed you of his visit to my office this afternoon concerning my former employee, Miss Lucy Smith. Her mother was a dear friend of your seminary days, I have been given to understand."

"That's right, Mr. Venezzia," Vincent said, explaining his acquaintanceship and belief in the unusual piety of the deceased woman.

"Like father, like son," Venezzia said ironically. "Should not the daughter be like the mother also?"

"She is very young," Vincent said, getting the clear implication of her atheistic, socialistic tendencies. "Perhaps in time the prayers of her mother and her own innate good sense will make her see the light."

"Perhaps," Venezzia said politely. "But I must explain my position to you lest you begin to believe that the Holy Father has conferred great privilege upon me in vain. And, too, I would not want you to think that I am a friend of the Cardinal only in terms of financial benefits. His principles, and yours, dear Monsignor, are very sacred to me."

"I'm sure of that," Vincent said with firm politeness. "But I must confess I do not understand what I know of your policies at the plant."

"I shall endeavor to explain. You must realize, my son, that all the skilled help at my plant—the pressmen and the machinists—are of the white race, highly paid and hard to get. Outnumbering them by sheer dint of the manual labor to be done in stripping, packing, and transporting the thousands of paperboard sheets we print are the colored help. Much of their work could be done by donkeys, believe me, and those I could import from the Italian Alps. Nonetheless, I need them and pay them the going rate for most paper-box plants in the city. The main point is that my skilled white workers will not eat with them or share their rest-room facilities. If I tried to force the issue, my skilled workers would walk out of the plant and there would be work for neither colored nor white. It is as simple as that."

"I see," Vincent conceded. "It is a real problem. May I be so bold as to suggest what conditions would be if a union were to be accepted in the plant?"

Venezzia sighed and opened his hands.

"I see that you have been somewhat indoctrinated on this matter by our crusading journalistic friend. However, I do not mind. Free discussion of these things is the breath of life itself. I pay my help just as much as they would get under a union setup. It is about these things like segregated facilities that we would have a strong difference of opinion. It will not work in my plant, good Monsignor, and I will not weary the point with further discussion of it."

Vincent got the point and saw the uselessness of pushing the matter further, but he wanted to make one more suggestion. He was a little apprehensive, too, lest the Cardinal's twenty thousand dollars should go glimmering. He saw the prudence of easing off the subject. He had a job to do for the Cardinal, and this had gone far enough.

"Thank you for being so frank and so patient with me, Mr. Venezzia. I have no commitments to the unions, yet I did appreciate a clarification from you because of Lucy. May I suggest my interest in starting some sort of evening classes for adults next fall in which perhaps we can take some steps toward mutual understanding among people like those who work in your plant—providing I can obtain the Cardinal's approval and obtain a little more money?"

Venezzia responded to this immediately.

"Excellent, excellent. That is the way to do it—gradual change— reform their thinking and make it practical for employers like myself to go along with the ideal Christian attitude in employee relations. I will offer to do something for you in evidence of my sincerity in this matter. A substantial contribution I cannot make at present because of this evening's commitment. But I will help you help this girl Lucy. She does not belong in my plant. She is an educated woman, a social thinker."

"What do you propose?" Vincent asked hesitantly.

"Why not let her set up such a course, under your guidance, and I will guarantee her salary for a year at whatever figure you think reasonable."

"That would be wonderful!" Vincent said. "Do you really think you want to do it?"

"I most certainly do."

"That would be fine. I have the office facilities available at night for use as classrooms. It would be just the thing—if she'll accept—it would be just the thing for us, for her, for you."

"I am glad you feel that way. You may count on my word," Venezzia said.

"Thank you, thank you," Vincent said, rising. "I must go now. You're an extraordinary Christian gentleman, extraordinary."

Venezzia bowed graciously and shook his hand.

"I do extraordinary things only for extraordinary people, Monsignor."

Arthur saw Vincent leaving and caught up with him at the door. They went out together and waited for the elevator.

"What happened?" Arthur asked. "Tell me, I'm about to bust!"

"Wait till we get downstairs," Vincent said softly as two other curates approached the elevator.

Later, on the street, in the sultry summer night, they walked toward the cathedral and he told Arthur the whole story.

"I simply cannot get involved in this union thing, Arthur," he insisted. "We might win a battle here and lose the Cardinal's war."

"That's fine—the Lucy thing, I mean, if she'll take it," Arthur said. "But what are we going to do about Tony? He's going to be in this thing up to his ears."

"He'll just have to do the best he can. I will not jeopardize the Cardinal's interests any further. And neither will you!"

Arthur nodded a little sadly, realizing the logic of Vincent's position but feeling confused. The union was right and Venezzia was right. What a mess. Poor Tony, poor Tony, he thought. Off on another goose chase.

"Arthur, I mean it," Vincent insisted, sensing the gravity of his friend's reflections. "We've got to stay out of it!"

"You know what you sound like?" Arthur said with a thin smile of resignation.

"What?" Vincent asked as they strode vigorously around the corner toward the rectory.

"Just like—a very reverend monsignor."

CHAPTER XXI

It Can't Happen Here!

Tony slept late Saturday morning and was buried in oblivion until he heard the majestic, melancholy notes from the piano in the living room. He blinked his eyes at the rays of light streaming through the venetian blinds and listened to the music, smiling at the thought of the big, Norwegian girl playing on and on.

He groped for his watch on the night table beside him. Eleven-fifteen! Had he slept that long—almost twelve hours? The events of the previous evening ran quickly across his mind: Teedee Quinlan, the new Monsignor's great money pitch, the bidding and rebidding —Venezzia's twenty thousand dollars. Yeh, and Tommy Naski, that was it! He had to get out to the south side right away and line up Lucy for Monday morning at the Roma plant. Stars and Stripes forever!

He settled back on the pillow with a deep sigh. One more brief respite before going into a drive for the day. Lying there, listening to the music, he felt more seriously the fullness of his manhood and knew in this golden morning moment the depth of his longing for a mate. This was the time, he sensed, when marriage must mean so much. To wake in the morning like this and find her there beside you or maybe out in the kitchen with the bubbling coffee and the sizzling bacon. This was the golden moment, but who, where, how? His life was in violent flux and there was no time or place for that kind of decision.

He rose, stretched, and hurried into the shower.

Later, dressed and shaved, he opened his bedroom door and

walked into the hall and to the kitchen. The table was set for one, and there was a note tucked under a large glass of orange juice.

Good morning, Tony. You needed all that sleep. Heat up the coffee, have some juice and muffins, I'll be back about three. See you for dinner at seven.

And don't forget to call our big money man, the new Monsignor! I heard all about it! Marvelous, what?

Love,
Mother Wagner

P.S. Take a peek out on the back porch. We have an artist in residence.

Artist in residence? He struck a match under the coffeepot, settled the gas flame, picked up his orange juice, and took a look out back.

It was the Venezzia girl, still a study in black, in front of an easel on the spacious sunny corner of the porch. She was painting the back yards in the summer breeze. There was a section of wooden fence and sky to the left she had swept into the painting. Dabbing away with white oils now, her stern little cleft chin, just like her father's, was angled upward.

He felt in a burst of intuition that there should be an easel directly behind her with a painter absorbed in her sheer black diminutive figure with the small transfigured, sharply chiseled features rapt and upward. He respected the spell of the moment and stood suspended himself until she caught the touch, the detail, and turned to her canvas for the almost mundane chore of putting the vision into reality.

She sighed and reached for a long black ivory cigarette holder on a small tray affixed to the bottom of the easel. As she took a deep, satisfying puff, he found his tongue and spoke in an unreal, husky voice.

"Did you catch it?"

She did not startle but rather held at the sound of his voice. After several moments of silence she inclined her head slightly toward him and said:

"Perhaps." There was infinite softness in her answer, but behind it a hard core somewhere, a restraint, a steel ball under folds of velvet. "You must be Mr. Lorenzo, the man next door," she continued, turning and smiling in a brief, pleasant flash.

He walked up to her and took her firm little hand in his.

"You're Rosa Venezzia," he said. "Mother Wagner calls you 'the artist in residence.' "

"Mother Wagner always says and does the gracious thing."

"Like your father," Tony said candidly. "Only in a different way."

"Yes, like my father," she said, arching her dark eyebrows. "You must have been at the fund-raising dinner last night. How much of the family's money did he give away this time?"

"A good chunk. Would you join me for a cup of coffee? Or is this a bad time?"

"It's a good time," she said. "I've been painting since eight and was about to take a few minutes."

He followed her into the kitchen, holding the door for her. He felt easy with her, not knowing why, but easy, with a quiet, growing excitement in him because of her presence.

"Long have I known thee in the great steel jaws . . ."

She seemed to sense his perception of discovery, and as he clinked the clean white cups she looked directly at him with the wide, sweeping whites of her eyes minimizing the dark center points.

"How do you have your coffee?" he asked.

"Black, no sugar."

He served her, and they sat quiescent in the big apartment which, bereft of the others and the blithe central spirit of the house, seemed like a long, cool tomb.

"You are a friend of Father Wagner's, I gather," she said softly.

"Yes, sort of. But mostly through Monsignor Whelton, whom I've known much longer."

"It is the opposite with me. Father Wagner has been a tower of strength to me, and the rising young prelate I know only casually."

A tower of strength. So that was it. Arthur was her spiritual adviser. He had collected her at Mother Wagner's, just like the others. Her widowhood, perhaps, and the problems of readjustment.

"Father Arthur's really a bright guy."

"More than bright," she said, slipping one of her gold-stamped Turkish cigarettes into the long black holder. He gave her a light in silence, waiting for her to say more.

"He is more than bright," she repeated, inhaling deeply and blowing out the smoke while beaming at him again. "His gay, provocative manner conceals a seriousness and spiritual depth which people like my father cannot believe exists."

"From what I could gather yesterday at the Roma plant," Tony said, "your father would appreciate him more in Europe than in America."

"That is correct," she said, smiling and showing small, even teeth. "Father Wagner told me about your visit after Mass this morning."

"You were at Mass that early?"

"I was. I attend his six-thirty Mass each and every morning."

"That's a nice habit," Tony said.

"It was not always thus. Only after Carlo was taken from me and I met Father Wagner."

"Carlo must have been your husband. I'm sorry . . ."

"He was my husband—and he was not," she said with easy bluntness. "He was a mechanic and a professional racing driver. My father did not approve of him and had our marriage annulled. Yet I continued to live with him because in my heart there was no annulment."

That explained why she still bore the Venezzia name, Tony thought. And it explained why she did not live with her father.

"Carlo was killed last July in the race from Naples to Rome. I was dead with him until I met Father Wagner at the art museum one day in February."

"You must have studied painting in France at some time or another," Tony said, changing the subject and recalling the warmth and richness of her color blending. "I was in hiding for some years and had a chance to do a lot of reading. I recall some critic of painting writing that you could always distinguish a French-trained painter from an American-trained artist by the handling and blending of color. There's a technique of glowing warmth and depth in the French training that local painters do not have, regardless of comparative talent."

"You are correct," she said, using that phrase again, almost with an urgent hint of another meaning. Correct, sympathetic, right for her, maybe. "You were in hiding a long time, Father Wagner tells me."

He blushed at this. Arthur had told her about the state pen.

"Don't be upset," she said sympathetically. "It is best that certain people know about it. It is best that they hear about it from your friends rather than your enemies."

"You are correct," he said with a relaxed smile.

She laughed good-naturedly, and they talked on and on, weaving in and out of each other's consciousness without any sense of time.

He told her about the intention to try to organize her father's plant, and she seemed mirthful, even sympathetic, about this revelation.

"It is better that you hear about this from a friend rather than an enemy," he said, provoking her rich, musical laughter again.

"I have not laughed like this in many months," she said.

"It's good to know I can do something to make somebody laugh."

"You have," she said. "We must talk again."

"We must."

"You may have to talk to me eventually, in any case," she said quite soberly. "I am the principal stockholder of the plant which you intent to ravage with your socialistic hordes. My mother left me slightly over fifty per cent of the stock in the Roma Company, you might be interested to know."

"Wow!" Tony said. "And to think you live in the room next to me! I'll have the pickets out there in Mother Wagner's hall!"

"Delightful!" Rosa said.

The phone rang long and then repeated long and insistently.

"That's probably Monsignor Whelton for me," he said, rising. "Will you excuse me? I was supposed to call him right after breakfast."

"Yes indeed," she said. "I must get my things together. I have a lesson at the museum at twelve."

He hurried down the hall to the phone. It was the Monsignor, and he wasted few words getting to the point of his call.

"Lucy's here, right here in my office. I've got a good job for her setting up a night school for adults and I want her to take it. She seems to like the idea. She can teach labor education and things like that. We'll get others to teach the English literature and the artistic things. Now, Tony, she wants to talk to you first. She says you've got something in mind—that labor-union job Father Arthur put you onto. I want to be perfectly fair. Will you talk to her? Will you come over here and talk to her? It's up to her, Tony. I don't want to interfere. It's up to her."

But he did want to interfere, Tony knew. He wanted her there at that center, and that knocked the organizational plans into a cocked hat. What could he do? He couldn't go against the Monsignor. He couldn't.

"All right, Monsignor, I'll be right over," he said. "Tommy Naski of the Allied Paper Workers does have a job for her, but maybe your deal will be better. I'll come over there now."

"Thank you, Tony," the Monsignor said. "I knew you wouldn't

fail me. Talk to her and try to get her to do what's best for herself
—for her future, Tony. I won't be here—so take Lucy out for some
lunch and call me later here this afternoon, if you will."

"Okay, Monsignor, I'll do that," Tony said with lame cordiality.

"How do you like it at Mother Wagner's?"

"It's fine, just fine."

"All right, Tony. Call me later. I've got to go now. Lucy will be
waiting."

That's it! he thought, after he had hung up, leaning his head
back against the wall and letting out a sigh of bafflement. No Lucy.
That's it.

He opened his eyes, and she was standing before him in the long,
dark, cool hall, her artist's paraphernalia tied up neatly—under her
right arm.

"What is it, Tony?" she asked with involuntary intimacy.

"Oh, we've had a little change in our organizing plans," he said
glumly.

"You've lost your contact in the plant, I'll wager. Cheer up. I'll
help you obtain another if you like," she added with a sympathetic
smile. "After all, it's practically my plant."

He laughed at her unabashed partisanship and disregard of her
father's interests.

"You're a real good sport," he said. "But Naski and I will have to
find another angle. There's no need for your becoming involved."

"I'm already involved," she said softly. "I've met you."

She reached over and pushed back a lock of his disheveled hair.
He felt the small, cool, white hand momentarily on his forehead,
flooding him with a wave of easement. Her face was close, angled
up toward him, the full, red lips immobile, the wide eyes approving.

He took the portfolio from her, placed it against the wall, and
kissed her, her slim, firm figure melting against him with a moan of
longing. They clung together, wordless and sweet, for what seemed
a long time. He was loosening the buttons on the back of her
black silk blouse in delicious delirium when she spoke, tolling the
knell of time and place.

"We must remember where we are and be respectful of the Wag-
ners," she whispered softly. "We shall see each other again if you
wish."

"I wish it, Rosa," he said, dropping his arms with a sigh. "I wish
it with all my heart."

"And so do I, dear Tony," she said, kissing him on the cheek, "for you are not the only one who has been in prison."

"Thank you, Rosa. Whatever has happened to us is good. But I wouldn't want to upset this lovely home for all the world."

"I know that," she said. "I know what you are like, or else I would have passed you by in the hall."

"Get going to your art lessons. I've got something to do for the Monsignor."

"Good-by for now, my dear," she said. "We shall meet again."

"Good-by, Rosa." He watched her go, the fires of longing simmering and burning low within him. "'I was in prison, and you came to me,'" he called after her.

"You are correct," she said, and went out of the apartment, her presence lingering in a delicate essence of expensive perfume.

CHAPTER XXII

A School Is Born

"HE'LL be right over, Lucy," Monsignor Whelton said, hanging up the phone. "I want to be fair about this and let you talk to Tony. I feel perfectly confident in leaving you both together. You're both level-headed and I know you'll make the right decision."

Lucy, sitting in an armchair in the Monsignor's office, stroked her long, masculine chin. It was all so bewilderingly attractive. An evening school of social studies and she in charge. It was something she always wanted to do—teach the workers themselves, study with them, thrash out ideas with them. The new world was theirs if they would only grasp the idea that they controlled the means of production, the tools, the labor that was precious capital itself; they could, by organization, by peaceful revolution, by second-guessing managerial methods, win themselves a larger share of the profits pie.

"Can I tell them about Karl Marx and R. H. Tawney and Adam Smith?"

"Why, why, yes," the Monsignor said hesitantly. "But you must remember that this school will be conducted under Catholic auspices. You must promise me to relate the best thinking of these people to the social thinking of the Church. And Marx especially—he must be subordinated and aligned to the social thinking of Pope Leo XIII and Pius XI, I must insist on this. There is good thinking in those men you have mentioned. But you must study Pope Leo this summer, and you'll find some good things in Pius X's *Motu Proprio*. And there is the spirit of your mother—you must respect that too.

She would be very happy to know you are teaching at a Christian school."

"I think I can do it," she said. "I've already studied *Rerum Novarum*. It's quite as progressive as much of the thinking of those I have mentioned."

"The social thought of the Church has always been progressive. Consider the medieval guilds—these were labor unions long before Sam Gompers was born. It probably isn't very well known, Lucy," Vincent proffered eagerly, "but Pope Pius X was as good a union doctrinaire as any Marxist you can name. He brought about the formation of a new organization in Italy consisting of three great unions—the Popolare, the Economica, and the Elettorale. And as early as 1912 he denounced the oppression of the Indians of Peru by the rubber merchants of that country."

"Very interesting," she said, smiling, beginning to be taken in by his infectious enthusiasm. That was the spell of this man, she now knew. He captured you in the rush of his ebullience and conviction.

She had been reluctant to come when Joan showed up in a cab that morning. Monsignor Whelton, anticipating this, had given Joan a message for Lucy to be used in a last-ditch situation.

"The Monsignor told me to ask you to come out of respect for his friendship for your mother," Joan had said.

"But I do hope we're not letting Tony down, Monsignor," Lucy said anxiously now. "I know he has plans for me to help him organize the Roma plant."

"You'll be helping him more in the school than out there," the Monsignor said with quick conviction. "While I cannot possibly become involved in anything like that—and must ask you not to, if you take this position—I see no reason why those people at the plant cannot come here and study. It will be their privilege as well as anyone else's." He raised his hands magnanimously in one last effort to nail down the lid of her acceptance. "Let some of them come in here—those who are interested—teach them how to be good union people, if you like. But teach them love of neighbor, not revolution. And then let the chips fall where they may."

"That sounds fair."

"Of course it's fair," the Monsignor said, rising. "I've got to get over to the Cardinal's residence right now. I want to tell him about all this. Can I say you're interested?"

"Why—why, yes."

"Fine. I do have a promise of some money to help with your salary, but in the long run we'll need the Cardinal's support and approval more than anything else."

He did not tell her of Venezzia's offer to pay her salary. It was a confidential matter. He'd have to raise the money for the school himself, in any case, and he had planned such a project with or without the boxmaker's philanthropy.

"Have a nice visit with Tony and I'll see you after lunch," he said, taking his straw hat off the hatrack and walking to the door. "I'll ask Joan to show you where our social-action bookrack is. We have a whole mess of things Father Arthur has been sending over. If you decide finally after talking to Tony, you can go right to work studying and planning. Joan will set you up at a desk out there."

"Thank you, Monsignor," Lucy said with quiet fervor. "You've made my day a very exciting one."

He paused at the door and eyed her shrewdly and with a compassionate half-smile.

"You'd be surprised, Lucy," he said gently, "how infinitely exciting every day can be—if—if it is dominated by the love of God. Your mother knew that excitement. And I cannot believe that you are not every inch her daughter."

"Thank you," Lucy said, her feminine emotion assaulting intellectual conviction. "That's a very nice thing to say."

The cool, flippant wind from the lake was good for Tony's fevered feelings and a brisk dustbroom for his mind as he turned off the boulevard and headed down Senate Street toward the youth center.

In the cold perusal of common sense, the amorous upsurgence in Mother Wagner's hall could mean only one thing for him: he'd have to move out and get a place of his own. This was no hit-and-run affair—this was Rosa Venezzia, and she did not confer her affection lightly.

Well, he'd see, he'd see—one problem at a time. Now Lucy—and the Monsignor wanting things his way and at the same time being very "fair." Well, he'd do it the Monsignor's way, there was no other way; if the Monsignor wanted her at the center and she wanted to be there, that was it! He and Naski would just have to get on as best they could at the Roma plant with whatever indirect help they could get from Lucy. Surely she'd offer that, at least.

Where could they go for lunch? he asked himself, knowing there would be tension and a "situation" in the Senate Hotel coffee shop if he went in there with a Negro girl. They could go to that big chain drugstore on the corner of Senate and Bellrose Avenue; they could sit at one of those shaky little metal tables and juggle a triple-decker sandwich and a milkshake. That would be best.

He went up the CYC staircase to the second floor. Down the hall and around the corner now with the slap-slap-slap of punching bags in the background. There she was, seated at a little desk in the reception room across from Joan.

Joan. *I was in prison, and you came to me* . . . The thought knocked about mockingly in his mind. She should have been the one in the long, dark, cool hall, but that was not to be. The exotic signora had filled the requirements of the romantic dream. Rosa was movement, disassociated from the past; she was the glamour of far places and the insidious ego-salve of aristocracy. She was the caviar where he had been drearily used to bologna; she was the champagne where the beverage had always been plain brown beer.

"Joan—Lucy," Tony said. "How are you?"

"Tony!" Joan said, smiling. "We keep running into each other," she added tentatively, almost lamely.

"The Monsignor get off to the Cardinal's office?"

"Yes, and I think you know he wants you to take Lucy to lunch."

"Hello, Tony," Lucy said, putting aside a pamphlet treatise on the papal encyclical *Rerum Novarum*. "The Monsignor took me up on a high mountain and showed me all the kingdoms of the world."

"So?" Tony asked with just a hint of a challenge.

"So I'm very hungry," Lucy said, rising. "Let's go eat."

"Can we bring you back something, Joan?" Tony asked.

"No, thank you. I have my lunch with me. I'll have to stand by right here in case the Monsignor gets an important call or calls in himself."

"That's a good girl," Tony said.

"That's me," Joan said with almost psychic insight into Tony's turmoil. "That's me," she repeated with a hint of sarcasm, "a good girl."

They went down the stairs and across the street to the drugstore.

He felt it best not to tell her about the job Naski had offered her. He simply could not chance frustrating the Monsignor's plans for her.

"This job with the Monsignor sounds wonderful. Tell me something about it," he said.

"I'm amazed at the whole development myself, Tony," Lucy said with intense, anxious sincerity, trying to explain herself to him. "You know how I've felt about the Church—the handmaiden of the rich, the opiate of the poor, and so on. This—this Roman-collared wizard got me over here this morning and exercised the same charm over me that he must have showered on my mother—even as a seminarian. I'm just under his spell, Tony; I just listened to him and was swept along with his vision. He makes his plans and projects seem so personally important to his listeners."

"That's the Monsignor all right," Tony said, chuckling. "But what about the teaching job? Does it appeal to you—everything else aside?"

"Everything else aside—it does. I'm trained, as you know, for something like this—a formal propagandizing job."

"You'll have to propagandize the Church, you know," Tony said with a cautionary twinkle in his eyes.

"I realize that—and so does the Monsignor. He tells me I can adapt the best thinking of the Socialists to Catholic thinking wherever possible. Pius XI himself does it, he told me."

Tony laughed at that. "The Monsignor is amazing! He'd have you baptize Marx and Engels?"

"He would. And there are some things in common with papal social teaching in those boys. After all, nobody has a monopoly on ideas."

" 'Religion is the opium of the people,' " Tony quoted. "How will you manage that one?"

"I'll just have to reserve my private opinions, that's all," she said with a sigh. "After all, I couldn't and wouldn't embarrass the Monsignor. But it's you and the Roma plant that worry me more. I wanted to help you out there. What are your plans?"

"Tommy Naski of Allied Paper Workers hired me last night. We're going to circularize the place Monday morning."

"Do you want me to be there? If you do," she said earnestly, "I'll turn this job down and—and get right over there."

"You don't have to go that far. If you can slip us a few sympathetic names and tell us a few angles on the injustices and inequities in the plant, that would be a big help."

"I'll do that," Lucy promised. "I'll write down some names and suggestions over the weekend. Are you sure that will be enough?"

"It'll be enough for now."

The stenographers and salesmen were giving him the once-over. The picture of a sleek-looking Italian sitting there with a tall, homely Negress. He could tell they thought she was either a whore or a shoplifter and he looked like a hood or a dope pusher. But what odds? he told himself. Thoughts do not kill or maim.

"Some of our fellow citizens are giving you the eye," Lucy said with wry yet humble percipience. "I like the way you just walked in here and sat down with me. That's the American dream in action."

"Some of our fellow citizens are ignorant, if you ask me. Let's finish up and get out of here. You don't have to be subjected to this."

"I'd rather stay," she said gently. "It never pays to run away. And I think if my people keep asserting their normal, everyday rights as American citizens, the time may come when these folks will accept us as we should be accepted."

"That sounds okay to me. To get back to the Roma plant—perhaps we can consult you occasionally as the campaign progresses. I know Naski will be anxious to know if you'll be available on a confidential basis later."

"Certainly," Lucy said. "And one more thing—Monsignor Whelton says I can have people from the plant come into the school. How about *that*?"

"You can have your cake and eat it too," Tony said, chuckling. "But watch out for Venezzia. He may put the pressure on the Monsignor through the Cardinal if you move too fast and too far."

"We'll worry about that when the time comes," she said as they rose to leave.

He left her at the CYC entrance. She shook his hand and thanked him for the lunch.

"And most of all thanks for helping me take the job," she added. "I'm still mesmerized by the Monsignor's eloquence, but I know the end product is right for me."

"We'll miss you out there, but you'll be pushing for us at this end, I know," Tony said. "So long, American-dream-in-action. I like that phrase. Go up there and try to baptize Marx and Engels. Then you can go out to the south side and explain the new synthesis to Vinegar Jack Regan, the oldest Irish pastor in the diocese."

"We'll get the Monsignor to do that," Lucy said, heading up the stairs. "I'll have enough trouble explaining the 'new synthesis' to my radical friends."

He waved at her, watching her climb the stairs to a new life, tall and stately, climbing with patient, long-limbed grace, like a Nubian princess.

CHAPTER XXIII

"Sarto, Not Santo!"

"Do you recall your last visit to this office, Monsignor?" the Cardinal asked Vincent.

How odd and wonderful to hear the Cardinal call him "Monsignor"! There was a touch of nostalgia in the Cardinal's hawklike features and a filigree of mirth. The face still retained its ageless quality of alertness, although the crow's-feet were deeper around his intense gray eyes.

While Vincent had seen the Cardinal many times and talked official business with him on the phone, this was the first time in more than five years that he had been in the *sanctum sanctorum* of his private office.

It was all the same—the gold wallpaper, the dark wainscoting, the *Crucifixion* hanging in its gold frame to the left of the desk.

It could have been yesterday—and it was—a long yesterday in the same reeling world of his old pastor, Vinegar Jack Regan, and the seething post-war city resisting and challenging constantly all attempts to widen the established beachheads of Christian living.

"I recall my last visit here, Your Eminence, as if it were yesterday," Vincent said.

"You have come quite a little way since then," the Cardinal observed with a twinkle in his eye as he fingered a sheaf of clippings from the morning press. "Suppose I had listened to your old pastor and packed you off to a monastery!"

"Was that what he really wanted, Your Eminence?"

"Yes, now it can be told—now that you're capable of assimilating something like this without bitterness—that was what he wanted me to do with you," the Cardinal revealed with a slow, rich chuckle.

His Eminence was in a rare good mood, chuckling and reminiscent. Things must have gone well at the bishops' meeting in Washington, but they had gone even better in Lakeport if the newspaper clippings and other personal reports he must have received were any criterion.

Vincent was further assured of this when Mrs. Rush, the Cardinal's long-time secretary, rapped lightly on the door and entered with a silver tray of coffee and muffins. There were two cups and saucers, Vincent was relieved to see, and as she poured the steaming, pungent coffee out of the luxurious silver pot the Cardinal spoke.

"You remember our new Monsignor, no doubt, Mrs. Rush?"

"I do, I do," Mrs. Rush said with snappy cordiality, bestowing on Vincent a warm, motherly smile. "I must tell you, Monsignor, that little speech of yours at the banquet brought tears to my eyes. 'The voice of one crying in the wilderness . . .' It was beautiful, just beautiful. I thought I was sitting in the cathedral itself, and so did everyone else."

"Thank you, Mrs. Rush," Vincent said, glowing more with pleasure than embarrassment at the compliment.

"All right, Mrs. Rush, all right," the Cardinal said with sonorous aplomb. "That's enough of that or we'll have to order a bigger biretta for our bright young man."

Her lips went a little tight as she poured the Cardinal's coffee and then Vincent's. She served them the tinkling cups, offered the muffins, which the Cardinal refused. She then offered one to Vincent, who seemed politely reluctant.

"Take one, take one," she snapped in her quickly commandeered manner of false pique. "I know what's good for you young clerics in midmorning. This one here was the same before he began to live on coffee and soup. You young buckoos need the energy. Take one!"

"Thank you, Mrs. Rush," Vincent said, smiling. "I believe I will."

"You believe you will!" she chided with an appraising grin on her taut, parchment-like features. "You're all so fancy in your manners these days, you young prelates. And you from the west side, where your dear, saintly Irish mother served her hungry neighbors with tea, soup, and Irish bread in the kitchen and you cleaning out the stables like Hercules in the back yard."

Vincent gasped with surprise, and the Cardinal laughed again.

"She knows you, she knows all about you," the Cardinal admonished. "Now, Mrs. Rush, leave us alone for a while or I won't play pinochle with you this afternoon."

"Who would you play with if not me?" Mrs. Rush arrowed as she moved toward the door. "A safe old lady that knows how to let you win."

Again the Cardinal laughed, waving her out debonairly and stirring his coffee.

"When Monsignor O'Hara arrives," he called after her, "give him a copy of *The Clarion* and tell him to read my nephew's editorial about women's hats while I get rid of this young whippersnapper!"

"Very well," Mrs. Rush said, resuming a prim, businesslike aspect as she softly closed the door.

The Cardinal stirred his coffee, black and without sugar, took a careful, pursing sip, and inclined his head toward the french windows to his right, which gave on to a stone balcony and a panoramic view of the lake.

His merry mood was ruminative, too, and the mention of his pinochle game set him musing.

"Have you ever heard the 'scandalous' story of my pinochle games with Mrs. Rush?" he asked, smiling with a slow, growing depth.

Vincent had heard the story vaguely, but he was eager to hear it from the lips of the Cardinal himself.

"Some version of it is around, Your Eminence, but I've never really got it in detail."

"Well, you know," the Cardinal began, "I've played pinochle with Mrs. Rush after lunch right here on this desk for many years. The word got around, as it always does. There are very few secrets kept in our big family.

"Emily Winant, the radical Catholic social worker, was out there preaching in Lakeport Park one summer evening. She was urging some of those bums that hang around there to come up to her Christian Community farm in the Tri-State Valley. They could rehabilitate themselves there, she urged, learn how to farm, boil the hooch out of their systems in the hot sun, sleep, think about their lives, maybe get closer to God. It's a fine idea, she has. I believe in it, I support it—back to the land and all that. Well, anyway, there was a Communist heckler in the crowd who shouted at Emily: 'Do you have the support of the Cardinal Archbishop?' "

"'I do,' Emily answered.

"'Well, how can you take money from a priest who plays cards with his lady secretary every day?' the heckler shouted."

"No!" Vincent said, failing to suppress a smile.

"Yes!" the Cardinal said, chuckling. "And you know what Emily shouted back at him? She's very quick on the draw, you see. She said: 'That shows how democratic he is,'" the Cardinal revealed, chuckling.

"Very good," Vincent said, daring to be clubby in the spirit of the moment, "very, very good."

"Yes, democratic, eh?" the Cardinal said with savor, drawing up into his ecclesiastical dignity again. "Democratic . . ." he repeated with a sigh.

"I think you were rather democratic in not honoring Father Regan's request to pack me off to the Trappists. Perhaps if you had sent me I might now be a saint."

The Cardinal's merry mood changed. He looked right at Vincent soberly now, looked through him with penetrating rays of gray.

"You can be a saint, Monsignor, here as well as there," he said sternly. "And you know that well."

"I know," Vincent said, admonished, but still wanting to express his view, however politely. "But it seems so much harder to know the odor of sanctity in the flurry and hubbub of a metropolitan city."

"Tut-tut, my son. You are still good at retort even to your highest superior. I might as well further inform you," he said, shifting back into a genial, ruminative mood and glancing again at a lead line of one of the clippings which bold-faced the figure: $50,000. "It was your pure, uninhibited spirit of retort, after you had been consigned to outer darkness by your old pastor, that engaged my interest in seeing that your crusading energies would be released into the proper channels. That is why I sent you to the Tri-State Valley and assigned you to the chaplaincy of the state penitentiary. Arrogant retort among my younger clerics is one thing, but purity of retort based on deep conviction is another."

"Thank you, Your Eminence," was all Vincent could bring himself to say. He knew this as a moment of triumph in which he had got as close to the Cardinal as most subordinates would ever get.

The Cardinal's judgment and selection of him had been rousingly, if temporarily, vindicated by the success of the fund-raising effort. The fifty thousand dollars, Venezzia's major contribution, and the eloquent snatches of Vincent's address glowed at the Cardinal out of the clippings which Father Arthur had so adroitly planted in the morning press. But the Cardinal himself had not attained his present position for nothing. He was equally adroit at fitting Vincent's success of the previous evening into the over-the-years jigsaw of his clerical career.

Vincent could see that Cardinal Wagner's well-aimed glances at the clippings were part of an orchestration and perhaps would not draw more than casual comment. If the fund-raising effort had been a failure, what then? The same recapitulation of his toils and troubles with Vinegar Jack and Tony Lorenzo could have been re-evaluated and focused into stern disapproval and rejection. But that was human nature, life itself, Vincent knew, and constituted no serious indictment of the Cardinal or any man of good will.

"I must return to the problem of personal sanctity for all of us engaged in busy apostolic life—especially in a large city," the Cardinal said.

He leaned back in his great red leather swivel chair, swung slightly to the right, and mused out of the french windows at the oceanlike sweep of the lake—a vast, green void of peace and tranquillity which was at marked variance with the fever and flurry of automobiles and trucks along the girdling lakeside boulevard.

"Look there, Monsignor," he said, nodding eagle-like from the aerie of his episcopal residence, "our city—the peace and yet the hurry of our lives."

"I see what you mean, Your Eminence, a striking contrast."

"I know of no busier, more burdened and harassed men than our Holy Fathers, the Popes—and I have personally been acquainted with three of them. Their personal sanctity, in almost every case, has been and is a living fact. Recognized and revered as saints, mind you, while they were still alive as busy administrators of not a parish, a diocese, but the whole world of Catholicism. I cannot exemplify these things too strongly to you and all my priests.

"Giuseppe Sarto, who will one day assuredly be canonized as St. Pius X, was, like our present Pius XI, a man of immense and indefatigable apostolic activity. It was my privilege as a young Monsignor like yourself to stand behind him during an audience when a group of admiring Italian peasants chorused: 'Santo! Santo!' at him. Do you know what he replied?"

Vincent shook his head slightly, eager for the answer.

" 'Not *Santo*—Sarto!' was his answer in firm yet gracious anger. But he was a saint—Benedict XV was a saint—Pius XI is a saint— some in greater degree than others, it is true. Do not ever, Monsignor, do not ever again suggest that we need a monastery for the pursuit of holiness. The monastery of the Popes is the world; ours is this big, busy, corrupt city!

"Corrupt, I have said—yes, yes, I know," he continued with a profound sigh, "I know what we have here. You are allowed, Monsignor, to do what you do because of the pervasive evils of our post-war times. I have no special funds for this downtown center of yours. My pastors complain that your centralized youth work is unnecessary. It can be done locally, they contend. They cannot afford the special collections you wring out of them with my approval."

"I've heard it all, over and over again, Your Eminence," Vincent said respectfully, "but the work goes on and we are getting results."

"I know, I know," the Cardinal said impatiently. "They are wrong. The children—white, black, yellow, and brown—must know each other as children of God. Our parish borders follow the geographical and political patterns of segregation. I know this, I know, and it will take years of forbearance, charity, and education to break all this social prejudice down, even among our own people. But you are proving something before their eyes—now—years in advance of the time of maturation. Continue to do so! Thank God! Thank God!" he concluded, rapping his episcopal ring against the glass top of his desk. "Wherever there is great evil, there is always correspondingly great good!"

Vincent knew he would never forget the way this prince of the Church rapped the desk again with the blood-glowing ruby of his ring, snarlingly defiant of the powers of darkness.

"I want the children off the streets. I want them together in friendship and understanding, away from the hoodlums, the beer trucks, the drunks and perverts. If the city government cannot do it, we will do it! We are doing it already—you are doing it! Your program has my blessing and my complete co-operation!

"Now tell me," he said, the inflection of his voice simmering into crisp officiousness again. "I have another appointment pressing me. What of the center? What are your new plans and needs?"

Vincent told him with almost intoxicated alacrity of his plans for an adult education center in the fall, an extension of the youth idea to working people at night, with the emphasis on social education rather than athletics. He told him also of Lucy and the Venezzia proposition to pay her salary.

"Venezzia must have taken to you," the Cardinal observed with raised eyebrows. "For him to come forward with such an offer after kicking through with a large donation for the seminary is indeed impressive."

"He wants the girl out of his hair at the plant—union-wise, that is," Vincent explained. "And at the same time I think his conscience bothers him a little all around."

"He is Milanese, you know," the Cardinal said urbanely. "High in the Church, yet with clever footwork also high in the practices of the market place. Achille Ratti could tell you how to handle him. He is one of them—from Milan, I mean. Many are privately devout but publicly would not hesitate to put the interests of nationalism and commerce above the apostolic requirements of the Church. Venezzia is a gracious juggler of God and Mammon. Thank him for the offer of the girl's salary at the adult center. But say he has done enough already and that I wish to handle the expenses of the school directly from this office."

Vincent was pleasantly stunned and relieved at the Cardinal's realism, or was it prudence?

"That would be much better, Your Eminence—no strings," he said.

"Precisely"—the Cardinal nodded—"no strings. This girl—you knew her mother? And a Negro at that? Do you think this will keep some of our white brethren away from the school?"

"It might at first, but I'm confident we can break it down. There'll be others on the faculty also. Father Arthur will teach, and the Jesuits, as you know, are always anxious to lend a hand at something like this."

"Father Arthur—*humph!*" the Cardinal said, making a droll face. "Did you see his latest? An editorial on women's hats! From the sublime to the ridiculous!"

"It's too hot for bomb-throwing, Your Eminence."

The Cardinal laughed heartily.

"My nephew is a good journalist but a bad diplomat. However, they're reading the paper—my pastors, I mean. I do wish, however, he wouldn't try to reform the world overnight."

"He's learning, Your Eminence. He's growing up."

"Well," the Cardinal snorted, "I won't be around forever. He'd better grow up soon or someone will send him out to the cows and chickens—where you went—after I'm dead and gone."

"I hope not," Vincent said, preparing to rise, sensing that the interview was over.

"Well, go along now. Don't let this colored girl start any race riots over there! And get yourself some red robes. You're a papal chamberlain now!"

"Thank you, Your Eminence, for everything."

The Cardinal waved him out with cordial gruffness.

"You won't be thanking me when you find out about all the work I've got for you to do. And that's another thing. You're getting too valuable to me around here. Hire yourself an assistant, a layman, if you like—a man. You'll be away from the center more often now on my business!"

"Oh?"

"You've let yourself in for it by being so handy with your tongue and raising all this money," the Cardinal concluded, tossing the clippings to one side. "Go along now. I'll be in touch with you."

"Very well, Your Eminence," Vincent said. "Good day."

"You'll find Monsignor O'Hara cooling his heels out there in the reception room. Tell him to come on in here and we'll see how and when we're going to collect all this money. It's one thing to raise it," he continued, swinging his chair toward the lakeside panorama again, "but it's another thing to collect it."

BOOK FIVE

The Making of a Liberal

CHAPTER XXIV

Assault on the Castle

AT FIVE-FIFTEEN on Monday morning Tony's alarm clock racketed suddenly in the dim, gray concrete vault that passed for a bedroom at the Lakeport Christian Union.

He punched at the alarm button quickly, almost viciously, and settled back on the pillows for a few moments.

"Oh, God!" he sighed—the sigh of burden in the morning.

He rubbed his hand over his chin. Good, he had shaved closely the evening before. He'd just have to douse his face, put on his clothes, and get out to the south side to meet Tommy Naski at the Splendid Restaurant on South Cowpens at Seventy-third.

"Splendid," he muttered, smirking at the four gray walls of the room. He glanced out of the small window beside his cot, and the El rattled by in the smoky gray of dawn. Gray, gray, gray.

Well, this was a lot better than trying to explain things at Mother Wagner's. He had packed his things and gone Saturday afternoon, directly after leaving Lucy at the youth center. He had left ten dollars and a note for Mother Wagner, who, luckily, had not yet returned.

"I'm going to be out all hours of the day and night on this labor organizing job," he had written, "so I better get a place where I won't disturb your lovely household. Father Arthur told me I wasn't to offer you any money or you'd be offended. The enclosed isn't for room or board. Why not buy yourself a pretty hat? Your son is an editorial expert on those things—he can advise you. I'll be in touch later. Warmest thanks for everything."

And Rosa? She had not returned before he left, either, and for that he was grateful. For Rosa, only silence. That was the most eloquent love letter he could write.

He shoved himself out of bed, put on his robe, whipped a towel off the iron rung at the end of his cot, slipped into a pair of wooden clogs, and went out into the deserted hallway, heading for the communal bathroom.

Later, dressed and shaved, he started out. The elevator door slammed open with a nerve-racking explosion, and the great yawn of the empty lobby opened before him.

He went over to the desk with his key and, waiting for the clerk, who was at the switchboard, glanced up at the large reproduction of an effeminate, long-haired Jesus which dominated the wall behind the desk. He wondered what Rosa would think of that. Michelangelo? Giotto? What would they think of it? The Jesus of the Christian Union, the Rudolph Valentino Jesus, monitor of the infinite two-dollar rooms.

The clerk pulled out a plug, put down his headphone, and came to the desk, a peepy little man, rigidly unctuous by habit and training.

"Good morning," he said. "Did you sleep well?"

"Very well," Tony said. "I'll be gone all day and can't be reached until late tonight. Will you kindly take any messages?"

The clerk glanced at the tag on the key: 972.

"Are you Mr. Lorenzo?"

Tony nodded.

"There's a message in your box now," the clerk said. "A young colored lady came in late last night after you'd gone to bed. She wouldn't let me call you."

He handed Tony the message.

"I couldn't let you go in there cold," the carefully written scriptlike hand explained. "I contacted Mr. Naski this afternoon, and he said he was meeting you at the Splendid Restaurant at six. I'll be there with a couple of Roma workers you can trust. I can't go to the plant with you for reasons you already know. But this I can give you at the start—a little push. See you at the Splendid. Regards. Lucy."

He stuffed the note into his coat pocket and went out to the street, smiling. This was more like it. What a kid! He hadn't expected this, but he should have. As if she'd let them stand out there like gawks, handing out circulars to an endless trickle of morose, sleepy

paper-box workers. The circulars, yes, in any case—a start—but to
have someone inside talking it up, maybe handing out union pledge
cards in the heart of the citadel. That was the jump they needed.

He boarded the south-side streetcar, and it clanked across the
viaduct to the south, the railroad always awake beneath them, and
around them the lights of tenements blinking on, the clink of milk
bottles as wagons clopped by, and the relentless devourer of darkness overhead, scattering the smoky gray, cracking its multitudinous
seams of silver light.

South Cowpens Avenue now; on, on into Browntown and the
workers rising, washing, eating, descending the bare, wooden stairs
to their daily doom of monotonous labor. The Splendid, a grimy
haven of coffee, eggs, and rolls, a respite from the routine and
monotony of the worker's day, loomed ahead at Seventy-third Street.

He got out of the streetcar, pushed through the revolving doors,
scanned the busy, clinking scene of predominantly colored workers,
and saw Lucy waving to him from a table in the far left corner. She
was sitting there with a lean, athletic colored boy and a thin, big-
boned white girl. Lucy fixed him with a wise old smile which, like
many another calisthenic of her spirit, could successfully transfigure
her long, homely, pock-marked face.

"Hi," she said. "Sit down. Naski's not here yet. Bicky will get
you some coffee. You know Bicky, don't you?"

He shook hands, noting the rapier build and feeling the steely,
panther strength of Bicky's clasp.

"I've heard about you," Tony said. "Aren't you one of Monsignor
Whelton's boxers?"

"I am, Mr. Lorenzo."

"He's a boxer for Mr. Venezzia also," Lucy said. "A paper boxer.
Bicky's been working at the Roma plant during the summer vaca-
tion. It was only recently I learned that he's one of Monsignor Vincent's boys."

"I'll get you some coffee," Bicky said. "Anything with it?"

"Yes, Bicky. A small orange juice and an order of English muffins.
Need some money?"

"We pay on the way out," Lucy said. "Naski told me to hold all
the checks. But here, I want you to meet Sophie Narleski. She's
from Milwaukee and is a fellow student of mine at the U. She's
been working in the stripping room at the plant with me this summer. Why, I don't know. She's a librarian and could do much better."

"Of course she knows why," Sophie said brightly, quickly. "Nice to meet you, Mr. Lorenzo. I'm so glad you and Mr. Naski are going to try to clean up that pesthole."

She sat down and kept on talking in a bright, zestful way that clearly signified she could go on for a long time.

"I'm studying for my library science degree. But my friend Emily Winant—'Blessed Emily,' we call her—who runs St. Martin's Center over in skid row, thought I should get away from books for a while and get right in here with Lucy, close to some real problems. So here I am! *And what problems!*" she exclaimed in a deceptively flirtatious way.

"We're happy to have you aboard," Tony said with a chuckle, feeling the contagious mirth of the woman.

Bicky was back with the coffee and juice.

"Thought you'd want this now, Mr. Lorenzo," he said. "I'll go get the muffins now."

"Thank you, Bicky," Tony said, seizing the orange juice eagerly. "You really don't have to wait on me like this."

"A pal of the Monsignor's is a pal of mine," Bicky said, flashing a stunning white smile at Tony.

"I don't know how palsy we'll all be after today," Tony said, sighing and dropping a sugar cube into his black coffee. "What do you think, Lucy?"

"I don't know what to think. I don't see why he should be upset. I won't be in the picture, and neither will the Monsignor, as far as I know."

"What do we do? What do we do?" Sophie asked briskly. "Tell me, I'm all ears. We've got to punch in at quarter of seven. Tell me. Do I plant a bomb or what?"

"Here comes Naski now!" Tony said, laughing, as he noticed big Tom clambering out of a streetcar with a large brown paper package under his arm. "He'll tell you what to do!"

Naski pummeled his way into the languid cafeteria atmosphere like a sudden squall on a placid pond.

"Good, good, you're all here!" he said, puffing toward them. "Hi, Tony," he said crisply, and then shook Lucy's hand, continuing a businesslike monologue as Bicky approached with the English muffins and two more cups of coffee. "You're Lucy, I know. Nice to see you and nice of you to call. We'll keep it quiet—no embarrassment for you with the Monsignor downtown. Who are these folks? Tell me who they are—and let's get going."

Lucy introduced them and he sat down, steering one of the cups of coffee in front of his great girth of body.

"Good, good!" he said heartily, adding three cubes of sugar to the coffee and emptying two of the midget bottles of cream into the steaming black brew. "Glad to have you both in the plant there pitching—we'd be lost without you—just out front beating our gums and waiting for the cops. Now here's what we'll do this morning! Tony, open up the package and dig out some of those pledge cards —they're right there on top of the letters. Folks—Miss Narleski, Mr. Brown—— Why, you're young enough to be my son, Mr. Brown. That's what I like, that's what we need—young people in the movement. I'll make an organizer out of you yet, Brown——What's your first name again?"

"Bicky."

"All right, Bicky, Miss Narleski, take about fifty of those pledge cards each, keep them out of sight. Sign them yourselves and get as many of the others inside to sign also. Read what it says there. It just says you want Local 397, Allied Paper Workers of America, to represent you with your employer regarding wages, hours, and working conditions. No dues, no initiation fees now—nothing. Just have them sign and we'll have a meeting later. They're all self-addressed and the postal permit is on there. Just have them drop the cards in the mailbox on their way home from work, and the cards will be in our downtown office in the morning. Don't collect them yourselves unless you do it after work. I don't want to get you fired. And don't give them to stool pigeons. Give them to people you can trust—we'll bring the others around later."

"That means the whole stripping room, eh, Lucy?" Sophie said eagerly. "All thirty-six of them."

"Good, good," Naski said. "And where do you work, son? Are you in the stripping room?"

"No, Mr. Naski," Bicky said. "I'm driving a tractor on the main floor."

"Okay, give them to the other lumpers maybe. No pressmen, though; no printers, right? They're getting the big gravy in that plant. They'll turn you in to Venezzia right away. Isn't that so?"

"That's right, Mr. Naski," Bicky said. "There's one or two that have been jumped. They're not too happy."

THE MAKING OF A LIBERAL

"Jumped?" Tony asked, eager to know, generously betraying his ignorance of plant conditions.

"He means there's been upgradings in jobs and wages without proper consideration for senior men and so on. Is that right, Bicky?"

"That's right, Mr. Naski."

"All right, Tony and I will be outside handing out the letters and cards to all that will take them. What should we say to the people, Lucy, besides the usual things?"

"Tell them about me being fired, of course," Lucy said, "for sticking up for their rights. Tell them this is America and segregation isn't right. Tell them about all the money Venezzia keeps giving away. Tell them charity begins at home."

"Say, that's good!" Tony said. "Charity begins at home."

"We'll use it!" Naski said. "I wish I had it in the letter. I wish it was in there. We'll put it in the next one. We'll put it in Wednesday's circular if all goes well."

"It's almost six-thirty, Mr. Naski, we better go," Bicky said.

"Yes, yes, get going. Take the bus like you always do. We'll grab a cab and be in front of the gate waiting for you. Take a letter and a card from us just like the others and do what you can inside. Call me at the office this evening. Will you do that, both of you? Call me and let me know what happens. The number is on the pledge card."

"Will do," Sophie said brightly as Bicky nodded.

"Good luck, Sophie, Bicky," Lucy said as they rose from the table. "It's so good of you to help us out by coming here."

"You're helping us," Sophie said, kissing Lucy on the cheek. "Let me know what you need in the way of books at the center. I'll help you get them."

"Yes, yes, I'll need your help, Sophie. Maybe you can give a course for me in the fall."

"No courses for me, Lucy. If the Monsignor starts a library or a bookstore, come around and see me."

"I'll remember that," Lucy said.

They went out of the cafeteria and joined a group of workers waiting for a bus.

"We'll have to go now, Lucy," Naski said, sloshing his coffee down in large gulps. "We'll let you know what happens."

"I feel like a wooden Indian, Lucy," Tony said. "But thanks, thanks very much."

"Not at all." She sat there in complete repose. "I'm so glad I had a chance to help."

"Good luck on the new job," Tony called over his shoulder as he and Naski left.

"The same to you on your new job," she said, clenching her fist and lifting it to him.

"There's a tiger behind all that gentleness," Naski said as he flagged a cab. "I saw that clenched fist—just like the Commies. But she isn't a Commie, is she?"

"She isn't now, I guess. She better not be, working around the Monsignor."

Back at Mother Wagner's there had been another early rising.

Rosa, walking down the hall on her way to attend Father Arthur's six-thirty Mass at the cathedral, saw the open door and empty room that had been Tony's.

So he was really gone! Had she found him and so quickly lost him? Gone without a word to her, but gone with a meaning for her?

Yes, yes, she knew there was a meaning. He did not want to see her there at Mother Wagner's. And she in the long loneliness of Saturday and Sunday night had decided to go herself.

Could she bring herself to seek after him? Yes, yes. She had never overtly sought a man in her life, but he was different. There was always one who was different, and that difference, a woman knew, is instant, abiding mutual love. She had had it with Carlo, but in a brotherly, protective sort of way. Yet with Tony the passion seemed there—the upsurgent flame of oneness was there, or so she deeply sensed in the brief encounter of their hallway embrace.

Thus, even on the way to Holy Mass, she knew the supreme desirability of this twofold love to a mature woman and she was determined to find him and find again the extension of their kindling love.

It all went together. On Saturday her art instructor had urged her to get a studio of her own. He had liked the back-yard painting, even though only three-quarters complete. Knowing she was a woman of means, he had suggested she really give more time to her talent.

She was too perceptive not to know that he was a friend of Father Arthur's and had been alerted to her need for a return to a firm, absorbing interest in a fruitful pattern of life. So she was ready for a place of her own again—more than they knew.

She closed the apartment door behind her gently and descended to the calm street of morning which led down to the side entrance of the cathedral and the lower chapel.

Perhaps Father Arthur would let her take him to breakfast after Mass and she would tell him then. Knowing him, knowing his blithe, wholesome interest in the things of art, she believed he would help her look for a place. Father Arthur would know. Some brownstone rooftop in the Lake Park section. Perhaps later that morning they could prowl the section together and find just the right place.

Mother Wagner would understand, after the first shock of revelation, just as she understood about Tony after she had assimilated his note and decided affectionately to go out and really buy a hat with the ten dollars he had left.

They came and went at Mother Wagner's, the deserving maneuvered from the streets of the city by the alert good samaritan who knew the rebuilding value of his mother's cool, commodious hospice. Rosa had been there since February, and that was a fairly long stay. She was ready to go now, ready to do her work. And, Tony, Tony, she thought with longing. Maybe Tony would be part of her new life too.

At the gate of the plant the listless morning faces, colored and white, dull with resignation, some flickering with interest at the pumping vitality of Naski's voice as he urged them to organization and deliverance from the very jaws of hell.

"You folks need a union in this plant!" Naski said. "And we're here to help you! Take this letter and card—read the letter, sign the card, and mail it in. We'll take care of the rest!"

Naski stood to the right of the gate, Tony to the left, handing them the folded letters with the card tucked inside.

"Remember what they did to Lucy Smith!" Tony said, handing the material to a stout, blank-faced Negress. "Without a good union, it can happen to you!"

"Ah know, Ah know," the woman said, taking the literature as the blank face lost its blankness and creased in a wistful smile.

"Here you are, mister!" Naski said to a gangly, sullen white man in denim coveralls. "You look like a machinist. You could be a leader among these people in a good union. Help them and yourself to get what's coming to you! Sign up now!"

The machinist snarled at Naski and with a quick, vicious motion of his hand knocked the literature out of the organizer's grasp.

"We don't want any union Communist bastards around here!" he said, moving significantly away from Naski and closer to Tony as he spoke.

Tony flared with anger and was about to grab him when Naski spoke, coolly, crisply.

"That's no way to talk in front of ladies!" he admonished, nodding politely to a queue of white girls who were approaching well within earshot. "If you folks had your own union in the plant you could bring him up on charges for talking like that."

"Ladies, we're one hundred per cent American!" Tony said, getting the pitch quickly. "And so was Lucy Smith. She tried to help you all, and look what she got!"

The four girls, attracted by the flattering initiative of Naski, took the folded letters with a certain docile compliance and went on in.

So it went as over three hundred workers entered the plant, the pressmen outwardly hostile, refusing or flinging down the letters, the colored and some of the whites taking the material in various degrees of indifference and sympathy.

Bicky Brown came through, throwing a quick wink at Tony and ignoring the proffered letter.

Sophie Narleski bounced up to the gate jauntily, wearing a big smile, accompanied by three white girls whom she seemed to know as routine workers.

"Venezzia's got lots of money for charity and for his skilled workers, girls," Tony said, handing them the letters. "But what about the manual laborers, the backbone of the plant? Thousands for charity, but very little for the stripping room!"

"Charity begins in the stripping room, girls! Form your own union now and we'll talk turkey with the boss. Sign the card and mail it in. We'll take care of the rest!" Naski added.

"*Won*derful, *won*derful!" Sophie purred, taking a letter as the others followed suit. She fixed her open, pseudo-flirtatious expression on Tony and exclaimed: "Isn't he handsome, girls!"

They went through the gate and into the yard, giggling and elbowing Sophie in obvious delight and approval.

"That's about it," Naski said as they circularized the last few stragglers hurrying in to work at sixteen minutes of seven. "Let's pick up the papers they chucked away. Never give them a chance to complain except about things you can answer."

They walked around the sidewalk, stooping and picking up the castaway sheets and cards.

Inside, the silent, steaming plant was coming to life. Tony heard the groan and stagger of the presses as the printers sent the big rollers on their morning trial runs.

While picking up a sheet near the gate he caught a glimpse of a swarthy giant standing on the shipping and receiving platform with folded arms, his riveting eyes filled with hatred and contempt.

"Hey, there's Zangora, the foreman," Tony said. "We've really made him very happy this morning."

"So it is," Naski said with a certain merry grimness. "Good morning, Mr. Zangora," he called jeeringly, holding up one of the circulars. "Would you like to read the news?"

"I have already seen your trash."

"Oh, one of the pressmen delivered your morning mail, eh?" Naski said, standing there as big and as defiant as Zangora. "I do hope you have an extra one for Mr. Venezzia."

"He will see it when he comes," Zangora said. "By then you will be in jail."

"He called the cops," Tony said anxiously. "What do we do now?"

"They always do that. We'll wait right here and talk to them. They won't take us in unless they have a warrant. And it's too early for Venezzia to swear out a warrant."

"What would the charge be?"

"Oh, trespassing, disturbing the peace, anything he can fake," Naski answered. "We don't have anything to protect us but our wits. Most of the individual cops come from laboring people and are pretty good at leaving us alone. But naturally a guy as powerful as Venezzia has the precinct captain in his pocket, and the heat can either come from him or City Hall."

"What about the law? Isn't there any protective legislation?" Tony asked.

"The law, my ass!" Naski put his great forearm around Tony's shoulders. "Let's walk up and down the sidewalk in front of the plant here. Some of the workers will catch a glimpse of us through those sooty windows, and it will have a good effect.

"Tony, labor legislation right now doesn't amount to a row of

dried-out beans. We're conspirators, Tony—we met in secret like
thieves at the Splendid Restaurant this morning. And until we get
some real protection from the federal government we'll always be
conspirators against management. They used to knock us out by
invoking what they called the common-law doctrine of conspiracy,
but since about 1850 we've been strong enough to keep the courts
from complying with management on that charge. There's been
safety in numbers, and the constant threat of strikes and the dis-
ruption of orderly municipal life has forced the courts to go easier
on us in most industrial communities."

"Then the strike is still our best weapon."

"Sure it is," Naski said, "and it always will be even if we get a
democratic administration in Washington someday and enact the
swell protective laws that are all set up down there and ready to
go."

"Do you think Al Smith would do it—grease the skids for those
laws, I mean?"

"Sure he would—right after election," Naski said wistfully. "But
—well—he won't be elected."

"Yeh, the country's not ready for a Roman Catholic President,"
Tony said. "That seems to be the general feeling."

"That's right. You ought to see what they've got ready for us down
there—a great law establishing the right of workers to organize and
requiring employers to accept collective bargaining. Think of it, Tony
—we're close to it—maybe four years or so away from it."

"Wouldn't that be something!"

"You see, Tony, we've already established that right to organize
by the law of the jungle, by sheer force, knuckles, and blood. First
comes the fact, then comes the law."

"You think we'll have to strike this place?"

"Of course we will," Naski said. "We'll have to win the confidence
of the majority and then strike the joint—that's our only weapon.
We start something inside the plant which brings everybody outside
the plant. Then Venezzia gets an injunction out against us. Then
come the cops on foot and on horseback and we have a helluva
time! He'll be standing up there in his plushy office looking out the
window at us—the ancient lord of the castle watching his vassals
work their truncheons over the skulls of the rebellious peasants."

"You make it seem like a historical movie," Tony said. "What happens then?"

"Then comes public opinion and whoever will help us among the prominent and the powerful."

"Here comes the squad car," Tony said apprehensively as the big black municipal sedan purred up to the curb beside them with four husky alert cops ready for anything.

"I'll talk to them. That looks like Sergeant Harrity beside the driver there," Naski said.

"What are you doing, Naski?" the elderly police sergeant asked casually, removing his hat and displaying a thatch of wheat-colored hair.

"Same old thing, Sarge." Naski leaned on the window sill of the sedan. "Just trying to give these people a chance to improve their lot."

"I know, I know," the sergeant said wearily. "Anything would be an improvement over what they've got. But I do hope we're not gonna have another hurly-burly."

"You mean like the one over on the west side two years ago—the Globe Paper Company?"

"That's the one."

"Were you in on that?" Naski asked. "I don't remember seeing you around."

"The whole force was in on it. You were in the lockup when I arrived, but there was still plenty to do."

"They've got a swell union over there now, Sarge, really they have. Everything going as nice and smooth as you please."

"So I hear," the officer said, mopping his brow with a handkerchief and putting on his hat. "But why do we always have to go through hell to get to heaven?"

"As long as the employer can use the injunction and the police against the people, there'll always be trouble. I don't want it any more than you do," Naski answered.

"Well"—the sergeant sighed wearily again—"getting back to the matter at hand—Zangora in there called and claimed you and this other feller are trespassing and disturbing the peace of the plant. Who is this feller, anyway?"

"He's my assistant, Tony Lorenzo—a very capable guy, and comes well recommended by the Cardinal's nephew, Father Arthur Wagner."

Tony, standing about three feet away and trying to look nonchalant, sensed what was coming.

"How long's he been with you?"

"Just hired him, Sarge. He managed a plant and served in the Navy before that. Matter of fact, he was Monsignor Vincent Whelton's assistant in the Navy chapel up on the northern shore."

"Yeh, I know who he is," the sergeant said glumly, taking his cap off again and removing a pad and pencil from inside the lining. "Hey, you over there, c'mere."

"Tony, come over here," Naski said, reddening.

"Where do you live?" the sergeant asked, writing Tony's name on the open pad.

"Right now I'm living at the Christian Union."

"How long have you been in town?"

"Less than a week."

"When do you report to your parole officer?"

"Hey, wait a minute, Sarge!" Naski said. "Let's be fair. He doesn't have to answer a question like that."

"That's right," the sergeant said, inflecting his parched voice insidiously. "He doesn't *have* to. We don't have any warrant—it's too early in the day. You always make sure of that."

"We have to be here early, Sergeant. We have to contact these people on their way in—right?"

"Wait'll Venezzia hears about this guy! He'll be right on Captain Hardy's ass!" the sergeant said.

"Are you gonna tell him?" Naski asked.

"I just turn in a report, that's all."

"What the hell has Venezzia got to do with Captain Hardy? He gets paid to protect all of us—not just Venezzia."

"That's right," the sergeant drawled cynically. "Anyway, you better get the hell out of here—and take your friend with you—before that warrant comes through."

"We'll be here when it's the right time to be here," Naski said calmly. "You can pinch us if you like, Sergeant, but we'll be sprung out of that goddamn lockup half an hour after you bring us in. I'll promise you that. I know you guys are only doing your job." Anger was rising in him now, slowly, relentlessly. "But I want to tell you something and you can relay it to Captain Hardy. We're not a band of Bolsheviks any longer. We're very well organized—we've got money and we've got power. And we've got a lot of fine people inside and outside that plant who believe in us and trust in what we're trying to do. We'll knock off that box shop—you can bet your ass on that!

"This guy here," he said, inclining his head toward Tony, "has paid his debt to society. He's got lots of ability and he's getting a chance to use his talents honestly and openly. And you guys are going to leave him alone!"

"We don't bother him as long as he toes the mark," the sergeant said.

"He'll toe the mark," Naski said, cooling. "You know, Sarge, it makes me laugh. The town is loaded with hoods and murderers and pimps and bootleggers—and you guys are all sweated up about a couple of mugs who are trying to improve the lot of a bunch of people imprisoned in a medieval sweatshop."

The sergeant smiled at this, and the other policemen could not suppress their grins.

"We're just doing what we're told."

"Yeh, I know." Naski shrugged his shoulders. "Okay, we're on our way now, but we'll be back."

"Just stay inside the law," the sergeant said, beckoning the driver, who kicked over the engine with a smoke-belching roar.

"I'll be glad to stay inside the law, Sarge," Naski said as they jolted powerfully away, "if I know what the hell the law is."

They were gone. Tony let out a pent-up sigh of relief.

"Phew!" he said. "You mean we have to fight *them* along with Venezzia?"

"Yeh, if they can catch us out on a limb," Naski said, looking after the speeding sedan with a thoughtful expression on his face. "There won't be any warrant until something happens. Venezzia's too smart for that. This is all part of the dance. The threats come first, then they lay back and wait for an opening."

"You talked right up to them. I was amazed."

"Yeh, I'm amazed myself," Naski said. "But it's the only way. You gotta make them think you're strong and on the come, or they'll walk all over you. Ten years ago I got a busted nose for talking to the cops that way. But they know we're stronger now. Hardy knows it. He knows the climate is changing in Washington and around City Hall or he'd-a had them take us in."

"Do you think they'll tell Venezzia about me?"

"Sure they will. Harrity won't, but Captain Hardy will. So what the hell can they do? Unless your skin is too thin. They'll be re-

ferring to you as a killer and an ex-con. Can you take it, feller?"
Naski rolled his eyes compassionately. "You can still get out if you
want to. I'll even get you another job—in one of our unionized plants
maybe."

"I'm in this thing to stay," Tony said.

"That's the style. Let's go down the corner and flag a cab. There's
nothing to do now but head for the office and await developments."

As they passed the gate, they could see Zangora still standing on
the loading platform with rigidly folded arms. His lips were taut
and his olive complexion metallic with rage and frustration.

"We've got to go along now, Mr. Zangora," Naski called with
mellifluous sarcasm. "I do hope everything is going along well inside.
And please give our best to that distinguished Christian philanthropist, that esteemed Knight of Malta, Nino Venezzia."

Following this scathing farewell, Zangora jerked his bull neck back
like a vulture and expectorated, his arms still rigid, his face still
malevolent.

"That foul scum!" Tony said, looking ahead intently, blacking
Zangora out of his mind.

"I'd just like one go at that big bag of guts!" Naski said with
frigid anger. "Just one go!"

"Maybe you'll get it before this is over."

"Maybe I will," Naski said as they walked away from the paper-
box citadel, across the moat of prevailing challenge, and into the
wide, steaming maw of the city that seemed so friendly and normal
in contrast to the excitement and tension of their morning assault.

CHAPTER XXV

Cardinal Red versus Deep Purple

WEEKS later, at six-fifteen on a chill, drizzly November evening, after Al Smith had fallen and Herbert Hoover had risen, after the Roma plant had been circularized, cajoled, harassed, wheedled, over and over again, after meetings had been held with sympathetic employees each week and still less than half of the box-shop workers were pledged to the union, after Rosa, dark Rosa, had finally reached him by phone in the cold, narrow tombs of the Christian Union, Tony, curious and apprehensive about a sudden telegram from the Monsignor, climbed the familiar staircase to the youth center.

The gym was a beehive of activity as he passed its wide, open doors. Kenney O'Byrne, thumping about in the ring as referee like a small black bear, was directing the workout of two flyweights who were sailing into each other's midriffs with gusto.

"That's it, that's it," Kenney was chanting as he weaved in and out of the range of their fire. "If you can take it in the breadbasket, those Golden Glovers can't hurtcha."

"Those Golden Glovers . . ." Kenney was referring to the inter-city amateur bouts which would take place in the Lakeport Stadium about mid-December. The CYC would have a strong team entered this year, and Bicky Brown would be one of the center's strongest contenders for national honors.

Wonder if he's in there? Tony thought, pausing and glancing around the gym. No sign of Bicky. He continued down the hall toward the Monsignor's suite.

To his right, near the entrance to the prelate's offices, he was

arrested by the freshly painted and paneled storeroom in which
surplus bleacher seats and ring equipment used to be piled in dust-
laden heaps. The door was slightly ajar and he could hear a woman's
voice—familiar, soft, persuasive, firm.

"I like that sentence from Pius XI's encyclical," she said, musingly.
"In fact I've got a confession to make. It's better than anything
I've seen in Marx with regard to the essential need for the organization of the workers into self-protective guilds or unions. 'The rich
have their own defenses . . .' That's from *Rerum Novarum*, a
section of which you've read in preparation for tonight's discussion.
What does that Latin phrase mean, Bicky?"

Bicky was in there! This was Lucy's class! Tony eavesdropped
with a warm, surging feeling of pride.

"I'm no Latin student," Bicky answered with a sure shyness, "but
it's right in the notes in the back of the pamphlet you gave us. It
means 'new ways, new things,' maybe new times."

"Excellent," Lucy said. "I think you could be as good a student
as you are a boxer."

"A paper boxer?" Tony asked impishly, sticking his head inside
the door.

"Tony Lorenzo!" Lucy exclaimed, flushed with pleasant surprise.

He looked around the gathering of about twenty students seated
in the one-armed classroom chairs. Sophie Narleski beamed almost brazenly at him, and he noticed several other workers from
the Roma plant.

"Won't you sit in?" Lucy asked. "We'd love to hear some comments
from one who is so vitally active in the field. Folks, this is Tony
Lorenzo, who is working very hard at organizing the Roma plant
on the south side. Some of the students here are among his sup-
porters. Will you stay and say a few words, Tony?"

"I wish I could. I've got to go see your big boss in there right away.
Can I take a rain check?"

"Certainly."

"Keep up the good work," Tony said, waving and smiling as he
withdrew. "Sounds real exciting."

"It all goes together," Lucy said with a meaningful look.

Tony continued down the hall, the feeling of uncertainty replaced
by a sense of exhilaration. She was right. It all goes together. And
the Monsignor was the sharpy of them all—this girl enthusiastically
teaching the papal encyclicals and Christian principles instead of

Karl Marx and class warfare. Maybe Vincent Whelton was the man to organize the Roma plant. He'd whip Venezzia into line real fast, Tony found himself thinking with involuntary admiration.

He rounded the corner to the reception room, where Joan was seated at her desk, sweet and open, always tentative, always intimately concerned.

They exchanged greetings and she asked if he could wait a few minutes. There was a clergyman closeted with the Monsignor.

"I hear you're having a hard time out there," she said after they had exchanged greetings.

"It's no bed of roses. We've signed up less than half the people, and that's about as far as we're going to get unless something breaks, something big."

"What does Naski think?"

"He says we just have to keep going along until we get a break, a big break."

"He should know," Joan said. "Bill Ryan says Naski has cracked a lot of tough nuts, but this one is the toughest."

"Yeh, the D.A.," Tony said with a curious smile in which there was lots of meaning for Joan. "I understand he and Naski are good buddies. It's good to know that."

"Bill Ryan's okay."

"How's it coming along?" Tony asked.

"Oh, we see each other quite a bit," she said with deceptive lightness.

"He couldn't have a nicer girl."

"I'm glad you think so." She lowered her eyes to the triplicate sheets in her typewriter.

To Vincent, his former roommate, the present Monsignor Robert Lambert of the Harbourton diocese, seemed considerably more cordial and indeed completely devoid of the sheathed hostility he had manifested on his last visit to the Christian Youth Center.

Could it be, Vincent mused as Monsignor Lambert told him of his visit several weeks ago to Washington with his Bishop, that he has grown fond of amateur pugilism and centralized parish recreation? Hardly.

"Vin, we were all so thrilled at the bishops' meeting when Cardinal Wagner told us the news about your appointment as a papal chamberlain to the Holy Father," Lambert said, his new cordiality sending a bit of a chill up and down Vincent's spine.

"It was nice of the Cardinal to do that! Was New York there at the time?"

"He was," Monsignor Lambert said. "And he wanted to know all about you. The Cardinal gave him quite a run-down, I must say."

"The Cardinal is extremely generous."

"New York expressed keen interest in your idea of centralized diocesan youth work as you have worked it out here; he seems to think it might adapt very well to the New York area."

"You could have given him an opinion on that," Vincent said without batting an eyelash. "Did you?"

"Come now, Vincent," Monsignor Lambert said lightly and without pique. "I've largely been opposed to the introduction of such methods in a smaller diocese like Harbourton. As the city grows— and it is growing—perhaps we'll change. As for participating in the Washington discussion, that was the primary duty of Bishop Sliney. I was merely there as his aide."

"What else was new down there?"

"Oh, there's a great deal of cautionary talk about spiraling investments and a possible blowup in Wall Street. Archbishop Peruzzi, the Apostolic Delegate, urged only blue-chip investments in stocks and bonds."

"Archbishop Peruzzi——" Vincent said, smiling with a flash of reminiscence. "He's your bird-watching colleague."

"You've got a good memory. And so has the Cardinal. Can you imagine—we were walking through the campus of Catholic University with the Apostolic Delegate, and Bishop Sliney saw a flash of color in a cherry tree. 'I wonder which species of bird that is?' the Bishop asked, half aloud. Do you know what the Cardinal said, fixing me with the most amused smile?"

"I can guess, I think."

"The Cardinal said: 'Ask Monsignor Lambert—he knows all about those things.' Remember!" Lambert reminded Vincent. "That was almost twenty years ago on the seminary grounds—the bird-watching tour with the Apostolic Delegate!"

"I remember," Vincent said. "Did you identify the bird this time?"

"No, my dear boy, not verbally," Lambert said, cannily savoring his action. "I let the Apostolic Delegate do the identifying. It was a Baltimore oriole."

"Life-first or year-first?" Vincent asked, smiling.

"Year-first, you old Irish omadhaun." Lambert laughed. "You and His Eminence are certainly a pair when it comes to remembering things."

Vincent had never seen Lambert like this—so well at ease and almost on the border of the affectionate. What was he really doing here? He could have said hello—if that was it—by telephone. And as for Vincent's appointment, Lambert had sent him a note about it on his return to Harbourton from the Washington trip.

He was soon to know.

"You're probably wondering what Bishop Sliney and I are doing in town. As you know, we've been closeted with the Cardinal this afternoon," Monsignor Lambert explained.

"Yes, Mrs. Rush called and said His Eminence wanted me to wait here for you."

"I do hope you won't mind the official touch, Vin," the Monsignor said. "That was the Cardinal's doing. I know you would have seen me anyway on an informal basis."

"Of course I would. What's going on?"

"Well, you know something about the labor troubles out at Nino Venezzia's Roma plant. He expects it all to worsen and anticipates a serious work stoppage."

"A strike? I really didn't know the union campaign was making that much headway. But what's it all got to do with us?"

Monsignor Whelton had every confidence in Lucy and Tony. Surely they hadn't involved him or the center!

"I'm free to tell you that both His Eminence and Bishop Sliney have received similar notes from Mr. Venezzia stating that he'll be unable to honor his fund commitments until the dispute is settled. He also respectfully stated that if there is a serious work stoppage his financial losses will make it impossible to make further contributions for some time to come," Lambert explained with a reversion to the more polar aspects of his temperament.

"That sounds like pressure to me," Vincent said candidly. "I didn't know the Bishop of Harbourton was involved in his benefactions."

"We have been for several years. While our contribution this year would not compare with the imposing sum you so charmingly encouraged him to contribute to the Cardinal's seminary fund, it would nonetheless amount to about five thousand dollars."

"I still think it's pressure," Vincent demurred, "although he's perfectly within his rights to take this position, and it does sound fairly reasonable if he has a work stoppage out there. I still don't see how this involves me."

Monsignor Lambert's jowls tightened, and the old skeletal set of face under the increased fleshiness of the years was evident.

"Yes, of course it's pressure, Vincent. We recognize that. The Cardinal and the Bishop are impatient with it, but you agree that Venezzia has a point. He was in the episcopal residence with us this afternoon and mentioned this girl—a Negress, I believe, a former employee at the plant—who runs your new adult education school over here. He was very sympathetic about her, thinks she'll do a good job and all that, thinks it's the right spot and the right technique, and reminded us that he encouraged you to hire her."

"That's all true, and she is doing a good job," Vincent said tentatively. "Does he object to her having students from his plant in her papal encyclical classes?" he added pointedly. "That was part and parcel of his own original proposal to me after the fund-raising banquet. I thought it quite statesmanlike of him at the time."

"He doesn't object strenuously to the idea at all," Lambert injected, "but he hints at possible collusion with one of the organizing fellows, who he says is familiar to you."

"Oh, he means Tony Lorenzo," Vincent said casually. "He was my chapel assistant in the Navy and later, unfortunately, became involved with the law. He served some time for bootlegging and carrying a gun—but that's all over now and he's straightening out very well. On the other hand, Miss Lucy Smith is doing a perfectly fine job so far with the classes and has taken an impressive hold on the papal encyclicals regarding labor matters. I'm beginning to hope she's working out her own conversion to the Faith."

"She's not a Catholic?" Lambert said, raising his eyebrows slightly.

"No, actually she's not," Vincent said firmly. "You may recall her mother—out in Splinterville, north of the seminary. She was an unusually devout woman. Father Carney might have told you about her when we were students. He and I used to go out there on the student mission band."

"I do seem to recall her now," the Monsignor said, wrinkling his brow. "How come it didn't take on the daughter?"

"Oh, the mother went before the father—one of those things— the old gent was a shiftless sort. But I'm inclined to think the mother's impress is taking in a delayed action perhaps," Vincent said. "But to get back to Venezzia. I'm positive there's no active collusion. Both individuals promised me they'd kept the center out of it, and I have every reason to believe they'll keep their word."

"The Cardinal seems to know about all this," Lambert said.

"I told him about it. We don't operate in the dark around here, Bob."

"I'm sure you don't, Vin. But I wish there were some way we could smooth things over. What can we do?"

"Watch and pray," Vincent said, half seriously, half facetiously. "These workers have real, serious grievances, the toleration of which they contend is unbecoming to a layman so prominent in the Church. I'm no advocate of rampant union power. Industrial strikes do hurt everybody involved, it seems to me. But then, the union people have no substantial laws to protect their interests and the strike seems to be their only effective weapon in the last analysis."

"I suppose you're right, but right now that donation looks awfully big up in little Harbourton—and it's about to fly right out the window."

"It looks big to the Cardinal also, I'll bet," Vincent said, stating the obvious. "What does he think about all this?"

"I'd say about the same way you do—to be perfectly frank."

"I'm glad to hear that," Vincent said with a sigh. "I'll promise you this, though: I'll double-check on the Smith-Lorenzo relationship and will make every effort to maintain our hands-off policy here at the center. We can't stop the workers from coming to the evening school, however."

"I know, Vin," Monsignor Lambert said, "but it is in the very nature of the setup for Miss Smith to be stoking the fires—however indirectly."

Anger flared for an instant in Vincent. He felt impelled to tell Monsignor Lambert to get out and mind his own business. But the Cardinal, he believed profoundly, would know how to handle this inter-diocesan matter, and Bishop Sliney, however old and conservative, would realize that this was not his concern.

Monsignor Lambert sensed the storm of Vincent's emotions and rose, offering his hand.

"The Bishop and I are taking an early evening train back to Harbourton, so I'd better get along. I'm sure you'll be in touch with the Cardinal's office on this matter."

"I'm always in touch with the Cardinal's office," Vincent said cryptically. "Nice to see you again, though, Bob. Do I hear rumors correctly? Is one of my former roommates soon to be an auxiliary bishop?"

"There has been something in the wind," Lambert admitted coolly. "Bishop Sliney isn't getting any younger and he is inclined to agree to the appointment of a coadjutor bishop."

"I hope it goes well for you," Vincent said. "I'll show you out the short way—through my private entrance."

"Excellent," the Monsignor said, taking his black felt off a neighboring chair and following Vincent. "Speaking of roommates, how is our editor friend? Not planning to burgeon out editorially on the labor dispute, I trust."

"He's fine. What he does over there is his responsibility. I have no pipe line in there."

"I understand," Monsignor Lambert said with hasty cordiality. "And thank you for filling in the details. Bishop Sliney will appreciate your candor, believe me."

"More than glad to do it, Bob," Vincent said.

"Thank you so much and keep up the good work," Lambert said with a ring of sincerity as he waved finally on the staircase.

Back in the office, Vincent let out a sigh. He didn't know whether to be indignant or just laugh out loud. But after all, the Monsignor had come at the Cardinal's request. Had the Cardinal wanted him to give Lambert his walking papers? Perhaps. He'd know later. In any case, he'd been able to get him out through the private entrance. He knew Tony would be sitting in the reception room waiting, and Monsignor Lambert was just sharp-eyed enough to come to the wrong conclusion about Tony's visit.

Actually he had asked Tony over to offer him the job which the Cardinal had authorized as Christian Youth Center assistant. Monsignor Vincent had heard that the organizational campaign was almost at a standstill and was surprised at Venezzia's apprehensiveness. Vincent had no ulterior motive in offering the job to Tony. He just thought Tony would fit it and could make something out of it.

He pressed the buzzer and picked up the phone.

"Joan," he said crisply. "Is Tony there?"

"Yes, Monsignor."

"Good. Send him on in."

"One more thing, Monsignor. Mrs. Rush is on the phone. It's important. I've been holding the call."

"All right, put her on."

He waved Tony cordially into the office and motioned to a chair at his left.

"Hello, hello, Mrs. Rush. I'm sorry to keep you waiting. . . . Yes, yes. Nothing serious, I hope. . . . Why, yes—the Knights of Columbus, Twenty-fifth Anniversary Dinner, Lakeside Hotel—eight-fifteen. That doesn't give me much time, but I'll hustle home now and dress. . . . Wear my robes—yes. . . . Yes, a check for the building fund and a little acceptance speech. I'll get something together. . . . Nothing serious is wrong with the boss, you say? What's he got—the 'accidie'?"

The Monsignor chuckled richly, and Tony was almost a little stunned by the episcopal timbre of the laugh. He had never heard Vincent Whelton laugh that way before. *Rerum Novarum*, new things, new ideas, new times . . .

" 'Banquet-itis,' you say," the Monsignor repeated with a big wink at Tony. "I'll get it too. Hot whiskey and early to bed. . . . It wouldn't be that twenty thousand, would it, now?" He chuckled again. "But that's really no laughing matter, eh? And we may get it yet! . . . All right, Mrs. Rush. Tell His Eminence I'll be right on deck. Good-by now."

Laughing, he turned to Tony. "The Cardinal is off his feed this evening, young man, and you may be the reason for it."

"How come?" Tony asked with an amused look on his face.

"Well, old Venezzia may take a walk on that twenty-thousand-dollar contribution because of all that labor trouble out there. 'Banquet-itis,' Mrs. Rush calls it."

"That's news to me—Venezzia's concern, I mean. I didn't think we were doing too well."

"That's what I thought too," the Monsignor said, shifting into gradual sternness. "But he's putting the pressure on me, in any case, through the Cardinal."

"What have you got to do with it, Monsignor?" Tony asked, alarmed.

"Not a darned thing, unless you and Lucy have been in collusion. And I can't believe that."

"She gave us a few pointers at the start, Monsignor," Tony hastened to concede, "just before she went to work for you. But since then we've kept our word to you."

"I believe you have. But I must reiterate my original stipulation to you, and I'll do the same to her. Keep the center out of it! The school is one thing, but active influence is another."

"We've kept our word, Monsignor, and will continue to do so."

"I've no doubt of it. In fact, I called you over here for another matter entirely. And then I received this other news."

"Oh?"

"Yes. There's a job here for you as my assistant if you want it. The Cardinal has authorized me to hire someone. He's pulling me out of the office quite a lot, as you can see. I had intended to grab a bite and attend the elimination bouts in the gym tonight, but that's out. I'll be at the K of C dinner."

"Thank you so much, Monsignor," Tony said, visibly moved by the offer. "I can't take it now—much as I'd like to. I can't leave Naski till this is over—one way or the other. Can I take a rain check, or do you have to have someone right away?"

"It'll keep awhile," Vincent said, sighing and trying to collect his thoughts. It was already after seven. He'd have to dash back to the rectory, bathe, and get dressed.

"How *are* things out there?" he asked anxiously. "Will there be a strike?"

"We can't strike with less than half the plant with us," Tony said. "If we get a big break, yes—but as of now, we couldn't shut down a single press."

"How long can this go on?"

"Indefinitely. Venezzia won't give, and neither will Naski."

"Oh, Lord," Vincent sighed. "It all seems so pointless. Won't he give you people anything? Can't you compromise?"

"He won't even talk with us."

"Well . . . I don't know what to say. You do have grievances out there—all this segregation business, and I suppose plant conditions are bad, and pay scales and all."

"They are," Tony said. "We'll just have to keep trying to wean people away from him. Will the Cardinal hurt us?"

"I don't believe he will. You're hurting him more than he's hurting you right now."

"I can understand that."

"Well, Tony," he said regretfully, rising, "I'm terribly pressed for time. Keep the job in mind and let me know what you think."

"I will, Monsignor; it sounds wonderful."

"I'll pay you at least as much as you're getting now, and there'll be more as we go on. I've got to go. Walk out with me?"

"Love to," Tony said, following him out the private way. "Say, Lucy's doing a good job of teaching over on the other side of the hall. I stuck my head in for a while."

"Yes?" the Monsignor asked as they hurried down the stairs. "Everything sound all right?"

"Couldn't sound better if she were wearing a wimple," Tony answered.

"I'm glad to hear that," the Monsignor said as they approached the cab stand. "And remember what I told you earlier. Otherwise you'll have me shipped out to the country, and I'm getting too old to start all over again."

"You didn't do a bad job out there," Tony said with a grin.

Monsignor Whelton punched him solidly on the shoulder.

"Can I drop you anywhere?"

"No, I'm heading across the boulevard to the park."

"All right," the prelate said, ducking into the cab. "Let me know about the job and—remember—in this union thing, you're completely on your own."

"I'll remember," Tony said. He crossed the boulevard to the outer stretches of Lakeport Park.

How about that? he thought triumphantly as he strode to the address Rosa had given him. Venezzia's worried. All we need now is a break, a teeny-weeny helluva big break . . .

CHAPTER XXVI

Love in a Brownstone House

ACROSS the park now, the rain gone, the towers of the city veiled with heavy mist, and to the west glimmerings of waning, red autumnal light, presaging a brighter day on the morrow.

Tony stepped vigorously along the concrete walk which bisected the northern end of the vast lake-front park. Within, he was stormed with a delicious feeling of just being alive and free.

The Monsignor's revelation that Venezzia was attempting to use pressure on the union was a sign, a break, the very first. And Monsignor Whelton's benevolent neutrality was most heartening of all.

Now the dark Rosa was waiting for him in one of those brownstone houses dead ahead. The mystery and the promise of her quiet, burning beauty beckoned him through the mist and the hush of the black velvet evening. It seemed a fitting climax to a breakthrough of hope.

He squinted through the haze, seeking some sign of drug- or variety store where he could phone Naski, who would be home by now. He was anxious to give him the heartening news of Venezzia's unsuccessful coup against the union.

There was nothing ahead, only brownstone exteriors and wrought-iron fences.

Near the exit to the street he saw the gallant, prancing bronze of General Sheridan's steed. Gathered around the gleaming marble slabs at the statue's base was a group of shabbily dressed men and women listening to a speaker.

It was a woman, large and brusque, her words ringing with passionate conviction. Sheridan Square! The radicals gathered here, he recalled, lancing with endless contentious talk the tumors of society.

"It was a good thing for Al Smith to run," she insisted vigorously, standing on one of the marble steps and clutching a faded woolen afghan close to her pale, high-cheekboned features, "and it was a good thing for him to be defeated—good for the humility of American Catholics, good for the prickling consciences of Protestant bigots."

She was a handsome woman in a lusty, masculine way. Her generous crop of dark brown hair flecked with gray was drawn back tightly into a neat doughnut of a bun, accentuating her full, reddish face and the intensity of her wide, green eyes.

"I HEAR THE POPE WAS GOING TO MOVE TO WASHINGTON IF SMITH HAD BEEN ELECTED!" a heckler shouted.

Tony recognized her now. It was Emily Winant, he realized with an electric thrill of excitement. Sophie Narleski had mentioned her, calling her "Blessed Emily" with a certain affectionate humor. Friend of the skid-row bums and Negroes, with settlement houses on opposite sides of the city.

Emily tightened her jaw muscles at the taunt and drew her shawl more tightly around her, gaining a height of angry dignity before answering.

"That was the most absurd smear of the entire campaign," she said softly, "and I refuse to lend it dignity by discussing it any further.

"As usual," she resumed in a conclusive tone of voice, "I invite you all to soup and coffee at St. Martin's Center on the other side of the square. Our beds are all filled up for the night, but we will try to scrape together twenty-five cents as lodging-house money for each of you who do not have a place to sleep. We do not offer you much, but whatever we have, we give you in the name of Christ Jesus Our Lord and Savior, Who commanded each and every one of us to feed the hungry, clothe the naked, and shelter the shelterless. All who care may join me in prayer that the sun of justice may shine on those who are heavily burdened. In the name of the Father and of the Son and of the Holy Ghost."

Tony blessed himself and joined in the Our Father and Hail Mary which Emily led in a calm, strong voice. And the murmur grew stronger as she prayed on; the murmur of misery and defeat sputtered and crackled from the dry lips of defeated men and women, rattling a handful of stony hopes against the misty, inscrutable skies.

Tony left the dreary petitioners and sought out 575 Sheridan Place, his mood more sober now. To his left he caught a glimpse of Emily Winant clutching her shawl and walking stolidly and alone across the square to her relentless nightly chores.

He found the number, climbed the wide brownstone steps, and tugged at a heavy brass ring which released a rich, calm chime somewhere in a cool, eternal distance.

The chime echoed into deep silence broken after several ghostly moments by soft, evenly paced footfalls. Someone was releasing intricate mechanisms of security; the large brass door handle turned slowly and a tall Nordic man in a dark gray suit, white shirt, and black tie appraised him carefully. He nodded his balding gray head slightly, hinting disapproval with the faint downward motion of his beaklike nose.

"Yes?" he said with a gentle coldness.

"I'm Anthony Lorenzo," Tony said with uncertain cordiality. "I believe Miss Venezzia is expecting me."

"Yes," the man acknowledged. "Please come in."

Tony followed him into a long wide hallway resplendent with black and white tiles. The butler took his hat and hung it on a throne-like mahogany affair replete with hooks, umbrella stand, cushioned seat, and hand-carved gargoyles. He motioned him toward a winding mahogany staircase gleaming with fresh wax.

"Miss Venezzia will see you in the library upstairs," he said with what seemed like a Swedish accent.

Up the waxen stairs and to the right now, the ex-convict, ex-hoodlum, ex-what-next, he mused. The stairs had been bare in the pen, he recalled, bare with the coldness of steel and the arctic vapors of despair. Here warm, here rich, here teased with anticipation, he wondered on the windings of his life.

"It's Mr. Lorenzo," he heard the butler say as he rounded his way into the warm, fire-glow embrace of the library.

She was at her easel near the fireplace, sheer black in slacks, sweater, and the bright darkness of her being.

"Tony!" she exclaimed, rising, wiping her hands on a color-blotched towel and hurrying to him. "I'm so glad you came."

She took his hand in her small warm hand and squeezed it in a firm clasp.

"Come," she said, leading him to a huge wide black couch. "Lars," she called gaily over her shoulder, "bring the martinis and things."

Lars nodded and was gone.

"Say!" Tony said, angling richly into a corner of the sofa. "Some castle!"

"Isn't it nice!" she said, pleased at his approval. "I just had to get a place of my own, you know, and this one was up for lease, furniture and all. A friend of my father went to Europe for a year. And Lars—well, Lars has been with us for years—with me, that is. He just ducked out on my father and came over here."

"How many rooms?" Tony asked with wide-eyed naïveté.

"Oh, I don't know," she said, raising her eyebrows, surprised at the question. She had never known the problem of room space. "Fifteen or twenty, I suppose."

Tony whistled, steadfastly simple, steadfastly impressed.

"It's a hotel!" he said. "Who else lives here?"

"Just me—and Lars," she said with easy unconcern.

He glanced at the painting. It was the back-yard scape, almost finished. She had obviously been touching it up.

He rose and took a closer look.

Lars was back now with a silver cocktail shaker on a silver tray. There were hors d'oeuvres on the tray also, little cheeses, anchovies, small crackers.

She was beside Tony as he stepped back, appraising the painting.

"I think it's real good, Rosa," he said spontaneously. "I really do. It's a little better than the usual. The place looks—well, it looks lived in—real."

"That's just the impression I tried to give," she said, smiling and taking a martini from Lars. "Thank you, Lars."

"Thank you," Tony said, taking the thin, cold glass.

Lars was gone again, and they were alone.

"Martinis," Tony said, elated, whiffing the wry bouquet of the gin and vermouth. "The drink of quick refuge."

She touched her glass against his lightly and looked at him the way she had in Mother Wagner's hallway.

"Martinis," she said with a little catch in her voice, "the drink of love."

They sipped and sat in silence, looking at each other, warmed outwardly and inwardly by the fire and the martinis.

"I've missed you, Tony," she said. "How have things been going?"

He shrugged his shoulders slightly, amiably. "They're looking better, but we still need the big break."

"I will help you when the time comes," she said with casual generosity. "My father is a fool to fight this thing."

She put her glass down on an end table and tossed her delicate jeweled hand in a small graceful motion that encompassed the room.

"You see," she said with childlike glee, "I told you we would see each other again."

"You did at that," Tony said, a little bewildered by the almost clear implication that this was all for him—and her.

They talked of many things—their early lives, the poor little rich girl of the Italian villas, the defiant little hood from the south side of Lakeport. They were warmed deeply by the crackling open fire and by the sweet inner fire of the martinis.

An hour passed, two; they probed the odyssey of their lives, the winding trails that had now merged. They glowed with satisfaction, leaning back on the wide, rich sofa. They savored patiently, with impassive joy, their irrepressible attraction for each other.

They were talked out. After a long, luxurious silence she turned from the fireplace to the caged fire of him and spoke.

"Now you must kiss me," she said, leaning forward and touching the middle of her cheek with her finger. "Right here."

He hesitated a moment, cautionary. She was Venezzia's daughter and there was so much at stake. Yet he believed her; this was no act, no sham. She was a rebel, an independent; it was in every flash and flare, in every controlled dark depth of her.

"You were not so hesitant in Mother Wagner's hallway," she said petulantly.

He leaned over and kissed her warmly on the cheek. She sighed and slipped into his arms. Their lips met hungrily, and as they clung together in a tight embrace the fireplace seemed circular around them, burning and burning with relentless intensity.

Somewhere in the cosmos of fire and kisses he asked about Lars.

"Lars is gone for the evening, my darling, do not fear."

Eternity of fire again, and all his longings sacrificial in the holocaust of her untiring love. The fire burned low; they slept.

Now cold and warmth. The chill of dying fires against one cheek, the moisture of her tears against another.

"Do you have a phone here, Rosa? I've got to make a call."

"Yes, in my room," she said, "but kiss me—I cannot get enough of you."

"You've got all there is," Tony said, kissing her on the cheek and rising. "I've really got to call this guy. He'll be sore if I don't."

"Come." She was on her feet, tightening the belt of her black slacks, smoothing her sweater.

She took his hand and led him to her room, snapping on the light.

"There," she said, pointing to an ivory-colored French phone beside her bed. "Excuse me." She was gone—into a combination dressing room and bath which adjoined her room.

Sighing, rumpled, unpressed, irritated by unwanted remorse, he slumped into a sitting position on the satiny four-poster bed and picked up the phone. He gave the operator Naski's home number and got through.

"Tony," Naski boomed at him. "For Christ sakes, where you been? Things are beginning to hop. Bicky Brown was warned about union activity today and thinks they're going to fire him. He's right here now, and we've got to work something out for tomorrow. Can you come over?"

"Yes, I'll be there in three quarters of an hour."

"Three quarters of an hour!" Naski exclaimed impatiently. "Where the hell are you—in Boston?"

"I'm on the other side of town visiting a friend," Tony said calmly. "I'll be there in three quarters of an hour."

"Okay, okay, we'll wait. Hurry up."

"Okay, Tommy, and look," Tony said. "Venezzia must be getting worried. He tried to put the pressure on us through the Cardinal and it fizzled."

"Yeh? Who told you that?"

"You guess and it'll be the right one."

"I get it," Naski said. "Hurry up over here."

Tony hung up and went over to Rosa's dresser, where he combed his hair and straightened his tie. She was beside him, an ensemble of black again, black pajamas, black housecoat, black slippers.

"Must you go?"

"I really must, Rosa," he said, taking her in his arms again.

"When will I see you again?" she asked anxiously, sticking him with the eternal question of a woman who has grasped at love, only to find it writhing for escape.

"As soon as I can, darling, honestly," Tony said. "But this thing is coming to a head and it's best—well, it's best I keep you out of the picture."

"All right, darling," she said coquettishly, leaning her trim little-boy head against his shoulder. "But you will phone me every night and let me know how things are?"

Every night. And he to her darling; and she to him darling. He was in the web now and he knew it with a chill of foreboding.

"I will, darling, I will."

"I'll walk you down the stairs."

The sweetness descended again between them as arm in arm they stepped down the winding mahogany stairs.

"You've got to get out of that rabbit warren you're living in," she said anxiously. "Couldn't you move in here? I've so many rooms—and really wouldn't have to see you much."

Tony laughed.

"You could pay me rent," she urged with charming, conscious naïveté.

"How much?" he asked.

"Fifty cents a week." She chuckled. "It would pay for the olives in your martinis."

"I'll take it up with your father over the conference table," Tony said, "if we ever get that close to him."

"You will."

He kissed her one last time, long and sweet and loving.

CHAPTER XXVII

"Hit the Bricks"

THE joom! The zoom! The joom-zoom, joom-zoom!

The presses were rolling, relieving for the moment the piano-wire tautness felt so intensely by both Naski and Tony Lorenzo as they stood on the deserted sidewalk outside the plant.

Around them swirled the chilly mists of an early November morning, and beyond the grimy windows, in the caldron of decision, Bicky Brown and Sophie Narleski were stirring the witches' brew.

Joom-zoom, joom-zoom, now quicker joom-zoom, now the rhythm joom-zoom, and the sudden ziss of steam from a vent, the rumble of a tractor lift, the thump and clatter of an empty skid.

"Let's have a cigarette!" Naski snapped nervously, shifting his dwindled sheaf of circulars under his left arm and fishing for a package.

"Here's one right here," Tony said, popping, gunlike, an open package of smokes in Naski's direction.

"Thanks." Naski took the cigarette and accepted a light. "You're goddamn chipper this morning. You got a new look on your face," he mused shrewdly as they walked along the sidewalk beside the plant. "You got the look of happy pleasure, in case you don't know. Where the hell were you last evening?"

"Now stop fishing, Tommy," Tony said with a chuckle. "I told you I was with a friend."

"Yeh, friend!" Tommy said. "Has she got a friend too? I'm about ready for something like that, and my old lady would kill me if she knew it."

"Never mind. I'm happy for other reasons besides that. I got the big feeling this morning, I got the real big feeling. Listen to the music of those presses, listen to them. Maybe they'll stop today—and not just for lunch—maybe they'll just stop and we'll have lots of company out here, maybe. . . ."

"Maybe is right. Keep it to yourself!" Tommy snapped. "Where the hell is that goddamn Wolfson with the signs? He should be here by now!"

"The signs?"

"Yeh, the signs," Naski explained. "I got Jakie Wolfson comin' out here in his pickup truck with signs—just in case."

"Good, good," Tony said. "You think of everything."

"Fifty bucks for signs," Naski said wryly. "Maybe my kids will use them for paper dolls."

They turned and walked back toward the main gate of the plant. Joom-zoom, joom-zoom, joom-zoom!

"There's something almost sweet and fresh about a big plant kicking over in the morning," Tony said. "I never knew it could be like that."

"It's not sweet and fresh for those poor bastards in there! It's sweet and fresh for Venezzia," Naski said. "Those presses may as well be printing money, stamping it out in there just like the mint. That's what's sweet and fresh, old buddy, those soapboxes in there. And we gotta see that the people who make them get theirs."

At the plant gate Tony saw the hulking figure of Zangora, the foreman.

"Hey, there's Frankenstein!" he said.

"So it is." Naski lifted his felt hat and bowed briefly at the waist. "A very good morning to you, Signor Zangora!"

"Good for me—not for you," Zangora said with a triumphant smile, clenching his fist and shaking it at the two interlopers. "We fix you to-day!"

"Oh?" Naski said with a cold, controlled smile. "Strategy, eh?"

"You see," Zangora said, nodding confidently as he walked back into the plant. "You see."

"Look out for tricks," Tony said as they wheeled and sauntered along the sidewalk again.

"Yeh, tricks." Naski spat. "I know I may not get the chance, but I'd like one shot at that big, arrogant guinea face."

"Be careful what you say about one of my fellow countrymen."

"Ah, you're not a guinea," Naski said, putting his arm around Tony's shoulders. "You're a noble Roman, you got mind and you got soul."

"Now I'll let you buy me some coffee, Polack."

"Good idea." Naski glanced at his watch. "It's quarter of eight now. Like we agreed last night, Bicky and Sophie will make their moves at break-time, nine-fifteen. Venezzia should be in his office by then."

"You really don't think Zangora will fire Bicky before that?"

"No. He'll wait for Venezzia. They'll want to make a real ritual of it—Venezzia, the kindly patriarch, walking through the plant and all that. That's what I figured out last night, and both Bicky and Sophie think it will be that way. We've got to take the chance."

"Good, let's get the coffee. . . ."

Jam-bam, jam-bam!

"Okay, Bicky, go get another load," Mack Carver called from the catwalk over the big two-color press.

"Okay, Mack," Bicky said cheerily as he sprung lightly onto the steering platform of the snub gasoline tractor parked beside the press. "Can I speak to you a minute?" he hollered up at Carver through the din.

"Sure, Bicky," Carver said, glancing at the moving cardboard sheets and then leaning over the railing. He was a tall, almost skeletal man with a chicken chest and deep-socketed sad eyes. He had been a union man, too, right from the start, and unique among the lordly pressmen, several of whom he had finally induced to sign pledge cards.

"If this thing I told you works out, will you go with us?"

Carver glanced back at the endless sheets which were sliding and rolling in precision order. He rubbed one hand along the black stubble of his chin.

"You mean hit the bricks?"

"I mean hit the bricks," Bicky said anxiously yet definitely.

Carver rubbed his chin again and made the circle of his face, wiping off a forehead dew of murky perspiration.

"I guess I better," he said with a smile. "I been with the union all the way. This is no time to turn tail."

Bicky grinned happily, sobered, then asked, glancing down the batteried line of presses: "What about the others?"

"Maybe half of them," Carver said, twisting and peering down the line. "Yeh, maybe half the boys."

"And the lumpers?"

"They'll go," Mack said. "That'll shut 'em down. They can't run these rigs without lumpers. I know I can't," he emphasized, nodding at two big stripped-to-the-waist colored boys who were lifting great stacks of printed sheets onto a skid at the end of the press.

"That's all I want to know," Bicky said happily as he stamped on the self-starter of the tractor.

"I'll be watching," Carver said, waving. "Go get me some more stock."

The little gasoline tractor coughed violently into motion, and Bicky steered out into the main aisle of the pressroom, a flat, empty four-wheeled truck banging noisily behind him.

He swung to the left past the time clock and Zangora's desk, where the huge, sullen foreman stood with folded arms, staring at Bicky with naked hatred as he passed.

Bicky, still elated, held the foreman's eyes for a moment and nodded at him with a completely servile yet pleasant expression. The foreman turned his head away with sharp arrogance and glanced up meaningfully at the moonish clock which hung high on the pressroom wall.

Bicky took a look at the clock too: eight fifty-five.

He burbled along and turned right, chugged past the huge gray sunken welter of the stripping room, and parked nearby.

To his left a man-high skid of gray paperboard stock, to his right the back entrance to the stripping-room pit.

He dropped to one knee and peeked under the skid. The union circulars were still secreted there. He rose and surveyed the tight metal band which held fast the skid of stock. He could get a pair of pincers from the receiving clerk at the other end of the storeroom, but this would be a good chance to look in on Sophie and the strippers.

He walked to the back entrance of the stripping room and paused at the small staircase that led down into an opaque universe of whirling gray paperboard dust.

Sophie was jogging some stripped boxes and tying them into bundles.

"Sophie," he called loudly. "Throw me a pair of pincers. I'll return them right away."

"Okay, Bicky. How's it going out there?"

"Good," he said, smiling. "Good all around."

The cloudy denizens of the room were looking up at him now, both colored and white folk having achieved a gray identity which they could not deter.

Bicky caught the pincers tossed by Sophie and waved cordially to the foreman, a short, pudgy gray man who hurried to the staircase.

"Hey, you," he shouted, "go where you belong. I've got orders to keep you out of here. Now git!"

"Okay, Mr. Vaughn," Bicky said, grinning. "Just borrowed some pliers, that's all."

When he reached the skid of paperboard he glanced back through the stripping-room door and could see the foreman talking to Zangora, who had obviously been lurking outside. With the ancient conversational gesture of the underling informant Vaughn nodded in the direction of Bicky as he talked.

This was it, Bicky knew. It must be after nine. He stooped again to the aperture underneath the skid and removed the union circulars. He placed them on the hood of the tractor and then applied his pincers to the taut wire band around the consignment of paperboard.

He forced the head of the pincers in under the wire and worked them up and down, loosening the band. He did this for several moments on both sides of the stack, slowly, almost dilatorily. He heard footsteps behind him but continued to pry at the metal binding without looking up.

"You!" he heard Zangora say. "Put down those pliers and come over here!"

Bicky turned, and the foreman was holding the circulars with a triumphant leer on his face.

"These your papers?" he asked.

"No, they're the union's," Bicky said, looking right at him.

"Never mind the fresh. You pass them out?"

"Haven't had much chance today," Bicky said lightly.

"I like to punch your face, fresh nigger."

"You say that again and I'll punch yours," Bicky said, tightening his fists. Zangora was big and there would be no boxing gloves, but the rising anger in Bicky leveled Zangora's image to midget size. But no, but no, a cool thought counseled, don't ruin it now, don't wreck it now!

"You come to my desk. You get your pay and go."

They were listening now in the stripping room; they were stripping slower now and listening. They had heard and they were alert.

"Anything you say goes," Bicky said. "And it'll always be like this without a union. Anything you say goes."

"Never mind," Zangora said, turning toward the aisle. "You come with me."

"Go ahead. I'm ready."

He followed Zangora past the stripping-room door, around past the front entrance toward which all heads had turned. Into the pressroom now, the ancient procession of a man about to be fired. As they neared Zangora's desk the break bell rang for the stripping-room gang. The rest of the plant would take their ten-minute break half an hour later.

Joom-zoom! Ram-bam!

They streamed out of the stripping room, almost fifty workers, black and white, heading for the latrines, a smoke, a swig of coffee, a bite of sandwich in midmorning.

"You stand right there," Zangora said, taking his seat at his desk and reaching for the phone.

"Hello, Mr. Venezzia's office, please," he said with a sweetness belied by the tightening of his jaw muscles.

Joom-zoom! Ram-bam! They were watching at the presses now. The stripping-room workers were boiling around the entrance to the latrines to the left and right of Zangora's desk; on the left the twin rest rooms for women, COLORED and WHITE, the same twin facilities for men on the right.

"Yes, Miss Amassa, yes. . . . In the pressroom? . . . Thank you, I will see him here."

To Bicky's left, halfway down the pressroom aisle, he could see the slightly bowed, dwarf-like figure of Nino Venezzia sauntering benevolently among his beloved pressmen. They were his pets, the skilled artisans of his paper-box products. To them belonged the high wages and the clubby democratic privilege of talking as equals.

"My door is always open to my pressmen," he was telling Carver meaningfully at that very moment. "You do not need a union as a go-between. My pressmen are the backbone of this plant. You and the others out here will find me a reasonable and generous man."

Carver had come down from the press, which was shut off and without printing stock because of Bicky's encounter with Zangora.

"What is your grievance against me, Mack?" the impeccably

groomed owner asked. "I have heard you favor the union and I know you have been active in unions at other shops. You are one of my best two-color men; I appreciate this and pay you more than the going rate for your craft—as is true of the other top men on the floor here. Why do you want a union? I do not understand."

Mack Carver yanked a clean gray cloth from the back pocket of his overalls and mopped his neck and brow.

"I guess you want an honest answer or you wouldn't have asked my opinion," he said. "You know the facts of life about pressmen, Mr. Venezzia. A top man can get just about the same money anywhere. I work here because the plant is handy to my house—and you do pay me more than I can get on the west side. But—and maybe you'll think I'm crazy—I can't be happy among people who are unhappy. Those lumpers there . . ." He nodded at the two big colored boys who were jacking up a full skid of printed sheets, securing it for hauling to the stripping room. "What chance have they got of ever moving up on the press?"

"You know the answer to that one already. Half my pressmen would walk off the job if I tried to break these others in."

"That's your problem, Mr. Venezzia. In a union plant it's no problem—most everyone gets the same chance. It's your problem in the stripping room, too, and out in the glue room, where you put your boxes together. Nobody's going anywhere but where they are. It makes for an unhappy plant. You've even got something to say about where a person can relieve his kidneys."

"I see." Venezzia nodded coldly. "You are from New York originally, no? But I must run my plant in Lakeport where certain types of workers do not readily mix."

"They'll mix," Carver said. "Give them the chance."

"Perhaps it would be better if you sought employment in a much more progressive atmosphere," Venezzia said pointedly.

"Perhaps it would."

Venezzia nodded and proceeded down the aisle.

Bicky saw him coming but was immediately distracted by a rumpus in front of the colored women's restroom. Sophie was making her move.

"Why can't I go in there if I want to?" she was insisting to the matron.

"You know the rules," the matron said nervously.

"There's no rule against nature. The other place is crowded and
I've got to *go!*"

"When you gotta go, you gotta go!" a plump colored woman
from the stripping room chortled in a rich contralto.

"You go in there and you're fired!" the matron said. "Those are
my orders."

"I'm taking orders from old Mother Nature right now!" Sophie
said, pushing abruptly through the swinging doors.

"MR. ZANGORA! MR. ZANGORA!" the matron called anxiously.

In the one-arm lunchroom with the coffee gone and the cigarettes
dead and dwindled in the ash tray, Tony glanced apprehensively
up at the wall clock. Nine-fifteen . . . Bicky and Sophie would be
going about their business.

Naski was in the phone booth checking with the union office,
and Tony could hear the bluff voice through the closed door.

"Oh, he should be here with the signs by now," Naski countered
to the office secretary with unvarnished sarcasm. "Well, he sure as
hell better be! I wouldn't want to have a couple of hundred people
on the bricks and no signs! What else is new? . . . Yeh, yeh, have
Tony call Father Wagner—urgent, yeh? . . . Okay, we'll let you
know what happens. Marry that telephone the rest of the afternoon
—stay right there. . . . Okay, okay . . ."

Naski slammed the receiver on the hook and banged out of the
booth.

"Hey, well-yo," he called to Tony as he hooked his big right thumb
toward the phone. "Give Father Arthur a buzz right away. I'll
head back to the plant. Jakie Wolfson should be there with the
signs. I keep telling myself we'll need them."

Tony hustled into the booth, fishing in his trousers for nickles.

"Tell him to pray for fireworks!" Naski called as he pushed out
into the street.

Tony chuckled as he dropped a nickel in the slot, but the chuckle
came out as a nervous little giggle. He'd make this fast. Only for
someone like Father Arthur would he have bothered to return the
call at a time like this.

The operator got him through to the *The Clarion* office. The re-
ceptionist put the reverend editor on the line.

"Tony, how are you? I was hoping you'd get the message. How
does it look out there?"

"We may know real soon, Father Arthur, right away quick, maybe."

"I saw Rosa this morning. She said she'd seen you and sensed something big was in the wind. But I'm not calling to talk about Rosa right now," the priest said apologetically. "I'm going out on a limb—a well-worn limb—to tell you that Venezzia was in to see the Cardinal again early this morning."

"Oh?" Tony said with controlled excitement. Maybe this was it. Maybe he wanted to sit down and talk things over. But it might be too late. . . .

"He's a clever guy. He's reversed his field for whatever it's worth. He brought with him a certified check for twenty thousand dollars in full payment of his building-fund pledge. He also enclosed a check for five thousand made out to the Harbourton diocese. What do you think of that?"

Tony whistled. "What do *you* think of it? You couldn't say prunes now if you had a mouthful of them."

"I'm afraid you're right," Father Arthur said, "but I'm pulling for you anyway."

"What about the Monsignor? How does he feel about it?"

"He had no comment, although I could see he was impressed by the gift and the strategy. He still wants you to take that job at the center—when you're available."

"I may be available real quick."

"All right, I won't keep you. Good luck and tell Naski to keep his guard up high."

"I'll tell him, Father—and thanks a million for the info."

"For you it's a pleasure. Good-by, Tony."

He hurried out of the lunch room and down the street toward the plant. Soon he could hear the joom-zoom of the presses and, opposite the main gate, on the other side of the street, he saw Naski leaning on the window sill of a pickup truck, talking to the driver.

In the rear of the truck were piled about twenty-five signs mounted on three-foot wooden handles. Naski motioned him over.

"Here, come over here and meet Jakie Wolfson, who gets paid for his signs, win or lose. Jakie, this is my assistant, Tony Lorenzo."

"So, hello, Tony," said the little nut-brown man with kinky black hair, shaking Lorenzo's hand. "So you're getting an education working for Kosciusko the Second, the Polish liberator."

"Yeh, and he also had a hebe selling him the instruments of war in the old days, I'll bet. Choice rusty cannon balls, ten per cent off, this week only."

"So, one gets rich and one gets famous," Wolfson said with a knowing smile and a wink at Tony.

Tony gave Naski the high sign with his chin, and they walked halfway across the street together. He told the big man about Father Arthur's phone call.

"Venezzia's a cagey bastard," Naski said. "That move is calculated to make the Church officials sit on their hands in case there's a strike. Do you think they will—the Cardinal, I mean?"

Joom-zoom, joom-zoom, joom-zoom! Tony cocked his ears at the presses. He glanced at his watch before answering. Nine thirty-five.

"I thought I heard voices," Tony said, touching his lips with his finger. "Inside—excited voices."

Naski listened now, his thick sallow face tight with concentration.

"Voices," he said, cocking his ear and scoffing good-naturedly. "I don't hear no voices. Who do you think you are—Joan of Arc? I don't hear nothing but the presses."

Tony listened intently again and felt an electric impulse starting at the base of his spine and spreading in prickly waves clear to his neck.

"What presses?" he asked Naski, giving him the elbow in the ribs. "WHAT PRESSES!" he said loudly.

"Jesus, they've stopped. Maybe it's the pressmen's morning break."

"The hell it is. They don't take their break until ten."

They heard the yelling now, Bicky's voice and shrill yells of support behind him, followed by a herdlike pounding of feet.

"HIT THE BRICKS!" Bicky hallooed from the shipping platform in the plant yard. He leaped to the concrete, followed by a dozen workers from the stripping room and as many more lumpers from the press.

"Hay-ah!" Naski said with an infinite sigh of triumph, and grinning from ear to ear. "They're coming out, Tony, they're coming out! Hey, Jakie," he yelled, racing to Wolfson's truck on the double, "hand out those signs to that good-looking colored boy. He'll distribute them! Bicky, Bicky!" He flailed his arms wildly. "Over here, the signs! Sophie, Sophie, the signs!"

"Glory, glory, hallelujah!" Sophie was singing, walking out of the plant yard arm in arm with two girls from the stripping room.

"All right, Tony, after the signs are passed out, Bicky will lead the pickets up and down outside the plant. Send any others that come out over on this side of the street. Tell them to go home after they've watched the show for a while. Tell them to come to the meeting tonight. Pythias Hall—seven o'clock!"

"Right," Tony said happily, taking a station by the plant gate as Bicky and about twenty others began to parade up and down in front of the plant.

ROMA PLANT UNFAIR TO ORGANIZED LABOR!
THE BOSS WON'T TALK TO US!

WE WANT TO WORK IN A PLANT WHERE AMERICANS
ARE TREATED LIKE AMERICANS

STRIKE! STRIKE! STRIKE! LOCAL 397
ALLIED PAPER WORKERS OF AMERICA

UNION NOW OR NEVER!
GIVE US A GOOD CONTRACT
AND WE'LL GO BACK TO WORK!

No more the joom-zoom, Tony thought as the workers continued to come out of the plant in a seemingly endless stream. At the grimy windows he saw several die-hard pressmen framing their bewildered faces, smoking and timidly eager to take in the show.

On the top floor the draperies parted and both Venezzia and Zangora peered anxiously out, re-enacting the interminable tableau of the baronial masters looking down on the boiling rebellion of the peasants and awaiting the arrival of the avenging knights-at-arms.

Tony sent those without signs across the street, relaying Naski's instructions.

No joom-zoom now, no hiss of steam, no jam-bam; hilarity and happiness effervesced about the streets, the snapping of weeks-long tension, the first wild intoxication of defiant freedom.

And now in the distance, the first chill of sanction, the knights-at-arms speeding to the succor of the besieged baron; now in the distance the eerie, augmenting municipal whine of a police car.

CHAPTER XXVIII

Bring Round the Stutz—and the Cardinal Too!

ON A bleak Monday morning in early December, Monsignor Vincent Whelton, having said the seven o'clock Mass and eaten his breakfast, settled back in an old brown leather armchair, deep in the stillness of his room.

In his lap glared the loud, fresh invitations of the Lakeport *Herald's* front page. He frowned at the trumpeting of Republican rectitude played by the swaggering, stodgy front-page editorials of the *Herald* publisher, Rear Admiral Elbert Flagpost, importuning the President-elect, Mr. Hoover, not to give in to "the insidious onrush of long-haired Socialists . . ."

"We did not win the day at Gettysburg, San Juan Hill, and in the dark forests of the Argonne in order to lose our birthright in Washington, D.C.

"You fed the people of Europe without Socialistic dogma. If we suffer a depression, you can feed the people in the American way—no doles, no handouts. If they don't work, they don't eat! That—take it or leave it—is America!"

The Monsignor lifted his eyes impatiently from the ringing rhetoric of the entrenched right wing and anxiously sought news of the strike at the Roma plant.

Nothing on page one. He opened the paper and scanned the news stories on two and three. Nothing there. On, on, through the thickets of ads and social news, on through Red Grange, Eddie Rickenbacker, Tillie the Toiler, Mutt and Jeff.

On the last page he found an item, three and a half inches of type at the bottom of the column, and just about to slip out of the news entirely.

ROMA PLANT STRIKE DRAGS ON

The Roma paper-box plant strike on the south side, engineered by the Allied Paper Workers of America, dragged into its fourth week without foreseeable progress on either the management or union side.

Over 300 workers, represented by a union-dominated minority of largely colored pickets, has been unable to force a conference with plant owner Nino Venezzia, eminent Lakeport businessman and church philanthropist.

In a statement to the *Herald* this weekend, Venezzia declared: "I categorically refuse to bargain with these socialist brigands and jailbirds who have temporarily disrupted the orderly production of my plant. Plans are in motion to hire a group of white paper-box workers from the southern part of the state. I applaud our city police who have maintained order during the strike and I believe them perfectly capable of handling this disturbance of civil peace, come what may."

"So that's it!" Monsignor Whelton said aloud, dropping the newspaper from his lap onto the thickly carpeted floor. "Brigands and jailbirds . . ."

Tony—the jailbird. Venezzia had been checking around. And new workers being imported from the southern part of the state. That would mean trouble, real trouble.

His eyes traveled around the room, lighting for a moment on the tickets for the CYC boxing tournament which would take place in the gym the following Saturday night.

Bicky Brown. No one had seen him working out lately. He was on the picket line, and his three-round match with Julie Rodriguez was to be the prime attraction of the evening.

The Monsignor had tried to get hold of him by phone and telegram but had received no answer. He'd better do something about all this—Tony, Bicky—this morning.

He hadn't even seen Arthur for several days, so busy had he been on the Cardinal's fund-raising business. And the Cardinal was in a box himself, with all of Venezzia's money firming up the fund—all that money for the Church—but maybe blood money before all this was over.

Now! Today!

Where would Arthur be right now? He glanced at the small brass travel clock on his dresser—eight-thirty. At the newspaper office. He could check downstairs.

Now! Today! He slipped on his suit coat, picked up his felt hat, topcoat, and breviary. He left his room and hurried along the hallway and down the stairs.

Across Lakeport Park, in the brownstone house, another friend of Anthony Lorenzo had been anxiously scanning the morning press. Nourishing her love for him on furtive late-evening visits and sporadic phone calls, she was now climactically filled with cold anger at her father's refusal to negotiate with the strikers.

Tony, wearied and discouraged by the long weeks of fruitless picketing, barren of hopeful phrases with which to arouse flickers of determination in the vacant, defeated faces of the strikers, had told her last night of the strike-breaking move which her father was about to make.

She had at first refused to believe this, knowing the inevitable violence and bloodshed that would result. She had consoled Tony with coffee, scotch, and kisses, and sent him home to his hotel, needing the solitude and the calm stretch of night in which to determine what preventive action she could take.

Brooding and turning on the decision, she had arisen early, dressed, and gone to her easel, where her new study, a portrait of Tony in oils, was vividly emerging.

Blending the gravity and merriment in his dark, handsome face, the mirth of a hinting smile, the sad, almost tragic aspect of his dark eyes, she had touched her canvas intermittently and whirled the decision about in her mind. Strong the strength of his cleft chin and created to her image, this image willed ironlike by her, the Renaissance prince with whom she was so passionately entranced.

With her mother's interest in the company willed to her, she knew she controlled the majority stock of the firm. She had rechecked all this with the firm of Woodall and Steeves only the other day, Mr. Woodall having assured her she was eligible to other privileges and influence besides the collecting of dividends and the clipping of coupons. She could, yes, sell her stock to such a group as the Atlas Paper Corporation if she so desired.

Sitting now over the news story and her morning coffee, she was further outraged by the publication of her father's intended course of action. She would call on him at the plant this morning!

In the hallway outside her study, Lars gently knocked along the black and white tiles with a dry mop.

"Lars," she called, setting down her cup with a punctuating clink of determination.

He appeared at the open door of the study, somber and prim in a gray cotton coat, the dry mop held lightly in his hands like a lance.

"Yes, Miss Venezzia—shall I remove the tray?"

"Do," she said, rising, "and bring round the Stutz. We shall call on my father this morning."

"Very well."

The emergency mass meeting of the strikers at Pythias Hall was almost over.

In the gray, bare, shedlike hall, its drab monotony broken only by the gold-trimmed banner of the local chapter of the Knights hanging from the wall behind the speakers' platform, close to three hundred strikers sat disconsolately on folding chairs or stood in the side and back aisles, adding their moods of grayness to the total atmosphere of gray.

"Don't forget," Naski said, holding up a marked copy of the Lakeport *Herald*, "Venezzia's liable to ship these scabs in any time. We want the picket line doubled today and every day from now on, and if you get the word that these scabs are on their way, the rest of you come a-running! There's not too much we can do against the army of coppers this phony philanthropist will have walled around the plant. But we may be able to scare some of the scabs away with yelling and shoving. At least we're going down swinging—if and when we go down. Right?"

"Right!" Bicky Brown shouted from the audience.

"Kee-reckt!" Sophie Narleski chimed in, and there was a general subdued ripple of approval.

"Remember this!" Naski pounded. "As long as we can keep those presses quiet, we're winning this strike! According to the estimates of our international union office, we've already cost Venezzia about a quarter of a million dollars. That's a lot of money gone down the drain, and you people are the ones who've done it by walking out and staying out. He can't go on losing money like that—he just can't.

He'll have to sit down with us sooner or later—and we'll win, we'll win it all."

They sat there nodding in subdued approval, but the spell of defeat and financial distress was heavy on them all. Naski sensed this keenly and he knew they needed more than exhortation and ideas to lift their spirits. He turned to Tony, who was sitting at a table beside the platform.

"Now that these folks have listened to all these battle cries, Tony, tell them the good news!"

"I'll be glad to, Tommy," Tony said, rising, smilingly eager to cast a little real bread upon the waters of their despair. "Tommy here knows what you're going through better than any of us. This isn't the first strike he's been through, you know. He's raised a fairly substantial sum of money by means of assessments from other unions in the Allied Paper Workers. You'll all be given weekly vouchers for grocery orders starting today—right here at 4:30 P.M."

This time the murmur of approval was brighter, sharper. Heads were lifted out of hands; slow, incredulous smiles creased formerly frozen faces.

"Yeh, food for your families," Tony said, grinning, "and the larger the family, the larger the amount on the voucher."

Cries of "YAY, MAN!" and "HALLELUJAH!" peppered the audience.

"WHAT, No GIN?" a big colored lumper shouted.

"No gin," Tony said. "You can redeem these vouchers at Kazmier's Market until nine tonight, but you can't sell them or trade them. You have to bring the chow home to your families—one signature on the voucher when you sign it here this afternoon and another identical signature when you redeem it at the grocer's. Okay?"

"OKAY!" "YAY, MAN!" "HALLELUJAH!"

In the rear of the hall the mobile, intent features of Emily Winant stirred with intense interest. She had come to the meeting as a sympathetic observer on the invitation of Sophie Narleski. She leaned over to Sophie now, holding together her shawl, and whispered a few words. Sophie nodded, raised her hand, and climbed to her feet.

"Yes, Sophie?" Tony acknowledged. "Go right ahead—the floor is yours."

"As you and Mr. Naski know," Sophie began in her irrepressibly chipper manner which tended to camouflage the seriousness of her spirit, "we have a royal rooter here today. She's known to many of

us because of her work with the down-and-out on both the west and
south sides. We're kind of down but not out—right, Emily? Brothers
and sisters of Local 397, I give you that great Christian friend of
the workers, Miss Emily Winant!"

Generating her magnetic calm, Emily got to her feet amid considerable applause, stamps, and whistles led by Tom Naski and
Tony. A deep smile and a more reddish hue tinged her full features
as she raised her hand slowly against the applause.

"It's a marvelous thing," she began gently, brightly, "to see hope
come back to people who were about ready to give up. I saw hope
born again here this morning. You're to be complimented for holding
out against an unjust employer this long. And you're to be further
complimented on the wisdom of your leadership which recognizes
that the courage of the spirit is closely connected with the welfare
of the body. 'Not by bread alone doth man live,' but man certainly
needs bread nonetheless. I just want to tell you and your leadership
that all our humble resources at St. Martin's Center here and on the
west side will be marshaled behind you for the duration of this
strike. We got hold of a small truck and it's filled with hot coffee
and sandwiches. You'll find all this waiting for you downstairs after
the meeting, and we'll keep the truck around the picket line for
you, too, as long as our money holds out."

There was another burst of applause at this.

Emily was about to resume, when a lanky, sullen pressman raised
his hand.

"Yes?" Tony intercepted, rising.

"Ah'd like to ask Miss Winant a question."

"Certainly," Emily said.

"Ah read someway-uh that the Cardinal is behind your work. Now
we hear, too, that old Nino give the Cardinal a big piece-uh change
to make him sit on his hands maybe. You think that's so—you think
that the Cardinal gonna hush his mouth for old Nino?"

Emily was more impressed than shocked by the question and so
was Naski, who glanced at Tony with sharply arched eyebrows.

The hilarity of the group subsided a little now, wilted by the
electric bolt of tension inherent in the pressman's question.

"That's a very good question," she began almost casually, "and I
feel no hesitation at all in trying to answer it."

The gray of atmosphere surged back into dominance around the
hall, the gray and a crackling stillness, the stillness and the gray.

"To begin with, where truth and justice are concerned, the Cardinal doesn't 'hush his mouth' for anyone. I've known him twenty years; I know what he's done for the people I try to help; I know of his love of God and his love for souls no matter what their creed or color. It's only natural for you to want to hear his voice in a crisis like this where the injustice seems to lie on the side of a prominent Catholic layman. I know about the big money gifts, and your suspicion is only natural, too. But don't forget this—the rich have always been expected to kick in heavily to the Church—and they do; they have for centuries—with 'conscience' money, even blood money, if you will. And it's well they do, for the poor, at least, receive much of that money back from the benevolent hands of the Church.

"Maybe Venezzia is playing a game of hush-hush with the Cardinal, however gracefully and indirectly. But it won't work. I know my man, and his voice will ring out when he believes the time is right."

The pall was still on them, she could sense. They believed her, but the pall of bewilderment and resignation to the buffets of power still hung over them.

"I know what you're thinking," she began again. "You're thinking the time for Cardinal Wagner to speak out is right now—before Venezzia brings in all these goons and scabs from the southern part of the state. And you're right, you're absolutely right. But I want to ask you something—you and your leaders. Have you gone to him with the facts? He's a big, busy man—maybe he doesn't know the facts. You don't think the Lakeport *Herald* is going to tell him the facts, do you? Rear Admiral Flagpost has acute astigmatism where unions and racial justice are concerned."

The tension eased and a small circle of smiles widened throughout the group.

"Tom," she said, directing her question at the union leaders up front, "have you gone to the Cardinal about this?"

"We've been talking about it," Naski said almost guiltily.

"The archdiocesan newspaper editor, Father Arthur Wagner, has been sympathetic," Tony said, "and I can't believe that Monsignor Whelton is unconcerned."

"You ought to go down there," Emily said. "I'll go with you if you like. We'll make an appointment and go down there to see the Cardinal."

"Sounds great," Naski said. "If these punks don't show up from down south, we'll do it this afternoon."

There was a general murmur of assent throughout the gathering, the resurgence of good feeling and confidence. Something had been done—the groceries; something more would be done—a visit to the Cardinal.

"We'll take you up on that, Miss Winant. And thanks," Naski said, glancing at his watch. "We'd better break this up and get over to the plant. Those pickets need relief."

"Don't forget," Emily said. "Coffee and sandwiches downstairs right away."

The meeting ended in a crescendo of applause for Emily Winant, who stood there impassively, bringing her shawl closer around her neck.

"Jesus Christ," Naski muttered to Tony, "she's a hot-shot—we oughta bring her in here every day."

CHAPTER XXIX

In Time of Peace, Prepare for War . . .

TURNING the corner which gave them a sweeping view of the plant, Naski, Tony, Emily, and the others, walking over from Pythias Hall, saw the extra police cars parked at the office entrance and knew with a mutual chill that the time of terrible decision was almost upon them.

The pickets were moving up and down in front of the plant, not leisurely as before, but with a jerking nervousness of glance and movement which told that they were conductors for new and ominous electrical power.

"What the hell!" Naski erupted as they quickened their pace. "That's Captain Hardy's car—the black Pierce-Arrow."

"It's an auto show," Sophie said. "Look at the Stutz Bearcat!"

Tony was looking, too, his eyes wide with recognition and surprise. The gray, sporty four-seater with the wire wheels belonged to Rosa. She had driven him home in it on occasion, and its identification in this particular place was unmistakable. She was up there now, talking to her father. She had said she would do something. She was in there now, he thought wildly, stormed with commingled warmth and fear; for him she was in there, for him!

Around the plant the walking police detail had been doubled, and in the plant yard, behind closed gates, they heard the whinny of a horse and the battering stamp of a well-shod hoof against the cobblestones.

"The mounties are there also," Emily said softly, "two of them. If we're going to the Cardinal, I suggest we go right away."

"They're up there making arrangements," Naski said. "Who's the Stutz belong to? Anyone we know?"

"It belongs to Venezzia's daughter," Bicky Brown said. "She was here once before, during the summer. There's a guy drives her, a lanky spook. He must be upstairs with her. He stayed at the wheel the last time, I remember. I could see him out the windows from the top of the press."

They heard the shrill, tinny honk of a pickup truck behind them as Jakie Wolfson drove up, beckoning to Naski. He parked discreetly across the street from the plant, where an empty, weedy lot stretched desolately toward the ruddy ruins of a brick kiln.

They went over to him, and Naski got inside. Tony stood beside the truck, glancing apprehensively up at the office windows, while Emily Winant and Sophie joined Bicky in the picket line, striding calmly, confidently, up and down, brooding the wings of their courage over the jittery pickets, settling their jerky pace into an easier gait.

"Here, this is urgent," Wolfson snapped, handing Naski a telegram. "You hired me to make signs, and your office is making a goddamn errand boy of me."

"You love it," Naski said dryly, taking the yellow envelope and tearing it open. Across the top was the downstate date line, the industrial town of Springville on the Missouri border, naming the time of origination at 7 A.M.

TWO TRUCKS OF SKILLED AND UNSKILLED SCAB PAPER-BOX WORK-
ERS LEAVING FOR LAKEPORT 10 A.M. TODAY. HEAR TRUCKS WILL BE
MET BY POLICE ESCORT AT LAKEPORT CITY LIMITS TONIGHT AND
LODGE IN TRUCKERS' CAMP. EXPECT VENEZZIA WILL RUN THEM IN
ON YOU EARLY TUESDAY MORNING. WILL CHECK FURTHER AND
ADVISE. BEST OF LUCK. YOU'LL NEED IT.

                              CHARLIE ANDREWS
                              INTERNATIONAL ORGANIZER
                              ALLIED PAPERWORKERS OF AMERICA

"Sonofabitch!" Naski said, handing the telegram to Tony. "Charlie got me the dope all right, and what's happening up in there really figures. Now we gotta fight Captain Hardy too."

"Wow!" Tony said, reading the telegram. "Venezzia's really moving now! Can Captain Hardy get away with this escort business?"

"Of course he can. All under the shield of law and order. I told you before, the unions don't have any laws to protect them. This conniving copper is on Venezzia's payroll, I'll lay you ten to one, and he can say he's protecting us as much as he's protecting Nino, you know that?"

"Don't you think we ought to take Emily Winant's suggestion and call on the clergy? I'll do what I can with Monsignor Whelton myself."

"I think the suggestion is still okay," Naski said, "but I've got to do more than that. I can't take any chances now. But call them over here anyway, Bicky and Miss Winant and the other dame—Sophie."

Tony waved vigorously, attracting the attention of Bicky and the other two. He motioned them over.

"What do you have in mind, Tom?" he asked.

"Well, I'm going to get together about forty of our toughest strikers and go out there to Truckers' Camp and face up to these babies. We may not be able to get too close to them because of the cops, and there may be trouble, but we've got to throw the fear of God into them somehow. Better that we go out there than just wait for them to come here tomorrow morning. This place will look like an Army camp by then—mounties and flatfoots all over the joint. You've never seen those mounted cops come charging in on strikers with billies swinging like I have. Jesus, if you were standing there with your hands covering up your head, you'd think you were General Custer!"

Tony laughed. The grim humor seemed very funny in a highly nerved-up sort of way.

"Jakie, you're gonna have to take me downtown. I'll hire a couple of trucks and we'll lay in some broken sidewalk bricks and some sawed-off broom handles. If the cops will let us get near these bastards tonight, maybe we can scare half of them all the way back to Springville."

"Okay, Tommy," Jakie said. "Better to try something than wait here and die by inches in the morning. I've seen that little show before. The owner stands up in the office window smiling like the cat that ate the canary, and the cops escort the scabs in like they were school kids lined up in the schoolyard, and you can either get your skull broken or just stand there and let all these phonies take over your jobs."

"That's the picture," Tommy said. "Bicky, come over here! Tony, go tell the girls you'll go downtown with them and see what can be

THE MAKING OF A LIBERAL

done with the reverend clergy. We'll run you down most of the way in the truck here, and you can join me later at the hall. We'll probably shove off from there about six-thirty tonight."

The whole thing was explained all around. Bicky ran off on his rounding-up errand, and Emily climbed into the front seat with Sophie. Naski and Tony sat in the back, slumped against the metal sideboards, scuffing among the extra picket signs for meager sitting comfort.

Off they went, north toward the center of town, with Tony casting alert glances at the Stutz and then up at the office windows. Rosa, Rosa, where are you now?

When Rosa appeared at the office switchboard with Lars she thought she was entering a police station, for standing and sitting around the rude benches that contrasted glaringly with the interior luxury of the owner's office were four big, beefy bluecoats in various stages of slouching boredom.

"Does my father need all this police protection?" she asked archly of no one in particular as the switchboard operator, recognizing her, got very flustered and buzzed for Miss Amassa.

"Two of us are up here with Captain Hardy, ma'am—just temporarily," one of the policemen, a sergeant, said, touching the visor of his cap. "The other two officers are on regular detail to maintain order."

"Captain Hardy!" Rosa said blithely, striking a haughty stance. "Isn't he the one some journalist recently called 'the richest cop in the world'?"

"I guess so, ma'am," the sergeant said. "Some smart-alecky writer did publish a lot of lies about the captain a while back."

"Lies, eh?" She lifted her eyebrows sharply as Miss Amassa appeared in the drab vestibule.

"Rosa darling!" she said, coming forward with a warm rush of welcome. "Such a pleasant surprise. Come in, come in!"

Rosa accepted coyly the buss on the cheek and the intertwining of the escorting elbow. Miss Amassa glanced at Lars, who had taken a seat on the bench beside one of the policemen. Her hand was on the rococo brass handle of the dark, paneled door leading to the regal inner offices.

"Will Lars be all right there?"

"It's all right, Miss Amassa," Lars said, looking a little more furtive than usual. "I'll vait here."

They entered the portals, stepping from the gray paperboard desert onto the lush oriental carpets of the Venezzia oasis. Stepping lightly along the hall carpet toward Miss Amassa's cubicle outside the private office, they looked like mother and daughter in their petite black severity of dress and stature.

"Your father has visitors, but they will not be long," Miss Amassa said, showing her to a seat beside the desk. "I will slip in and tell him you are here."

"Thank you, Pia."

Miss Amassa knocked lightly on the door marked "Private" and went in. Rosa heard the determined rasp of her father's voice, and for an instant her bravado collapsed. The Siamese cat confronts the leopard in his lair. But she must do it! Her father's refusal to sit down with the representatives of his plant's union was preposterous stubbornness. And now this madness of bringing in strikebreakers, scabs, from downstate! There would be bloodshed, with that big cossack of a police captain maintaining "law and order."

When Miss Amassa entered, Venezzia was approving the details of the truck itinerary from the city line.

"Yes, Captain, that is good," he said, squinting out of his runty eminence and oversize shirt collar at a diagrammed sheet held in his hand. "West on Bellrose Avenue and south on Lakeport Boulevard. That will be fine. Do you think we will encounter any opposition along the way?"

"They might make a run at us even tonight," the captain said calmly. He was a short, thickset man of pinkish complexion, resplendent in the blue and gold stars of his rank. On the right side of his chest the great star of the city police shone in gold like the exalted medal of an emperor.

"I'll have two carloads of men there, fully armed and with riot guns. There'll be four cycle police on hand also. We'll be ready."

"I'm sure you'll do your best to maintain the civic peace," Venezzia said. "And you can tell your men they'll get their ten dollars each as usual for extra duty. And I've made arrangements for my clients to have cases of Lacto delivered to the families of all policemen who are detailed by you to help us out during this strike. You'll be asked to make up the list, Captain, and be as generous with it as you like. Order what you think you need—a carload, even two."

"That's very nice," the captain said casually, pursing his mouth in a little deprecating gesture. "I'm sure the wives of the men will appreciate the soap powder on washday."

At the back of Captain Hardy's mind was already the notion that he could order two carloads of the soap instead of one. The first would be used for patronage, the second could be sold wholesale for perhaps several thousand dollars. Surely old Venezzia would make no objection.

"Your daughter Rosa is here," Miss Amassa whispered.

"She is!" Venezzia said. "This is quite a surprise. Captain, you must meet my beloved but extremely independent daughter."

"It'd be a pleasure, Nino," Captain Hardy said with a show of spaced yellow teeth. "But I must get back to the division immediately after."

Nino rose and extended his hand, bringing it across the corner of the desk with an almost arthritic effort.

"My congratulations again for your willingness to maintain order in the public interest," he said with apparent conviction.

"I'm just doing my duty."

Rosa entered as they were shaking hands, and greeted her father with a knowing smile.

"Ah, Papa," she said lightly, kissing him on the cheek. "I see you have the military on your side in this your own civil war!"

"Rosa, my baby," Nino said, holding her at arm's length as he looked her over. "Just as pretty as your late mother—and as quick of speech. Captain Matthew Hardy," he said, tossing one hand limply toward the municipal baron of the south side, "meet my daughter Rosa."

Rosa snuffed out a handshake with a fetching, childlike curtsy to the police captain, her extreme distaste for him camouflaged cleverly in spontaneous charm.

"A pleasure to meet the daughter of such an eminent man," the captain said with his glossiest pink smile. "Now I must go. I'll be on hand early in the morning. And if anything develops tonight, feel free to call me at home."

"Thank you, Captain," Venezzia said. "Thank you for everything."

The captain waved with a pudgy, well-manicured hand and, slipping his braided cap off a festooned mahogany hatrack, strode mightily out of the office.

When the door closed behind him, Rosa took a seat beside her father's desk as Nino slumped into his thronelike swivel chair with a deep, tension-releasing sigh.

"Are you sure he hasn't forgotten something?" Rosa asked.

"What's that, my dear?"

"His butcher knife."

Nino glanced at her harshly, the tension returning. He rubbed one hand across his face, withdrawing to a redoubt of fatherly affection, and then said with an effort at tenderness: "Have you come here to visit with your sorely harassed father or to add your voice to the chorus of my enemies?"

"They are not your enemies," she said. "They are your employees and should be your friends. Instead you will not even give them the courtesy of a hearing. If a mad dog barked, you would listen. But for those unfortunates who have deprived themselves of bread in defense of principle you have only a sword."

"I, too, have some principle, my daughter. This is my plant and they have transformed it into a ghostly ruin. I seek only to bring it back to orderly function."

"Is it *your* plant really, Father?" she asked meaningfully.

Father and daughter held each other's eyes steadily, sustaining a channel flowing in two directions with bitterness and defiance.

"So that is the purpose of your visit," Venezzia said.

"It is. I have spoken to my attorneys about this matter, and they assure me that my majority control of the stock in the Roma plant entitles me to a voice of influence in the current crisis."

Venezzia was calmer now, even docile, but not, Rosa was quick to note, indicating any fear of defeat.

"I have always believed that you should have an opinion regarding the management of our affairs here," he said graciously. "Hitherto you have not evidenced the slightest interest in the conduct of the company."

"Hitherto," Rosa repeated coldly. "But I will not stand by while you play the role of medieval potentate and grind your employees into the dust merely because they have seen fit to organize a union."

"What do you propose to do?" Venezzia asked tentatively, a hint of sarcasm and slyness in his question.

"If you will not call off your scab labor and foul municipal dogs and confer with your struck employees as befits a Christian employer and gentleman, I propose to sell my stock to the Atlas Paper Corporation—a company, I need not remind you, which has nothing but good feeling toward unions in all its plants."

"Mmmmmm . . ." Venezzia said, plucking at his small bird-of-prey face with slow, appraising movements of his hand. "I must confess you would be perfectly within your rights to do so—your mother, contrary to my wishes, saw to that. She was a stubborn woman, your mother, and it came through in you, my dear. Stubbornness, if misdirected, is bad, very bad."

"I am no longer a child," Rosa said angrily. "I am the majority stockholder of this plant and you will do what I say—or else . . ."

"I protected you as a child," he said with a sly smile. "I will protect you now."

"Protect me?" Rosa asked haughtily. "Against what?"

"You shall see," he said, reaching for the buzzer.

He knows! He knows! she thought wildly. He knows about Tony and me. But how could he? How could he know—unless he had Tony followed, or both of us. He knows, he knows! The fury grew underneath her dark, impassive hauteur. If he, her father, was capable of such ruthlessness, so was she.

She sat tight-lipped, waiting with him for Miss Amassa, eying the gleaming Renaissance dirk with the jeweled handle, eying the weapon which he used to open letters, seeing it monstrously in his narrow, pointed chest.

"Miss Amassa," Nino said casually as his secretary appeared in the doorway, "bring me Confidential File Z, and ask Lars to come in also."

Lars! Not him, not Lars!

"You are in the wrong country," Rosa said with controlled malice. "You would be much more useful in the Soviet Union."

"I find my talents, daughter, much more fruitful here. Would you like a little sherry? It might steady your nerves."

"I provide my own sherry," she said.

Miss Amassa returned with the folder, and Lars shuffled in behind her, his sullen, expressionless face frozen in the direction of Nino.

"Sit down, Lars," Nino said, opening the folder. "You may go, Miss Amassa."

Pia cast a look of profound anguish at Rosa as she left with unusually quick steps.

"Must it be necessary for me, my dear, to document the history of your relationship with one whose unsavory record of crime and murder surely should have indicated to you that he would not stop at employing you as a union instrument in our current dispute?"

"I don't know what you are talking about!" she said fiercely. And then to Lars: "Lars, go down to the car and wait for me. Immediately."

Lars shook his head slowly, woefully.

"If you persist in your projected arrangements with the Atlas Corporation during the current strike or after," her father said, putting on a pair of tortoise-shell glasses and squinting wisely at the contents of the folder, "I shall be forced to release a story on this material to the press.

"You are my daughter, but to save this plant from hoodlums and Socialists, I am prepared to risk the humiliation, in the service of truth."

"Truth!" she said scornfully, rising. "You don't know what truth is. I admit nothing—to you or anyone else. I will not befoul myself in your presence any longer. You!" she said, confronting Lars. "Give me the keys to my car."

Lars handed her the keys, turning his long, empty face away.

"You treacherous scum!" she said bitingly, and struck him across the face with her open palm.

"See here, see here!" Nino said, rising. "I command you to be seated and finish this discussion."

Rosa turned and riveted her father with a hatred that had all the focused darkness of her being in it.

"I would command you, my father, to go straight to hell—except —and God help you—you are already there."

She turned vigorously and walked out the door, slamming it resoundingly behind her.

CHAPTER XXX

Lost and Found

CHILLY, the diamond brightness of the lakeside boulevard in early December married the worry-weather of Monsignor Whelton's mood as he walked briskly toward his office at the youth center.

His phone call to Father Arthur had revealed that the priest-editor was at the printer's and would go from there to the Cardinal's residence at ten-thirty. Vincent left word with Arthur's secretary that he would try to see him there.

It was now nine-fifteen; this would give him time to check his mail at the CYC office and perhaps say hello to Lucy. She would need steadying now more than ever, he knew. She had stayed out of things pretty well and given her best attentions to the adult education center, which was burgeoning rapidly, courses in public speaking and English composition having already been added to the curriculum by popular demand. It was such a bright, heartening thing, the way the adult center had developed and fitted in. There was no end to its possibilities, he thought with a glow of excitement. It might even become as big or bigger than the athletic program. And it had all started because he wanted something for Lucy to do, something that would get her thinking away from the Marxist and toward the Christian idea.

"*Deo gratias,*" he formed soundlessly with his lips, and, walking briskly along the boulevard, he felt an easement of tension regarding the factory crisis out south. Something good had come out of it already—Lucy and the school.

"JESUS IS COMING—ARE YOU PREPARED?" a squat, beet-faced lady hawked at him on the corner of Senate and Lakeport, brandishing a gospel magazine under his nose.

"If I'm not, may God have mercy on me, madam," he said, pushing on past her gently with a smile.

In his mind he could generally read what was in the publication without opening its pages—a bright, vigorous, untrained mind, devoted totally to the Bible and interpreting it with highly individualistic bias—with most of its sulphuric commentaries directed against the Catholics and the Jews.

But to hear that phrase, "Jesus is coming," bugled on the streets during the holy season of Advent, the period of liturgical and spiritual preparation for Christmas, was so apt, so good, that he warmed to it.

For in all the phrases of the Proper which he read each Advent morning at Mass was the spirit of "coming." "Come, small Lord, nor tarry longer . . ."

Let her shout, let her shout it out all over the city, what most Catholics were too shy and too proper to do, he thought.

"JESUS IS COMING," he heard her trumpet again in the distance. "ARE YOU PREPARED?"

Down Senate Street and up the familiar bare stairs to his office now, and no pounding, no two-stepping in the gym. The boys were all at school. The clash and clank of a mop pail signified that Stringbean Lincoln was plying his trade. And ahead he heard the elfin lightness of Joan's typewriter pattering away at his letters.

Joan, he thought, always there, always working, Tony withdrawn remotely from her life and the young district attorney seeing the gold of her and desiring to pan the nuggets of her life into his own personal vaults. Well, he's a fine young man, this Bill Ryan, a fine young man for her.

He slipped his key into the lock of the private side entrance, knowing that Joan would hear the click of the lock and be in with his mail before he could reach the desk buzzer.

No sooner had he hung up his topcoat and hat, seated himself, than Joan rapped lightly on the door and entered with the mail.

"Joan, my girl, how are you this morning?" he said, smiling and taking the folder.

"Fine, Monsignor, and yourself?"

"Umph!" he said, making a bland face and opening the folder. "We'll see what the day will bring. Have a nice weekend?"

The folder was fat with ticket returns for the Saturday-night boxing tourney, checks for the same from many who could not come, and several invitations to speak at testimonials and conventions of business and civic organization.

"Bill took me to the hockey game Saturday night," she said.

"Bill, she calls him!" he said, slipping on a pair of eyeglasses without looking up from the mail. "I can't call the district attorney by his first name, but my secretary can. That's the way it goes." He sighed good-humoredly, looking up.

"Of course you can," she said, laughing. "He adores you, thinks you're going to be Pope or something."

"So," the Monsignor said, taking warmly to the flattery. "The way things are going, I might get sent back to the Tri-State Valley. How'd you like to toll that church bell for me down there on a cold December morning?"

"That wouldn't be too bad," she said. "At least then you wouldn't have to worry about whether or not Bicky Brown will be available for the fights Saturday night. Have you seen the morning papers?"

"I have," he said glumly. "Who does Venezzia think he is—the Doge of Venice?"

"It's beginning to look that way. The word's around about all that 'hush' money. I heard Bill talking about it with Judge Conlon in the Garden Club after the game."

"So that's what they're saying," the Monsignor said, sighing and setting down his glasses. "I might have known."

"Of course they're saying it. It's general knowledge all over town."

"Well—maybe we can find out what's on the Cardinal's mind this morning. Take these letters and checks, Joan. Acknowledge the letters, deposit the checks."

"Yes, Monsignor. One more thing—Lucy's waiting to see you."

"Oh—good—send her in."

"Yes, Monsignor."

Lucy came slowly in, long and gaunt and sad.

"Have a seat, Lucy," the Monsignor said. "What's on your mind?" As if I don't know, he said to himself, as if I don't know. . . .

She sat alertly on about three quarters of the straight-backed chair, pausing reflectively before she spoke, like an actress waiting for the audience to settle after the curtain has parted.

"Monsignor Whelton," she began firmly, "when you hired me I promised you I'd stay out of the Roma situation. I have done so, with but one minor infraction. I gave the organizers some contacts and information at the beginning but have maintained hands off ever since."

"That's perfectly understandable, Lucy. I'm grateful you told me, but I wouldn't hold it against you at all. You've done a tremendous job in organizing the adult education school and in getting it off the ground. I really think you've found your niche. Don't you agree?"

"I love my work, Monsignor, but I must ask you to let me resign —immediately. I've seen the morning papers and I've talked to some of my neighbors who are on strike. I cannot remain here in peace and security when they will have their jobs taken away by scabs and while they will be brutally beaten by a group of mercenary police if they make an honest, manly protest.

"I have made arrangements for an excellent Jesuit college instructor to take over my class. And I am sure that things will run quite smoothly until you can find another director. I only ask that you give me your blessing so that I can go and be with my fellow workers when they need me most and when everything in me needs them."

Vincent, regarding her intently, was smitten by strong emotion. As a seminarian he had watched at her mother's deathbed; as a priest he had been fingered by Providence to attend her father's shoddy demise—all, he deeply believed, foreordained. He thought of the Portuguese proverb, "God writes straight with crooked lines." This girl was sent to him—she was in his life, come weal, come woe.

"My dear child," he said, leaning back in his chair with a wry, compassionate smile, "I am deeply proud of you and your decision, and I know both your mother and father must be. Go with my blessing, by all means, and stand by your fellow workers and your friends. But remember this!" His voice grew stronger now, tinged with righteous anger and indignation. "Up to this point I have gone about my business for the Cardinal and stayed out of this thing, believing, one way or another, that Venezzia and the strikers would come to terms. It has gone far beyond that, gone awry to the point of Christian outrage. And I will do every type and kind of thing that I can—with the Cardinal and elsewhere—to exert pressure on Venezzia and the police and stop this brutality, this job-stealing, before it takes place. I mean that I will do these things today—this morning, I am due at the Cardinal's residence at ten-thirty, in fact. I wanted you to know that before you go. The Church makes haste the press."

slowly, it is true, but when it is ready to move there is no force on earth that can stop it. Remember that! Lucy, remember that!"

Lucy's eyes were glistening with happiness now and her long, homely face had lost its caste of sadness.

"I am very happy to hear those words, Monsignor, but I am not especially surprised," she said, smiling. "I would not have stayed with you had I not recognized the bigness and love with which you serve these children and all these people who come to the adult center. I have one more thing to request. I have studied, discussed, and finally taught the social teachings of the Popes these many weeks. I like what the Holy Fathers have to say. There is, if I may say so, a socialism of Christian love—a passion for the dignity of the individual and a relentless disapproval of the exploitation of the weak by the powerful. I have also come to like what they believe about the approaches to Almighty God. I would like, Monsignor, to return to the religion of my mother in which I was baptized and in which I received my First Holy Communion. I would like to do this before I join my friends on the picket line."

Te Deum laudamus . . . We praise thee O God, Vincent thought.

"I have prayed to the poor souls in purgatory for that intention, Lucy—and to your mother that she would intercede with Our Lady for you. You are going home today in more ways than one. I'll be glad to ring up the cathedral rectory and make an appointment with one of the fathers for you."

"What will be involved?" she asked shyly.

"A general confession, Lucy, a firm purpose of amendment; you'll be absolved and he'll give you the Eucharist right there in the cathedral if you like."

"You are a priest, Monsignor," she said softly, averting her head, her pock-marked features tinctured with both hope and embarrassment.

"So I am. And it would be a great privilege to receive you back. I'll be glad to hear your confession here, and then we'll go over to the cathedral for Holy Communion if you like."

"I would like that."

"Very well." He pushed the buzzer, and Joan opened the office door.

"Joan, under no circumstances am I to be disturbed until you hear the buzzer again."

"Yes, Monsignor."

When Joan was gone he sensed Lucy's uneasiness, which is invariably the first fruit of spiritual honesty. He could not bring her immediately into the mechanical overture of confession. The tundra-like stretch of absence from the faith of her childhood could not be suddenly bridged by the down-hinging of her knees. He must talk to her awhile, fan with the sweet breath of tradition the livening coals of her resurgent belief.

"You know, Lucy," he began in a chatty way, "perhaps you are not aware that you have, by your request for the Sacrament of Penance today, conformed to a Christian custom as old as the Church itself. I mean that you have gotten the feel of the Church most deeply in asking for a specific confessor and in letting that confessor know who you are. In America most Catholics are too self-conscious to accept the traditional idea of a spiritual mentor or 'ghostly father,' but in Europe the custom still flourishes. It really is a ridiculous self-consciousness on the part of Americans, because most mature priests have heard just about everything there is to hear—in the confessional box, that is. We do not easily blush at what meets our ears and are always able to rise above the personal identity of the penitent."

"I think I understand," Lucy said, relaxing. She was always responsive to ideas—the ideological approach—and Vincent had gauged her rightly. "We had that kind of confessional intimacy among the Marxists. Self-analysis and self-blame were standard procedure, even on the personal level, and sometimes we had to do this almost gospel-mission-style, on the floor and in the presence of other members of the group."

"I've heard about that. Thank God you've been able to bring yourself to confess under the auspices of the greatest social revolutionist of all, Who gave this terrible power of hearing and forgiving sins to priests alone when He said: 'Whose sins you shall forgive, they are forgiven them: whose sins you shall retain, they are retained.'

"Now examine your conscience for five or ten minutes, trying to recall what you can remember of serious sin."

He placed a high-backed brocade chair between them, saying, "You can use this as a prie-dieu when you are ready. This way, I will not be able to see your face during the act of confession, which is the proper thing where a lady penitent is concerned. Let me know when you are ready to begin."

He picked up his breviary, opened it to a page marked by a

red ribbon, swung his chair away from her, and absorbed himself in its pages.

Lucy went to her knees, crossed herself, and, bowing her head in her hands, roamed and ranged back through the years of her late teens and twenties, spearing her more glaring peccadilloes of pride, lust, and defiance of God with the sharpened stick of remorse, gathering them into the rucksack of her renascent belief in the Galilean with an ecstatic lightness of heart.

"I am ready, Monsignor," she whispered huskily after several minutes.

Monsignor Whelton lifted a small stole from his desk, kissed it, and placed it around his neck.

"You remember the form?" he asked softly.

"Yes. Bless me, Father, for I have sinned," she began, crossing herself. "It has been about twelve years since my last confession . . ."

He closed his eyes and listened, bowing his head close to his chest, cupping his chin in his right hand.

"These are the serious sins I remember . . ."

There were the usual transgressions in the teen age and early twenties of an emancipated Marxist intellectual. The free love with venturesome white boys at summer discussion camps. The sporadic bouts of heavy drinking, heavy talk, and prolonged affairs in furnished rooms—all part of her defiance of religion and white arrogance, he knew—and as she ranged into her thirties, her preoccupation with the flesh receded, replaced by intense acts of pride and bitterness against what she believed to be the hypocrisy and intolerance, the crass materialism of priests, politicians, and prelates.

On and on she recited, the soft sure voice behind the back of the chair, the sweetness of her sorrow overwhelming the bitterness—and yet he noted an edge of hardness there, a cartilage of cynicism and wariness in the pure, offered lamb of her submission.

"I take full blame for all my sins, Monsignor," she concluded, "but I would be less than honest if I did not insist that the pressures caused by hypocrisy and indifference among your own people toward economic and interracial problems were often a spur to my defiance of morals and conventions. That is all I can remember, Monsignor, and for all these sins I am heartily sorry and I beg the forgiveness of God."

"I will give you absolution, my dear child," Vincent said. "But first let me remind you that no one, not even the saints, has a monoply on virtue. We are all sinners in one way or another—pride, selfishness, lust, social injustice, whatever it may be. Let any of your bitterness that may remain be resolved in this knowledge.

"The remembrance of excessive sexual indulgence may be particularly remorseful for you, as it is with so many who realize that the body is the sacred temple of the spirit and must be treated with dignity and respect. Yet, as I have implied, even the saints had their problems with the flesh. St. Bernard plunged himself into freezing water to cool the fevers of the senses; Benedict rolled in a thorn bush. Tradition tells us that the great Church father, St. Jerome, 'evoked the dances of Roman virgins' while fasting in the Judean desert. I tell you these things to help offset the grim fixation on continence which the sometimes overemphasized teachings of our great St. Paul have imprinted on the American Catholic consciousness. It appears to intellectuals like yourself, I know, that the Irish-Catholic emphasis on censorship of lurid public entertainment, books, and public morals often seems contradicted by a private addiction to alcoholic and sexual excesses among the Gaels. But the Church, I insist, is greater than any of its racial components; its spirit is the spirit of charity and forgiveness, since it best understands the nature of man as a fallen creature who has the means of salvation at hand.

"Our Lord, the Good Shepherd, rejoiced over the return of one lost sheep and seemed to favor it over the entire flock who were settled and secure. He did not say 'Marry or burn,' but rather let His feet be washed by the scarlet woman, Mary Magdalene, whom He turned from the error of her ways. He rejoices over you now, my dear child.

"For your penance I want you to say a rosary each evening for a week. You can say ten Hail Marys before you take Communion at the cathedral this morning, and thus start your penance. Now say a good Act of Contrition."

"O my God, I am heartily sorry . . ." she began.

He raised his hand in the act of absolution.

"*Absolvo te,*" he began, making the sign of the cross over her as she completed the Act of Contrition.

"Now go in peace, Lucy," he said softly. "I will see you in the outer office."

"Thank you, Father," she said, rising tall above him, her long taut face tear-stained but joyous. "Thank you from the bottom of my heart."

Monsignor Whelton nodded with a slight smile and turned swiftly to his breviary, feeling a peach stone of happiness swelling in his throat.

CHAPTER XXXI

Epistle to Nino

As HE left the cathedral vestry after giving Lucy Holy Communion, Vincent quickened his pace down the side aisle, free now, more anxious than ever to see the Cardinal. It was ten thirty-five by his wrist watch, which he read with a squint as he left the candlelight aura of the sanctuary and proceeded into the almost cavernous blackness at the rear of the cathedral.

To his left in the middle pews he caught a glimpse of Lucy bowed deep in thanksgiving, and ahead, as his eyes got used to the darkness, aided by the dull, filtered daylight through the stained-glass windows, he saw a lone young woman sitting in frozen meditation in one of the very last rows.

As he passed, she lifted her head slightly, sensitive to his quick tread, and he recognized the face of the Venezzia girl, whom he had seen casually at Mother Wagner's apartment. The dark, molded beauty of her face was damp with tears. She gave him no sign, lowering her face again, and he went on, wondering at the pervasive challenge of this entire day.

He went out the side door, his hat on now and his topcoat collar buttoned close to his neck against the chill grayness of the December morning. Diagonally across the street and on the lake-swept corner the towering brick chimneys of the cardinal's residence loomed out of swirling mists in a mongrel impression of both factory and manor house.

He crossed the street, clanged through a wrought-iron gate at the driveway, and headed for the breezeway door, to which he had a key.

There was no need to use the key which the Cardinal had given him so that he could come and go on official business without revealing his presence to those waiting in the main reception room. Arthur was standing there in the half-open door.

"Come in," he said with a sigh of relief. "I'm on pins and needles. Unk is down with a heavy cold and won't see anyone until after lunch. There's a delegation from the strikers out there waiting—including, of all people, Emily Winant. Your friend, Tony Lorenzo, is there also and Lucy's pal—Sophie. . . . Let's duck into the kitchen and get some coffee," Arthur continued, moving him along toward the back of the mansion.

As they walked along the long dark hall Arthur told him about the dramatic telegram from the union official downstate, the impending invasion of the strike-breaking workers who would rendezvous at Truckers' Camp, and the union's plans to intercept the scabs that night with sawed-off broomsticks, bricks, and what not against the armed might of Captain Hardy's uniformed details. All this as it had been retailed to him by Tony Lorenzo.

Vincent assimilated the news with a grunt, his face clouding with anger. Arthur took him warmly by the elbow as they entered the spacious, high-ceilinged kitchen, where a pot of coffee was slowly perking on one of the many gas jets which crisscrossed the stove.

"And guess who else is out in the lobby? Monsignor Robert Lambert, rising young chancellor of the Harbourton diocese."

"He's after the check," Vincent said glumly.

"Exactly. He was on his way back from Milwaukee and phoned his Bishop. Says Bishop Sliney wants him to pick it up."

"We've got to stop that somehow," Vincent said. "We've got to persuade the Cardinal to return that money if Venezzia goes through with this strong-arm stuff. The story's all over town. They're calling it 'hush' money."

"I know," Arthur said, filling two white mugs with steaming black coffee. "You've got to get upstairs and see Unk before it's too late. We'll talk to Mrs. Rush."

"Does the Cardinal know about all this dirty business?"

"I really can't say. Nobody knows what's in the Cardinal's mind— not even Mrs. Rush. He's probably seen the papers this morning, however."

"Probably. Where is Mrs. Rush now?"

"She'll be in here soon to fix up a tray," Arthur said. "Maybe she'll let you take it up."

"To the Cardinal's bedroom?" Vincent asked hesitantly.

"To the Cardinal's bedroom!" Arthur said testily. "What's wrong with that?"

"Well," Vincent said, smiling, "I do have some fund-raising reports for him."

"Any checks?"

"Yes, about thirty-five hundred in checks."

"Good, we'll tell that to Mrs. Rush. She knows the importance of money and how much it's always needed around here."

"S-a-ay! I almost forgot!" Vincent exclaimed, sipping his coffee. "I just saw the Venezzia girl sitting in the rear of the cathedral, sitting in the dark there looking as if there were a contest going on."

"There's no contest," Arthur said somberly. "Or if there was, it's all over. She came to me this morning all upset. She tried to force the old man to call off his dogs. She has controlling stock in the place, she tells me."

"I thought you were at the printer's! And I was looking for you, you scoundrel!"

"I always tell my secretary to say I'm at the printer's in the morning. It saves so much unnecessary explanation. Actually I was at the printer's early and found Rosa waiting for me in my office when I got back."

"How did she make out? And why all this sudden interest in the problems of the working class? I didn't think she was the type."

"Well—I'll tell you once, and don't ask me for details. She and Tony have been very involved."

Vincent set his cup down on the stove with a loud clink.

"They met at my mother's and liked each other. They have been getting together at a place Rosa took over recently. But she isn't as naïve as you might think. She really is genuinely outraged at her father's unchristian conduct. She's been feuding with him for a long time over the way he treated her husband. She was certain to make a move against him in this situation—Tony or no Tony."

"What about her own conduct?" the Monsignor asked grimly. "Does her father know about that?"

"Yes. He knows all about it. He had them spotted. Her butler was in the old man's pay. The old man snuffed her out with threats of publicity."

"I've heard enough," Vincent said. "Where *is* Mrs. Rush?"

"She'll be in. But don't think too badly of Rosa and Tony—they've been very foolish and reckless, but these things happen. Rosa went to confession to me. I think she'll straighten out pretty well."

"Confession," Vincent said glumly. "What is this—a day of retribution? I received Lucy back into the Church only a short while ago."

"No!" Arthur said. "Congratulations. That's marvelous—thank God, thank God!"

"I simply can't understand why Tony would let himself get involved with this girl and in this situation," Vincent said, shaking his head and sighing. "He's erratic, I guess, just erratic."

"You've been a priest long enough to know that love doesn't care for the rules in many cases. When it happens, it happens, sometimes regardless of persons or circumstances."

"Let's talk about something else," Vincent said. "This whole problem is crying for action. We've got to do something—now!"

There were quick, light footsteps in the hall.

"Perhaps this is Mrs. Rush now," Vincent said.

"That's not her step," Arthur said with irritation.

"Who is it then?" Vincent asked impatiently. He could stand all this complexity, human vicissitude, and indecision no longer.

"It's probably Monsignor Lambert looking for me and a cup of coffee."

"I don't want to see him," Vincent said, eying the narrow staircase which led up through the old-fashioned servants' quarters to the second floor.

"What are you going to do?"

"I'm going up there," Vincent said grimly.

"Without the tray?"

"Damn the tray!" He strode to the staircase, climbing out of sight quickly.

"Hi, Art," Monsignor Lambert said, rounding the corner into the kitchen as if expecting others. "Mrs. Rush said I could have a cup of coffee. Didn't I just hear you talking to someone?"

"Yes." Arthur reached for the coffeepot and a clean cup. "One of the fathers. He's gone upstairs."

Lambert accepted the explanation with a knowing smile. Monsignor O'Hara, the chancellor, and the ancient seminary prof, Father Carney, who had taught everybody, from the Cardinal down, lived upstairs. The explanation would have to suffice.

"I'm sorry the Cardinal is under the weather," Lambert said stirring his coffee. "Do you think he'll see anybody at all today?"

"I don't know. Personally, I'm inclined to doubt it. Do you have terribly important business with him? Perhaps you'd do well to catch him in a better mood."

"You're probably right," Lambert said. "But I was just so handy here, and Bishop Sliney would be so happy to get the Venezzia donation, which I'm informed is now in the Cardinal's hands. The Bishop authorized me to pick it up if possible."

Arthur paused, restraining a surge of anger. He controlled himself and then said casually, "You certainly must have gotten the news fast. I understand the checks are on hand and, knowing the Cardinal, he probably hasn't done anything about them yet."

"To be perfectly frank," Lambert said in a friendly, conciliatory way, "I got the news from Venezzia himself. I had occasion to call him this morning to convey the best wishes of his friend, the Apostolic Delegate—Archbishop Peruzzi, you know——"

"Yes, the bird watcher," Arthur said with undisguised acid.

"A fellow bird watcher," Lambert corrected with icy meaning. "At any rate, I ran into Archbishop Peruzzi in Milwaukee, and he told me to give Venezzia a call. The old gentleman informed me about the check at that time."

"Have you seen the morning papers?" Arthur asked petulantly.

"Yes. It's most regrettable—this threat of violence. Venezzia himself seems terribly upset about the whole thing. He said he'd take me out to lunch but wouldn't want to risk embarrassing me at this time. He'd be glad to take the strikers back—even give them a raise, he said—but wants no part of the union."

"But the strikers are the union now," Arthur said vigorously. "They're part and parcel of the union. They won't deal any other way."

"That may be. But it all seems so ruthless. A few union officials putting all those people out of work and precipitating mob violence. For what? A little power? A handful of union dues?"

"There are bigger things than that at stake," Arthur said. "But then you and I have never seen eye to eye on the social order anyway. So why don't we just drop the subject?"

He wanted to hit that long, cold, arrogant face. He clenched one fist until the knuckles were white. A priest hit a priest? Yes—his checks, his bird watching, and his clubbiness with Venezzia. Working people were jobless, hungry, many of them Catholics; soon their heads would be broken, along with their hearts, if something wasn't done.

"God help you, Monsignor!" he said with clipped, searing anger. He turned and walked out of the kitchen and down the hallway with stinging tears in his eyes.

Striding down the upper hall toward the Cardinal's bedroom suite, which he knew was in the front of the building, facing the lake, Vincent felt the old chill of indignation that had swept him into the Cardinal's presence when as a young, crusading cleric he had run afoul of Vinegar Jack Regan and the corrupt district attorney.

He was no blithe young cleric now; he wore the red necktie of the Monsignor, with the added authority and power bestowed on him as the Cardinal's official "voice" throughout the archdiocese. But he knew he could still be "cashiered," as it were, and consigned ignominiously to the "outer darkness" of the archdiocese if the Cardinal frowned upon his temerity in bursting into the bedroom where he lay uncomfortably ill.

But he had more constructive "official" business this time. The thirty-five hundred dollars in checks was nestling inside his coat. There were significant commentary and promises to go along with the donations. The seminary fund was steadily growing, and that might divert the Cardinal from the grippe and the intrusion, Vincent thought with some comfort as he approached the wide mahogany sliding doors which gave on to the sitting room of His Eminence's lordly sleeping quarters.

He knocked vigorously but briefly and paused. No answer. Perhaps he was asleep or couldn't hear the knock across the large ante-room with the door of his bedroom possibly shut tight.

He placed his hand in the shiny brass aperture on one of the sliding doors and drew it back slowly. It opened easily—no rattle, no squeak.

The luxurious sitting room, rich with cardinal-red drapes and carpeting, kingly with gold brocade sofas and chairs, authoritative with a shimmering mahogany conference table at its center, was empty and still as a chapel. At the far end the door to the bedroom was half ajar, and Vincent detected the rustling of paper. The Cardinal was reading in bed.

He crossed the room, took a deep breath, and knocked on the half-open door.

"Yes?" came the crisp, hoarse answer.

"It's Monsignor Whelton, Your Eminence," he said softly, grasping the knob and pushing the door open. He was still determined to talk to the Cardinal even if he asked him to leave, but it looked much better. "I'm sorry to burst in on you this way while you're sick. But it's terribly important that I see you."

"Important, is it?" the Cardinal snapped. "And me about to go down for the third time in a sea of catarrh. Well, come in, come in."

He was propped up on three big pillows in a huge four-poster bed, canopied with cardinal velvet, his breviary balanced on his lean, updrawn knees. He was thickly clothed in white flannel pajamas, with a white, tasseled stocking cap pulled tightly down over his ears, accentuating his hawklike features.

As Vincent walked toward him he swung a huge white flannel square of cloth out from under the pillows and blew his nose mightily into its folds.

At the foot of the bed, Vincent was taken mirthfully by his droll Dickensian appearance and fought back a smile.

The Cardinal stuffed the handkerchief back under the pillows, coughed with a deep laryngeal rumble, and severed Vincent's face with a baleful glare.

"Well, don't stand there gaping like a seminarian at a papal audience," the Cardinal snorted, waving him around the bed. "Get yourself a chair and sit down here."

"Yes, Your Eminence." Vincent pulled over a straight-backed chair. "I wanted to talk to you about some of these checks—thirty-five hundred dollars in all this weekend. Some of them are confidentially offered and require special handling. That's why I didn't give them to Mrs. Rush."

"Humph!" the Cardinal said, his eyes again on his breviary. "You've got something else on your mind besides checks. Those could have waited until this afternoon or tomorrow, and you know that very well, Monsignor."

Vincent was silent, shattered by his quick, deep perception.

"Well, what is it, boy, what is it?" the Cardinal resumed, more settled now, more comfortable, his genuine affection for Whelton rounding the edges of his irritation. "Yes, my Chrysostom, my golden-mouth, I've heard a lot of things about you, but never that you had trouble locating your tongue. How did you expect to find me," he continued wryly now, "in long red woollies? I have an eminent Roman confrere—who shall be nameless—who was surprised once in long red woollies. How do you like that?"

Vincent was chuckling now, eased by a man who knew when dignity could go too far or rather when humanity was in danger of being totally withdrawn. And now, in the settled, middle distance of their meeting, the administrator, the man who constantly had to get up the money, appeared casually.

"Show me what you have there." He snapped shut his breviary, gracefully turning out the long, lean hand of an El Greco painting. "Let me see the gleanings of your weekend eloquence," he added with a sly wink, "then I will listen to the real reason for your visit—your inevitable petitions, in one way or another, to needle the social conscience of Holy Mother Church."

"You have me there, Your Eminence," Vincent said, handing him the envelope containing the checks. "Although I did think it neces-sary to be present when you looked over the signatures of some of the donors."

"We shall see." The Cardinal dumped the checks into his lap and adjusted at some familiar check point on his long nose the old steel frame reading glasses he wore, a feature of which were dingy wind-ings of white thread around the ear pieces. He browsed through the checks in silence, seeing meanings in signatures and amounts which were the fruit of decades of schooling in church fund-raising drives.

"Most of these are from the St. James Club," he said. "I take it you were received very well over there, Monsignor."

"I was," Vincent said, "largely because I spoke officially for you, Your Eminence."

"Humph!" the Cardinal snorted. "You charmed them—don't give me that old bull. They're all Knights of Malta and St. Gregory over there. They usually give little but perfunctory compliance to any cleric with less rank than a bishop. Monsignori are a quarter a dozen to those boys.

"What's this—what's this? Venezzia again!" the Cardinal said, screwing up his features and squinting at a thousand-dollar check on imprinted St. James Club stock which bore the signature of "Nino Venezzia, Treasurer."

"Was he present at the dinner?"

"No, Your Eminence, but Judge Conlon, the club president, told me the money was appropriated on the original motion of Venezzia."

"Humph!" the Cardinal said again. "Methinks he doth protest too much."

"Methinks the same, Your Eminence," Vincent said, springing to the opening. "Have you seen the morning paper regarding the latest developments in the Roma strike?"

The Cardinal put the checks back in the envelope, stuffed it under the bottom pillow, and then looked out over his glasses at Vincent with a glance that was both a wise and chastening reminder of his official identity. With his other hand he fumbled under the pillows for a moment and drew out a raggedly torn newspaper clipping. He touched the nose clamp of his glasses once more and peered at the clipping, which he held lightly on highly drawn knees.

"This part here," he began coolly, "what does it mean? 'Plans are in motion to hire a group of white paper-box workers from the southern part of the state. . . .' "

"A delegation from the union, headed by Emily Winant, is downstairs waiting to give you full details," Vincent said.

"Yes, I know Emily is down there. Mrs. Rush told me. They're down there and you're up here for the same reason," he added. "Now I want to hear it from you. Just what is going on? I don't want opinions or crusading blather from you or anyone; I want the facts. What is going on?"

Vincent related the facts as he had heard them from Arthur: the hiring of the two hundred non-union workers from downstate—he refrained specifically from calling them "scabs"—the telegram from the union official alerting Naski to the rendezvous at Truckers' Camp. All, all, he told to the alert prince of the Church, who turned the newspaper clipping slowly round and round in his hands with shrewdly pursed lips and occasional bleak glances at the Monsignor.

When he spoke of Venezzia's alliance with Captain Hardy, the Cardinal interrupted: "I know all about him—what else is there?"

There were the sawed-off broomstick handles and brickbats of which Tony had spoken to Father Arthur. "And the strikers are determined to have the showdown out at Truckers' Camp tonight. They feel there'll be less police to contend with and that they may be able to scare these hirelings off. But wood and bricks are no weapons against pistols and riot guns. Heads will be broken and maybe worse, Your Eminence. Can't we do something—anything— before it's too late, to get Venezzia to sit down with the union?"

"Action, action," the Cardinal snapped, "all you young pups want is action! Tell me this: has the man offered anything to the strikers independent of the union?"

"I can't say for sure. But the general opinion is that he would take them back and give them a raise in the bargain—without the union. Yet there would still be racial discrimination probably—separate facilities and no chance of advancement for the colored. At least, that's the way it's been."

"What else do you hear, Monsignor?" the Cardinal asked with a smile.

He decided not to tell the Cardinal about Rosa, her intervention at the plant, her involvement with Tony. Besides, it wasn't relevant to the public problem. She had made her bid privately and the scandal was, for the present at least, a private thing. But Judge Conlon's remark about "hush money" to District Attorney Ryan was entirely relevant. He'd let the Cardinal have that one with both barrels.

He told him the story as he had heard it from Joan—tale-bearing, it was true, but he was determined to bear tales from here to Rome and back again if he could dent the Cardinal's armor of noncommitment and discern somehow, whether or not he would move against Venezzia.

"Judge Conlon said that?" the Cardinal asked with a flash of anger.

"Yes, Your Eminence, in a box seat at the stadium. And if they're saying it there, they're saying it everywhere!"

"THEY'RE NOT SAYING IT ABOUT ME, BECAUSE IT'S A CONFOUNDED LIE!" the Cardinal exploded, throwing aside the coverlets and swinging his feet into a pair of slippers. "Reach me that bathrobe on the chair there, Monsignor."

Vincent helped him into an ancient blanketlike bathrobe with broken belt loops and two buttons missing.

"Get on that phone and get Arthur and Mrs. Rush up here right away. Tell her to bring her book."

The Cardinal shuffled off to the bathroom, and Vincent, his veins pounding with elation, had to restrain himself from running to the telephone.

Seated at the head of the conference table in the sitting room, with Mrs. Rush beside him, sharp pencil in hand, the Cardinal tossed his head, swinging back the tassel of his nightcap, gave one great blow of his nose into the large flannel kerchief, and was ready for business.

Standing at the foot of the table with arms folded, Father Arthur Wagner smirked briefly at Vincent, saw the red flush of his happiness, and returned his gaze intently to his uncle, curious as to the nature of the tactic.

"Write this down, Eva," the Cardinal began, glancing up and away toward the wide french doors which brooded like a landscape painting filled with the gray sweep and petulance of the lake shore.

"To the Honorable Nino Venezzia, K.M.—Dear Mr. Venezzia: The bearer, the Very Reverend Monsignor Vincent Whelton, has my authority to deliver the contents of this envelope and to discuss the implications of the letter should you be at all interested in doing so.

"In view of your high standing and generosity as a lay servant of Holy Mother Church here and on the Continent, it is a most unpleasant duty for me to have to return you the enclosed checks. After much consideration of the circumstances, publicity, and damaging gossip which have surrounded and emanated from the current labor dispute at the Roma plant, I have no recourse, as spiritual leader of this archdiocese, but to head off any scandal which may be associated with our fund-raising efforts by declining your generous donations.

"The pragmatic necessity of unchristian and uncharitable segregation at your plant, Mr. Venezzia, is your personal business. Your adamant refusal to sit down and discuss your personnel problems with what appears to be a legitimate, well-intentioned union, possessing the loyalty and confidence of a majority of your workers, is again your right as a capitalist and citizen. And now I am informed that you are willing to risk almost certain violence and bloodshed by bringing in a corps of strikebreakers from downstate. That, too, is your business, and it is no right of mine to interfere directly.

"But when all this enigmatic conduct of an outstanding layman and Knight of Malta begins to reflect on the integrity of the Catholic archdiocesan leadership and, indeed, upon the sincerity of the affection which I feel for all working people, whatever their religion, white or black, I have no recourse but to take whatever action I believe necessary to preserve good will and to further implement the traditional fact that Holy Mother Church is the refuge and protector of all—not just the privileged few.

"I am, therefore, returning the enclosed checks, one for twenty thousand dollars made out to the Cardinal Archbishop, and the other for five thousand dollars addressed to the Bishop of Harbourton. In the latter instance. I take full responsibility, since the Harbourton diocese is under my jurisdiction. I will go further than that with the good Bishop Sliney, who is an old and revered friend of mine. If necessary, I will make good this five thousand dollars for him out of my own personal funds.

"I cannot convey too strongly my sense of shock and outrage, for what it is worth to you, that a layman so highly placed in the esteem and honors of the Church should conduct his business affairs with such ruthless and brutal disregard of the most obvious concepts of Christian charity and social justice.

"Toward this end, I must inform you out of courtesy that I will release copies of this letter to the local and national press this evening, in time for the morning editions.

"Again, my regrets that this action must be taken—and believe me, the seminary building fund could use this money—but there is no other recourse under the existing circumstances.

"I repeat, you may feel free to discuss this letter with my personal emissary, Monsignor Whelton. Respectfully yours in Christ, Arthur Cardinal Wagner, Archbishop of Lakeport."

Vincent let out an audible sigh and blessed himself when the Cardinal finished.

"Oh, you're pleased, are you?" the Cardinal snapped. "Well, we'll see, we'll see what will happen now. Eva, type this up right away, enclose the checks, both of them, and give the envelope to the Monsignor here. Arthur?"

"Yes, Your Eminence?"

"Get a carbon of the letter from Mrs. Rush and prepare some releases for the papers. Keep in touch with Monsignor Whelton, and unless something good develops, give the story to the papers before midnight."

"With pleasure!"

"Never mind the editorial comments," the Cardinal said. "Is that squirt from Bishop Sliney's office still down there?"

"Yes, Your Eminence," Mrs. Rush said.

"Don't tell him a thing. Pen a little memo to Bishop Sliney from me, asking him to sit tight on all this. Enclose a carbon copy of this letter."

"Yes, sir," she said, rising. "Is that all?"

"Yes," he said, handing her an envelope from his folder. "Here are the checks—both of them from Venezzia. Oh," he added, rubbing his eyes and smoothing his black bushy eyebrows in the same motion. "Put Bishop Sliney's letter in one of those envelopes you can't hold up to the light. Seal it well and give it to Monsignor Lambert without comment. That'll send him off to Harbourton as if the Old Nick had hold of his tail. He's a little too ambitious for my taste."

Arthur repressed a snicker, and both Mrs. Rush and Vincent smiled.

"What are you all grinning about?" the Cardinal snorted, rising and snuffling. "Get on about your business—all of you," he added, picking up his personal folder. "You'll be the death of me; I'm going back to bed."

"Do you want your coffee tray brought up now?"

"Never mind the coffee!" he said, his hand on the knob of his bedroom door. "Get Father Carney across the hall to fix me up some more of that hot Irish whiskey and lemon. It's the only thing that'll make me sweat."

"What will we tell Emily Winant and the others?" Arthur called after him.

The Cardinal paused at the half-opened bedroom door. There was a touch of wistfulness in his long, gaunt features.

"Tell her to go back to her soup line with my blessing," he said with a tired smile. "And tell the others to watch and wait. I've done my best."

Monsignor Whelton rushed forward, went down on one knee, and kissed the Cardinal's ring.

"Umph!" the Cardinal snorted. "You think that'll do it, do you?"

"I do, Your Eminence," Vincent said, rising. "God bless you!"

"And, Mrs. Rush," the Cardinal sighed wearily before pushing on through the door, "no more calls or visitors. Not even the Holy Father would I see the rest of this day."

BOOK SIX

The Guerrilla Bishop

CHAPTER XXXII

Utopia Round the Bend

ON A wet September morning in the year of Roosevelt, 1936, Monsignor Vincent prickled with excitement in the taxi which padded patiently over the gleaming rain-sheen of the boulevard toward his ten o'clock meeting with the Cardinal at the Senate Hotel.

Arthur and Tony would be waiting for him with the script for the labor-convention address which he was scheduled to deliver at two. But there was something urgent about the meeting with the Cardinal which distracted him from all that.

What could it be? All the Cardinal had said was "Be there" on the phone early that morning. Be there, be there, of course, but for what, why? The plans for the seminary dedication banquet on Saturday night were complete. The armory would be filled with visiting Cardinals, bishops, clergy and civic dignitaries and the new seminary itself would be solemnly dedicated on Sunday afternoon.

There was the labor-convention speech. The Cardinal hadn't said yes and he hadn't said no. Vincent had written him a note, telling him he had been invited to speak by Tom Naski, who was now international president of the Allied Paper Workers. "No priest has ever addressed a formal labor convention in the city of Lakeport," he had written frankly to the Cardinal. "If I am permitted to address them I will confine myself to comments and current interpretation of the Holy Father's labor encyclical, *Quadragesimo Anno*."

Slap, slap, slap, past the huge citadel of the Lakeport *Herald* with the late news bulletins crayoned on huge panels. The lead items caught his eye and needled him drolly:

3RD ANNUAL SOCIALISM DAY!
COMMIES AND PINKO CRACKPOTS
ALL WELCOME!

WHY?

(1) PRESIDENT IN TOWN TODAY
COMING FROM WARM SPRINGS

(2) ALLIED PAPER WORKERS CONVENTION
AT STOCKYARDS HALL!

WILL MERGE WITH CENTRAL LABOR ALLIANCE (CLA)
"BIRDS OF A FEATHER FLOCK TOGETHER!"
SEE AFTERNOON HERALD FOR LATEST DETAILS!

The President! He had forgotten about that. Arthur had mentioned F.D.R.'s visit a few days ago. The realization sobered the mirth he had felt upon reading Flagpost's anti-liberal headlines.

F.D.R., the Cardinal's great and good friend! No, no, he dared not think about it! The day, the times were too crammed already: the rapid expansion of the Christian Youth Center and the adult education school, the fund raising, the new seminary, the labor convention.

He blotted the staggering program of commitments out of his mind. Only in the cool clarity of morning did his schedule confound him. He blinked and shook his head. You can't think about all these things. You can't fit them all in if you think about them. Do them, do them, that is all. Schedule them and do them, otherwise be overwhelmed, freeze in a corner somewhere at their increase and multiplication. Then nothing would be done! Nothing.

Nearing the Senate Hotel, he breathed a silent prayer to the Blessed Mother, *The Magnificat*, his favorite, easing prayer in time of inner tumult.

"My soul doth magnify the Lord . . . for He that is mighty hath done great things to me . . . He hath put down the mighty from their seat, and hath exalted the humble . . ." Put down Venezzia, who was so clubby with the union now and was cutting somewhat of a figure as a liberal. Took in the union, begged the Cardinal to accept the checks. "He hath filled the hungry with good things, and the rich He hath sent away empty . . ."

The cab jolted to a stop in front of the Senate Hotel. Vincent pressed a bill into the palm of the cabdriver, signified no change, and hurried onto the thick rubber tarmac, fleeing the chill pesterings of rain and the canker worm of indecision.

"Father Wagner and another gentleman are waiting for you in the lobby," the lean, red-jowled doorman in the faded uniform of a South American general whispered as he held open the door.

"Thank you, Mack," Monsignor Whelton said. "How's the missus? She still up north in the San?"

"Yes, and doing fine, Monsignor," Mack said with a smile.

"Good. I'll remember her at Mass tomorrow."

"Thank you, Monsignor. I'll write and tell her that."

He strode on in, his brief case tight under his arm.

Father Arthur and Tony were almost immediately at his side.

"You've got ten minutes before you see the Cardinal," Arthur said briskly. "The labor boys have a suite upstairs where we can go over the speech. Tony's got the key."

"Yes, yes. I want to see it," Vincent said as they walked toward the elevator. "We might as well be ready in case you get the green light. I haven't heard a thing from His Eminence on it. Have you?"

"Not a thing," Arthur said. "But no news is good news."

"Tony, how are you?" Monsignor asked, smiling and grabbing him by the elbow. "How are things at the center? I haven't been in since Monday. This seminary banquet and dedication have me buried."

"Fine, Monsignor, fine," Tony said with subdued happiness. He had taken the post as the Monsignor's administrative assistant after the Roma strike had been settled and was supremely happy in the job. "Your old friend Venezzia spoke at our labor-management forum the other evening, and he sounds like Frances Perkins."

"Who said the leopard does not change his spots?" Arthur said as they stepped into the elevator.

"That gentleman isn't a leopard, he's a chameleon," Monsignor Vincent said with a faint smile.

"Times have changed," Arthur said with undisguised glee. "F.D.R., the New Deal, the Wagner Act, *Quadragesimo Anno!*"

"Listen to that litany of the common man!" Tony said.

"Yes," Monsignor Whelton said with the resonance of elation. "But I still don't like that term 'the common man.' 'Common' had a—well, a common flavor. Christianity seeks to develop the uncommon man —the saint, as it were. It's the type and kind of term that can be grossly misunderstood in some quarters."

"Don't worry about terminology," Arthur said as they left the elevator. "Just be grateful the little guys in this country are finally getting a break."

"Yes," Vincent said with a rather arch sigh. "How did you and Tony come out with the speech? Did you work in those quotes from the encyclical—especially that one I marked up for you?"

"It's all in there," Arthur said. "If you get to talk, you'll knock them dead."

"You'll fracture them," Tony said with a grin.

"I'll fracture myself if I don't find out what's on the Cardinal's mind." Vincent followed them into a comfortable two-room suite.

"I think I can guess what's on his mind," Arthur said, beckoning Vincent to the sofa in front of a coffee table and slipping an eight-page manuscript out of a manila folder. He placed the script in front of the Monsignor and sat down beside him as Tony pulled up a padded footstool.

"Well, the President's coming through," Vincent said tentatively, taking his heavy black tortoise-shell glasses out of an inside pocket and squinting at the first page of the script. "I saw all that quite nastily displayed on the *Herald* news bulletins as I passed."

"Yes," Arthur said. "I've got a bulletin for you—and it isn't nasty. I think you're going to get to see the President with the Cardinal. I have to be there to handle the press in case the Cardinal makes a statement. My guess is he'll invite you along."

"No!" Vincent looked up with childlike happiness in his face, which was not without a touch of awe. The President! The golden voice he had first heard on a tinny little street radio from the Democratic convention in 1928. The voice of hope and indomitable courage, calling the American people out of the wastes of economic recession and fear, leading them into the lands of plenty which were rightfully their own. The President—in person. F.D.R.!

"Yes," Arthur said with a triumphant smile. "And prepare yourself for something else. As you know, Auxiliary Bishop O'Hara has been bedridden for over a year now with a stroke. He hasn't been available for his duties as vicar-general nor for Confirmations. There's going to be a new auxiliary bishop around here, and Mrs. Rush hinted something to me last evening. Will you still speak to us if we have to call you 'Your Excellency'?"

Vincent didn't know what to say. He felt the thrill of anticipation but refused it. There was too much on his mind. Yet Arthur's perceptions about the Cardinal's moves had rarely been wrong.

"We already have a new bishop in the Harbourton diocese," Vincent said, bowing low over the manuscript. "He's been handling Confirmations up here," he said softly, evasively, "our former roommate."

"Yes, our former roommate, the Most Reverend Robert Bird Watcher Lambert. But he's Coadjutor Bishop with full right of succession to old Bishop Sliney. He simply can't continue to fill in here."

"We'll cross that bridge when we come to it," Vincent said with sustained evasiveness. "This first page looks good: 'Man is born to labor, as the bird to fly . . .' That's cited from *Rerum Novarum* in the Holy Father's latest, eh? It's one of my favorite quotations. Who put that in there—you or Tony?"

"Tony," Father Arthur said. "Hurry up. You only have five minutes."

"'The trade union,'" Vincent read with a little oratorical flair, "'given the present state of affairs, is a necessary but not an ideal solution. . . .'"

"Do you think we ought to quote that—after all, this is a labor convention?"

"Read on, Macduff," Arthur said pertly.

"Oh, I see," Vincent said. "You apply that differently to America. 'But in present-day America the will of the people has overwhelmingly approved the integrity of trade unions as the standard-bearer of social justice for those who earn their bread by the sweat of their brows—this we see in the smashing victory of a federal administration dedicated to the service of human rather than corporate needs across our land; this we applaud in a leader who is determined to make the abundance of our great land available to all and not just the privileged few. This we see in the monumental vision and utility of the great and vigilant Wagner Act. . . .'"

Vincent read on in silence, finishing the text, making several minor markings with his pen.

"Fine, fine," he said. "I'll go over it more carefully after lunch. And I like that quotation from Daniel Webster with which we close—I like it very much."

"You can thank Father Arthur for that one," Tony said. "It's a real crowd-pleaser."

"Here, before we go upstairs"—Arthur pointed to a phrase on page five—"read that sentence: 'The strategic necessity of implementing the Wagner Act at this time . . .'"

"The stra-getic necessity . . ." Monsignor Whelton began.

"Pronounce that again," Arthur said.

"Stra-getic . . ."

"You've got a block on that word," he said gently. "Change it to—oh—compelling. And, for heaven's sake, if you have to ad-lib at any point, don't be using that phrase 'type and kind.' It's sheer affectation and has no meaning."

"All right," Vincent said sternly, flushing a little. "Let's get on up-stairs. Do you think I should show a copy of this to the Cardinal?"

"No. Not unless he asks you. Don't go begging trouble. Tony, you keep those extra copies of the speech for the press out at Stockyards Hall. Don't release them until I call you out there."

"Right, Father. I'll say good-by to you now, both of you. And see you out there," Tony added, crossing his fingers. "I hope."

"We'll be there," Arthur said confidently.

"I hope so," Vincent said with a sigh, rising.

Tony took his brief case and started for the door, turning before he went out.

"I hope it works out, Monsignor," he said with deep affection. "You'd make a great bishop."

The Monsignor smiled slowly, gratefully.

"Pray for me, Tony," was all he said as he waved him out of sight.

"Now that Tony's gone," Arthur said, "just a few more things be-fore we go upstairs."

"Spare me, please," Vincent said, slipping his glasses into a leather case and putting them away. "It's all too much for one day."

"You're right." A sympathetic smile touched the corners of Arthur's mouth. "But I'm trying to prepare you. You may be taken into the councils of the big boys and you'd better be ready."

"All right, all right," Vincent said impatiently. "I know there's a meeting of the bishops up there—an executive meeting—the Cardi-nal told me that much this morning. But I honestly don't know what the meeting's for. Can you tell me?"

"I'm trying to," Arthur said. "As you may have noticed in the papers, all hell has broken loose in Spain. The thing is fiendishly mixed up, and the Church is considered by some as the big black beast, dead on the bull's-eye and directly in the line of fire."

"Looks like another Mexico on our hands."

"Worse than that," Arthur explained. "The final alignment will be between Stalin on one side and Hitler and Mussolini teamed up on the other."

"A plague on both their houses," Vincent said.

"That's the Cardinal's thinking. He detests Hitler and Il Duce just as much as he hated Stalin—calls Der Fuehrer an 'upstart paper-hanger.' But the Church is still in the middle in this Spanish thing. Most of our big boys have come in for the seminary dedication Saturday—and they'll probably discuss policy. They know Unk's got the President's ear. Thus the importance of discussing things informally here, instead of Washington, where it's actually much harder to get to the President."

"What do you expect me to do?" Vincent asked.

"I want you to be informed before you go in there. Listen and learn. Remember what the Cardinal's attitude is, and if you're asked, try to make a vigorous yet not too radical statement."

"I've already said it," Vincent snorted. "A plague on both their houses."

"Yes, but that's not enough of an answer."

"Well, what do the eastern boys think?" Vincent asked. "Are you sure Spain will dominate the talk? What about the 'radio priest' up in Detroit? He's really been knocking the Jewish brethren lately. Won't he be a topic of conversation?"

"Don't worry about the 'radio priest'—both Chicago and Boston would keel-haul him if it weren't for Detroit. And Detroit will be here—out of deference to him 'the voice of destruction' will not be discussed. After all, Burke is boss in the automobile city and has a right to handle that fellow in his own way."

"Do you think he dislikes the 'chosen'?" Vincent asked.

Arthur sighed impatiently. "There it comes again—the great sensitivity. If I disagree with you, does that make me anti-Irish or anti-Catholic?"

"No," Vincent said with a tentative smile.

"No two priests in America have spoken up for the Jew more than you and me—in the name of interracial justice. But Burke has a right to resent any slurs on his ability to handle the 'radio priest.' Any of those autocratic editorials from the Jewish press as to how

THE GUERRILLA BISHOP 358

to handle that fellow are taken as a personal challenge on Burke's validity as a competent ecclesiastical authority."

"I understand," Vincent said. "But the whole thing is most regrettable. Where *do* the eastern boys stand on this Spanish situation?"

"Well, let's tick some of them off," Arthur said, taking an anxious glance at his wrist watch. "Cardinals Burke of Detroit and Ronan of Philadelphia are ultra-conservative. They'll go with those who are protecting the interests of the Church. O'Connell of Boston isn't here, but you know him, an aristocratic snob. He'll be orating about his love of Spain as the land of his late friend, Cardinal Merry del Val; he'll be making statements about the godless Communist hordes as he walks up the gangplank on his way to Bermuda this winter."

The Monsignor chuckled. "He's the one they call 'Gangplank Bill,' isn't he? Those Boston Irish have a good sense of humor."

"O'Connell's young auxiliary, the fabulous Walter J. Bannon, will be here, however. He's the one who fits so well with Cardinal Pacelli—worked with him in the Papal secretariat—a real comer.

"One of my old professors at the American College in Rome visited me recently, Vin, and told me the following story. I had heard hints of it but I don't think I ever mentioned it to you. Bannon, it seems, is quite a versatile guy. He's had a pilot's license, for example, for years. When the Pope had all that trouble with Mussolini on the Concordat, Bannon flew news of the Holy Father's denunciation of Il Duce right out of Italy and spread the story all over the world. That was the only way they could get the word out. I guess the radio was dead and the Vatican itself was surrounded by blackshirts."

"He must be quite a guy," Vincent said with deep interest. "Is that story true?"

"That was the way it was told to me," Arthur said.

"Will Bannon have a sort of proxy for Cardinal O'Connell at the conference?"

Arthur smirked. "Are you kidding? Nobody has a proxy for O'Connell—but nobody! And besides, Bannon doesn't need anybody's proxy —even as an auxiliary bishop. He really can run with the ball—all by himself. Can you imagine what he'll be like if he should get New York someday?"

Vincent nodded with involuntary admiration.

"And New York isn't too well these days—he won't be here, by the way—but he'll go with Unk. Next to Unk—and I'm, of course, prejudiced—Cardinal Dwyer stands in closest with F.D.R."

"Which way will they jump?"

"Cardinal Wagner still rules the roost. These three—Bannon, the Apostolic Delegate, Archbishop Peruzzi, and Unk—will play cards together, and the others will probably go along. But Unk is the man with the President, and that will be the clincher, I'd say."

"We're running late now," Vincent said. "What about the President?"

"Well, it looks as though he's walking a tightrope right now. He's got the pinko liberals on one side who'll be screaming for the loyalists and a tremendous block of Catholic Democratic votes on the other, urging the support of Franco."

"Franco—he's the Moroccan general who has the army in his pocket?"

"Yes, and a loyal son of the Church who will protect its interests but who will also play ball with Hitler and Mussolini."

"Wow!" Vincent said. "Let's go!"

"Wow is right," Arthur said, turning the doorknob. "You got the story now. Play the rest of it by ear and keep an eye on the Cardinal. Right?"

"Right," Vincent said with a sigh, following him out the door. "God help us. What a world. We're talking heaven-on-earth over here, and all hell is breaking loose over there!"

" 'My kingdom is not of this world . . .' " Arthur said with a smile as he pushed the elevator button.

Vincent put his arm around Arthur's shoulders, giving him a brief yet iron squeeze with his pitching hand. "How right our Blessed Lord was, how very right."

CHAPTER XXXIII

The Ball and the Cross

"ELEVEN," said the elevator boy.

"Are they in the Presidential Suite?" Vincent asked.

"Yes," Arthur said, "down left here."

"Well, the President won't be here, will he?"

"No, he'll be across town at the Lakeside Hotel. He'll have to see the chief rabbis and the heads of the ministers' associations, too, don't forget that. And every Democratic pol in Lakeport will be ducking in and out for an audience. How'd you like to be in his seat?"

"No, thanks, mine is hot enough."

At the end of the hallway they approached a staircase with black wrought-iron railings and gleaming brass knobs. Standing sentinel by the stairway that led to the suite was a big, burly policeman who touched his hand to the peak of his cap as the clergymen approached.

"Good morning, Fathers," he said with a touch of an Irish brogue.

"Good morning, officer," Arthur said. "Keep an eye peeled for Communists. You've got half the American Church in there."

"I will that, Father," he said with a chuckle.

The great sliding doors to the foyer of the suite were shut, but they could hear the hum of voices and subdued laughter as they approached.

"We'll go in the back way," Arthur said. "The Cardinal has his own room there and Mrs. Rush will probably be standing by." He looked at Vincent, who was grim and tight-jowled, and turned on that impish smile again. "Unless you want to walk right in and confront all that red and purple?"

"The back way sounds like a fine idea. Besides, the Cardinal will probably want to talk to us in private."

"Talk to *us?*" Arthur raised his eyebrows. "Talk to you, you mean. You're the ball carrier in this club. I just run interference."

"Interference is a good word for you," Vincent said pertly. "You've got your finger in everything and you never miss a trick."

"That's the life of a newspaperman."

"Yes—and the Cardinal's nephew, to boot. Is this the door?"

"Yes," Arthur said, knocking.

Amid the pause, while the signal of admission was sent and received, Vincent felt the overpowering sense of expectancy. The repressed exultation at the possibility of what lay in store for him behind that door was almost too much. He didn't know whether to laugh, cry, or pray. He set his teeth tightly and held onto his dignity as the sound of footsteps came toward the door.

The door clicked, swung open.

"Come in, both of you," said Mrs. Rush. "The Cardinal has been inquiring about you."

She ushered them into the room and beckoned Vincent to an armchair next to a tall one at the head of a round walnut table.

"You, you big omadhaun," she said to Arthur, "can sit over there on the other side of the table, where I can keep an eye on you."

"You've done pretty well in that department for years."

"I've had to or you'd have disgraced us all long since," she said with a smile of affection. Then with a hint of better things: "But you're doing fine nonetheless, and even His Eminence has remarked about it."

"Glad to hear that. How's the meeting going?"

"Oh, they're just getting under way, having their coffee and their little jokes about this and that."

"Who else is here besides the big brass, Mrs. Rush?" Vincent asked.

"Our friend is out there," she said slowly, "the new Coadjutor Bishop of Harbourton."

"No!" Arthur said.

"Yes. By special invitation of the Apostolic Delegate. The Cardinal agreed with his idea that one or two young bishops should sit in."

"You can't beat our old roomie," Arthur said, shaking his head. "He's always right there when big things are happening."

"He's a very capable young man," Mrs. Rush said.

"He is," Vincent agreed firmly. "Bob Lambert is a fine priest and a fine administrator. On the conservative side, yes, and perhaps partial to wearing the gumshoes. But a very solid item, always was. Correct, Arthur?"

"I guess so," Arthur conceded. "He's just never been my cup of tea." Now he looked at Mrs. Rush with a twinkle in his eyes. "Which other young Bishop, if any?" he asked.

She looked steadily, reprovingly, right back at him.

"Oh, you'll see," she said. Then she shifted her gaze to Vincent and smiled at him in a motherly and admiring way which brought the color to his cheeks. She sat down at her typewriter and banged away at a half-finished letter.

Muffled sounds from the conference room betrayed no laughter now as the conversations among the prelates took a more sober turn. Now footsteps, the turning of the knob. The door swung open. It was Cardinal Wagner.

"Oh, you got here, did you?" he said. "Did you think you were to attend a parish penny sale that you could be so leisurely about showing up?"

"I'm sorry we're late, sir," Arthur said. "It's really my fault. Monsignor Vincent was here on time, but I briefed him a bit on who would be present at the meeting. I didn't think you'd want him to come in cold."

"Very well," he said curtly. "Pull up a chair, both of you. I can't spend much time in here. Mrs. Rush, give me that letter to sign and then take it down the hall and mail it while I talk with these two."

"Yes, Your Eminence," she said, whipping the letter out of the typewriter, attaching it to an envelope, and bringing it to him for his signature.

With the camouflage of discreetly lowered eyes, Vincent found himself looking at the Cardinal's face as he fished out his thread-wound glasses, adjusted them near the end of his nose, and with shrewd, boring focus perused the letter. The aristocratic, hawklike face was showing its age more than ever, and in a different, alarming way, Vincent noted. There was a sagging of the jowls, a chalkiness, and for the first time in his long association with the Cardinal he could hear his breathing—short, somewhat labored.

"Fine," the Cardinal said, signing the letter. "I'll keep the carbon here, Eva. When you get back make another copy from your notes on my official stationery. I'll give that one to Peruzzi. But this one must go to the Holy Father, registered air mail. Clear?"

"Yes, Your Eminence." Mrs. Rush took the letter from him and crossed to the corner for her hat and coat. Years of service to the Ordinary of the archdiocese had taught her the meaning of dispatch. She was out the rear door and gone in a matter of seconds.

"Well, now," the Cardinal said with a sigh. "Let's get on with our business." He moved the carbon copy of the letter to one side and took off his glasses, swinging them first at Vincent and then at Arthur. "You're both here," he continued. "What is it you want of me before I tell you what's on my mind?"

"I'm here to handle any press problems you might have," Arthur said. "Vincent?"

"One thing, Your Eminence," Vincent said. "Is it going to be all right for me to talk to these labor people this afternoon? We're just about ready to go, but of course I need your approval."

"Did you think I had forgotten your request?" the Cardinal said, irked, yet softening.

"No, Your Eminence. But it's just that time is running out and you have such a heavy schedule today."

"I want you to do this thing right," he said with slow, careful emphasis. "It's perfectly all right that you're the first priest to address a formal labor convention in this archdiocese. But if I'm sending you in there, you're going in big and you're going in heavy!"

The Cardinal paused and glanced at the carbon copy of the letter.

"You're going up on that platform," he said, rapping the table with his episcopal ring, "as Auxiliary Bishop-elect of the archdiocese of Lakeport. You can also tell them, Arthur," he continued, smiling, and motioning with his right hand, "that this new Bishop is now vicar-general of the archdiocese along with his other duties. Now are you ready to address the Allied Paper Workers in convention assembled?"

"I'm overwhelmed, Your Eminence," Vincent said, his eyes growing uncontrollably misty.

"Well, stop being overwhelmed. We've got too much work to do." The Cardinal rose, showing a mien of deep satisfaction. "Kneel down and I'll give you my blessing."

"Thank you, Your Eminence," Vincent said, kneeling. "That is exactly my deepest wish."

The Cardinal glanced at Arthur, who was confusedly stormed with joy for Vincent and remorse for his own indiscretions which had seemed to prevent his formal advancement in the Church.

"You don't have to go through all this again, my nephew," he said with a reproving yet affectionate smile. "The same cable from the Vatican which approved my designation of a new bishop also carried your appointment as a papal chamberlain with the title of Very Reverend Monsignor. So kneel down with our new Bishop and we'll get on back to the meeting."

"No, Unk!" Arthur said with sheer astonishment and a touch of irrepressible mirth.

Vincent knew a surge of triumph that engulfed his own joy.

"Yes," the Cardinal said sternly. "Kneel down!"

"Yes, Your Eminence," Arthur said, kneeling beside Vincent.

They blessed themselves, the Cardinal intoning: "Almighty God, allow me to paraphrase the words You uttered to Your divine Son as I call Your blessing down on these two holy fathers who have been bestowed new honor and authority at the will and pleasure of the Holy Father, Pope Pius XI. These, then, are my beloved sons in whom I am well pleased. Bless them with courage, the light of the Holy Ghost, humility, teach them to be as is their great sponsor, the Holy Father, *servum servorum Dei*, each a servant of the servants of God.

"God bless you both," he whispered, touching each of them on the forehead as they kissed his ring. "Now come with me."

He opened the door to the vast conference room of the Presidential Suite where some of the great powers of the American Catholic Church were gathered around a shiny oval table, listening to the sure, modulated voice of a rotund Irish auxiliary bishop as he read from a prepared typewritten memo.

"That's Auxiliary Bishop Bannon of Boston," the Cardinal whispered. "He's acting as conference secretary."

They caught the phrases of Bannon, whose back was directly to them at the head of the table. He had not yet sensed their presence. "Spain and the Church in turmoil, yes. But General Francisco Franco, an estimable son of the Church, in reasonable control. There is, too, the manifest good will and fairness of our great President, who must try to be the all-wise civic father to all of us—Catholic, Protestant, Jew, liberal, conservative, and reactionary alike—he must serve us all and take into conscientious regard our over-all interests in a seething, unhappy world.

"But happily, to serve our cause of non-intervention and lighten the consequences of controversy, there is the *cordon sanitaire* of the

British naval blockade and the iron vigilance of the French border patrols. . . ."

Around the table Vincent could see the two cardinals, both stout men of beefy, medieval visage, unlike the Teutonic hawk of Lakeport. Both of them he recognized from newspaper photos, the amiable Burke of Detroit, the joke teller, who dozed behind erratic eyelids, and the alert if fatty features of Philadelphia's Ronan, who darted his eyes suspiciously at their appearance in the doorway.

To the right of Bishop Bannon another episcopal back was visible: patient, contained, the Apostolic Delegate, Archbishop Peruzzi.

On various soft and straight-backed chairs along the walls were several monsignori, among whom Vincent spotted the wide-eyed, apprehensive face of the Coadjutor Bishop of Harbourton.

"There's our old roomie," Arthur whispered. "He thought he had this Olympian session all to himself."

The Cardinal was ahead of them now, leading the way as Bishop Bannon, sensing his entrance, stopped reading and turned his head.

"Your Eminence," he said. "I'm glad you got back here for the conclusion of all this."

"A thousand pardons, Bishop," Cardinal Wagner said. "And you, my dear colleagues, forgive me. I've a couple of young whippersnappers here whom you should put immediately under surveillance. A new auxiliary bishop and a new monsignor, both in my archdiocese. Perhaps you'll bear with them while they sit over there with our bright young Coadjutor Bishop from Harbourton."

There were general smiles and nods of approval, all in courtesy to the host Cardinal, and, irrepressibly, a sense of benevolence toward the young who were on the same ladder which the men at the oval table well knew.

"Please continue, Bishop Bannon," the Cardinal said, taking the seat to his left. "And do, please, forgive the interruption."

"Not at all. Not at all, Your Eminence."

The Bishop droned on about the need for prudence and nonintervention as long as General Franco held the initiative and the British blockade endured.

Bishop-elect Whelton caught a cordial signal from Bishop Lambert, who moved over on the sofa and beckoned both him and Arthur to sit beside him.

"God love you, Bishop!" he said in a whisper, touching Vincent's sleeve with genuine feeling. "You must give me your episcopal blessing later."

"Thank you, Bob. And you must give me yours. This is the first time I've seen you in the purple."

Bishop Lambert nodded and then reached across, touching Arthur, who smiled back wryly.

"Three roommates," Bishop Lambert whispered. "Two bishops and a monsignor. Congratulations, Art!"

"I just got in the back door," Arthur said, thumbing toward the Cardinal's private room.

Vincent had never known more elation. The spontaneous warmth of the usually cool Lambert was just the right, crowning touch. He and Arthur would simply have to get to know him better. After all, there was so much to do together, so much to do.

". . . and after serious deliberation of all the factors, in executive session early this morning, your steering committee, composed of Cardinal Wagner, Archbishop Peruzzi, and myself, respectfully urge that these recommendations of policy on the part of the American bishops, with regard to the welfare of the Church in Spain during the present civil conflict, be agreed upon by you and forwarded forthwith to the Holy Father."

When he had finished, Bishop Bannon paused urbanely, setting down the memo. "Is there any comment or any objections before we take a vote?" he asked in a soft, casual voice which was not calculated to encourage much discussion.

There was silence, almost a somnolent silence, while the three members of the steering committee watched alertly. Cardinal Wagner looked quickly at Bannon over his glasses, as if to say: "Lock it up, lock it up."

Peruzzi swept the table with the dark, Latin searchlight of his eyes and then, sweeping around the walls, rested on the "bird watcher" and his two former roommates, giving the three a benevolent smile.

But rotund Philadelphia, with all the prickling restlessness and suspicion of a thin man, was not to be denied. He snorted impatiently at the dozing "Friar Tuck" from Detroit to his right, and poked him rudely in the ribs.

"John, John, wake up," he said petulantly. "We've got decisions to make here."

"Oh-oh," Detroit said, shaking his head and blinking his eyes, "yes, yes. I'll go along with that—sounds fine. We'll watch how Franco goes, and the limey blockade is there, too, and the French will hold at the border. I'm sure, too, that Cardinal Wagner knows the wisest course with the President."

"All well and good," Philadelphia's Ronan snorted, impatient to remind them of his authority and viewpoint. "But I still think we could send the Navy in and clean those Bolshevik scum out of Madrid—the marines, perhaps, a landing party. They're desecrating our churches, shooting our priests, violating our nuns. Surely, in the name of humanity, Roosevelt would be willing to go a little further. We can't expect Franco to work miracles even if he does have help from Italy and Germany."

Bishop Bannon nodded carefully, diplomatically.

"I'd like to say a few words on this out of deference to the sincere views of my dear old friend, the Cardinal Archbishop from Philadelphia," Cardinal Wagner said. "It is just and proper that there should be preventive action. But that we have. Britain has vital interests over there—Gibraltar and the Mediterranean life line which must be protected. F.D.R.'s strategy is of a more long-range character. To wit, world peace. Franco is working for our cause within—Britain and France without."

"Yes, but the blockade hampers Franco's allies as much as it does the Russians," Ronan said.

"Yes and no, Your Eminence," Cardinal Wagner said. "Hitler and Mussolini with superior air transport are getting in there strong. Russia, too, could go in that way, it is true, and will. But only on a limited basis, it is predicted, because of internal troubles and the pressure of Japan on its Siberian borders."

"Then we should lift the blockade and let the Germans and the Italians come in by sea," Ronan said.

"It can't be done. There's too much danger of general war. And you must remember, Roosevelt has other elements in this country to appease—great blocks of good citizens who believe differently than we do about this conflict. Neutrality is best, Your Eminence, especially since Franco holds the initiative. And that means we go along with the President on non-intervention. Can we get this thing moving now?"

"All right, Arthur, all right," Ronan complied with a pout. "You always seem to have the practical diplomatic solution with that Teutonic mind of yours. The Irish, you know, used to run the American Church until you came along."

There was subdued laughter at this, and even Cardinal Wagner chuckled.

"I don't run the American Church, Harry," he said amiably. "The Holy Spirit runs it. You know that."

"Yes, yes, I know," Ronan said with droll reluctance. "But what do these young fellows think over there? They must have some ideas. How about an opinion from them? After all, they're going to be running things when we go along."

"An excellent idea," Bishop Bannon said.

"Indeed," Cardinal Wagner said. "Well, we can't have too much discussion on it. We've got to get over to see the President. There's the new Coadjutor Bishop of Harbourton. What about it, Bishop Lambert?"

All eyes were on Bob Lambert now, and he responded to the occasion with cool, unrattled grace.

"Thank you, Your Eminence," he said. "I like the general policy fine. It is certainly realistic. I wonder if we couldn't push it a little further and organize more material unofficial support for Franco. After all, he is our modern crusader over there. And a devout Catholic, too, I am informed. Why couldn't our home folks give him the same support they gave the Allies during World War I: food baskets, clothing, money, creature comforts for the soldiers? We could organize such a program in the parishes, parochial schools, and colleges."

"Yes, why not?" Ronan asked. "I like the attitude of this young man."

Cardinal Wagner blanched a little. "Our modern crusader!" Lambert had touched on one of his pet peeves—Franco's authoritarianism and his chumminess with the tyrants Hitler and Mussolini.

Arthur glanced at Vincent and could see that he was prickling with a desire to speak.

"Well . . ." the Cardinal said with obvious disapproval. "Let's hear from another new bishop on the subject. Gentlemen, this is Auxiliary Bishop-elect Vincent de Paul Whelton, my new vicar-general, who's been doing a splendid job with our young people in the archdiocese. You've perhaps heard by now of the Christian Youth Center. What is your opinion, Bishop Whelton?"

Bishop Whelton. The salutation fell on his ears with the thrill of newness. He arose and cleared his throat.

"Thank you for the opportunity to express myself, Your Eminence," he began. "I suppose a newly elected bishop should be seen and not heard for a while. But here goes.

"I can't quite agree with my esteemed colleague from Harbourton. I think we've got a strange kettle of fish over there. Franco happens to be on our side in his personal religion and support of the Church. But, from what we can gather, he is not the most democratic leader in the world, and he certainly is friendly with those two in Germany and Italy—neither of whom is a bargain where human freedom is concerned. I wish we could say, 'A plague on both their houses,' but we can't! So we have to go along with fascism—a social evil, with its anti-Semitism, ruthless nationalism, and worship of rule by force, which is just as evil as the Communist crowd.

"If we have to go along with him—and it appears we do—let's not sacrifice long-range principle to temporary practical policy. After all, the Church has been persecuted in various countries for centuries and has emerged in those countries stronger than ever. That goes for the Church in Spain also. We may have to go along with Franco, but we don't have to canonize him. That's all I have to say."

There was silence when he had finished and sat down. Mixed approval and yet an arrested atmosphere, almost of admiration.

"You've said a lot," Ronan snorted with a smile that conveyed he was more charmed than irritated. "How long have you been a bishop?"

"Just a few hours," Cardinal Wagner answered with a droll smile.

Bishop Bannon held a look of careful scrutiny in Vincent's direction. "Where have you been hiding him, Your Eminence?" he asked, smiling and turning again to the conference table.

"Oh, he's been around."

Mrs. Rush opened the rear door and paced quickly to Cardinal Wagner's place at the table, whispering anxiously to him.

"Yes, yes," the Cardinal said, nodding, "all right, right away. . . . Gentlemen, give us your okay on the letter to the Holy Father if you will. I'll contact Boston and New York by phone personally. Cardinal Dwyer, I believe, will go along with the majority here. I'll make a special effort to bring Cardinal O'Connell around myself— and so will Bishop Bannon," he said gently, firmly. "There's a police escort waiting for us downstairs to take us to the President. We've got to go—now!"

Bishop Bannon asked for and received a favorable vote from the group of cardinals and bishops.

"Your Eminence," Arthur asked, rising, "does the committee want a press release prepared on this meeting?"

"No publicity, Arthur. That was all decided this morning. Arthur, by the way—my opinionated nephew," he said, tossing his hand at *The Clarion* editor, "has just been made a papal chamberlain. He's done some consistently good work for us over the years in the Catholic press here."

More nods of approval and kindly smiles as Arthur blushed and acknowledged.

Bishop Lambert was at the conference table, chatting with Cardinal Ronan now, having left the sofa without comment after the exchange between him and Vincent.

"You're to come with me in my car, Bishop Whelton," the Cardinal said. "Arthur, you go on ahead in a cab. The press will be there, and do what you can to steer things."

"Yes, Your Eminence," Arthur said, hurrying to the back room with Vincent for the Cardinal's coat.

"You didn't give your blessing to Bishop Lambert," Arthur said with a grim smile.

"I noticed he ran away. Perhaps later on."

"I'll take one, Your Excellency," Arthur said, kneeling.

Bishop Whelton gave him his blessing in the name of the Trinity and then added, "I honestly don't think I'd be doing this if it weren't for you."

"You would have made it anyway," Arthur said, rising. "In fact, I think you'd go a lot farther if I weren't around at all."

He handed Vincent the Cardinal's coat and hat after helping him on with his own.

"Now you're the highest-ranking coat-holder I know," Arthur said.

Vincent swung at his shoulder and missed.

"Get on over there to F.D.R. and cut the bull," he said.

CHAPTER XXXIV

Art for Father Art's Sake!

ON THE sidewalk in front of the Senate Hotel, Tony remembered the extra copies of the speech he had ordered mimeographed at the office. He'd go down there now, get the extra speeches, and put in a call to Tommy Naski, who would be anxiously awaiting an okay on the Monsignor's appearance. But what news? Tony didn't know himself and wouldn't until Monsignor Wagner called.

At least he could tell Naski the speech was ready and the likelihood was, according to *The Clarion* editor, that the Cardinal would let Monsignor Vincent talk. He could tell him, too, that the Monsignor might be a bishop-elect by the time he got out to Stockyards Hall, and that would be a considerable lion to parade before the delegates.

On the street floor of the CYC his attention was caught by the sight of an unusual number of people, in festive mood, moving among the bookshelves of Watch and Pray, the combination library and bookstore which Sophie Narleski conducted under the auspices of the CYC. The self-conscious name of the bookstore had been wished on Sophie by a colleague who had more influence with the Monsignor than she had. Sophie now comically referred to the name of the bookstore as "Stop, Look and Listen."

Through the bright, wide windows he could see a number of well-dressed people balancing cups and saucers and plates of cake in their hands and eying a series of oil paintings which were hung on the bookshelf ends and along the walls.

Standing in the middle of the floor, chaffering and gesticulating to the ancient librarian who was her co-worker—a Miss Brigetta O'Laughlin—was Sophie herself. She was dressed in a dark blue cocktail dress, but the angling and swaying of her big, bony body as she talked gave Tony the impression that she might just as well be in the stripping room out at the Roma plant preaching the gospel of unionism to any and all who would listen.

Tony pulled his hat down over his eyes and quickened his pace through the common foyer, where the staircase led up to the CYC offices on the second floor. But Sophie, even in the midst of a complicated discussion, was all eyes.

"Tony, Tony," she called, waving wildly and rushing to the door of the bookshop. Out into the foyer she charged, taking him by the arm. "Tony, how are you?" she asked ebulliently. "I know the Monsignor's terribly busy and won't be here, but you've got to come in and say hello—at least for a minute."

"All right, Sophie. Just for a minute. I've got to get out to Stockyards Hall and line up things for the Monsignor's speech. What's going on? What's all this? It's all so gay, so arty here."

"We're having an exhibit of modern Christian art," Sophie said proudly. "Didn't you read my memo?"

"No, I'm sorry, I didn't, Sophie. I've been helping Naski out at the convention the last several days and I've hardly looked at my mail."

"Come on in in back first," Sophie said gleefully. "I want to hear all the dirt, all of it. I'm starved for gossip, simply starved. And old lady O'Laughlin is driving me right out of my mind. She's got a real bug on the Oblates—the Third Order of Benedictines for lay people, you know. They're coming through here all the time. And *I* have to wait on them while Brigetta holds court—tea, hotel rooms, special books at extra discounts—she's driving me out of my mind!"

Tony found himself laughing as Sophie led him around behind the stacks, away from the guests, to a small secluded room where she made up invoices, packaged up books, and frequently had herself a quiet cup of coffee.

"Sit down, sit down," she said. "One cup of coffee and there's some cake I snitched from up front." She poured him a cup of coffee from a small aluminum pot. "Here now, drink this. And don't think I'm down on the Benedictines too much. It's just Brigetta—she's actually psychopathic on the subject. She forgets we have to please the Jesuits, Franciscans, and all the others. They buy books, too, and they stop in Lakeport between trains, just like the men in those little black hoods.

"But tell me, tell me," she said with her indefatigable ebullience, "what's what, who's who? What's this we hear about the Monsignor? Pretty soon the purple? Tell me, Tony, or I'll never consent to marry you in my whole life. Tell me . . ."

Tony laughed again. Sophie was good for the soul. She could bring merriment to any atmosphere, and it was always good and unselfish.

"It looks good, Sophie," he said seriously. "I just left Monsignor Vincent and Father Arthur. Arthur thinks it has come through. We just may have a bishop in the family."

"Thanks be to God!" Sophie said. "Oh, this is wonderful, wonderful. Oh, I'll let Brigetta put her Benedictine friends up in my apartment for a week if this is true. I'll move out and let her load the place up! Oh, Tony, Tony . . ."

"Yup," Tony said. "And the Cardinal's going to take him along to see the President this morning, I think. And then of course there's this big labor thing this afternoon."

"Oh, day of days!" Sophie said. "Wait'll Lucy hears about all this. She'll have kittens right on the spot!"

"Now tell me—and I've got to go," Tony said. "Who's the painter? Who painted all this stuff? What's it all about?"

"You'll never guess," Sophie said in more sober tones, looking at him shrewdly. "It's the Venezzia girl—Rosa. She's back from Italy with all these religious paintings and a few others besides. Father Arthur called me and asked if we'd give her an exhibit. Brigetta, who's quite an expert on religious art, and I looked them over, and here they are! She's a very gifted girl, very gifted indeed. I didn't think old Venezzia had it in him!" she concluded with a flash of Rabelaisian drollery.

Tony smiled thinly. Rosa back after all these years. She had refused to see him after the strike and had gone away, leaving a dull ache that had finally mellowed and dissolved. Even now the sudden awareness of her return, of her presence outside in the bookstore, aroused no disturbance in him. It had been just one of those flaring, tempestuous affairs without any hand holds of continuity to keep it going. Religion, he knew, from her devotion to Father Arthur, was the big thing in her life. Freedom—whatever that was—was the big thing in his.

"How is she?" he asked coolly. "What's she look like now? She was a real classy dame when I knew her. She roomed at Mother Wagner's while I was there, you know."

"I know," Sophie said meaningfully, raising her eyebrows slightly. "I know you liked her, Tony, we all knew," she added gently. "We know she liked you, too. But let me prepare you—you'll never know her—she's so changed. She went into a convent in Italy—some order that takes widows. They let her paint and teach, which she did. But she left; she settled some things within her, I guess, and then picked up and came back here.

"She still looks like a nun: straight hair, no powder or lipstick, no fancy furs or exotic jewelry. She's made up with her father, too. The old tyrant is getting along in years and she can see, as we can, that he's made some restitution out at the plant there."

"I wish her well," Tony said with a sigh. "But now I've really got to go, Sophie."

"That's the spirit, Tony," Sophie said, taking him by the arm as they walked out to the front of the store. "Father Arthur wants to get her to teach art here in the adult center. What do you think?"

Tony smiled and shook his head, knowing Sophie was feeling him out. "You kill me," he said, squeezing her arm. "All this lightheaded pretense about gossip and things, and yet there's always a method in your madness. If you're asking me, I think she'd do a terrifically fine job. And that's Lucy's department, anyhow. I have nothing to say about it."

"Lucy wanted to know," Sophie said apologetically. "Your attitude will make her very happy."

"Lucy happy, you happy, Rosa happy," Tony said with mock impatience. "Look, there's only one person around here I have to make happy, and you know who he is! Get it?"

"I get it," Sophie said. "What about Joan Linehan?"

"Never mind. She's got the district attorney to fight her battles."

"That's right," Sophie said, running her voice up the scale a few notes.

"You never give up, do you?" Tony said pleasantly. Joan was always there, it seemed. Why didn't she get married? The D.A. would be governor or a federal judge eventually. Yet she wouldn't even accept an engagement ring from him, and he was stronger for her than ever.

"Joan never gives up either," Sophie said almost defiantly. "But come and say hello all around quickly and you can go. We have to have some kind of executive here from the center. It will look bad otherwise."

"All right, Sophie, all right. You goddamn women will run this place right into the ground."

"Shhhhhhh!" Sophie said. "Here comes Brigetta! She's going to pounce right on you."

Tony withdrew from drollery, seeing the pert old wren of a librarian descending upon him. He recalled that she had been the Monsignor's librarian for many years in her little hole-in-the-wall shop on the sixth floor of the building. He had seen her at a distance, and even close up at affairs where she had paid her devoirs to the Monsignor. But he had always shied away from her chaffering intensity about "liturgical" books and "the devout life" and the names who were important in the Catholic field of books. Names that were unknown in the labor movement or the liberal movement—names that, nonetheless, he knew were important in their own field, a big field, the field of the human spirit. But she was a favorite of Monsignor Vincent de Paul Whelton, and, over and above the respect he owed her because of her age and sex, he owed her his loyalty and courtesy because of the Monsignor.

"Mr. Lorenzo, Mr. Lorenzo!" she exclaimed in a shrill yet well-modulated voice. "I did hope you would drop by." She clasped his hand. "I just knew the Monsignor would send someone important," she said, glaring at Sophie and still holding onto his hand. "And, sure enough, he sent us his executive assistant. He's such a considerate man—born to be a bishop, I always tell him. He's an Oblate, you know, a member of the Third Order of St. Benedict. Do you know about this tremendous spiritual force among the laity, Mr. Lorenzo?"

"I've heard about it." He had seen her literature plastered all over the adult education bulletin boards. "We must be 'content with circumstances,' mustn't we?"

"Oh!" she exclaimed, taking his arm with the graciousness of a duchess. "You've read my notices. Come now, you must meet Miss Venezzia and take a look at her work."

Tony threw a wink at Sophie, who shrugged her shoulders and rolled her eyeballs.

"What's this? What's this?" Tony asked, bringing the gnomish old lady to a halt in front of a large oil painting of a back yard with lines of pure-white wash billowing in the wind against a bright blue sky.

"That's something from what I call Rosa's 'Lakeport Period,'" Brigetta said. "Isn't it remarkable? Of all her non-religious pieces, this one stands out."

"It's the color blending and the sheer realism," Tony said, stormed for the first time with emotion. "Is it for sale? I like it very much!"

"Of course it's for sale," the old lady shrilled authoritatively. "She wants fifty dollars for it, but—well, perhaps she might let it go for less. No one is buying today. Just drinking coffee and talking."

"I'd like to buy it—now, at the listed price," Tony said, taking out his checkbook. "I'd like to make a present of it to the boss. I think he'd like it. It would remind him of his old neighborhood. And it is so well done."

"Of course, of course," Brigetta said excitedly. "Sophie, Sophie," she commanded, "bring a receipt book immediately!"

Sophie brought the receipt book with an amused docility. Tony now knew what she was up against, and nothing could be done about it short of a happy death for the old lady.

He gave them the check, and they pasted a little label marked "Sold" on the bottom panel of the frame.

While Brigetta directed Sophie's movements in imperious tones, Tony took a good look at some of the religious paintings on either side of the back-yard scene. There were portraits of nuns in various stages of age and repose, lights and shadows, with the emphasis on the latter, and over all a nice communication of a focused characteristic in the face of each—the sensual contesting with the ascetic, and each a mirror, it seemed to him, of Rosa's spiritual conflict.

There were traditional and interpretive profiles of the saints and two or three madonnas, attractive in color blending if not always in force of personality.

"Now the artist shall meet her patron," Brigetta said. "Come."

Tony threw another wink at Sophie, who seemed ready to run and hide. Brigetta walked ahead, and Tony beckoned to Sophie to follow.

He saw her now against the back wall, surrounded by coffee-sipping guests—students and older devotees of religious art, they seemed, some of whom he had observed hurrying determinedly about the corridors on adult education nights.

"Rosa, Rosa," Brigetta called, riding roughshod over her dilettante admirers. "Mr. Lorenzo, our executive director, is here representing the Monsignor. And—we have a surprise for you—he has purchased your back-yard painting for our beloved director-general!"

Their eyes met now, and between them passed a world of things no other could ever understand. She was calm, she was cold, with a restraint built up by years of long preparation for this meeting, but it was all there nonetheless.

"How are you, Rosa?" he asked warmly, ignoring the blandishments of Brigetta and extending his hand.

"I'm fine, Tony," she said softly. "It's been a long time."

"Indeed it has," he said, feeling the limpness, the coldness. "But I see you haven't been idle."

"Nor have you. I'm so happy you bought the painting."

"For the Monsignor," he said.

"Yes," she said, "for the Monsignor."

"You two know each other!" Brigetta exclaimed, crestfallen but courteous.

"Yes," Rosa said, "I've known Tony for some years. We are mutual friends of Father Wagner."

"Yes, yes, I see," Brigetta said without enthusiasm.

"Well, I really must go now," Tony said. "The Monsignor is speaking at the labor convention, and I've got to do a little advance work for him."

"Yes, of course," Rosa said. She seemed so drab, so unadorned, and yet the same. A flicker of passion stirred in him and died as she looked at him so oddly, coldly, almost with hatred and a little disgust, it seemed. He had the awful feeling she believed he had befouled and betrayed her. He wanted to get away from that look, as far away as he could.

"It's a fascinating show," he said to Sophie. "I hope you sell them all."

"I'm so glad you came in," she said. "You brought some life into the whole thing, even if it was hard on you," she concluded sympathetically.

"Thanks, Sophie. I'm glad I saw the exhibit, really glad. Good-by now."

She watched him go, happy in her heart that he had gone through it all—now—today.

CHAPTER XXXV

Paving the Way

In a large conference room at Stockyards Hall big Tom Naski, president of the Allied Paper Workers International Union, sat at a paper-strewn table with the union's executive committee and thrashed out final details of their move to join the new giant industrial federation, the Central Labor Alliance.

Perspiring and in his shirt sleeves, pressed and tensed on all sides with the encyclopedic detail of the convention, the indefatigable political maneuvering, the overeating and late-night drinking sessions, he glanced balefully at the three dissenting members of the committee and quickly determined his strategy.

He had to get a favorable vote on the recommendation to affiliate with CLA fast. It was lunch time now; the President's motorcade would drive through the stockyards at one-thirty, and the vital afternoon session, in which the convention would vote on affiliation, would begin at two. The Monsignor was scheduled to speak, along with the well-known president of CLA, burly, beetle-browed Edward L. Ferris, leader of the United Underground Workers across the nation.

He'd heard from Tony, who was on his way out, but he still didn't have the final word, which must come from Father Wagner. The press boys were clamoring for advances on the speeches—Ferris's speech they had, but Monsignor Whelton's he could not release, nor would he have it until Tony arrived.

He ticked off the votes he had at the table: Ike Jansen from Oregon and the West Coast Division was against affiliation, so was Mrs. Tilly Veblen, president of the Southern Division from Nashville,

Tennessee. Billy Conlon from New York, president of the Eastern Division, would go with him. That was two against two.

The tie-breaker was Jakie Wolfson, vice-president-at-large, the former sign painter whom Naski had moved up in the union for just such eventualities as this. But Wolfson was, for the first time, being very stubborn. He had fought privately with Naski against affiliation, fearing a loss of identity of the union and also possessed of a deep personal dislike of Bible-quoting Edward L. Ferris, who was reputed to be secretly anti-Semitic in spite of his high-sounding liberal phrases. Naski had been diplomatic about Wolfson's objections for a while, even his resentment of the invitation extended to Monsignor Whelton as a featured speaker.

"Why not invite a rabbi and a Protestant minister as well?" he had importuned in front of Mrs. Veblen, a devout Baptist, and Jansen, a Lutheran.

"Go get them for me!" Naski had exploded. "We'll feature them every bit as strongly as Monsignor Whelton. But there isn't one—Catholic, Protestant, or Jew—of any stature that will come out here and break the ice. They think we're a bunch of goddamn Communists and they're afraid of what the Lakeport *Herald* will say. It's as simple as that."

"Then why have anybody at all?" Mrs. Veblen had remonstrated. "It will only create ill feeling."

"There'll be no ill feeling," Naski had said with a sigh. "Monsignor Whelton is one of the best-loved men in this community—by all faiths. Now I'm not going to discuss this any further. Your convention committee invited him to speak and you'll just have to take it or leave it."

"I'll leave it," was Mrs. Veblen's reply. "And I'm against affiliation one hundred per cent."

"Me, too," said Ike Jansen.

"And me." Wolfson rolled his cigar around in his mouth.

"This is ridiculous!" Billy Conlon said. "Monsignor Whelton runs a youth and adult education center which has fought racial and religious discrimination for years. He's a big man, loved by all who love people. And, furthermore, we've got to affiliate—we need the strength of union to help organize the unorganized—especially in areas like yours, Mrs. Veblen, and yours too, Ike. You know it's slow going in the South and the Northwest—we need help all around, and Mr. Ferris can get it for us on a clean, democratic basis."

"He's anti-Semitic," Wolfson said.

"That's a goddamn lie!" Conlon shouted.

"There are no Jewish officers in his entire international," Wolfson insisted.

"You're too goddamn sensitive," Conlon said. "And you do your own people a disservice by being that touchy. There are no Jews in official capacity in the Underground Workers because there just aren't enough of them to get together within the outfit and push for their own. What the hell do you think Ferris is running—the garment workers?

"And another thing—Naski is right on this religious-speaker deal. You and Mrs. Veblen go out and get a minister and a rabbi of some prominence to come in here and talk to us! Go ahead! The welcome mat is out! I don't mean to say they're insincere or anything like that. But they're cautious—they're waiting for somebody to break the ice. And they know that if they come in here and talk the Lakeport *Herald* will roast their tails off. The *Herald* will do the same to Monsignor Whelton if the Cardinal allows him to speak. Just wait and see."

"Jesus Christ!" Naski said, glaring at Wolfson. "You better find out what they're paying sign painters these days. I've had enough of this malarky!"

Watching them now, delaying the vote as each sullenly surveyed the other and Wolfson stood fast, chewing on his cigar, Naski decided to make his move at the first opportunity.

There was a knock on the conference door.

"Come in," he snapped.

Bicky Brown attending his first international convention as business agent of Local 397 at the Roma plant, popped his head in and flashed his scimitar smile.

"Hey, boss, Father Wagner's on the phone."

"Good," Tommy said, relieved. "I'll take it in the other room. Let's take a ten-minute break," he added. "I'm sure we can get together. Jakie, I want to see you in that little office in five minutes." He glanced meaningfully at Bicky.

"What for?" Jakie asked arrogantly. "You know where I stand."

"Look, Jakie," Naski said, coloring. "It's my privilege as president of this international union to ask for a private conference with any member. You are a member of this international. I want to see you out in that little room there in five minutes."

Jakie glared his defiance, then went slack and sullen.

Naski turned to Bicky as he approached the door. "Bicky, you stay here. If Mr. Wolfson needs reminding, I want you to remind him that he has an appointment with me in five minutes. Is that understood?"

"Right, boss," Bicky said, tightening his jaw muscles.

Naski hurried out the door.

"Great, great," he said on the phone after hearing all the news from Father Wagner. "We came up with a barrel of gold—a priest was good enough, but already he's a bishop. I knew he'd make it, we all did! Great, great, absolutely great!

"Oh—Bishop-elect, we call him. I get it. And he's in with all those big shots visiting the President, eh? . . . Buffet lunch with F.D.R.? That's the pay-off. First thing I'll do is ask him for his autograph. . . .

"Yes, do you think we should have a press conference? . . . Oh, I see, the Cardinal! . . . Just let the speech do the talking. All right, that will be good. But I've got to tell you what's been going on here. We've had some opposition in the Executive Committee. . . . Yeh, a Catholic priest—they're touchy. They're touchy about Ferris too. Don't want to affiliate. But we will—everything will go off all right, I'll see to that! Don't bother the Mon—I mean the Bishop-elect— with it. We'll have him meet Ferris and they can go up to the platform together. . . . Real big stuff, right, Father? . . . What? I should call you 'Monsignor'? How come? . . . Wonderful! Congratulations, Monsignor, congratulations! I'm astounded. I thought they'd send you to Leavenworth first! Oh, the two of you—a bishop and a monsignor! Great, great, absolutely great. . . .

"No, Lorenzo isn't here yet. He'll be here any minute. . . .Yeh, the mimeographed copies. Yeh, he's got them. . . . We'll give them right out to the press. . . . Wait'll you get here. . . . Okay, Father— I mean, Monsignor—I don't know what the hell to call you guys. Don't acquire any more titles until this convention is over. You'll have me tongue-tied. . . . Yeh, Bishop Whelton will be along in the presidential motorcade. Okay, okay . . . Yes, good-by, Father—I mean Monsignor. Oh hell, good-by and thanks, thanks an awful lot. . . ."

Naski hung up the phone and mused a minute, his big, strong face touched with a little awe and wonderment. That man a bishop! It couldn't happen to a nicer guy. And F.D.R. in town the same day, the convention going on, and this man who fought for social justice for Negroes and labor unions a bishop, a Catholic bishop, appointed by the Pope to a hierarchical group not very famous for public espousal of social justice. They were more famous for coming out against sin—and, yes, communism. You could always take the episcopal whip to that sore horse and sound as if you were really leading a crusade. But unions, and the public espousal of their cause —most of the cardinals and bishops wore a union label on their B.V.D.s, but that was it!

However, things were getting better. Whelton's appointment was maybe a sign of change. If he spoke out—he would do so, Naski had to admit, with the Cardinal's obvious approval—others would. Maybe more young bishops, monsignori, and priests would spring up across the land and take up the oratorical cudgels for organized labor and a liberal social-action program.

"Give them a chance," he whispered to himself, rubbing his chin and reminding himself to sneak in a shave before the afternoon session began. "Give them a chance. After all, labor has just come into its national and formal recognition with the advent of Roosevelt and the Wagner Act. They'll begin to understand we're not all Communists and racketeers. Give them a chance, they'll understand . . ."

There was a knock on the door.

"Come in, come in," Naski said gruffly.

Jakie Wolfson came in, sullenly chewing on a cigar, followed by Bicky Brown, who took a position like a plain-clothes man at the door.

"Sit down, Jakie. What I've got to say to you won't take long."

"Well, make it fast, Tommy," Jakie said tentatively, half defiant, half anxious. "We gotta vote on that measure. The others are waiting."

"I'll make you fast," Naski said grimly. "I made you and I'll unmake you right now! Bicky, lock that door."

Bicky turned the key in the door ominously.

"Hey, wait a minute," Jakie said. "I got my rights under the international constitution."

"You'll get your rights," Naski said. "Bicky, pick up that phone. Call Mack Carver at the gate and tell him to have a cab standing by, ready to go."

"Right, Tommy," Bicky said, picking up the phone.

"Now, Jakie, here's the story. There are big things happening today. Monsignor Whelton's been made a bishop—he's coming here in the President's motorcade—and last, but not least, we've got to affiliate with CLA for our own good and the good of the entire labor movement. Right now you're holding all this up by siding with those others in there."

Jakie took the cigar out of his mouth, pursed his lips, felt the winds of personal trouble blowing, and decided to try to salvage the situation without complete loss to his own position.

"I'm not that hard to get along with," he said. "We been pals a long time, Tommy. I'll go along with you if you'll promise to support me for re-election as vice-president."

Naski brought his open palm down on the surface of a small, rude writing table.

"I'll go along with you on *nothing*, you kike sonofabitch. You're a disgrace to your race. Now listen! There's a cab waiting downstairs and it's for you. But you're gonna need some help to get into it." He stood up, took off his suit coat, rolled up his sleeves. "If you don't go in there and vote for recommendation on affiliation immediately," he said, sticking his malletlike fist under Jakie's nose, "I'm gonna knock the living shit out of you right here and now. That's it! Which will it be?"

"Now, look, take it easy," Jakie said as the cigar trembled right out of his hand. "No trouble, Tommy, see? I'm whicha, I always was. I'll go in there right now. Let's get this thing goin', Tommy, let's get movin'. I'm whicha see, I'm whicha!"

"You better be," Naski said, letting out a gust of air and rolling down his sleeves. "Get the hell back in there—you go with him, Bicky. And another thing, if you say one more goddamn word against Bishop Whelton, I'll skin you alive. Clear?"

"Okay, okay, Tommy," Jakie said, rising and picking up his cigar. "It's all set. I'm sorry, I'm whicha, I tell you. . . ."

"*Screw!*" Naski said, thumbing vigorously at the door.

After they left, Naski slumped into a chair with a tension-breaking sigh. "Jesus," he said, talking aloud to himself, "all this energy to squash a fly. But there's so much at stake, so much . . ."

He picked up the phone and asked for Mack Carver at the gate.

"Mack, cancel that cab, I won't need it now. . . . Any sign of Lorenzo? . . . Oh, good, put him on . . .

"Tony, for Christ sake, where you been? . . . You got the speeches? . . . Good . . . Yeh, I talked to Father Wagner. He's a monsignor now. How about that? . . . Yeh, it's a fact, and the other guy a bishop. . . . Yeh, it came through. Great, huh?

"Look, I've got to wrap up this vote for recommendation right away. I'll meet you in the little anteroom here. Don't give anything out until Wagner gets here. . . . Yeh, if you meet any of the press boys, tell them you've got a big story for them. . . . Yeh, he'll be here in about fifteen minutes. They can wait that long. . . . Okay? . . . Yeh . . . Yeh . . . Oh, that little bastard Wolfson gave me some trouble. . . . Yeh, imagine! He's cooked now, all through. . . . How'd you like to be an international vice-president? . . . Yeh, yeh, I'll see you."

He slipped on his coat, pushed a comb through his hair with two quick strokes, tightened his tie knot, and went out of the room.

"Titular Bishop of where?" the reporter asked Monsignor Wagner.

They were in the press room, and the feeling ran high because the news was running high. The presidential motorcade was soon to arrive in its swing through the stockyards and the south side of Lakeport.

After all, that was where the Democratic votes were concentrated, among the industrial workers, the Negroes, the railroads, the little people who made things go. The Lakeport Demo pols knew this and had persuaded the President to make this one big swing, which would touch the west side, too, before boarding his train for Washington. The money people were on the north side, and if some were for F.D.R., fine, but time was of the essence and you had to go where the votes were now and always.

Arthur looked at Dick Rakow, sharp-eyed, supercilious political editor of the Lakeport *Herald*, who was writing things down on the back of a mimeographed copy of the Bishop's speech. Around him, alertly, the others scribbled, too; Paul Aiken from the small but vigorous Lakeport *Daily Eagle*, Bill Johnson from the AP, Rolly Baldwin from UP, a man from the INS, and an urbane individual named Morehouse from the weekly news magazine *Event*.

"He's been appointed Titular Bishop of St. Perpetua's Church in Rome," Arthur explained. "Every bishop has a titular church in Rome, but Bishop Whelton, you understand, is now Auxiliary Bishop of Lakeport and vicar-general of the archdiocese under the Cardinal Archbishop."

"I see," Rakow said. Then with an insinuating smile which served well his publisher, Admiral Flagpost: "Now tell me, or tell us, why this speech here? How come? Is this official? Did the Cardinal send him here? I mean to say, does this mean that the Cardinal endorses the Paper Workers' probable affiliation with the pinko Central Labor Alliance?"

Arthur paused, suppressing his personal reaction to the "pinko" tag which was so sweepingly typical of the *Herald*. He wrinkled his brow and framed a careful answer.

"The Bishop-elect was invited to address the convention by the union's speakers' committee. He was invited to talk on any subject he chose," Arthur said slowly, carefully. "He decided to comment on the papal encyclical *Quadragesimo Anno*, which is really a freshening and bringing up to date of Pope Leo's earlier *Rerum Novarum*. He asked the Cardinal Archbishop's permission to give the speech and the request was granted. But—and let me emphasize this—his presence here constitutes no official endorsement on the Cardinal's part of his or any of the proceedings of this convention."

"Good, good," Paul Aiken of the *Eagle* said, writing rapidly with the rest.

Rakow of the *Herald* still had a smirk on his face.

"You mean to tell me, Monsignor," he began knowingly, "that on this precedent-setting occasion—the first time a major clergyman has formally addressed an international labor convention—we are to attach no special significance to the speech?"

"I've told you the situation exactly as it is," Arthur said. "You have a copy of the speech and you can read it and interpret it. There's nothing hidden, nothing ulterior in all this."

"But you've just told us he's coming out here in the presidential motorcade," Rakow pursued. "Isn't that significant?"

"He's with the Cardinal Archbishop, Mr. Rakow," Arthur said with a sigh. "And I'm sure you know that the Cardinal has never had any self-consciousness and reticence about his admiration and respect for F.D.R."

"That's true, that's true," Rakow said in a cold, insinuating tone of voice. "Our paper has appreciated his sincerity, and there is no greater admirer of the Cardinal than Admiral Flagpost, despite their difference of political views. May I ask you this, then?" he continued. "Will the Bishop make any ad-lib remarks over and above the text?"

"I can't give you an absolute answer on a question like that," Arthur said, glancing at his watch and looking over at Naski and Lorenzo, who were standing by restlessly at the press-room door. "As far as I know, he'll stick to the text. But that's rather an unfair question. Any speaker has a right to make extra text observations which may be occasioned by unforeseeable circumstances at a gathering like this."

"Thank you, Monsignor," Rakow said. "That's all for me."

"Anything else, fellows?" Arthur asked. "I've got to get downstairs. You too."

"Will the Bishop make any statements for the press before or after the speech?" Johnson of the AP asked.

"No, definitely no statements," Arthur said quickly. "I can tell you that. There'll be no statements. We'll stand on the text."

"One question, if you will," asked Morehouse of the news weekly *Event*. "Is there any rapport on the speeches or personally between Edward L. Ferris and Bishop Whelton?"

Arthur smiled at that one.

"They both quote the Bible occasionally, I'd say," he quipped. "But actually they've never laid eyes on each other."

There was general laughter at this sally, and it wrapped the conference up nicely.

"That's right, boys," Naski interjected. "Come on, let's get going or we'll miss the President. He's due right now!"

"Thanks a lot, fellows," Monsignor Wagner said. "I hope I've given you some help."

"You have, you have," white-haired Paul Aiken said cordially. He was the senior political correspondent in the press band. "Thank you, Monsignor, thank you very much."

CHAPTER XXXVI

The Big Pitch

THE President is coming!

This great, electric fact supercharged the atmosphere and the crowds of delegates and stockyard workers who thronged the corrals and cobbled alleys around the stockyard gate and all along the way to the wide pavilion outside Stockyards Hall.

Coolidge, Hoover, F.D.R.—what difference did the name make? What difference did it make whether you were Democrat, Republican, Socialist, or Independent! When the President is coming, you feel the spine-tingling thrill of something great happening to you, something solemn and something gay, something of bugles and drums, something of Old Glory breathing gently or flapping wildly in the breeze.

Bishop-elect Whelton, sitting beside the Cardinal's chauffeur in the long, black Packard, sensed all this as the presidential motorcade swung toward the stockyard gates amid the cheers and halloos of hundreds who lined the tenement-cliffed south-side streets.

The Cardinal's car, fourth in line behind the mayor and the governor, wheeled on slowly, majestically, as His Eminence and Auxiliary Bishop Bannon of Boston, seated in the parlor-car atmosphere of the rear cushions gazed quietly out the windows at the demonstrations and spoke in calm phrases which were at variance with the whooping jubilation along the presidential route.

Vincent glanced at his watch. He had ten minutes to get upstairs and run over his speech before going on. Arthur said he'd wait inside the gate for him. He'd better make his excuses as soon as they pulled up and get in there.

"Your Eminence," he said, "I've got to get on up in there. Will you and Bishop Bannon excuse me?"

"Yes, of course," the Cardinal said as they slowed to a halt.

"Awfully good to have been with you, Bishop Bannon," Vincent said.

"My pleasure, Bishop," Bannon said, appraising him shrewdly. This was no underling, he knew; this was someone moving up—a heavyweight in the making. "Do a good job in there."

"I'll try, sir."

"Go, now," the Cardinal said, beckoning him away casually. "Give it to them straight—don't talk too long—get in and get out—it's always best."

"Yes, Your Eminence," he said, turning around and looking at the brooding, hawklike face. "Thank you for everything, sir."

"Go on, go on," the Cardinal said.

He opened the door and hurried out into the crowd, stretching his neck for a glimpse of the main entrance as the crowd surged and roared against the cordons of police around the President.

F.D.R. was calling for silence now, and over the boiling crowd a simmering calm descended.

Pushing through the crowd, he caught snatches of the mellifluous voice bringing them all into intimate contact, or so it seemed, with his deepest thoughts and feelings.

Vincent paused near the entrance, caught with the others in the web of casual yet deep-striking eloquence as the President leaned on the shoulder of a stalwart secret-service man and gave out with the fevers and the hopes of America's promise. This he did for three minutes, which seemed like an eternity of eloquence—the interdependence of all our workers . . . the need for organization to protect individual rights . . . the recognition that our civilization cannot endure unless we, as individuals, realize our personal responsibility to and dependence upon the rest of the world . . .

The remarks were over and the President, amid great tumult, was shaking hands with various personages who were torpedoed through the crowd by flying squads of police. Vincent caught a glimpse of big Tom Naski in that group.

Heady with the whole wild atmosphere, and feeling the throbs of the Paper Workers' brass band which was playing "Hail to the

Chief," he pushed his way through to the main entrance and saw Arthur waving vigorously at him near a side door.

"Hurry up, hurry up," Arthur said, grabbing him by the elbow. "I've got to get you upstairs before the newspaper boys spot you. They're dying to ask you questions."

"Gosh," Vincent said, stepping into a little elevator with Arthur, "how can I make a speech after all this!"

"You can, you can," Arthur said.

In a small waiting room behind the auditorium stage Bishop Whelton took one last look at his speech.

"What's this, what's this?" he asked Arthur, looking up suddenly from page nine of the manuscript. "I didn't notice this before. 'As soon as feasible, enlightened management should consider a form of annual wage guarantee which would carry workers through slack periods of work and production, keep them working the year round, sustain their morale, and firmly stabilize labor-management relations in a radiant atmosphere of confidence and trust.' Wow! Where did you get that one?"

"Just get up there and say it, Bishop," Arthur said. "That's the semi-private thinking of the academic labor crowd and of some of the big union leaders like Murray and Ferris. Just speak it out loud and strong at the proper moment. You'll hit every front page in America with it, and it will catapult you into the forefront as a progressive spokesman for organized labor. That's the big pitch, my dear Bishop-elect, and you've got to make it, as high and as hard as any fast ball you ever threw at St. Brendan's College!"

"Why, it's tremendous!" Vincent said, for the first time drawing himself up to a new height of dignity and authority, which Arthur immediately noticed. "It's simply a tremendous concept!"

"Now you're talking like a bishop," Arthur said with a smile.

Bishop Whelton read intently now, boring through the final pages, his face touched with deep seriousness.

"Splendid, splendid," he said when he had finished. "Closing with the Webster thing is fine. I do think, on second thought, that guaranteed-wage thing is a long way off, but the idea is so good, there's no harm in proposing it at all."

"That's right," Arthur said."

Someone knocked briskly at the door.

"There they are now. Ready?" Arthur asked.

"Yes, yes indeed," Vincent said, feeling the butterflies flutter in his stomach.

"Come in, come in," Arthur said.

Naski entered the room, followed by Lorenzo, who was remonstrating with several reporters.

"You'll have to ask him yourself, fellows," Lorenzo said. "No, you can't come in here now. He's going right up to the platform."

He closed the door with some difficulty.

"Your Excellency," Naski said. "My heartiest congratulations and good wishes."

"Bishop—Bishop Whelton," Tony said, "we're all so happy for you."

"Thank you, Tony," he said, grabbing his shoulder with the pitching grip. "You're all part of it," he said with a generous sigh. "You've all helped to bring it about."

"Let's get on in, Your Excellency," Naski said. "Mr. Ferris is already on the platform, and we'll get right under way."

"Splendid," the Bishop said in a lordly baritone as Arthur smiled again at the readiness with which he had donned the episcopal manner.

"Now remember, Bishop," Arthur said, "no statements. Tell them it's all in the text."

"Yes, yes, of course. Let's get along."

They followed Naski and Lorenzo out into the backstage area. Dick Rakow from the *Herald* thrust his way through to the Bishop.

"Bishop Whelton," he began quickly before anyone could interpose, "would you mind saying something about that set annual wage idea? Have you talked to Phil Murray or any of that pinko group around the Labor Department?"

"I've talked to no one," the Bishop said politely but tersely. "I just thought it was a good idea to throw out for discussion."

"Thank you, thank you, Bishop," Rakow said. "May I ask if the Cardinal has read this text?"

"Sorry, no statements," Arthur said quickly. "Gentlemen, you'll have to go with the text."

"That's correct, gentlemen," Bishop Whelton said as they approached the stage, where a great hubbub of delegates could be heard settling into their chairs while the union band played "The Sidewalks of New York."

"You'd think you were Al Smith," Arthur whispered as they walked onto the stage amid the lilting New York City anthem.

The Bishop chuckled richly and with a new episcopal depth. "There's only one Al Smith," he added a little pompously.

Naski hurried ahead to the right of the rostrum, where he confronted a mountain of a middle-aged man with a thick unmanageable crop of black hair and coal-black piercing eyes.

"Mr. Ferris," Naski said, stretching out his arm gracefully, "I want you to meet our other guest speaker, the brand-new Auxiliary Bishop of Lakeport, Most Reverend Vincent de Paul Whelton."

"I've heard about you, Reverend," he said gruffly, extending a black, hairy hand. "It is indeed a great privilege to meet a man of God on the platform of organized labor."

"I've heard much more about you," the Bishop said, taking his hand, while the Lakeport delegates, spotting his familiar figure, began to whoop it up. "You've done so much for your people, so very, very much."

"It needed to be done, Reverend, and it would have been done eventually anyhow. My humble people who work underground like moles were bound to win because of their meekness." He paused now, looked right at and through the Bishop, and said without a shred of self-consciousness " 'Blessed are the meek, for they shall inherit the earth.' "

"Yes, and the labor movement, if I may say so," the Bishop said, responding alertly to the biblical wave length, "deserves an epithet from those same Beatitudes: 'Blessed are they that suffer for justice' sake, for theirs is the kingdom of heaven.' "

Ferris nodded his huge head, peering intently out of his cage of hair. "On earth, Reverend."

"Yes, of course," the Bishop said politely and without challenging the meaning of the exchange, "the kingdom of heaven on earth—within certain bounds, of course. I mean there will always be sickness and trouble of one kind or another—death and taxes, as it were."

"Yes, of course," Ferris said. "Won't you be seated?"

They sat down beside each other, and Naski took over the huge gavel at the rostrum.

"The Bishop sure had to wriggle out of that one," Lorenzo whispered to Arthur from a row of folding chairs behind the front line of guests and international officers.

"Yes," Arthur said, "but you'd think he'd been a bishop for quite a while—to hear him talk. That's what cripples me. He's taken to this thing so fast."

Tony put his head in his hands and suppressed a fit of laughter.

"Wonderful, wonderful!" was all he could concede in the suppression of his mirth.

Naski called the convention to order, and some deep-chested wife of a local union president favored the assemblage with a loud but faltering rendition of "The Star-Spangled Banner."

The report of the Executive Committee secretary, Billy Conlon, was called for, and Billy arose, sawed off and nervous, sensing the glares of Mrs. Veblen and Ike Jansen behind him, knowing he had to tuck in the recommendation of affiliation during his report.

Mrs. Veblen looked down the line of seats at the Bishop, in a rage of frustration and anger at the turn of the vote. Wolfson, that worm, she thought, sold us out. She glanced about for him. He was nowhere to be seen, having ducked out to the Cowpoke Inn, where he could have a few drinks, chew a few cigars, and stay out of the line of fire.

Her eyes returned to the Bishop and were aglow with hatred of the power and panoply of Rome. They've been trying to control the human race for hundreds of years, she thought, and now they're sticking their fat, jeweled fingers into organized labor. Power attracts power. They always go where the power is, the fat, smug devils. And that big turk Naski is their agent, that big, slobbering brute!

Her inner hatred and frustration were consuming her. She dug her nails deep into her black leather bag, leaving indentures there.

"You all right, Tilly?" Ike Jansen asked, seeing the blanch of her cheeks and fearing she was about to faint.

"Yes," she said through clenched teeth. "I was just looking at that big Roman pig over there. Naski had no right to do it, no right at all. Why don't they stay where they belong?"

"Easy now, easy now, Tilly," Ike said. "It was all done by invitation and by democratic process, we have to admit that. It ain't right to favor them over everybody else, but it's done and we have to go along."

"We have to go along with that other black monster, too," she said, nodding at Ferris.

"Yes, yes, I know," Ike said, recoiling from her vehemence, "but maybe it's for the best; things always happen for the best."

"Oooh," she said in one venomous spate of rage, "I'd just like to go over there and spit in his face. He has no business here, no business at all."

"Easy, Tilly, easy now. I'll get you a glass of water."

He leaned over to the rostrum for the water pitcher and a glass.

Billy Conlon, reading now the vote on the recommendation for affiliation with CLA, stopped suddenly and looked at Ike apprehensively.

"Go right ahead, Billy," Ike said reassuringly. "I just want some water for Mrs. Veblen."

"Oh, oh, fine," Billy said, resuming the reading of the resolution.

He read on quickly, concluding the report. Naski was ready at the rostrum as Billy finished. He called and gaveled immediately for a vote of acceptance, and all those in favor said "Aye" with a deafening roar. There was only one "No!" and it was uttered in a shrill, defiant feminine voice directly behind him.

"The ayes have it," Naski said, glancing over his shoulder somewhat sheepishly at the glaring lady vice-president. "It is a vote and so ordered," he concluded, turning again to the convention assembled.

Now he introduced the craggy leader of the Underground Workers, who took his place at the rostrum with an austere, shuffling dignity amid a wild demonstration of music, snake-dancing, and a great show of signs for CLA affiliation among the several hundred delegates.

Bishop Whelton took this opportunity to lean back and catch Arthur's ear.

"Who is that woman down on the left there?" he asked. "She's obviously very hostile to Naski and the whole idea. In fact, I've felt the sting of a few scorching looks myself. Who is she? What is she about?"

"She's the opposition," Arthur whispered. "Naski told me she's on the Executive Board and she's against both affiliation and *you!*"

"Me!" the Bishop snorted. "I never laid eyes on the good woman in my life."

"Well, she's agin you—anything in a Roman collar. I'll keep an eye on her while you're talking. We don't want another Abraham Lincoln operation!"

"Stop the comedy," the Bishop said, irked. "What shall I do? This business is unnerving."

"Just ignore her," Arthur said. "Do you see who's sitting beside her now?"

Naski had sat down beside Mrs. Veblen, folding his arms grimly like a great Praetorian Guard.

"Oh, that's fine, fine," the Bishop said, relieved.

Edward L. Ferris was calling for unity now in gruff, slow tones. "Labor is coming of age . . . we must meet this great challenge of our maturity with unity and co-ordination for the common good, not only of our members, but of all America. . . ."

He talked on in this vein for about ten minutes, urging immediate affiliation, and both Arthur and the newspapermen seated in the orchestra pit were playing their waiting game of alertness for the inevitable quotation from the Old or New Testament.

"And when we march together . . . stand together, fight together . . . for the abundant life . . ."

"Everybody's using that Roosevelt word 'together,'" Arthur whispered to the Bishop. "It's in your speech, too, you'll notice."

"Splendid," the Bishop whispered in elation, and there was the texture of the episcopal in the way he pronounced "splendid," Arthur noticed. "It's the type and kind of word that arouses a general emotional reaction in one's audience," he added.

"Yes," Arthur countered, "but watch out for that 'type and kind' —I warned you, remember?"

"Yes, I know . . ." the Bishop whispered impatiently.

"So that when your single democratic will declares for affiliation with the Central Labor Alliance today," Ferris gruffed on, "truly can we all say together in the words of Ruth, who waited patiently amid the alien corn, 'Whither thou goest, I will go . . . thy people shall be my people, and thy God my God!'"

He bowed his great, hair-wild head as if in prayer, lifted it slowly amid a powerful dramatic silence in the hall. Then he waved his horny right hand and stepped back from the rostrum, releasing a crescendo of applause, stamping, and whistling, deafening in its impact.

When the demonstration had ceased, Naski stepped jubilantly to the rostrum, knowing that affiliation was practically assured. He glanced over at Bishop Whelton, who simulated dignified calm, looking out at the audience and holding the manila folder lightly on his lap.

He brought the gavel down twice, calling for order and attention.

"Our next distinguished guest speaker . . ." he began, going on to tell them of Bishop Whelton's background of charitable activity in the city, his athletic prowess as a collegian, and now the double

honor that had come to him as Auxiliary Bishop-elect and vicar-
general of the archdiocese.

When he had finished, Vincent walked to the rostrum amid vigorous applause. He spread his speech out on the reading triangle,
slipped on his heavy black tortoise-shell glasses, which gave him a
stern, professorial look, and, clearing his throat, began.

"'Man is born to labor, as the bird to fly . . .'" he said, reading
the words softly yet clearly, holding out the lure of his eloquence
as the delegates leaned forward in their chairs. Louder now, gradually, yet full and richly, he explained his belief that the Popes,
particularly Leo and Pius XI, had laid out a Bill of Rights for labor
which had anticipated the Wagner Act by many years.

"'The rich have their own defenses,'" he cited from Leo, and
then went on, paraphrasing: "Laboring people must seek their
economic strength and security in organization and collective bargaining as you have done and as others are doing across our great industrial nation. . . ."

He talked on, implying his strong approval of their interest in
consolidating their forces with the Central Labor Alliance.

"I have no authority to endorse officially your possible affiliation
with CLA," he said, taking off his glasses and departing from his
text.

Arthur and the others on the platform grew more alert. The Monsignor had not expected an ad-lib sequence this soon.

"But I know that in unity there is strength," he said, turning to
Naski, who was again sitting stolidly beside the ashen Mrs. Veblen.
"And I personally share the confidence of your great President, Mr.
Thomas Naski, in the ability of our distinguished previous speaker,
Mr. Edward L. Ferris, to serve your national interests in a God-
fearing and utterly devoted manner."

He paused, sensing a cloud of approval about to burst but feeling
the need of some kinetic phrase to set off the downpour. He gripped
his glasses in his right hand, pointed them directly at the audience,
and thundered:

"If I were a delegate sitting down there," he began, swinging his
arm and the pointer of his glasses in an arc toward Edward L. Ferris
and Naski, "I know who I would be with up here!"

The cloud broke; the applause mounted and roared for a full
minute as the Bishop nodded sternly in approval.

"My God," Arthur whispered to Tony, "the *Herald* will run us out of town!"

"You taught him all this, now listen! It's great, great!" Tony said, watching the reporters furiously scribbling down the ad-lib endorsement.

Naski was radiant, stamping his feet with approval, and the great shaggy head of Ferris nodded slowly.

The calm again and, with glasses donned, Bishop Whelton resumed the reading of the text, discussing the idea of the assured yearly wage. ". . . a visionary, far-off reality, perhaps, but one which you and the CLA should consider in the planning stages right now," he said, mixing the text with an ad lib. "It's the *type and kind* of idea which it is *stragetically* necessary to execute," he said involuntarily, casting all of Arthur's semantic cautions to the wind, "through some nationwide organization, involving other unions interested in the same ends. Thus the possible intrinsic value to you of affiliation with CLA!" he said, abandoning all practical pretense as to his attitude on affiliation.

He talked on about the fight labor had to make for its integrity when there were no protective laws and cited the Roma dispute and the difficulties attendant upon that bitter episode.

"If ever there was any doubt that the Catholic Church was unsympathetic to the cause of organized labor, it was dispelled once and for all by the statesmanlike action of our great Cardinal Archbishop of Lakeport in throwing his unstinted liberal support to one of your local unions in that agonizing strike. That, my friends, is a matter of record!

"I believe with all my heart and soul that among the ministers and rabbis of the Protestant and Jewish faiths there are forces working strongly in your behalf. For, after all, do we not serve a common God who created all men in his image of dignity and freedom, regardless of race, creed, or color?"

This brought the applause again and softened the anxiety of Monsignor Wagner. Naski smiled appeasingly at Ike Jansen, who nodded benevolently. The big union president's attempt to smile at Mrs. Veblen, using the same wedge of Bishop Whelton's oratory, drew only another glare.

The Bishop rolled on to his conclusion, savoring with keen anticipation the final quote from Daniel Webster.

"In closing, I cite the words of a former great American senator and

Secretary of State who expresses most eloquently the deepest feelings of my heart and those of my Church for organized labor. I quote:

" 'Labor is one of the great elements of society—the great substantial interest of which we all stand. Not feudal service, or predial toil, or the irksome drudgery by one race of mankind subjected, on account of their color, to another; but labor, intelligent, manly, independent, thinking and acting for itself, earning its own wages, accumulating those wages into capital, educating childhood, maintaining worship, claiming the right of the elective franchise, and helping to uphold the great fabric of the state—that is American labor; and all my sympathies are with it, and my voice, till I am dumb, will be for it.' "

He stepped back a little from the platform, gathering his sheets into the manila folder and taking off his glasses.

"God bless every one of you," he said with emphatic finality.

He stood there as the applause and cheers, so generously given by these several hundred delegates, broke around him like an electrical storm. He took the outstretched hands of Tom Naski and Edward L. Ferris, who were immediately by his side. The three clasped hands for the news photographers, who popped and flashed their instruments directly and alertly upon them.

"Fine, fine," Edward L. Ferris said, "a golden tongue indeed."

"Bishop, you were great," Tom Naski said, squeezing his hand until it hurt, "absolutely great!"

"Well, thank you, thank you," the Bishop said. "It's so very easy to talk to this type and kind of an audience."

Arthur and Tony were there beside him, beaming with pride. He acknowledged the applause with several waves of the hand, and it subsided gradually, leaving an atmosphere of electrical warmth throughout the auditorium.

"Your Excellency," Naski asked avidly, "will you be able to stay until we take the formal vote on affiliation? We'd like to give you some refreshments afterward if you could so honor us."

The sage admonition of the Cardinal rang through Vincent's mind like an alarm bell: "Get in and get out."

"Thank you so much, Tom," he said, "but some other time. Monsignor Wagner and I have to look after arrangements for the Cardinal's banquet Saturday night. I hope that you and some of your group will be there."

"We'll be there, Your Excellency," Naski said, "we bought a whole table just to help out."

"Splendid," the Bishop said. "Well, we'd better get along now, Monsignor. Mr. Ferris, Tom, it's been a pleasure."

"It's been more than that for us," Naski said. "Your speech has practically assured us of a favorable vote on affiliation."

"I merely suggested the same," the Bishop said with a roguish smile.

"A potent suggestion indeed," Ferris said. "It's been a privilege, Reverend."

Arthur was inclining his head toward the press section, where several of the boys were making their way to the stage.

"Well, good night, now," the Bishop said.

They started off the stage, occasioning a new burst of applause, scattered but vigorous. The Bishop waved again, loving every second of the limelight.

He had just stepped into the wings behind Tony and Arthur when Mrs. Veblen blocked his path, her face a mask of blanched hatred, her hands on her hips.

"I beg your pardon, madam," Vincent said gently.

"You ought to beg my pardon," she said through taut lips. "And the same to all of us. You have no business here—you—Roman pig!"

Vincent flushed, stunned by the insult, and repeated, trying to move past her:

"I beg your pardon, madam."

With one last focus of hatred she drew back her head and spat upon his cheek.

"You uncouth bitch!" Naski said, moving toward her.

The Bishop stopped him with one powerful thrust of his right arm.

"Madam," he said softly as his temples pounded with barricaded rage. "It is a privilege to endure the same insult that our great Lord and Master underwent for all of us on the way to Calvary almost two thousand years ago. A very good night to you!"

He accepted a handkerchief from the shaking hand of Monsignor Wagner, wiped away the spittle, and walked past her into the wings and down the auditorium stairs.

CHAPTER XXXVII

Tower of Babel

IN THE cab later they rode north along the lake in silence. It was a good calm, too, Arthur sensed, one that came gradually but strongly out of the inner and outer turmoil that had surrounded Bishop-elect Whelton.

The Bishop was reading his breviary and turned, after a while, from the daily text to some familiar section, thumbing the pages calmly, surely.

Arthur had a pretty good hunch as to the specific nature of the Bishop's reading, which a quick glance at the breviary page confirmed. It was the pure lyric of praise, the crystalline canticle uttered in an inspired burst of birdsong by Mary when she had learned she was to be the mother of God:

> My soul doth magnify the Lord
> And my spirit hath rejoiced in God my Saviour! . . .
> For He that is mighty hath done great things to me
> And blessed is His Name . . .

Bishop Whelton read on, seeking peace in one of his most favorite citations. Arthur could see the anxiety and humiliation recede from his features as he read.

> He hath put down the mighty from their seat
> And hath exalted the humble . . .
> He hath filled the hungry with good things,
> And the rich he hath sent away empty . . .

The new papal chamberlain took the over-all hint and slipped his own breviary out of his brief case. He had read about half of his daily hours in the morning, would get some in now, and catch the rest before retiring, like many another priest, with alert glances at his watch.

Thus did two men of God drink of the words of the Holy Spirit amid the purring of the tires along the lakeside boulevard. All the calm after the earsplitting jubilation of the convention, all the putting on of the sweetness of Christ after the spitting hatred of Mrs. Veblen and the ominous clouds of headline print that would surely break out in the Lakeport *Herald.*

"*Ad flumina Babylonum . . .*" Monsignor Arthur read in the great psalm of Jewish exiled loneliness for the mother country. "By the rivers of Babylon, we sat and wept when we remembered Sion . . ."

He read on for several minutes that seemed like a suspension of time. He heard the snap of the Bishop's breviary closing and promptly closed his own as Vincent spoke for the first time since they had entered the cab.

"'He hath put down the mighty from their seat . . .'" the Bishop said with a budding, kindly smile.

Arthur reached over and grabbed him by the elbow, relieved.

"Yeh," Arthur said. "He and Mrs. Veblen, eh?"

"My God," the Bishop said, "that woman must be a mental case. Imagine—all that hatred for us—like a powder keg!"

"She's apparently been storing that up for years. I'm glad, at least, that the reporters weren't on hand."

"Do you think she'll go around blatting about it to the press?" Vincent asked.

"I doubt it very much. She's probably overwhelmed with remorse right now. That will be her next violent reaction, I'm sure," Arthur said. "Besides, if she did sound off, you'd come out very well. That little other-cheek remark you made would look awfully good in print."

"Never mind," the Bishop said impatiently. "We've set enough type for one day!"

"Speaking of print," Arthur said, "we ought to stop and get a paper. The early editions of the evening *Herald* should be hitting the streets soon," he concluded, glancing at his watch and noting it was a quarter of four.

"We'll see them later," the Bishop said with a sigh. "We'll ask the gentlemen to drive right on by the city. We'll go out to the seminary grounds and have a look at the new building."

"Fine," Arthur said. "How is it coming? I haven't been out there for weeks. I hear the Cardinal has them working night and day so that things will be ready for the dedication Sunday."

"Yes, the Cardinal is determined to dedicate the seminary on the golden anniversary of his priesthood, which, you know, is that day. They've got the floodlights on at night and they're spreading that pink Italian stucco all over the place."

"Think they'll make it?"

"Yes," the Bishop sighed. "Yet I fear His Eminence will hear the last few bangs of the hammer while he's reciting the dedication blessing."

"Tower of Babel?" Arthur suggested with a smile.

The Bishop chuckled. "There's more to that statement than you might think. Those Italian artisans who work with the stucco don't speak much English, and between them and the Irish hod carriers there's often been something less than communication. In any case, we'll have a look," the Bishop concluded. "Driver, keep right on going north on the drive and take us out to the new Wagner Seminary."

"Yes, Father," the driver said.

Walking up the ramp of Union Station toward the incoming taxi stand, the young Coadjutor Bishop of Harbourton was a tall, dark study in episcopal dignity. He had the tickets and compartment reservations on the Washington Special for Archbishop Peruzzi and Bishop Bannon, who were soon to arrive.

To his right he could hear the chime of parking trains. They were rolling slowly in the cool darkness of the passenger platforms, and their creaking and chiming made a sad, discordant symphony which evoked a touch of melancholy in him.

Why must he and Vin Whelton always end up at swords' points? They were always on opposite sides of the fence, he reflected with a sigh. Could it be because of the Cardinal's nephew? Arthur was always the gadfly, always suspicious of the conservative point of view —and always the red mantle of the Cardinal's power loomed in the background as a resource of refuge and protection for his aggressive attitudes.

Actually he admired Vin Whelton—his generosity of heart, eloquent tongue, his courage and indefatigability. He had admired these qualities even when they were seminarians, but there was always the "best friend" Arthur between them.

Well, he thought, long may he reign, but the Cardinal could not live forever. Then we shall see what Arthur will do on his own, then we shall see! God forgive me for feeling this way, but I do, I do.

He had noticed, too, the sinking vitality of Cardinal Wagner. The spirit was as fervid as ever, the mind still honed to razor sharpness. But the deepening circles under the eyes, the slight shortness of breath, and the slowing of physical movement—these were apparent to all.

He thought with glowing warmth of his growing friendship with the Apostolic Delegate, Archbishop Peruzzi. They had gone bird watching together in Lakeport Park while Bishop Bannon had joined Cardinal Wagner in the presidential motorcade.

They had seen a red-winged blackbird amid a horde of English sparrows, and that was about all. But the walk around Hancock Lagoon in the exhilarating spring air had been a pleasant one.

Archbishop Peruzzi had also observed the Cardinal's declining health and had mentioned that His Eminence had been to a heart specialist recently.

"The appointment of young Whelton as vicar-general is perhaps significant," Peruzzi had said. "As you know, the vicar-general becomes administrator of the archdiocese upon the demise, God forbid in this instance, of the Ordinary."

"Does such a designation have much to do with the practical naming of a successor?" Bishop Lambert had asked in the easy intimacy of their stroll.

"Eet does and eet doesn't," the Apostolic Delegate said with the beginning of a shrewd smile. "There are no royal families in the hierarchy, you know. Such a decision must come from the Holy Father on the recommendation of the principal American bishops. Yet I cannot but approve of the Cardinal's good judgment in the case of young Whelton," he continued, twisting a little wire of envy in the breast of Lambert. "He has perhaps too much a mind of his own for such a young bishop and is unduly influenced by the—shall we call them liberal elements?—but his ability and eloquence and drive are what we need among these rising young bishops here in America."

Bishop Lambert nodded and was silent as they continued their walk. The Apostolic Delegate looked at him with the same shrewd smile.

"I have observed similar qualities of achievement in the new Coadjutor Bishop of Harbourton," he said, touching Lambert affectionately on the shoulder and kindling a laugh which grew steadily and mutually between them.

"One red-winged blackbird and a thousand sparrows!" the Archbishop had quipped as they crossed from the park toward the Senate Hotel. "Such is the human equation also."

It was then that Peruzzi had asked him to pick up the tickets at the railroad station for Bishop Bannon and himself.

The relentless hawking of a newsboy on the taxi ramp lanced now into Bishop Lambert's consciousness. What was that he was saying?

"LAKEPORT HERALD! THREE-STAR EXTRA! CATHOLIC BISHOP ENDORSES LABOR ALLIANCE! READ ALL ABOUT IT!"

With a glance at the empty cab entrance, Bishop Lambert hurried over to the newsboy and bought a paper.

"Thank yuh, Father," the newsboy said. "YUXTREE! YUXTREE! LAKEPORT HERALD," he caterwauled as others converged on him for the first afternoon edition. "READ ALL ABOUT IT! WELL-KNOWN LAKEPORT CLERGYMAN SAYS POPE SUPPORTS LABOR UNIONS!"

Bishop Lambert took one look at the front page, saw a three-column picture of Whelton joining hands with Ferris and Naski, folded the paper, and hurried back to his post at the station entrance.

Well, now, he thought, shaking his head, pumping an emotion of righteousness up and over his twinges of envy. Well, now . . . he thought as Cardinal Wagner's black Packard swung into the ramp entrance from the street, bearing Peruzzi and Bannon.

He called two redcaps and motioned them over to the slowing Packard. They aided the chauffeur in removing the bags from the trunk of the limousine, and Lambert opened the rear door, greeting the prelates.

"Everything's ready, Your Excellencies. I have the tickets and reservations right here," he said, patting his inside coat pocket. "May I suggest we'd better step along? You have only ten minutes until train time."

"Yes, yes, of course, Bishop," Bannon said, alighting and straight-

ening out the folds of his smartly cut black topcoat. Peruzzi was next,
and they hurried into the station as the newsboy sounded off again.

"YUXTREE, YUXTREE! LAKEPORT HERALD! NEW CATHOLIC BISHOP
SUPPORTS PINKO LABOR ALLIANCE. READ ALL ABOUT IT!"

"What's this, what's this?" Bishop Bannon said, pausing.

"Yes, what ees he saying?" Peruzzi asked anxiously.

"It's Bishop Whelton's speech at Stockyards Hall," Bishop Lambert
said. "I think the *Herald* is giving the speech a hard time."

"Do you have a copy of the paper?" Bishop Bannon said tersely.

"Yes, Your Excellency. Right here."

"Well, bring it along with you," Bishop Bannon said, moving
again as the Apostolic Delegate nodded sternly. "We'll have a look
at it on the train."

"Yes, Your Excellency," Lambert said, turning to the redcaps, who
had paused also. "Right this way, boys. Track 14, the Washington
Special."

They moved down the ramp and across the station floor in silence,
their ears fused into one as the mocking caterwaul of the newsboy
sounded clearly behind them in the middle distance:

"YUXTRA, YUXTRA! NEW LAKEPORT BISHOP ENDORSES LEFT-WING
UNIONS! READ ALL ABOUT IT! HEY, LAKEPORT HERALD OUT! YUXTRA!"

CHAPTER XXXVIII

Onion Soup

"THAT'S right, Mr. Krivitz," Bishop Whelton said into the telephone. "That's the right inscription on the watch. I'll read it back to you so there won't be any mistakes. Ready?

"'Ad Multos Annos on Your Golden Anniversary as a Priest of God.' Right? . . . Now, underneath: 'From Your Devoted Clergy of the Lakeport Archdiocese,' Right? . . . Then today's date—abbreviated. Right?

"That's what you have; that's precisely what Monsignor Wagner gave you on paper. Good . . . It'll be ready by four this afternoon? . . . Good. I'll pick it up—yes. . . . Oh yes, Mr. Krivitz, it's got to be ready at four. The banquet is tonight, sir. Yes, at the armory. . . .

"Why silver? Well, His Eminence expressed a preference for silver, Mr. Krivitz. . . . Waterproof, yes, it had to be waterproof. . . . Yes, I know it's a golden anniversary, Mr. Krivitz," Vincent concluded with a touch of impatience. "It's just that His Eminence wants a silver watch. . . . Yes, I'll be over with Monsignor Wagner at four. . . . Yes, thank you very much. Good-by."

Well, he thought with a sigh, the watch is ready. And I'm ready —for the cleaner's!

He could not resist a smile, thinking of Mr. Krivitz's bewilderment concerning the silver watch on the golden anniversary. He was the most exclusive jeweler in town, but certainly his curiosity should have been moderated by the fact that he was selling, without discount, a six-hundred-dollar Swiss watch.

Vincent, who had not seen the Cardinal since the Stockyards

speech, had got the word on the watch from his old seminary professor and sponsor, Father Carney, who lived across the hall from
His Eminence.

The new Bishop had sought out Father Carney after the latter's
early Mass at the cathedral and chatted with him in the vestry,
gently laying his vestments away in the deep, aromatic cedar
drawers. It was two days following the labor-convention speech and
he had the double anxiety of wanting to divine the Cardinal's reaction to all the strident publicity in the *Herald* and to determine
the suitability of the gold watch he and Arthur had ordered with
money collected from the pastors and chancery priests.

Arthur had said the Cardinal definitely needed a new watch and
they had ordered a gold one from Mr. Krivitz for Saturday delivery.

"No, not gold," Father Carney had said, slowly, shatteringly.

"But it's his golden anniversary, Father," Vincent had said.

"Throw your right arm out as if you were making a gesture up
on the platform," Father Carney said with sly mirth. "Throw your
arm out for your old speech teacher," he added.

Vincent did so, revealing the shiny gold band of his watch.

"Now do you see why His Eminence prefers silver?"

"I see," Vincent said. "But he's a cardinal—people are prepared
to accept a little ostentation from a man in his position."

"Are they?" Father Carney said firmly. "You get him a silver watch.
And you might get yourself one later on. People notice everything—
especially those not of our Faith. Nobody knows that better than
the Cardinal."

"All right, Father," Vincent said with a slight shrug of his shoulders.
"I'll change the order today."

"Make it a waterproof watch while you're at it—if you want a
further suggestion."

"Waterproof?"

"Waterproof. The Cardinal is never late for an appointment. And
he often wears his watch when he's in the tub."

Vincent chuckled at that one.

"You know all about him, don't you?"

"I've been around him off and on for many years," Father Carney
said with a steady gaze out of watery blue eyes. "And I know something about you too. You've certainly made me feel a little better,
the way you've come along. I haven't forgotten that you should
have gone to Rome on that scholarship, you know. And it was your

involvement with me and my missionary work that put the clincher to you."

"I never looked at it that way at all."

"I know, I know," Father Carney said, sitting on a hard wooden chair near a small porcelain sink used for rinsing out the cruets before and after filling them with altar wine.

Vincent, grateful that Father Carney had taken his respite before going up to breakfast, waited for the old seminary professor to speak, hoping he would reflect something of the aftermath of the convention publicity.

There had been a seeming conspiracy of silence regarding comment on the speech scareheads among the clergy, but Vincent had received very complimentary phone calls from the mayor and District Attorney Ryan, both of them avid New Dealers. Arthur had reported great enthusiasm among the labor union and Lakeport University set—but only silence thus far from the man who had sent him up on that platform—the Cardinal. Admiral Flagpost himself had refrained from formal editorial comment, perhaps out of deference to his friendship for His Eminence. On the other hand, the liberal Democratic tabloid, the *Daily Eagle*, had applauded the endorsement of the Central Labor Alliance and hailed Vincent's call for a fixed annual wage as "epoch-making."

"Sit down here a minute, Bishop," Father Carney said, motioning Vincent to a nearby wooden stool in a disarming tone of voice, both good-humored and reverent. "You're getting to be quite a 'bleeding heart,' aren't you? You always were, in a way," he mused, "always were. The mission out in Splinterville while you were a seminarian, the state prison, the youth center here. But I didn't think you had national and even global aspirations."

"I have no aspirations like that, Father."

"I didn't mean it quite that way," the old priest said with affectionate concern. "I think you're fulfilling something or other in yourself by speaking out the way you do—especially on that liberal line—which is quite unusual for a Catholic priest. You know. You'd probably be much more popular if you'd swing along with the extreme right wing the way that feller up in Detroit does. He goes after 'the money-changers in the temple' and gives the Jewish financiers a little jab once in a while."

"I couldn't do that," Vincent said. "I think you'll agree, Father, it's a most unchristian and uncharitable tack."

"It is, it is," Father Carney said, "and I'm not suggesting that you do anything like that. I don't have any patience with anyone, priest or layman, who stirs up racial hatred. But the American Church is still strongly conservative, strongly right-wing. You're heading for trouble backing these labor boys—even if they're right, even if they're one hundred per cent right!"

"I certainly wouldn't make any statements without the Cardinal's tacit approval."

"I know that, I understand," Father Carney said with a hasty note of confidence. "And the Cardinal knows it too."

He paused, sensing Vincent's growing anxiety.

"He liked your speech, by the way," the priest said with a smile. "He talked to me about it the next morning. He was in bed—he's slowing down a little, you know. I brought him a hot Irish whiskey and he had the papers there in his lap—the *Herald*, the *Eagle*. He thought you went a little too far, but he blamed that on your enthusiasm. He's all for those unions getting together. He thinks you're right in emphasizing the spirit of the Holy Father's encyclicals. He likes that idea of a guaranteed annual wage, and I think he's really proud that one of his own priests stood up there and championed it."

"I'm so glad," Vincent said with relief. "I was worried, I was really worried."

"Well, you should be. You should be worried and you should be more careful what you say the next time he lets you speak. He could have done all that himself, you know, but he wanted you to do it. You know what he called Hitler—and it hit the world-wide press. He called him 'an Austrian paper hanger,' and the world listened and applauded. But he's the Cardinal, don't forget that. He's the Archbishop of a great archdiocese. He's undoubtedly the greatest churchman in America. I mean he can get away with being outspoken much easier than you. He knows that—that's why he's worried. But he likes what you said and he'll back you to the hilt."

"God bless him," Vincent said.

"Yup, he'll back you. I know it because I heard him doing so."

"Yes?" Vincent asked.

"Yes, and keep it under your hat," Father Carney said, rising. "Bishop Bannon called him from Washington. Said he and the Apostolic Delegate were upset about your remarks. Thought they were a little brash for a fledgling auxiliary bishop. Thought they'd give people the impression the Church was taking sides."

"The Church is taking sides," Vincent said. "It always has."

"Yes, but not usually on the side of the Socialists. We make haste slowly, remember?"

"I remember," Vincent said, laughing as he thought of his first pastor on the south side. "Have you forgotten I received my baptism of fire under Vinegar Jack Regan?"

"I haven't forgotten," the priest said with a rather mellow smile. "He was good for you, Vincent. If he hadn't stuck the gad in you, you might still be out there running a parish. And not a bad life at all for any priest, may I remind you, not a bad life at all."

"They're the backbone of the Church, those guys."

"Well, I'm going up to breakfast now," Father Carney said with a sigh. "Hobble on up—a little gruel, a little coffee, and my old black pipe. That's all I need."

He turned to go, and Vincent asked him a question.

"Father, please tell me if you will what the Cardinal said to Bishop Bannon?"

Father Carney paused at the narrow staircase leading up to the cathedral rectory, and with his eyes twinkling through narrowing lids declared:

"His Excellency, the junior Auxiliary Bishop of Lakeport, desires to know what His Eminence, the Cardinal Archbishop of Lakeport, said to the astute and powerful Auxiliary of Boston. Quoth he to he, Your Grace, as follows, but in much nicer words: M—Y—O—B. Good morning, Bishop Whelton," he said, curtsying like a leprechaun and shuffling slowly up the stairs.

Bishop Whelton chuckled in his office now, recalling the wise old drollery of Father Carney, the majestic loyalty of the Cardinal. He simply could not tell Mr. Krivitz the real reason for the specification of the silver watch. It might be misunderstood.

He took off his glasses and glanced around his CYC office. What next? Yes, final arrangements with the caterer. Joan was to take care of that. He'd call her in now.

His glance swept the wall to his left, noticing a change. There was something missing. Yes, that big, garish reproduction of the Sacred Heart which Joan had picked up for him at some second-hand sale years ago. It was a horrible likeness of the Lord and yet a familiar old friend. Where was it? Out for reframing perhaps.

He leaned to his right and pressed the desk buzzer.

Joan appeared, smiling, always avid, anxious to serve. Out in the reception room he heard the sound of voices—Tony, Monsignor Wagner, others, female voices . . . What were they doing out there? He was supposed to meet Arthur at Krivitz Jewelry later.

"Oh, we've got visitors?" the Bishop said tentatively. "Do I hear the Monsignor out there?"

"Yes," Joan said with winsome evasiveness, closing the door behind her. "Now about the caterer, Your Excellency . . ."

"Yes," the Bishop said with mock glumness, "the caterer indeed!"

"Well, Mr. O'Laughlin said the only change on the menu he gave you will be French onion soup instead of bouillon. He said he doesn't have enough bouillon stock on hand for such a large number, but plenty of onion soup."

"Plenty of onion soup, eh? What's going to be on the printed menu?"

"Mr. O'Laughlin says it appears as 'Soupe du Jour.'"

"Oh, fine, fine," the Bishop said. "They're cute, those caterers." He glanced up meaningfully at the empty wall space. "Now, tell me, where's my picture—the Sacred Heart thing—what's happened to it?"

"Just a minute," Joan said, opening the door to the reception room.

In they came with solemn gaiety—Rosa Venezzia, Lucy Smith, Sophie Narleski, and behind them Tony and the Monsignor bearing a large painting covered with gray cheesecloth.

"Make way for the episcopal gift horses!" Arthur said.

"Well," the Bishop said. "What's all this?"

"You're to be present at an unveiling, Your Excellency," Tony said.

"Splendid," Vincent said, going along with it.

"Right over here," Joan directed, pointing to the wall where a square dust line and picture hook invited the cortege to cover a certain glaring nakedness.

They hung the picture carefully, making certain the cheesecloth stayed in place.

"Now, will the artist step over here?" Monsignor Wagner said, smiling at the shy, severely dressed Venezzia girl.

She took her place to the right of the painting, smiling hesitantly but fixing her beautiful dark eyes, with the whites still so prominent, on the Bishop. There was pride in her aspect now, pride that her work should be bought and given to this prominent man, pride that it might hang in his office. But the apprehension lingered within her too. Perhaps Tony would have been wiser to have selected one of her religious things. There was a portrait of St. Vincent de Paul hanging with the others down in the bookstore. She had heard that the Bishop had been named by his mother after that French minister to the lowly.

"Now, Mr. Lorenzo," Arthur said, "the floor is yours."

"Your Excellency," Tony began eagerly, "the painting you are about to see is perhaps the best work of Miss Rosa Venezzia, whose interesting exhibit is hanging in our bookstore downstairs. She has graciously consented to unveil her painting for you. We are presenting it to you, all of us here at the center, in honor of your well-deserved appointment to the American hierarchy—and we—well—we hope you like it and we hope it will always remind you of our love and admiration for you."

The Bishop's eyes were misty now as Tony nodded to Rosa, who carefully removed the cheesecloth from the painting, revealing the rickety grays of the back porches, the billowing whites and pennantry of hung-out laundry, the soaring dome of blue sky.

"Well," the Bishop exclaimed graciously, "it's lovely—it's the west side! Congratulations, my dear," he said to Rosa, putting on his glasses and moving closer to the painting. "What do you call it?"

"Just 'Monday Morning'!" she said.

"I was hoping you'd see the west side in it," Tony said.

"You ought to," Arthur said. "It's my mother's back yard."

"Of course, of course," the Bishop said, up close now and squinting. "It's a wonderful job, Miss Venezzia; such warmth and—such rude reality."

"I'm glad you like her work," Arthur said. "Tony is thinking of hiring her as your art director here at the center. Sophie and Lucy think it would be a good idea also."

The Bishop looked closely at Rosa for perhaps the first time and was taken with the comeliness all packaged up in a strange, burning austerity.

He took her hand, patting it in a fatherly way.

"I think it would be a splendid idea, Miss Venezzia," he said. "When would you be available?"

"I'm available now, Your Excellency," Rosa said with rather vigorous coyness. "I've discussed an outline of lectures and workshop sessions with Lucy, and I can go to work any time."

"That's right, Your Excellency," Lucy said. "She's all ready to go."

"Splendid." The Bishop turned to Tony. "Tony, get her an office somewhere. Do you have one available?"

"We may be able to set up a workshop for her in the front left corner of the gym," Tony explained. "She and Lucy have been looking it over. But that will take a few weeks. In the meantime we can fix her up a desk in Lucy's office."

"No, no, that will never do," the Bishop said impatiently. "Lucy needs more elbow room than that, and so does Miss Venezzia. Put her in one of those offices in back there," he continued, pointing to the hallway which led out of his office to the private back entrance.

Joan looked at Tony hurriedly and with a little alarm. She would practically be in the Bishop's private office!

"Okay," Tony said somewhat coolly. "Then we'll go ahead with the workshop project and get her out where there's some light and space.

"You'll be right in with the Bishop here for a while," he said gallantly to Rosa. "But you can close your door and have as much privacy as you like. We're all a big team here, all one big family."

"I shall try to be a dutiful daughter in this new family," Rosa said with gentle winsomeness. "Thank you so much, Your Excellency."

Sophie Narleski rolled her eyes at Lucy.

"Happy to have you aboard, as we used to say at Pondview Naval Station, eh, Tony?" the Bishop said merrily, punching Tony on the biceps.

"That's right, Bishop."

"Monsignor, we've got to go—it's almost four and the jeweler is waiting—not to mention the caterer and all those last-minute things at the armory."

"Yes, we'd better get along," Arthur said. "Rosa," he continued, walking over to her and taking her hand. "You're all set now. You've landed the big boss as a patron, and he's the one, he's really the man to have on your side."

"I'm so happy," Rosa said through a delicious tear-mist. "And you, Monsignor, how lovely of you to share your friends with me!"

Tony glanced at the painting apprehensively. It had all been his idea—buying the painting for the Bishop, that is. But it had not worked out as simply as he had expected.

There was the painting. If it could only talk, the laundry would not seem so fresh and sweet. "Monday Morning," yes, and Monday night, too, love around the painting, under it, above it, in the brown-stone house; Rosa and Tony blended with the oils, Chanel No. 5, and the heady musk of a woman before, during, after love.

Now she would be in the Bishop's office, the ex-nun, the ex-love—cold, cold, cold . . .

"All right," the Bishop said, "thank you all. We've got to go."

They said their goodbys and filed out, leaving the Bishop with the Monsignor and Joan.

"Come, we'll go out the back way here," the Bishop said, picking up the snub black homburg he had bought for the Cardinal's dinner.

"Joan," he called over his shoulder with a droll expression on his face, "I'm very fond of the fancy new painting, but . . ." He pointed to an empty wall space to the right of his desk. "Get hold of my old friend, the Sacred Heart, and hang Him right up there!"

A sea of black, silver, and white as the band played "The Blue Danube."

The armory was almost filled now, the wide, gray hall festooned to its girders with the symbols of the land and the Church—crosses, stars, and stripes mixing the sometimes unmixable, the Church and the state. The followers of the Prince of Peace, breaking bread to-gether in the Hall of War.

A rising tide of Roman collars and tuxedos filled the tables. Cigar smoke billowed; conversation mounted to a vast bee-hum as a bat-talion of waiters moved swiftly to the initial task of dishing out the onion soup.

"They're playing the Cardinal's favorite song," Arthur said, stand-ing with Vincent to the right of the head table, where the Cardinal would enter from the street. "Yum-dum-da-da," he hummed merrily. "Da-da-da-dum."

"What's that smell?" the Bishop asked, crinkling his nose.

"That's the onion soup."

"Does it usually smell that strong?"

"I guess so," Arthur said. "Remember—they make it with onions."

"I suppose so, but it smells exceptionally strong. Remind me to pass up the soup."

"Say, what were you talking to Mr. Krivitz about while I was looking at the watch? What was that big book he was showing you?" Arthur asked.

"He was showing me his Cantabridgia University yearbook, Class of

'97," the Bishop explained. "He's quite a liberal, you know. Said he was very much interested in my speech at the labor convention and asked me all about the center."

"He's got loads of money," Arthur said. "He might send you over a donation."

"Well, I don't know about that. In case you've forgotten, we handed him a check for six hundred dollars for the watch. Anyway, it was very interesting."

"What was—his picture in the yearbook?"

"Yes," the Bishop said. "His was the only picture on the page. The page was unnumbered, and there were perforations in near the binding so that you could tear it out if you didn't like Jews. That's what he told me and that's what he showed me. How do you like that?"

"Gosh, no!" Arthur said in some amazement.

"Gosh, yes. But he says things have changed since then. It's hard to believe, though, isn't it? A great university like that! He said he didn't mind all that too much, because he knew he was part of the wearing-down process—part of the drip against the stone that would wear down the prejudice. He said Jews know how to handle that. They persistently, consciously go where they're not wanted."

"Catholics have been up against the same type of thing for centuries," Arthur said. "In Boston the Yankees used to put up signs around their property saying 'Dogs and Irish keep out!' They probably still feel the same way, but the Irish have outbred them and outvoted them!"

"Say, there's our former roommate," Vincent said.

"Where?"

"Sitting at the head table with old Bishop Sliney."

They both waved at Bishop Lambert, who smiled at them cordially.

"Don't forget now!" Bishop Whelton said. "Cardinal Ronan on the right, Cardinal Burke on the left."

"Check. Where's the watch?"

"It's in the little compartment underneath the rostrum. Here comes the Cardinal now!"

Vincent gave the high sign to the orchestra leader, who had been on the alert. He cut short the playing of "The Blue Danube" and raised his baton. He brought it down quickly, and the band broke into the pompous yet majestic strains of the well-known Holy Name march written by William Cardinal O'Connell of Boston.

"O Holy Name of majesty and power . . ." the band played as Vincent and Arthur hurried to meet the Cardinal and the entire assemblage arose to its feet with vigorous applause. "O Holy Name, of God's own Son, In every joy and every weary hour, Be Thou our strength until life's war is won . . ."

The Cardinal moved in slowly, tall, lean, still the courteous embodiment of a medieval prince, the circles under his eyes deeper, his breathing shorter, as if he had been exerting himself, but still the prince, taking the genuine wave of affectionate applause lightly, waving at old friends and smiling along the way to the head table.

"Right this way, Your Eminence," Vincent said, helping him up to the dais at the head table.

"Oh, it's you, eh? My proud 'bleeding heart,'" he said, turning to Cardinals Ronan and Burke, who carried their great flesh genially along behind him. "We should have given your text to Roosevelt and let him deliver the speech. It sounded like it came out of the same office."

"Quite an inaugural message for a brand-new bishop," Cardinal Burke said with a twinkle in his eyes.

"You keep on talking like that," Cardinal Ronan said with glum good nature, "and your superior here won't be able to raise a nickel."

Bishop Whelton accepted it all with a good-natured smile, assisting each to the platform.

"Fierce is the fight," the band played on, "for God and the right," echoing the pompous tones to which a thousand parochial-school bands across the nation had marched, "Sweet Name of Jesus, in Thee is our might . . ."

When the cardinals were seated, the other head-table guests took their places—the mayor, the police commissioner, the adjutant general representing the governor, Nino Venezzia, old Father Carney, and, down at the end, the Cardinal's droll classmate Vinegar Jack Regan.

The Cardinal beckoned to Vincent.

"Tell Vinegar Jack to move down here next to Cardinal Burke," he whispered. "That's Bishop O'Hara's seat, and he won't be able to make it. He's still under the weather. Regan will tell a few of his stories and keep Burke entertained."

"Yes, Your Eminence," Vincent said, preparing to turn and move down the line.

"Come here, come here," the Cardinal said, beckoning him closer.

"Don't go away yet! I—uh," he began, clearing his throat. "I liked the speech. A little too strong, but strong meat won't hurt them once in a while. Otherwise they get to thinking we look in all directions before we'll say a word in public. I don't like gumshoeing—I never have."

"Thank you so much, Your Eminence."

They were playing "The Blue Danube" again. The Cardinal paused, a nostalgic crinkle forming around the corners of his mouth.

"They're playing your favorite song, Your Eminence," Vincent said.

"Yes, yes, I know," the Cardinal said gently, raising his hand and waving acknowledgment to the orchestra leader. "I danced to that music once—as a very young man in Vienna. I danced around a polished floor as lightly as a wren."

"Is it true what they say about the Danube, Uncle?" Arthur asked from behind Vincent.

"Oh, you're here, are you?" the Cardinal said gruffly. "At least I can keep an eye on you. I don't know whether it's true or not about the Danube. I never got that far." There was the hint of a mischievous twinkle in his eyes.

"You," he said to Arthur, shifting back into gruffiness. "Go tell Vinegar Jack to move down next to Cardinal Burke. I want His Eminence to hear some of Regan's stories."

"Yes, sir," Arthur said, moving down the line.

The Cardinal again beckoned Vincent down low to him.

"I wanted to get another word in. Listen carefully," he said. "After we get the ordinations out of the way in June I'm going to celebrate my jubilee in Rome. I want you to come along and see the Holy Father with me. This trip," he concluded with a deep, tired sigh, "just might be my last."

"I'd love to go, Your Eminence," was all Vincent could say.

The Cardinal leaned over to Burke now, obviously telling him about Father Regan, who was making his way down the line.

Bishop Whelton moved to the right and paid his respects to Bishop Sliney and his former roommate.

"You got quite a lot of publicity on that speech, I see," Bishop Lambert said. "Gosh, you're dishing out a strong meat. Do you really want all that to come to pass?"

"I wouldn't say it if I didn't mean it," Vincent said politely.

The Cardinal was at the rostrum now, giving the blessing before meals. "Bless us O Lord," he intoned solemnly, "and these Thy gifts which we are about to receive from Thy Bounty, through Christ Our Lord. Amen."

Most of the six hundred diners went avidly at the onion soup.

Vincent, moving down the line to a seat with Arthur, saw the Cardinal push aside the soup. He noticed that Cardinals Ronan and Burke did the same. He had heard that men who go to public dinners frequently eat little or nothing at those affairs. He glanced at Bishop Lambert and saw him spooning up the limp onion shreds with the alacrity of a youthful appetite.

He seated himself next to Vinegar Jack, who was tasting the soup cautiously and telling Cardinal Burke a story. Arthur took a sniff of the soup, pushed it aside, and, glancing at Father Regan, threw Vincent a wink.

"Yir Eminence may have heard this one," Father Regan began. "'Tis about a monk and a bowl of soup, appropriately enough. As you know, the monks are not a-tall encouraged to complain about their food and usually accept what is put in front of them, be it steak or gruel. It seems as how this bowl of soup was served to our monk with a dead mouse floating around in the middle of it. After giving the matter much thought, taking into account his vow of humility and his habit of contentment with circumstances, he turned to Brother Cook, who was passing by with the soup kettle, and declared, pointing to the monk beside him: 'Frater John has no mouse in his soup!'"

Cardinal Burke sputtered until tears bowled down his great fat cheeks like small, bright diamonds. Cardinal Wagner looked, nodded amiably, took a sip of water, and repeated the joke to Cardinal Ronan on his right.

"Not bad," Arthur said, poking Vincent lightly. "Did he used to tell jokes like that when you were his junior curate?"

"I was his walking joke," Vincent whispered.

"Gosh, when do we eat?" Arthur said, taking a sip of water.

"They're bringing in the chicken now."

"I hope so," Arthur said. "Even the onion soup is beginning to look good."

A note was being passed down the table toward Vincent. Arthur took it from the adjutant general on his left. Vincent glanced at it and saw his name and title written on a plain white folded piece of paper. He opened it.

"Your speech was excellent. Spoken like a true bishop—a spokesman for truth and justice before the councils of men. I continue to be your admirer and I am grateful that you have found a place for my daughter in your fine educational organization. You have made her very happy and have restored a beautiful ideal of hero worship to her life. Call on me when you need me. My resources are at your command. Nino Venezzia."

The Bishop warmed with gratitude at that gracious gesture from one he had supposed to be an old enemy. He looked up, caught the eye of the birdy old man in the overwhelming bands and plumes, and waved cordially to him.

"Venezzia's giving you the rush again," Arthur said, tasting a little of the onion soup.

"I thought you were ducking the soup."

"Everybody's eating it. It can't be too bad—and those waiters with the chicken are awfully slow."

Vincent noticed that many of the people now moving down the aisles weren't waiters.

"Say, a lot of the guests are getting up and going out."

"Ulp!" Arthur said, spitting out the soup and pushing away the bowl. "It's the soup, Vin. They're all heading for the john!"

"Oh, my God!" Vincent said as Vinegar Jack rose, his face turning green.

"Can I help you, Father?" Vincent said, rising also.

"I'll make me own way, Bishop," Father Regan said, swallowing and stumbling along the line to the end of the platform.

Bishop Lambert went past in a hurry, his face bloodless and lips set tight.

The Cardinal, too, had noticed all this, the flurry to the back of the hall, the rapidly emptying tables. He glanced sternly at Vincent, who rose and sought out the headwaiter near the orchestra.

"Play something, keep playing," Vincent commanded the orchestra leader. "There's something wrong with the soup!"

"For heavens' sake!" he said to the headwaiter. "Get rid of that onion soup. You've poisoned the entire attendance here!"

"It can't be! It can't be!" the headwaiter said frantically. "We made it this morning!"

"GET RID OF IT!" Vincent said angrily as the headwaiter hurried off, conferring with his fellows as he went.

He debated whether or not to make an announcement and decided it was best to warn the late-comers. He strode to the microphone, observing that the hall was half empty now.

The Cardinal was calm and spoke tersely as he passed.

"It's the soup. You'd better warn the rest of them."

Bishop Whelton signaled the orchestra into silence and gave out the warning about the soup, which was received with a general "You telling us?" attitude.

Arthur was next. He had taken one sip too many. He rose, his face in a cold sweat, and hurried off the platform.

"Sit down," the Cardinal said to Vincent, "there's nothing you can do."

"I suppose you're right, Your Eminence," Vincent said, sitting and signaling to the orchestra to begin again. "But the whole thing is frightfully embarrassing."

The Cardinal had an odd, amused expression on his face as the clerics came and went on the floor in front of him.

"Look at Father Quinlan there," he said, leaning over to Cardinal Ronan and nodding toward a huge red-faced priest who was hurrying down the middle aisle. "I haven't seen him move that fast in years."

A reporter from the Lakeport *Herald* approached the head table and addressed Cardinal Wagner.

"Your Eminence," he began, "do you think this soup has been poisoned as the result of some kind of plot on the part of the German Bundists to wreck your jubilee ceremonies?"

"I don't think anything of the kind," the Cardinal said. "The caterer served us rotten soup—that's all there is to it."

"Can I have a copy of the speech you'll deliver this evening, Your Eminence?"

"I won't say much now," the Cardinal said. "I think we'll just call the whole thing off. These poor folks are sick and upset. Bishop Whelton, get hold of Monsignor Wagner and ask him to give this man a copy of my speech. You can say," he added, inclining his head toward the reporter, "you can say I'll deliver the address at the dedication ceremonies tomorrow afternoon."

"Thank you, Your Eminence."

Vincent went looking for Arthur and found him standing against the outside wall of the men's room, holding his head, moaning and laughing at the same time. Around him the guests were milling in and out of the rest room.

"What's so funny?"

Arthur nodded toward the door.

"You can't get a stall in there for a thousand dollars."

In the distance they could hear the Cardinal dismissing the gathering with brief, sympathetic remarks.

"The Cardinal wants you to give the *Herald* reporter a copy of his address. He says he'll deliver it tomorrow."

"Good, good," Arthur said, his forehead still in his hand. "You'd better get back to the head table. Give the Cardinal the watch before he goes."

"Yes, I'll do that. Where are you going?"

"Back in there," Arthur said weakly but amiably.

Vincent took him by the elbow and helped him through the crowd to the doors of the men's room.

Through the hum and the buzz of mutual sympathy and occasional outbursts of temper there suddenly came the thump of a fist pounding against a door.

"Open up! I'm a Bishop!" commanded the unmistakable voice of their former seminary roommate.

"You may be a bishop," answered the firm, brogued voice of Vinegar Jack Regan, "but I'm an irremoveable pastor!"

CHAPTER XXXIX

Cardinals Die in Threes

THERE was one empty chair at the captain's table.

Through the starless Atlantic void somewhere off Nantucket Light, the trim, black sword that was the S.S. *Contessa* thrust and plunged toward the port of New York and the end of an eight-day voyage from Naples.

Captain Vincento Cordoni, a small gold-hooped barrel of a man, lifted his tiny goblet of B&B, smiled compassionately at Vincent and Arthur, calling for a toast.

"To the Cardinal," he said in gracious, faultless English, nodding to the Venezzias also and the other guests, "as if he were here."

"To his speedy recovery . . ." Bishop Whelton acknowledged, sipping the rich, mellow brandy mixture.

They drank in silence while around them in the main salon the gaiety of the last night aboard effervesced in laughter, dancing, and catchy music.

Rosa, in severe unrelieved black and without make-up, sat between Monsignor Wagner and her Father, her eyes constantly on the Bishop, intensely alert to serve.

"It was so good of you to come to dinner with us," Venezzia said to the Bishop. "I am sure you might have preferred to stay with His Eminence."

"He insisted that I come," Bishop Whelton said. "And the same with Monsignor Wagner. He wanted us to be here."

"That is typical of his graciousness," Venezzia said.

"Tell me, Your Excellency," asked a tall, white-haired man with

square, ruddy features, "did the ship's physician have anything en-
couraging to report this evening?"

"Dr. Montessi believes there has been a slight improvement since
the attack three days ago," the Bishop explained. "Unfortunately he
believes the Cardinal's age and his enormously active habits will
militate against a more progressive recovery, however."

"Will His Eminence rest in New York for a while?" the tall gentleman asked. "I know the President will be gravely concerned about
his health."

"What do you think, Monsignor?" Vincent asked Arthur.

Monsignor Wagner framed his answer carefully for the presidential aide who was returning to Washington after a series of confer-
ences with the Pope regarding policy toward both sides in the Spanish
Civil War. He was perhaps apprehensive in a purely pragmatic
political way lest the Administration should lose a powerful native
spokesman against intervention.

"I'm quite positive he'll insist on going direct to Lakeport by train.
'If I'm going to the Lord,' the Cardinal told me last night, 'I'm going
from my own bed.'"

There were wistful smiles amid the group at this.

"Did he seem upset at the news of the death of his old friend,
Cardinal Metucci, while we were in Rome?"

"He did," Bishop Whelton volunteered. "And you perhaps have
all read in the ship's newspaper that Cardinal Burke is very ill."

"Cardinals die in threes," Nino Venezzia said soberly.

"Tell me about that if you will," the man from Washington asked.
"Is that a Church superstition?"

"It's, I suppose, an old saying rather than a superstition," Nino explained. "It symbolizes, of course, the Holy Trinity, and there have
been triple deaths among cardinals over the centuries."

"It's a lovely yet sad phrase!" the emissary said.

"Let us pray it does not obtain in this instance," Bishop Whelton
said.

This was all too much for Monsignor Wagner, and he was irked
that Nino had paraded his erudition.

"I do hope you will excuse me," he said, rising. This was the first
time he had really faced the reality of the Cardinal's possible death.
It was the wild terror of imminent loss he felt as he walked away
from the table and out of the salon—loss of the Cardinal, loss of his
uncle. They could have the diocesan newspaper, the "Very Rever-

end" before his name; they could keep all the snail-pace conserva-
tism and the gumshoeing on public issues. They could send him to
the Tri-State Valley or the island of Molokai. What difference did
it make to him? But spare the Cardinal, O Lord, do not take him
away from us, his heart cried out in anguish. Thy will be done, but
please, dear God, he prayed in emotion-stormed contradiction, do
not take him away!

He walked along the deck now in the darkness, seeing the friendly
wink of Nantucket Light off to his left and hearing the far-off cry
of gulls, a distant, churning of sough and sigh as of breaking surf.

He stopped and leaned on the railing now, the dance music subdued in the salon behind him, and below him in the cabin a great
man lying still, trying to get it all back, trying to match again, to well
up the vitality which would complement the never-ebbing strength
of will.

The lighthouse winked faithfully as the great vessel throbbed on
toward New York.

"Lead, kindly light," Arthur found himself thinking, recalling Cardinal Newman's heartening silver verses, "amid th'encircling gloom
. . . lead Thou me on . . ."

"Don't get so upset," said the calm, confident voice of the young
Bishop at his elbow. He had sensed Arthur's anguish and had
promptly followed him out of the salon. "He wouldn't want you to
take it this way."

"I know he wouldn't," Arthur said. "But he's always been so strong,
the strength of all of us. And now he's weak and failing. He just
seems to be going down, down, down . . ."

"He won't let go—not yet, at least," Vincent said, striving to con-
vince and steady himself. "If we can get him back to Lakeport he
may be all right."

"I'm glad he wants to go home. To his own home, his own
room . . . To Father Carney, Mrs. Rush, my mother. He'll want
them all around him at the end."

"He'll want you around him too."

"I know that," Arthur said. "He's always been so good to me and
I've given him such a hard time."

"You've been sincere in what you've done," Vincent said. "Don't
forget—he trusted you; he trusts you to bear up under all this too.
We'll do a turn about the deck while you get rid of those onions

around the eyes. Then we'll go see him, stand the long watch with him. What do you say?"

"Yes, I think we ought to do that," Arthur said, brightening a little, deeply inhaling the sharp sea air and striding along beside the Bishop.

" 'The night is dark and I am far from home,' " he quoted to Vincent with a sigh as the lighthouse ray white-scarred the heavens for an instant, " 'lead Thou, lead Thou me on . . .' "

"What are you typing, may I ask?"

Rosa looked up from her portable with a smile. The Hon. Lawrence A. Royten, confidential messenger to the Vatican, held his scotch and soda in hand and focused a smile of polite curiosity on his strong, chiseled features. Beside him in the luxurious first-class suite stood her father, who had invited Royten in for a drink after the farewell dinner.

"I am getting together some social-action notes for Bishop Whelton from various European periodicals of direct or indirect Catholic sympathies," Rosa explained with the low-key reverence with which she invariably spoke of the Bishop. "Monsignor Wagner marked them up for me, and it may be that His Excellency will find them useful in future speeches."

"May I read this one?" he pursued amiably, leaning over her shoulder.

"Why, of course," Rosa said. "There's nothing secret about them. This is a French labor writer quoting St. Jerome."

" 'Opulence is always the result of theft,' " Royten quoted aloud, " 'if not committed by the actual possessor, then by his predecessors.' "

Nino Venezzia laughed heartily.

"Now, Mr. Royten," he said, "you can perhaps begin to see why I finally submitted to the unionizing of my plant."

"Will the Bishop really quote something like that?" Royten asked with a wry smile.

"Not directly," Rosa answered with deep seriousness, wrinkling her brow in thought. "But it gives him insights and ideas, I would say. It gives him a sort of springboard."

"Yes," Royten said, turning to Nino again, engaged by the technique. "I suppose he could get at usurious practices and things like coupon clipping which is excessively done at the expense of low wages and poor working conditions."

Nino laughed again. "If His Excellency were to hear your comment he might seek to engage you as a speech adviser."

"I already am doing all the advising I can handle," Royten said.

"Come, sit down with me, Mr. Royten," Nino said with a gracious flourish of his right hand. "Little did I dream when I did business with your paper mills in Seattle that I would one day live to see you serving as presidential messenger to our beloved Holy Father."

"You may have had quite a little to do with it, Nino," Royten said, taking a seat on the wide cloth-of-gold sofa. "I did give your name, among others, when asked for Catholic references by the President's office."

"I was approached," Nino said with terse geniality. "You, of course, received my heartiest recommendation."

Rosa continued her typing at the desk in the corner, but she was all ears. She had suggested this conference to her father earlier that day. After all, if the Cardinal did pass along, Bishop Whelton would become administrator of the Archdiocese. But that would not be permanent unless it were made so. She had hinted to Nino that Royten and the President might be helpful in insuring a liberal, Administration-minded successor to the President's sympathetic friend, Cardinal Wagner.

"We have Rosa to thank for our reunion in the Eternal City," Nino said, taking a sip of his scotch. "It was she who persuaded me to accompany the Cardinal on his jubilee visit to the Vatican. I have Bishop Whelton to thank for regaining the love of my daughter. Her devotion to him has resulted in a share-the-wealth love for her old father with whom she has not always seen eye to eye," he concluded with a chuckle.

"Now, Father . . ." Rosa admonished, looking up from her typing.

"Now, daughter . . ." Nino returned whimsically. "Will you not indulge an old man's happiness at the return of his daughter to his bosom in the late winter of his life?"

"I'm sure she does," Mr. Royten said sympathetically. "But tell me, Nino—I am most concerned about the Cardinal's illness and I know the President is. I talked to Washington this morning on ship-to-shore phone. His Eminence has on occasion been such a fearless and profound spokesman for the liberal element of the Church—and of course has been a cementing force in Church-state relations in an otherwise ultra-conservative hierarchy group. What will we do—to whom can we look—if Divine Providence should take him from us in this crucial hour of world events?"

Nino paused. Rosa stopped typing and brought her alert head over to the periodicals on her right so that she could see their faces.

"That is a very difficult question to answer," Nino said slowly. "And the decision will ultimately be made by the Holy Father on the recommendation of the principal American bishops and the Apostolic Delegate."

"Is it true that Bishop Whelton will administer the archdiocese should the Cardinal pass away?"

"Yes, that is true. He is vicar-general and would run the archdiocese until a permanent ordinary is appointed."

"But we must moderate our hopes, I suppose," Royten said. "He is such a young man!"

"That is true," Nino agreed. "His youth might tell against him— and, I dare to add, his strong advocacy of liberal ideas in a traditionally conservative atmosphere."

"What other alternatives might there be?" Royten pursued avidly.

"Cardinal Dwyer of New York will be in an excellent position to determine the ultimate choice, I would hazard the opinion. While not yet a wearer of the red hat, he is perhaps the most influential member of the hierarchy in America, next to Cardinal Wagner. He is close to the Apostolic Delegate and a favorite of the Holy Father."

"And a good friend of the President," Rosa interjected firmly, "may I remind you, Father."

"Yes, my dear, of course," Nino conceded with a chuckle. "Mr. Royten is surely aware of that."

"Yes, there is great rapport between them," Royten acknowledged, "similar to the friendship between F.D.R. and Cardinal Wagner."

"But what of other candidates?" Royten asked. "Is there another among the younger crowd who might be appointed?"

"Yes, yes, there is a possibility," Nino began, angling his head intently. "There is Bishop Robert Lambert, the Coadjutor of Harbourton. He is one of the brightest young lights in the hierarchy—and a conservative, too, scrupulously correct, efficient, highly regarded by the older crowd. And, I am told, a great favorite of the Apostolic Delegate."

"Mmmmmm . . ." Royten said, puffing out his lower lip. "I hadn't heard about him."

"Oh, Father," Rosa insisted strongly. "How can you possibly compare him with Bishop Whelton?"

"Yes, surely, as a public figure . . ." Royten began.

Nino interrupted them both politely.

"He must be considered," he said flatly. "And it is more in Bishop Whelton's behalf that I emphasize Bishop Lambert's prominence." He nodded reassuringly at his daughter and took the wraps completely off his intentions. "For whatever it is worth to you, Larry"— he used Royten's first name now in a resumption of easy familiarity that harked back to their business deals together—"in your possible representations to the President on this matter, I must advise you that Bishop Whelton has predominantly but one great and good friend among the hierarchy, and that is our dearly beloved Cardinal, who may now be facing his Maker. On the other hand, Bishop Lambert, because of his painfully discreet approach to Church policy, internal and external, is powerfully connected with elements who will, as a matter of course, assume greater influence and authority should the Cardinal expire."

Royten was deeply absorbed and impressed. Here, more than the American press would ever know, was the heart of his mission. The glowing hospitality of Pope Pius XI and his deep appreciation of the President's defiant good will in sending a personal messenger to the Vatican were one thing—the statements, the press stories and photographs, the hopes for peace and good will among men—all that was one thing; but here in the intimate experience and insights of a powerful lay son of the Church lay the practical fruits of his mission. Here, as the sleek, black S.S. *Contessa* plowed through the coastal waters of the homeland, here at the gates of New York, with the physical journey and protocol ended, here lay the heart of his confidential report to the President.

"Is there a likelihood, a chance, may I ask," he queried intensely, "that Cardinal Wagner will make some formal or informal designation of Bishop Whelton as his successor during his declining hours?"

Nino looked shrewdly into the amber depths of his glass.

"Very unlikely, I would say, my dear Larry, very unlikely. May I put it this way? Do you suppose that F.D.R. has earmarked a successor? This is the unfailing and forgivable ego of public figures who are extraordinarily eminent. None of them—politician or prelate —will allow themselves to believe that another can adequately fill their shoes. It has ever been thus," he concluded with a sigh. "It will ever be so. You have heard the expression in business, Lawrence, I am sure. 'Shirt sleeves to shirt sleeves . . .' This principle is similar. It is most difficult for a big man to prepare the way for a successor. And often, as it happens, when such a designation is attempted, it is too late."

"Yes, you have a point there," Royten conceded. "Then whatever we do, we must do on our own and in the interest of preserving present co-ordination with Administration. From our point of view, that is."

"I would say you are correct," Nino said. "If the President desires such a liberal continuity in the hierarchy as—well, let us be candid —such as Bishop Whelton . . ."

Rosa brightened at this, and the complex love for her father was radiant in her face.

". . . then let the President use his influence powerfully and discreetly in this behalf."

"I understand now," Royten said. "I understand. I'm very grateful for all this, Nino. You've given me added food for thought in the preparation of my report to the President."

"I'm happy to think I may have served you in this regard," Nino said. "Yet I doubt if such an aspect could properly be expressed in a formal report."

"Yes, yes, I know," Lawrence said, correcting himself. "It must be informally presented but no less effectively, I assure you."

"My daughter and I are happy to hear that," Nino said as Royten rose. "You will do well to take our rising young liberal Bishop into the private counsel of the President."

"I'm sure of that. Well, it's been lovely—and profitable—I must get back to my cabin. I have some more packing to do."

When he had gone, Rosa got up and kissed her father resoundingly on the cheek.

"Father, you were wonderful!" she exclaimed. "You fill me with shame and humility for the way I treated you in past years."

Nino shrugged his shoulders, suffused with pleasure at his daughter's long-denied obeisance.

"I do it for you and your mother," he said. "But I do it, too, for the Cardinal and the Bishop. What has been achieved by them must not be allowed to deteriorate."

"Thank you, my dear Father, thank you so much," she said, her eyes shining.

"One last drink and I shall retire," Nino said, pouring a dollop of scotch into his glass. "You too, my dear?"

"Yes, Father."

He poured her a drink of the scotch.

"To the Cardinal," he said, raising his glass, "that his life or his memory may endure, according to the will of God!"

"To my Bishop also," Rosa said, touching his glass with restraint and good taste, the meaning of which remark, however, was unmistakable.

"And to your Bishop," Nino said with a slow, shrewd smile. "He will make, God willing, a splendid Archbishop of Lakeport."

CHAPTER XXXX

There Goes Lakeport!

THEY say, they say, what do they say? . . .

On a moth-soft morning in May 1940, a year after his uncle had become a legend and a myth in the Church forever, Monsignor Arthur Wagner sat at his typewriter in *The Clarion* office and thought about what everybody else was saying and what he was going to say in his weekly editorial.

Roosevelt was saying to England, "Sail on, oh ship of state, sail on . . ." Churchill was saying, "Send us the tools and we'll finish the job." The America Firsters were saying, "Convoys mean shooting and shooting means war." The interventionists were saying, "I'm sittin' and knittin' a mitten for Britain."

They say, they say, what do they say? . . .

The brawl and the broil of committees for and against war, for and against the Allies, clouded over America in an incessant ear-splitting dissonance of chicken-cackles. He would say that, put it into the present tense, set it down.

"Committees, committees," he began. "The country is crawling with committees: for and against the Allies, for and against Britain, the Russians, the French. . . . But what are the issues? Are our merchantmen being ruthlessly torpedoed, our sailors boiling in oceanic eruptions of oil? Is there in full swing a fascistic conquest of the world? And must we wait at the water's edge to defend Fortress America?

"What does the Holy Father say about all this? What does the

President say? Here are two world leaders who do not need committees to clarify the issues . . ."

The phone on his desk rang briskly. He picked it up. It was Tony
calling from the center.

"Monsignor," Tony began excitedly, "there's an item about the
Bishop in the religious section of *Event*. It's just on the stands!"

"Yeh, what, Tony, what—what?"

"Well, they ran a column-wide picture of him and underneath
there's the cutline: 'New Archbishop?'—with the question mark."

"What's the story say?"

"It says news of a meeting of the Apostolic Delegate and the principal members of the hierarchy is around Washington this week. The
meeting is allegedly scheduled this week and they'll come up with
a recommendation to the Holy Father on the Lakeport archdiocese."

"Yes, the meeting's due," Arthur said. "It's really due."

"What do you think?" Tony asked anxiously.

"What do I think?" Arthur repeated. "What do we all think—and
hope—and pray? Nothing to do now but sit tight. Did they mention
our friend up the lake?"

"No, they didn't mention Bishop Lambert at all."

"That's bad," the Monsignor said. "I wish they had. I wish they'd
mentioned him. These news magazines can be way off at times—and
the Bishop's good copy. The Cardinal always told me never to calcu-
late too closely when an ordinary is being appointed. Even my late
uncle wanted Boston originally, you know. And everybody thought
he was going to get it, too. But Lakeport it was. . . . Where are
you now, Tony?"

"I'm at the center. Are you going to the budget conference at the
chancery?"

"Yes, stop by. I'll meet you downstairs in the coffee shop," Arthur
said.

He loomed again over his typewriter and the editorial. He knew
exactly what he wanted to say. Neutrality, yes, but not the neutrality
of selfish nationalism—AMERICA FIRST—ME FIRST!

Roosevelt had the idea—aid, "short of war"—help your friends but
try to stay out of it.

Impossible! Probably. But you couldn't sit by in some weird mys-
tique of Washington's Farewell Address; you couldn't "keep clear of
entangling alliances" until you were the last succulent morsel to be
gobbled up by the predatory dogs of fascism.

America First! So many anti-British Catholics, priests, prelates, laymen were bitterly against any form of aid or intervention at this time. France had fallen, Hitler had risen, the Japs were stomping around arrogantly at the approaches to the Philippines, and the great cities of England were augmenting rubble heaps.

The Irish-Americans, strong in the East and even here in Lakeport, were confusing their insular enmity against Britain with the stark and pressing threat of fascism to world freedom. The vociferous Coughlinites, even without the now muffled voice of their strident Roman-collared leader, were howling against the Jews and British imperialists, with communism leering from every New Deal wood-pile, they insisted.

Few if any Catholic publications in the country would come right out and say, "Let's look at this thing—let's use our reason instead of our emotions." He detested this state of mind—that England was again leading us into war.

It was the same old split—right down the middle on the Spanish Civil War. The sideshow was over—Spain had its benevolent dictator now. By sheer accident of Franco's religion and the Roman Catholic warp and woof of the country, the Church, at least, was still a force for good in that war-ravaged land.

He had been editorially silent then, but how could *The Clarion* avoid it now? Bishop Whelton—yes. But would it really hurt him—even this weekend? The Bishop agreed with him entirely and had put it on public record in a speech before the Foreign Policy Association, calling for responsibility in world affairs rather than "melting-pot prejudices."

He would take for an editorial theme the anti-nationalist words of Pius XI in his Christmas message delivered as early as 1930.

He typed away, working all these ideas in and weaving them around the percipient words of the former Pope, who had said:

"Even more difficult—not to say impossible for peace to last between people and States—if in place of true and genuine love of country, there rules and abounds a hard and selfish nationalism which is the same as saying hatred and envy, in place of mutual desire for good . . ."

That should take care of the America Firsters, and he wouldn't have to mention them by name.

He heard the door of the office open and close. It was Father Ed Saulnier, his managing editor, back from the printer's.

"All we need now is your editorial and we'll have a newspaper," he said with his characteristic, genial glumness.

"It's right here," Arthur said. "Have it for you in a few minutes."

"Careful now," Father Saulnier said, describing with his right hand a little skullcap circle around his head.

Arthur laughed. Saulnier always did that at press time to warn the Monsignor away from any editorial opinions that might prejudice Bishop Whelton's chances of the archepiscopal appointment.

"Okay, Mr. Skullcap," Arthur said. "We're taking on America First this week. But I'll show a carbon to His Eggs first—for an okay—okay?"

"Okay." Father Saulnier slumped down to his desk. "Have your spies and informers told you about the story that just broke in *Event?* I saw it at the printer's. They're predicting he'll get it this weekend."

"Yes, Tony called and told me about it. What do you think, Ed? Advance publicity like that always makes me uneasy. And they didn't mention the fellow up the lake."

"I don't like a buildup like that myself. Afterwards, yes—not before. It can be the kiss of death. But he should get it—he really should."

"Yes, he should," Arthur said wistfully. "The Cardinal never did say much about it before he died. After the ocean voyage he declined steadily for over two years. But his confidence in the Bishop was unmistakable. Unk was wiser than all of us. He knew that Vin hadn't been a bishop long enough to designate as Coadjutor. And he knew that dead men tell no tales and that a word from him might hurt Vin more later on—when he was gone and had become someone you reverently and admiringly remember but do not obey. Vin himself never mentions it, but his heart is set on the job. Lakeport's his baby, his whole life."

"Yup," Father Saulnier said glumly. "Now, get going—you're holding up the works."

Arthur resumed typing furiously and finished the job. He ripped the sheets out of the typewriter and went through them with a pencil for several more minutes. He rose and threw a copy on Saulnier's desk.

"Have it set, Ed. But don't let it run until you hear from me."

"How long will that be?"

"A few hours maybe. I'm going over to the chancery now."

"G'by," Father Saulnier said, casting a baleful eye at the copy and marking it up for type.

"So long," Arthur said, taking his hat off a hook. "I'll see you at the printer's this evening."

"Yeh, g'by, Father Churchill," Saulnier said without looking up.

At the reception desk in the chancery office Joan Linehan kept her fingers going on the typewriter keys in spite of the enticing aroma of coffee Mrs. Rush was preparing far down the hall in the kitchen.

To her left in an enclosed cubicle, with the door shut tight, Rosa Venezzia was going through the morning mail—a chore, Joan could not help reminding herself, which was once Mrs. Rush's for the Cardinal and hers for the Bishop at the youth center.

Rosa with her nunnish dedication and indefatigable service to the Bishop—her savoir faire and considerable personal wealth also being tributary factors—had steadily moved in close as the Bishop's confidential secretary. From the moment when the Bishop had assigned her to the small rear office at the center, which she still shrewdly occupied, through the jubilee trip to Rome, she had inched into his confidence and his trust.

To be sure, the Bishop had his close clerical assistants: the young Monsignors Galvin and Fortuna as chancellor and vicar-general, respectively; and Monsignor Wagner was still perhaps his most intimate adviser on the affairs of the archdiocese and the world outside the Church. But Rosa, who sought nothing for herself, gave her salary to the Bishop's charity fund and daily offered herself to complete, dedicated service to His Excellency, the administrator of the archdiocese—Rosa was in there close.

With but a word, a hint, a memo, a shuffled appointment, a delayed or hidden letter, she could be and was the most powerful if unobtrusive influence on the Bishop.

Perhaps Mrs. Rush had been the same with the Cardinal. Joan knew that she, herself, had never approached that status. She was not the aggressive, completely dedicated type. There were always the outside interests—Tony Lorenzo; Bill Ryan, the D.A.; the home and babies looming—always making such a rigid orbit of dedication as Rosa's impossible to her being.

Rosa, too, understood this and treated her with civility, knowing she was not a rival. Toward Mrs. Rush, whom the Bishop kept on because of her personal abhorrence for retirement, she was benevolently patient and tolerant. Mrs. Rush, the secretary emeritus to the Cardinal, was the only one allowed to enter the Bishop's office with-

out an appointment or a prior buzz. Rosa had seen to that. Even
Monsignor Wagner and Tony, to their initial chagrin, had to be
announced and okayed. But Mrs. Rush, sassily ignoring Rosa when
she felt like it, had the privilege of rushing down the familiar hall
to the Cardinal's old office, to bring the Bishop coffee, ice water, an
occasional letter, or just a bit of urgent gossip if she so pleased.

Joan heard the tray clinking along the side hallway now. Mrs.
Rush was coming with the ten o'clock coffee. Had she seen the latest
copy of *Event* which was open, displaying the Bishop's turtle visage,
on Joan's desk? Rosa certainly had, for she had put through a call
to her father in Washington, D.C., less than half an hour ago.

Mrs. Rush rounded the corner with the tray, her wrinkled, bony
being sparkling with pert energy.

"Fine, fine, fine . . ." she said as Joan cleared away a space on a
neighboring table. She set down the tray and rayed a shrewd glint
down the inner hall toward the Bishop's office.

"He's in there now," she chaffered merrily. "Fine, fine. I have
those little Danish pastries you and the Bishop like," she said, raising
her voice, making sure that Rosa could hear her behind the closed
cubicle door.

"You and the Bishop . . ." Joan chuckled, wanting to kiss her. It
was so sweet of her to put it that way.

"Have you seen the story in *Event*—about the Bishop?" Joan asked
as she took her coffee and a roll from the tray.

"Yes, I've seen it," Mrs. Rush said casually, pouring black coffee
for Rosa. "I do hope the Bishop won't get too keyed up. There's
no one in the world who wants him to get the job more than I do,
but I put little stock in publicity. The newspaper boys had the Cardinal, God rest his soul, going to Boston years ago."

"Is that so?" Joan said, taking a dainty little bite out of her pastry
as she seated herself again at her desk. "Well, do you think it will
hurt?"

"I don't think it will hurt or help," Mrs. Rush said brusquely,
taking the coffee and approaching Rosa's closed door. "I think whatever is, is already, and it would take a lot to change it. Those boys
down in Washington will know what they're doing—don't you worry,
my dear. Put it in the hands of God," she concluded, pausing, looking
over her shoulder, and screwing up her face with a sweet elfin quality. Then she said in a warm, urgent voice, hardly above a whisper:

"But the Cardinal loved him so! Pray to him—he's in heaven—he'll get what's best for our Bishop."

Joan smiled with deep affection for this shrewd yet affectionate old woman who had served the Cardinal amid the great of Church and state for more than two decades.

"I'll pray that way," she said. "And I'll pray, too, that he gets it —okay, Mrs. Rush?"

"Of course, my dear. I want him to get it too—so much!"

She balanced the coffee cup in one hand—Rosa never took sweets or anything eatable between meals—and rapped pertly on the door.

"Come in," Rosa said coldly yet politely. She had heard it all, all the cautious banter from the old lady, all the sickly piety from the Irish girl. Of course he would get it—who else? She alone knew how much he wanted it—how much it meant to his whole life. The magazine was right—he would get it—he deserved it; he was the logical choice. What she had done for him—outside of the usual routine services for which these others were hired. Who did they know and what resources were at their command?

Her father, gone to Washington as the Bishop's lay representative on the Pope's Refugee Fund Committee, would not sit idle. The Bishop would get it! He would, he must!

When Rosa saw Mrs. Rush head down the hall with the Bishop's coffee tray, she picked up the folder containing his mail and hurried after her.

When they entered his office, he was puzzling over some balance sheets, his heavy glasses adding considerable sobriety to an already sober mien.

"Yes, thank you, Mrs. Rush," he said without looking up as she poured his coffee.

On his desk Rosa and Mrs. Rush could see a copy of *Event*, open to the pertinent page. Rosa placed the letter folder near the magazine.

"I simply don't know what I'm going to do about this parochial-school budget. You know, we lost a good deal of money on the boxing show this spring, and I've had to use some of our educational funds to keep the center going. It's perfectly legitimate, Monsignor Galvin tells me, but there still isn't that much money to go around."

He took off his glasses and reached for the coffee with a sigh. A more affable mood seeped through him as he sipped the coffee and nipped at the Danish pastry.

Mrs. Rush and Rosa both stood there in what seemed, for a moment, something like an awkward, competitive silence.

The Bishop broke the ice forthwith.

"What would the Cardinal have done about this budget problem?" he asked Mrs. Rush jovially.

"How much money is involved, Your Excellency?" she asked crisply, getting right to the heart of the problem.

"About sixty thousand dollars."

Rosa, fuming at these very confidential revelations to one she considered an "honorary" secretary, walked to the left wall and straightened out the gold-framed painting of St. Vincent de Paul which she had done herself and given to the Bishop last Christmas.

"Go to the bank and borrow it," Mrs. Rush said.

"I would in a minute if it weren't for this indecisive state of affairs." He nodded at the open copy of the news magazine.

"Well, it'll be all over soon," the old woman said, moving toward the door. "We're all praying for you."

"Thank you Mrs. Rush. I need those prayers."

"And remember," she said, "if it's the will of God, you'll get it."

"I'll remember," the Bishop said as she left.

He picked up the folder and perused the letters: invitations for speaking engagements, a pious letter of complaint about a priest who was maintaining a racing stable, various offers of professional services . . .

"The letter from Bishop Sliney is probably the most significant," Rosa said.

"Mmmmmm . . ." the Bishop said, his glasses heavy on him again and the episcopal seriousness in focus as he scanned the letterhead of the elderly Bishop of Harbourton.

"Well . . ." he said, looking up from the letter. "This is another matter for Monsignor Galvin at the budget conference. Bishop Sliney insists that his diocese has ten thousand dollars due its own building fund from the seminary building-fund pledges we got down there. He said this was the kickback percentage agreement with the Cardinal."

"It was," Rosa said. "Monsignor Galvin has verified that agreement. There's a letter of confirmation from the late Cardinal in the files."

"I know that. I understand," the Bishop said. "But the debt for the new seminary is so overwhelming that we simply can't send out that kind of money. We've written to Bishop Sliney to that effect, but he insists that they must have the money and that we honor our pledge."

"What about the carbon-copy note, Bishop?"

"Yes, yes, I see it: 'Carbon copy to Most Rev. Gaetano Peruzzi, Apostolic Delegate, Washington, D.C.' I wonder whose idea that was? And it couldn't have happened at a more critical time!"

"I'll give you one guess."

"Yes, I suppose the Coadjutor Bishop down there has put the pin right in me. But they still won't get the ten thousand dollars because we haven't got it to spare."

"I am sure, Bishop," Rosa said consolingly, "that Washington realizes the debt involved in the Cardinal's new seminary. You did not run up all this debt," she concluded almost savagely, "someone else did. That is very obvious."

"It's very obvious to me that Bishop Lambert is keeping this issue alive," he said with another sigh. "Now where is Arthur and those people from the center? The morning is running away from us."

"I'll check right away," Rosa said, hurrying down the hall to her office.

"There's still so very much to be done," the Bishop said, sighing and removing his glasses. Around him were seated the three monsignors: Galvin, Fortuna, Wagner. He had heard their reports on various fiscal matters—Galvin on the schools and parishes, Fortuna on the marriage court and charitable institutions, Wagner on the diocesan press and fund-raising drives. "When things get more definite," he said, giving no relief to the supercharged electricity of the atmosphere, "we can talk about that new diocesan high school, these settlement houses we'd like to have on the south and west sides as adjuncts of the center, a clubhouse for our servicemen downtown— that's something we really ought to get on with. . . . There's so much to do, so much . . ."

He glanced at Tony, Sophie Narleski, and Lucy Smith, who were seated against the wall to his left.

"Tony, what about it? Is there a chance we can recoup some of our CYC budget losses on the boxing show with that barbecue-banquet idea you have for July Fourth?"

"Yes, Your Excellency," Tony answered. "If we can hold it in Lake-port Stadium on a good night and bring in some big-name entertain-ment—all donated to the cause, of course."

"I'm sure we can get the talent," Monsignor Wagner said.

"Well, go ahead with it, Tony," the Bishop said. "I'll discuss the matter in more detail over at the center when this picture here is clearer."

He turned now to Lucy, who was looking at him with a great doglike focus of burning compassion on her long pock-marked face. The Bishop's features were a sickly white now, and there was a film of perspiration on his brow.

"I'm not going to ask you if the adult education school is making any money, Lucy. Of course we don't expect that, and you're doing a splendid job. Would you like to say something about next fall's program?"

"Yes, Your Excellency," Lucy said with avid enthusiasm. It was so good of him to have business as usual when anyone could see his every nerve was vibrating with tension. "I just wanted to say we're doing very well with those two-dollar stipends for evening sessions. I know the total isn't much, but it helps pay the light bill."

The Bishop nodded affably. The three or four hundred dollars per semester was a drop in the bucket, but Lucy had the right spirit.

"And I want to tell you that we have made final arrangements for a seminar series of lectures on mental illness. These will take place this coming fall."

The Bishop chuckled, relieving the tension a little. "We'll all be ready for them about then."

Rosa, standing in the shadows behind the Bishop's desk, found herself looking at Tony. For just a moment he caught her eyes and held them. In spite of themselves and the long, cold, final estrange-ment, there flickered once again the question. There always would be that hint of a question between human beings who had once been so close. She turned away from him coldly. She had her life there in front of her—service to the Bishop—a nun might sense the dedi-cation of it, a lover the inner satisfaction. She took Communion from him at the railing each morning and thanked God each night that she had found her niche in life.

But now, now, all this anxiety and indecision. Surely her father would call from Washington soon.

Monsignor Wagner, also glancing at his watch, fished for the copy of the editorial in his coat pocket. He'd have to call Father Saulnier soon or they'd have to hold up the press run. He had sensed the arctic zone projected by Rosa, seeing her cold glance at Tony, and he was sympathetic to the latter. She had been giving him a little of the ice, too, lately—anyone, he was beginning to see, who was at all close to the Bishop.

He knew a twinge of anguish in this growing recognition. She had been close to him as a soul for some years. He had seen her through a lot of rocky times as her spiritual adviser and had paved the way to the actual position she now occupied.

But she did answer some legitimate need in the Bishop and she seemed to be happier in her work than she had at any previous time. Perhaps it was all for the best. And if Vin was pleased with her total dedication of service, that was what mattered most.

"Now, Sophie," the Bishop said, nodding affably to the pert and beaming librarian, "how are we doing between hard covers?"

"We're breaking even, Your Excellency," she said briskly. "Actually we'd probably make a profit if you didn't insist on that free library and information service. But that seems to be most popular, and if it's what you want we can only keep it going as you see fit."

"Splendid," the Bishop said. "Keep it going. The flow of truth and correct information is so tremendously necessary," he added a little pompously and a little vaguely.

Rosa glared at Sophie for what she thought to be her impertinence in talking up like that to the Bishop. The Bishop set them up and built them up, and they all talked like executives after a while. If His Excellency took his hand away, they'd all fall flat on their faces, she thought fiercely.

The buzzer on the Bishop's desk zitted with sharp brevity. He picked up the phone. It was Joan telling him he had a long-distance call from Washington.

Her father, Rosa knew, her heart beating wildly. But it was only eleven. It was too early. The bishops would still be in session. Maybe Nino had been tipped off in advance. What possible news now? What news?

"I'll take it in the small office in back," the Bishop said. "Rosa, hold this, please, until I can get to the other phone. Will you all excuse me, please? I won't be long." He caught Arthur's eyes sternly and beckoned him along.

Arthur followed him out of the office and down the hall to a small private office where the Cardinal used to see people when he did not want them to be seen by others.

They were all looking at Rosa now as she held the phone. She held it primly until the Bishop started talking, and then placed it carefully in its cradle.

Sophie, sitting far to her left, could not resist a catty whisper to Lucy: "If we weren't here I'll bet she'd get herself an earful!"

The two young monsignors talked softly to each other, anxious for the news, but equally anxious to be on and about their daily work.

Rosa hurried out of the office and down the hall. Her father would probably want to say a few words to her also. She lingered alertly outside the door. If the Bishop wanted her, he'd call her.

"Yes, Nino," the Bishop was saying in an attempt at casual tones which were betrayed by a catch in his voice. Now his face tightened as he hugely willed to control himself. His face tightened and he said with the old authority as Nino began to talk:

"Yes, go on. . . . Well, of course they won't let the cat out of the bag. . . . Yes, I'm sure you've been very discreet in your inquiries. . . . Of course they've decided already. They're always prepared before going into executive session. . . . Yes, Mr. Royten, the President's personal representative to the Pope . . . Yes, I know he's a friend of yours. I recall meeting him on the boat. . . . He's seeing Archbishop Peruzzi this afternoon, yes. . . . No, I hadn't heard about the President's letter concerning me. . . . Why, that's splendid of F.D.R., very generous, indeed. I don't think it will hurt at all. He and New York are on the best of terms. . . . Nothing like that hurts —unless it's been done too late. . . . He sent the letter two weeks ago? . . . Well, perhaps it was in time."

Monsignor Wagner stood by, rigidly alert, eager to talk to Nino. The President had written a letter—obviously—but when, to whom? The Bishop was right. It couldn't hurt, especially with Archbishop Bannon, the new Archbishop of New York, sitting in.

"All right, Nino," the Bishop said with a sigh, letting out some tension. "You'll see Royten later. Here, I'll let you discuss it with Monsignor Wagner. . . . Rosa, yes, we'll put her on. . . . Here, make your arrangements with Monsignor. . . . Yes, call us after lunch some time. . . . I'll keep the Monsignor with me here today. . . . Yes, thank you, so much. Here's the Monsignor. . . .

"Nothing definite yet," he said, handing the phone to Arthur.

"Hello, hello, Nino . . ." Arthur began. "What's this about the President?"

The Bishop turned the knob and walked out of the small office, seeing Rosa immediately.

"Rosa, you'll want to talk to your father. There's nothing definite yet. The Monsignor's on the phone now. He'll turn it over to you as soon as he's through."

"Yes, Your Excellency."

"Oh, and another thing," the Bishop said, turning. "You'd better tell the cook we're having two more for lunch. I want Arthur and Tony around here if the news finally breaks."

"Yes, Your Excellency," she said obediently, but with inner reluctance. She knew how to be his secretary—that, she had learned. You never voiced your objections outwardly to something that was very close to him. You had to bring things around—slowly yet relentlessly. She could not possibly say: "But wouldn't it be better if you were alone when the news comes?" That is what a wife could say, but not a private secretary, who is, in a way, a wife, in her service, loyalty, but only in companionship as a by-product.

As she entered the little office, Monsignor Wagner was still trying to get the picture straight on the President's letter.

"Oh, I see, Royten arranged it. Yes, just a short note to the Holy Father with a carbon to Archbishop Peruzzi. . . . Yes, a week ago . . . Well, it could have helped—if it weren't too late. . . . Yes . . . No, it wouldn't hurt, it wouldn't hurt at all. Everybody knows he's a liberal—why hide it? And here comes the greatest liberal in America, a friend of the late Cardinal and Archbishop Bannon; here comes the President of the U.S.A. and says: 'Sure he's a liberal, we'd love to see him as Archbishop of Lakeport.' It can't hurt him, can't hurt him at all, Nino, and you've done a wonderful job in setting it up. . . . Yes, here's Rosa, right here. . . . Yes, sometime this afternoon, you think. . . . Yes, if Royten can find out . . . Fine . . . We're all on pins and needles. . . . Thank you. Here's your girl, right here."

He met Monsignori Galvin and Fortuna in the hall as they were leaving. Lucy and Sophie were behind them.

"The Bishop says there's nothing definite yet, Art?" he asked anxiously. "How does it look?"

Vincent obviously hadn't told them about the President's letter.

"It still looks good, I'd say, Jim," Arthur said. "But we won't know until this afternoon—if then."

"We'll probably see you at dinner," Monsignor Fortuna said.

"Right, Al. We might know then."

"We'll be praying for him," Lucy said.

"Banging on the doors of heaven," Sophie added.

"Thanks girls, thanks," Arthur said. "Tony will probably let you know later."

Know, know, know . . . When and what would they know?

He rapped lightly on the Bishop's door, turned the knob, and went in. The Bishop was signing some letters and Tony was scrutinizing a financial report.

Arthur glanced at his watch. Almost eleven-thirty. He'd have to get an answer on the editorial right away. He sat down beside Tony and slipped it out of his pocket. Before perusing the editorial he jotted down a sentence on one of his personal cards and passed it to Tony.

Tony looked at the note hurriedly, anxiously, as if it were a sudden development. His grim olive features relaxed; his face softened with a smile.

"The death house was never like this!" was the message on the calling card.

"There's nothing in the mail this morning?" asked Bishop Walter Sliney, the ancient and venerable Ordinary of Harbourton.

Seated in his office with him, reviewing the morning mail and the day's business, young Bishop Lambert assumed he referred to the hoped-for check from the archdiocese of Lakeport.

"No, not that one, Bishop," Lambert said. "He'd be just about receiving our last letter today."

"Well, there never should have been any need for this exchange of letters. If the Cardinal hadn't passed on there wouldn't have been any trouble. But with this young loud-mouth who has opinions on just about everything—different from us all—I might have expected a delay."

"Do you suppose the Apostolic Delegate will do anything about the carbon copy?" Lambert asked, skirting the edges of a subject that weighed heavily on his mind.

"Of course he won't. He knows the bonded indebtedness of the new seminary," the old Bishop grumped. "But it was a good suggestion of yours to have me send it along. It will have a salutary effect on Bishop Whelton."

He cleared his throat now, thinking of the story about Vincent which he had read in the news magazine that morning. Despite his irritation at not receiving the fund-drive check, he was still a good sport.

"I don't think I would have let the carbon copy go if I had seen that story in the news periodical previously."

"Yes, I see what you mean," Bishop Lambert said, feeling sheepish about it himself. But he knew he had acted out of a primary sense of rectitude and with no direct consciousness of foul play. Bishop Whelton should have made some attempt to fulfill the pledge, even partially, within the past year. And to add fuel to the fire, it was no great secret that he had transferred over fifty thousand dollars in educational money to his own pet project, the CYC. This was legitimate, of course, as the CYC could be loosely considered educational. But one could seriously question whether this appropriation should have been made at the expense of more serious obligations.

And if one obligation, such as the Harbourton commitment, was being neglected, the chances were that others were receiving the same short shrift, Lambert reasoned.

"Do you think he'll get the appointment?" Bishop Sliney asked, getting right at the question that was uppermost in their minds.

Bishop Lambert took a quick look at his superior. No, it was not a loaded question. The old Bishop knew, as Lambert himself did, that it would be unusual for the committee to recommend a man who had recently been appointed a coadjutor and had a fine diocese ready and waiting for him on the death of the elderly Ordinary. He was not putting his Coadjutor on the spot.

"He has a very good chance, I'd say," Bishop Lambert said as the old prelate furrowed his brow impatiently. "Wouldn't you say so?"

"Yes, I'd say he did," the Bishop said gruffly, striving to be generous. "After all, he was close to the Cardinal—he served him well. And he's done a fine job with that youth thing—blazed a trail there, I'd say. New York has one now, Cleveland, Philadelphia, Boston. You're starting one here."

"Yes, but no boxing," Bishop Lambert said with a smile.

"Oh, a good knock on the head wouldn't hurt our boys once in a while," Sliney said. "Those sixteen-ounce gloves are like sofa pillows."

"Come, come now, Bishop," Lambert said. "You agreed. No boxing."

"Do you think all this liberal business will hurt his chances?" Lambert pursued.

"I don't think it will help. It never hurt the Cardinal, but he was already the boss. There is a difference," Bishop Sliney said. "And there's always been general agreement that advance publicity is bad. You never know where lightning will strike. I had a small diocese up in the Dakotas before I got this job."

"Did you want it?"

"I wanted Toledo, Ohio, with all my heart—I'm from up that way, you know. I wanted it and I thought I was going to get it. Well," he said with a philosophical sigh. "They put Wilkins in there and they split this hunk off the Lakeport archdiocese, and here we are."

"Have you ever regretted it?" Bishop Lambert asked.

"I did for a while," the old man said nostalgically, "but you know, once I resigned myself to the will of God, this place grew on me and I—I grew with it. I've been very happy here the last twenty-odd years."

"I'm glad to hear that."

The Bishop scrutinized Lambert closely now, a mixture of curiosity and admiration.

"I think you'd be happy here too—for a while, that is," he said exploringly. "You're going to need a larger place than Harbourton in which to flex your apostolic muscles, Robert. As you know, we won't grow much bigger here—there's nothing west of us but prairie and nothing east of us but the Lakeport archdiocese. You'll move on to greater things, I'm sure."

"Thank you for your confidence, Bishop," Lambert said.

"It 'tisn't confidence, it's recognition. Tell me—and I'm going to put this to you quite bluntly—you are, I know, very friendly with the Apostolic Delegate. You explore nature together or something. . . ."

"We're bird watchers," Lambert said. " 'Birders,' they call us."

"Yes," the Bishop said, chuckling, "sounds infernally silly, but I imagine it's quite relaxing and interesting. But tell me, have you been felt out at all, in any way, concerning the job down the lake?"

Bishop Lambert answered without hesitation: "I can honestly say I haven't. The Apostolic Delegate has never mentioned the appointment to me in any way, shape, or manner. He has mentioned Vin

Whelton in the past, but largely in a complimentary manner. I was talking to Archbishop Peruzzi on the phone about three weeks ago. You'll recall you asked me to call him on the Peter's Pence item. You wanted a month's extension, hoping the check would come through from Lakeport so that you could tuck a little extra into what we collected through the parishes."

"Yes, yes, I remember. What did he say that was unusual?"

"Nothing about the appointment."

"Did he say anything that might at all be unusual? Think now, boy, they sometimes have a way of letting you know what's on their minds."

Lambert wrinkled his brow in thought. There was something Peruzzi had said, something he had emphasized. He had noticed the emphasis but had seen no significance in it at the time. He had shrugged it off and gone back to the completely absorbing routine of his episcopal duties.

"Yes, yes, I have it," Bishop Lambert said.

The wizened old Bishop leaned forward in his great red leather armchair. Here on the borders of senility and in the objective quiet of his personal closeness to God was a brief adventure and excitement which stirred the tired chemistry of his blood.

"He asked about your health," the lean, young Bishop said.

"What is so unusual about that?" Sliney said, a shade of disappointment touching his features.

"Wait a moment, Bishop," Lambert said, the excitement stirring in him deeply now, his pulses beginning to throb. "When we were through talking, he asked about your health again, soliciting greater detail."

"Did he?" the Bishop asked, looking off at a picture of the Little Flower, who was his favorite patroness. The first wild thought died. No, not me, he knew. I am too old, too old. They were considering this boy—even now—even now. They wanted to know if I could manage alone until another coadjutor is chosen.

"Archbishop Peruzzi is a man of few words," the Bishop said, turning to Lambert again. "He is not given to repeating questions about one's health without a purpose."

"That is true," Bishop Lambert said in a whisper, his voice having suffered almost a stroke of recognition.

The Bishop paused and looked at him with deep compassion. He had grown to love this young man over the years of his association since Lambert's first diocesan assignment to the marriage court.

"Have you been to the chapel since breakfast, Bishop Lambert?"

"No, Your Excellency."

"Then you'd better get on in there now," he said sternly, yet not without warmth.

Bishop Lambert plumped to his knee and kissed his ring in silence. He rose and stepped back, ready to turn.

The old Bishop's watery blue eyes were again lifted to the dainty, girlish picture of Thérèse of Lisieux, the Little Flower.

"I have asked my patroness to send you a rose today," the old Bishop said, "if it is the will of God."

The old Bishop, confounded with nostalgia and a warm light of understanding, was about to speak again to Lambert when there came a light but definite double rap on the door of the office.

"That will be Father McElroy, my son," Bishop Sliney said with a touch of apprehensiveness. "I instructed him not to disturb us unless it was important. See what he wants."

Bishop Lambert went to the door, opened it, and conversed briefly with Father McElroy. He closed the door and returned to the Bishop's desk.

Lambert's lips were dry, his throat tight. He summoned the message with a great effort at self-control.

"Its Archbishop Peruzzi from Washington, Bishop," he said, adding with a renewed attempt at an official manner. "For you, sir. Would you like me to step outside?"

"No, no, my boy," the Bishop urged with a kindly smile. "Sit right down again. Sit down."

He reached for the battered old perpendicular phone which he had never replaced with the French types now in service throughout the chancery building. He gripped the brass-blotched pipe of it solidly, pulled it to him, and removed the ponderous earpiece.

"Yes, yes, Archbishop Peruzzi," he said cordially, surely, his voice and feelings perfectly under control. "This is indeed a pleasant surprise. . . . Yes, I've been feeling quite well, thank God, Archbishop. The old oak learns how to bend with the wind. . . . Yes, yes, excellent, doing an excellent job. He's right here now. . . . Yes, why, yes, if you don't care to tell him directly. . . . Well, it's nice of you to say that Archbishop."

The weathered old face grew light with wonder and reverence

now as he listened to the Apostolic Delegate's reason for calling.

"Well . . ." he said, looking over at Lambert with shining eyes, eyes made bright with both light and a sudden mist of tears. "Well, Archbishop," he commented softly, "glory be to God. . . . Yes, yes, he'll hear formally by mail tomorrow. . . . Amazing are the ways of God, Archbishop. . . . Yes, yes, we never know—Toledo, Harbourton, Lakeport—how little the faithful know the obedience of those to whom they must be obedient. . . . Yes, yes, I'll tell him. . . . Glory be to God. . . . Thank you so much for this great privilege. . . . Yes, yes, I'll be able to manage fine until we get a new man. . . . Yes, thank God it's settled. . . . Good-by now, Archbishop. Thanks for the news."

Silence, heavy yet golden, within the ancient Bishop's office, and the young Bishop slumped in an armchair, head in hand and bowed to his chest.

"Well, my son," Sliney said softly. "I guess you've gotten the gist of the Archbishop's message. The word has come. The decision has been made. God has touched you, my son."

He arose from his creaky, splintered swivel chair and scuffed around to Lambert. He sank, with shortened breath, onto one knee and looked up at Lambert with a smile.

"May an old man ask the first blessing of the bright new Archbishop of Lakeport?"

Archbishop-elect Lambert could not find words to pierce the cloud of gratitude and bewilderment which engulfed him. He found instead swift, sweet refuge in tradition and ritual.

Over the bowed, wrinkled head which loomed low to kiss his ring, he intoned and signified with his hand the cruciform blessing. A stillness of wonder and grace flooded the room, evoking an eloquence of silence and mutual understanding which all attempts at words could not convey.

"Bishop, will you take a look at that editorial I handed you at lunch? Father Saulnier is holding the presses over at Crowley Brothers and he's about to jump into the form himself," Monsignor Wagner said. "I've got to have an answer, yes or no."

They were sitting in the Cardinal's old suite on the second floor. Mrs. Rush had served coffee, and the three of them—the Bishop, Arthur, and Tony—had reminisced about the old days, evoking a golden mood which needed only the good long-distance word from

Nino Venezzia to make those nostalgic moments perfection itself.

"Yes, yes," the Bishop said, patting his side pocket and taking out the two stapled sheets of copy paper. "You and Tony keep on," he said genially and with a touch of urgency, as though reluctant to let the golden moment go.

He slipped on his glasses and perused the editorial as if he were going to read it aloud.

"But what would you and Naski have done out there at Truckers' Camp if the Cardinal hadn't interceded in the strike?"

"We'd have had a battle royal with the cops and everybody," Tony said. "Somebody would have been killed."

"To say the least," Monsignor Wagner said, adding with a sigh, "All's well that ends well. It would be a lot easier today. With that majority you had, you could force an employer to bargain collectively with you—under present federal law."

"Yeh," Tony said. "And imagine how things change! Mr. Venezzia's gone completely liberal and is down there right now in Washington pitching for the boss."

The Bishop raised his eyes from the editorial.

"I hope the Lord is pitching for me."

"I'm sure he is, Vin," Arthur said soberly. "One way or the other."

"One way or the other," the Bishop repeated with a deep, sad sigh. Then alertly: "This is a splendid editorial, I think. It gets right to the heart of the entire controversy on intervention."

"Thank you," Arthur said, relieved. "It's similar to what you yourself said before the Foreign Policy Association. 'Intervention is no longer a debatable question. It is a fait accompli.' Remember?"

"I remember too well—right now!" the Bishop said with a touch of regret. "Perhaps it would have been better unsaid in the light of the present indecision."

"You had to say it, Bishop," Tony said. "It was you—no one else would have spoken out like that within the Catholic hierarchy. If they're going to hang you for that, they could hang you for a lot of things."

Arthur was a little taken aback at Tony's bluntness. But the Bishop's face relaxed into a smile. The turtle's head emerged from a gloomy shell, bright, alert.

"I believe you're right, Tony," he said. "I believe we've got to stand or fall on the pattern of what we say. . . . I do like this editorial very much," he went on. "Have you read it, Tony?"

"Yes, I read it before lunch. I like it so much I think Monsignor Wagner ought to run it on the front page in bold-face type, over the Bishop's signature."

The Bishop chuckled richly. "That's all we'd need at a time like this, Tony."

"If we did that," Monsignor Wagner said with a facetious smile, "I'd have to pull out that story about the Catholic Army Veterans and the Coughlinites picketing the British Consul."

"That might be a blessing in itself," the Bishop said. Then he shifted, as was his frequent and unpredictable bent, into his own private and redundant idiom as he expressed himself finally on the editorial:

"It is the type and kind of editorial I would have liked to write in every manner and way, but . . ." He paused now, and the pressure of the hour and the decision from Washington were resurgent throughout his being.

"But I do think it would be wise to hold it off for a week or so until something definite is decided. The fat may be in the fire, but the steak is still in the pan."

"Very well, Bishop," Arthur said, concealing his disappointment.

He could not see what difference it would make now. The paper would not be out until tomorrow, and the decision would have been made by then. Yet there was always the possibility of a postponement. Yes, yes, the Bishop was undoubtedly right. For when he was prudent about controversial statements—which he usually gave without hesitation—there was doubtless a need to be prudent.

The Bishop placed the editorial to the right of the desk, for Rosa entered with some letters to sign. She came in her darkness and grimness, Tony noticed, pretty despite the stealth and the almost insidiousness of her movement. Had he been intimate with this woman, this relentless machine? Yes, yes, he had.

While the Bishop signed the letters, Arthur glanced at his watch, thinking of Father Saulnier waiting and some way to get to a phone. He could leave with Rosa, use the pay telephone in the waiting room. He did not want to chance tying up the Bishop's line.

Rosa noticed the editorial and picked it up.

"May I look at this?" she asked politely.

The Bishop nodded and continued applying his broad, bold strokes to the crested stationery.

The Monsignor and Tony watched her now, fascinated, as she

read the editorial with devouring intensity, her face firming with anger as her eyes roamed down and through to the next page.

The Bishop finished signing the letters and passed them over to her.

She took the letters after setting the editorial down again, keeping a taut, slender finger on the surface of the sheet.

"Is this going to run tomorrow, Bishop, may I ask?"

She framed the question with cold, repressed anger, confident she could ask him something of urgency to her, ignoring the editor and Tony bluntly as though she were alone with the Bishop.

"No, it isn't," the Bishop said tersely, a little taken aback by the revelation of their confidential status to his two old friends. "Monsignor Wagner and I have already discussed the matter."

"I should certainly hope it wouldn't run," she said, looking up at Monsignor Wagner and making her hostility quite clear.

This was the first time she had shown her hand directly to Arthur, he knew. There had been many indirect signs of her growing coolness and possessiveness of the Bishop since their return from Rome almost a year ago. A rejection of him as a confessor and mentor, which, while hurtful perhaps personally, he could understand because of the awesome sovereignty of the individual soul. But then the vagueness over the telephone concerning information he wanted from the Bishop. The enforced embarrassment he felt at not being able to pop in and out of the Bishop's office—the need for being announced, listed in the appointment book. Now this, out in the open now, the resentment and the hostility.

"What is your basic objection to the editorial, Rosa?" Monsignor Wagner asked with considerable restraint.

She turned to the Bishop. "May I answer this question frankly, Your Excellency?"

The Bishop raised his eyebrows and shrugged his shoulders slightly. "Yes, of course," he said. "We've been all through it. But go ahead, Rosa. We're all in the family."

"You know perfectly well, Monsignor," she said, her dark eyes burning into his soul, "this isn't the time for such a statement as this. It's—it's positively reckless and terribly, terribly inconsiderate of you to burden the Bishop with such a decision when so much is at stake—here and now. . . ."

Arthur's face was bloodless. He had the words to answer her but could not bring them to his throat. Perhaps she was right. For anybody else but the Bishop she was right in what she said, he knew. But he could not rebut the fury of a righteous, respectable woman. Thank God, thank God the Church has had the wisdom to set them apart from our altars, our lives. . . .

"And another thing . . ." she went on.

Tony reacted more intimately, aghast and irritated at her savage frontal attack on the Monsignor. He might have had to listen to that phrase all his life had things gone differently. "And another thing . . . and another thing . . ." Yet, strangely, warmly, he thought of Joan; Joan downstairs, sweet and submissive, yet strong; Joan, a woman who knew woman's role and nature, he thought with a need of flight to her, away from this glowing black core of power which he had known so closely.

"This is the very kind of thing that has"—she almost said "held back the Bishop," Arthur knew—"that has made so much anxiety necessary on this day of all days for our Bishop."

Day of all days, day of all days . . . The phrase rang like a knell through the wide, opulent sitting room which looked out with such sweep on the infinite silver prospect of the city and the lake.

"Rosa," the Bishop snapped, "that will be enough."

She paused, flushed, knowing she had said too much, but simmering still with anger and resentment.

"You may go," the Bishop added icily.

"Yes, Bishop," she said with taut features.

She picked up the letters and walked out of the suite.

Calm after storm and prickling embarrassment among old friends.

"I—I shouldn't have let her talk," the Bishop said, removing his glasses and rubbing his eyes with a sigh.

"It's just as well, Vin," Arthur said with bowed head. "Better out than in."

There ensued an awkward, writhing silence in which no one knew quite what to say. When the telephone rang long and insistently they turned to its summons eagerly, suppliantly, reprieved from tension as the final answer loomed.

The Bishop did not pick up the phone. He turned to Arthur, his face an answer itself in petition and trust.

"Arthur," he said hoarsely, "take it in my bedroom. If it's Venezzia, tell him I want him to give you the news."

"All right, Vin," Arthur said, rising. "I'll handle it for you, as before."

"As before," the Bishop said, smiling confidently, and adding, as Arthur placed his hand on the brass doorknob of the bedroom, "and, dear old friend, win or lose, I want you to run the editorial in bold-face on the front page."

"I'll be happy to do that, Your Excellency."

The phone rang again—long, strident, insistent.

"And be sure to do this," the Bishop said with a smile at Tony before he turned to Monsignor Wagner again.

"Be sure to sign my name—at the bottom of the piece."

Monsignor Wagner nodded, blinked the scalding tears from his eyes, and hurried into the bedroom.

This is the warmly human action-packed —often violently exciting—novel of three men who chose different paths within the Catholic Church by which to follow their destinies.

Father Vincent Whelton was a maverick liberal, spokesman for the underdog, loved by all. His path led him on a crusade against political corruption.

Father Arthur Wagner, editor of the archdiocesan newspaper, made his way along a parallel route, which had its own kinds of blind alleys and soul-wearying detours.

Father Bob Lambert had a goal that could be reached only by shrewdness, scholarship, and an aptitude for progressing smoothly through the labyrinth of Church politics.

Deft characterizations and contrasts in spiritual values—as well as the moving story itself—distinguish this new novel by the author of *No Lasting Home* and *A Certain Widow.*